A Dance with Fire

This book is a work of fiction. Any reference to historical events, people or places are used fictitiously. Other names, characters, places and events are products of the author's imagination, and any resemblance to actual events or places or persons, living or dead, is entirely coincidental.

Softcover Cover design and typography image by: Storywrappers
Hardcover design and typography image by: Moonpress.co
Edited by: Lisa Nieves
Map design done in: Wonderdraft
Formatting by: Aleera Anaya Ceres

This book is for the oppressed.
For the silenced.
And for those who wish to be seen.

Fae Elementals Glossary and Pronunciation Guide

Kingdoms, Cities, and Landmarks

Illyk: *Eel-ick*
Tuath: *Two-ahh-th*
Dana: *Day-nuh*
Vellm: *Vey-mm*
Ielwyn: *Eel-win*
Teg: *Teh-gg*
Orknie: *Orc-knee*
Lake Degara: Lake *Dig-are-uh*
The Arcana: *Arc-ay-nuh*
Lywyth River: *Lee-with*
Tir na Faie (also known as the Feylands): *Tier Nuh Fey*
Ley Line: *Lay Line*
Castle Aileach: *Castle I-lick*
Terrlyn: *Tear-lynn*

People

Shula Azzarh: *Shoe-luh Uh-zarrh*
Piriguini: *Peer-ee-gween-ee*
Ryker Valda: *Rye-curr Vahl-duh*
Clay Valentino: *Clay Valen-tee-no*
Julius Darah: *Jewel-ee-us Dare-uhh*
Valerio Ashera: *Vahl-eer-rio Ah-sheer-uh*
Weylyn Xanth: *Way-lynn Zanth*
Uric Adriel Nova: *You-ric Ay-dree-el No-vuh*
Orna: *Or-nuh*
King Amos Ashera: *Ay-mose Ah-sheer-uh*
Emperor Robert Laurel: *Robert Lore-rel*

Terms

Esses: (Pronounced like S. S.) A derogatory term for the Fae. Originally Seelie Scum, later shortened to S.S., then 'Esses'.

Mana: (Pronounced Mah-nuh) The word to describe the Fae entity/deity/god. It is magic, nature, and the elements, as these are holy amongst their race.

Ilyk
The Lagnh Sea
Gyshapur
Kaym
Vellm
Bazra
Kayron
Valley of the Dead
Barrenhorn
Telshaw
The Arcana
Myrim
Ielwyn
Badfa
Ojor
Wintshore
Loren
Castle Aileach
Crystal Forest
Bridgertown
Tuath
Minn
Hiel Lake
Lywyth River
Seirz
Arcancliffe
Covenglen
Vallart
Solle
Zaen
Teg
Lake Degara
The Arcana
Dana
Port Bay
Clyhr
Port Lays
Orknie
Eul
Porir
Verdt
Terrylyn
Wyrshl
Ley Line
Crimson Court
The Iron Mountains
Western Waters
Gold Court
Tir na Faie
The Feylands
Sombhra Mountains
Jade Court
The Seelie Court
The Pool
Elin Ocean
Obsidian Court
Nach es Forest
Sapphire Court
The Unseelie Court
N
W
E
Nymph Island

Trigger and Content Warnings

A Dance with Fire contains dark and **graphic** themes such as:

Sexual themes

Alcohol consumption

Descriptive violence

Gore

The death and loss of loved ones

Grief

Racism of Fae within a fantasy setting

The genocide of the Fae people in a fantasy setting

Post traumatic stress and trauma

Allusions of an attempted suicide in a character's past

The abuse and torture of main and side characters

The attempted sexual assault of a side character in Chapter 43, *WANTED: Alive and Intact.*

If such material offends you, please do not pick up this book and/or proceed with caution. Your mental health and well-being always comes first.

A Dance with Fire is part of a six book series and does not end in a cliffhanger. It is in 3rd person point of view and while each book will follow the story of a different Elemental, there will be scenes with several POV's throughout, including villains'.

Piriguini's Circus

The shadows clung to Shula's small body, hugging her close to the brick wall and hiding her from the emperor's soldiers. She knew they were out there looking for her, and it wouldn't be too long until she was found. The blood splattered against her legs and the hem of her tattered night shift would be sniffed out by the hounds. Even if she'd run through puddles of water and mud in between dark alleyways to hide her scent, they would find her.

The emperor always found those like Shula Azzarh.

Her heart beat like a panicked baby bird in her chest, struggling to break free with every gasping breath. She thought if she had a heart attack now, it would spare her the pain of when they came and took her away in iron cuffs.

Her hands trembled from the icy bite of cold and fear. She couldn't pry her fingers off the pearl and diamond necklaces she'd pilfered from the old woman. It'd been a good idea a few hours ago. The woman was dead, after all, and Shula needed the jewels more than the dead human did if she wanted any chance at survival in a world that hated her kind.

Freedom seemed so far away, though, and nearly impossible to picture beyond the blur of her tears. She tried to shake that notion off and tried to imagine what her Papa would say.

"Anyone who claims something is *impossible* doesn't know how to get creative."

But he'd died right along with Mama just a few days ago. What did they know, anyway?

The wounds of her parents' absence still rubbed her soul raw and made tears stain a sticky pathway down her dirty cheeks. Even her ears hurt every time her hair grazed their sensitive tips. She fought back the urge to touch the bloody wounds and took a breath.

She had to get out of there. Sitting still would only get her found that much faster, but where could she go?

Shula tilted her head to the side, listening to the sounds of the city. Street urchins ran between alleyways, their bare feet slamming against puddles and mud with distinctive squelching noises.

She could trail beside them. The emperor's soldiers would never know, and her scent could get lost among them to confuse the hounds.

She'd be just another orphan running the streets. They wouldn't look twice because she fit in so well with them. Her clothes were tattered, her body almost skeletal with malnourishment, making her appear younger than she really was.

The light of stars and the flickering flames of street lamps beckoned her from her hiding spot at a cautious pace. Every step of her shaking legs was harder than the last, and she almost bolted back to the protection of the shadows once again.

She forced herself to follow the sounds of other kids, stepping out of the alleyway in time to see them barrel past her, their laughter trailing behind them like will-o'-the-wisps. Shula followed, letting her arms pump at her sides, trying to mimic their enthusiasm. Every step was painfully jarring against her body and sent blood rushing through her ears.

She had no idea where they were going, but if they could lead her to freedom, she'd follow them to the edge of the world. They noticed her behind them and waved her over with quick gestures of their hands.

"Come on! They're here!"

Hands tugged on her arms and pulled her forward when all she could manage was to gape, all fear momentarily forgotten.

She'd heard of the infamous Piriguini's Circus before, whispered like legends through the reservation camps she'd grown up in. But nothing could ever prepare her for it.

It was colors and lights and an opulent world beyond anything she'd ever seen. It was women with beards that touched the ground and twins joined at the hip and head. It was acrobats and people taller than her fitting their entire bodies into boxes. It was magic openly celebrated.

That scared her most of all.

Magic burst from every corner of the place. It rose in tendrils of flickering flames and streaks of fireworks across the sky that reminded her of the extinct faerie lights from her dreams.

She wondered how a place like this could exist without the emperor's soldiers bursting in and taking them all.

Because this was faux magic, and the humans didn't fear that of their own making.

Her feet dragged her past wonder after wonder. Shula didn't confine herself to the shadows, and despite her barefoot, haggard appearance and the blood on her hem, nobody stopped her.

Here, she was invisible. Here, she could fit in and claim the magic inside her to be as fake as their own.

Here, she would find freedom from hunger and fear.

Freedom from those who wanted her dead.

Illegal Fae

10 years later...

Sometimes, Shula couldn't stand the stench of smoke.

The way it wrapped around her lungs and threatened to suffocate them. It reminded her of another time, another life when she'd been someone, *something* else. Yet it was smoke she inhaled deep into her lungs, and a smile she plastered onto her face as she peered behind the thick velvet curtains that separated her from the crowd.

"It's a crush."

Shula let the curtain flitter closed, blocking the assault of smells and memories. "Of course it is," she responded to her friend, Fantasia, rather arrogantly. This was her sixth and final show of the night and the busiest so far. "Everyone wants to catch a glimpse of the infamous fire dancer."

Shula had made sure of it; in the ten years since she'd joined Piriguini's Traveling Circus, five of those years she'd juggled while dancing for coins or scraps of food. Then she moved up to doing simple parlor tricks *while dancing*, until she ascended rank and became one of the most popular attractions in their pilgrimage.

It was rarer *not* to sell out an entire show. At least, that had been the case. Lately, tensions were high across the empire of Illyk, but that was nothing new. It was normal to see the emperor's soldiers about everywhere they turned, and the men in steel armor never failed to create problems for the circus when they passed through the kingdom of Tuath.

The sight of them no longer made her as nervous as they once had, no matter that they'd gotten more aggressive and determined throughout the years. She'd lived with the circus so long, Shula no longer knew what it was to fear for her life. It was dangerous to deem herself safe when she really wasn't.

She never would be.

Because Shula Azzarh was Fae in a world where it was illegal to be.

"Break a leg." Fantasia squeezed Shula's arm, bringing her back to her current reality. Her name had just been announced, which meant it was show time.

"Break yours first." Shula slipped past the curtain before she could hear Fantasia curse out her reply. And once she stepped out before the crowd, her entire world shifted. Silence blanketed over the entire crowd because it was what her presence commanded.

Shula was under no illusions; she knew what she looked like, knew how beautiful she was no matter how hard she tried to diminish it so others would never know what she truly was. It was hard to hide the beauty of a Fae, and her low riding harem pants, sparkling top that cut off midriff, sheer veil that obscured half her face, and golden circlets around her wrists and bare ankles, did nothing to hide her allure.

For a moment, the only sound that echoed through the large tent were the soft jangles of the circlets sliding up and down her arms. Then there was a silence so profound that no one even dared to breathe. It was part of the magic of her act. She entranced like a snake charmer, and everyone sat at the edges of their seats to watch what she'd do next.

And she didn't disappoint.

Fire erupted from her fingertips and soared high through the tent. Sharp bursts of heat flowed all around her, and then she began to move. Body undulating like the waves as she danced across the ground, stomach and arms rolling. This moment was magical. It coursed through her veins, a current of power that was desperate to be unleashed. With every breath she took and every snap of her wrists, fire encircled her body. It slithered like a snake, long lines of golden and red streaks lighting up the darkness.

The gasps were lost to her and so was the applause. In that moment, there was nothing but her confidence in the dance, in the way her body became one with the fire. She was flame itself, flickering movements and passion. Blazing heat and brightness. She captivated hearts just as easily as she could destroy them beneath the inferno of her sensuality.

Fire fell from her fingertips, drawing figures wherever she traced them. She knew the brightness illuminated her. She knew it made the dark of her skin glow like burning embers. It lit up her eyes. They were so enthralled with her and she with them.

She moved in tune to the rhythm of the drums resonating around her. She swiveled her hips, rolled her entire body to look like the flickering of flames. She was the Fire Dancer, her black hair billowing down to her waist. The bangles decorating her wrists slid up and down the length of her arm. Her feet stepped quickly, carefully, and each step was a quick succession on the ground that burned, leaving the markings of her footprints onto it.

As the tempo picked up, so did Shula's body. She moved around, throwing fire balls through the air to form floating and flying figures. The beat of the drum became a savage thing inside her, through her bloodstream. She lost herself in the music, felt it rush through her, whispering in her ear, caressing her bare and exposed skin. The warmth of the flames grounded her. It lit something in her. Perhaps it was the magic of her very own blood that demanded release.

And as the final notes rang, she threw her hands above her and all the wisps of fire that danced freely joined together above, reforming and reshaping into a massive image behind her.

The finale would surely capture them all.

Her hands shot up at the same time the wildfire imploded upwards. It fragmented in streaks until they formed the blazing image of a dragon. The bursting sound of applause echoed through the tent just as sparks rained around her body.

Chest heaving, she dipped into an elegant curtsy and, in a swirl of silky material, walked away.

"I swear, they only come to see your big finish," Fantasia greeted Shula on the other side of the curtain, her small button nose scrunched in amusement.

"It is a pretty great finish." Shula wrapped her arms around her friend's shoulders. "You know they come here to see you too, Fanny." She knew she had to reassure her because Fanny was as delicate as she looked. As Shula's exact opposite, she was small and rail thin and completely flexible. Her blonde hair was cropped near her scalp and her cutting, white cheek bones were covered in sticky glitter. Silk ribbons adorned her spandex clad body, red silk tied around her wrists that flowed down at her sides and looked like rivers of blood.

Shula hated how her mind thought of that. Of blood and fire and iron. There was little else that haunted her nightmares and she hated that the memories made an appearance while she was awake, too.

Shaking off her morbid past, she forced the smile to stay on her mouth. She hadn't crumbled all those years ago, hadn't given into what had happened then, and she wouldn't do it now, either. She'd been a child then, alone and afraid, with nothing in her pockets but stolen pearls and the bloody night shift on her back. She was different now. The infamous Fire Dancer of Piriguini's Circus. She'd made a name for herself and had been safely hidden from the emperor's soldiers for years.

"Wait for me and we can go get some sugared scones." Fanny slipped from Shula's hold and pushed aside the curtains. It was her turn to go on, and a small peek at the crowd showed that they'd diminished slightly compared to only a few moments before. Fanny threw a knowing look over her shoulder, lips pursed, just before she disappeared into a sea of velvet.

Shula peeked out to watch Fanny take her position. Her act was Shula's favorite because the woman was *flexible.* She could fold her body into epic proportions, twist and mold herself and fly over the audience from rope to rope. It was wild. It was free.

Fantasia did her act with the same freedom she lived through life. With wild abandon. For a moment, Shula's own heart lurched, and she wondered what it would be like to feel that. To not wander with a mask placed carefully over her entire self. To be genuinely happy with life and to not hide the most essential parts of herself from a world that wanted her dead.

She supposed she would never know what it felt like, to fly like a bird, to soar and freefall knowing that you could catch yourself on the way down.

And Shula would just have to live with that.

Davina's Fortune and Tarot Readings

Fanny looped her arm through Shula's with an energy that buzzed between them like lightning. She bounced excitedly on the balls of her feet before tugging her away from the main white-and-red tent. Midnight had long left them and their final acts had been performed. The circus was still bright with activity and excited spectators ran across the field.

The smell of popped corn, sugared pastries, caramel and chocolate covered fruits, and fresh flavored waters hung in the air. Her stomach growled loudly and Fanny chuckled, changing directions so she was pulling her towards the section where the foodstuffs were sold.

"Dessert first," the small woman declared.

"You know me so well." They stopped before a stand that sold fried balls of salted dough covered in sparkling white sugar. The pastries glittered like diamonds and were as beautiful as they were delicious.

"How many will it be?" the surly man named Wells asked with a bored voice.

Fanny unhooked her arm from Shula's and placed her hands defiantly on her hips and stared at the much taller, bigger man. "Now, don't take that tone with me."

He scratched his scraggly hair and muttered, "Sorry, Fanny. It's been a rough day."

Traveling to Tuath was always stressful. It was where most of the emperor's soldiers were stationed and it always took so long to get there. Shula understood his weariness. She felt it herself down to her bones.

Soldiers were everywhere, scattered all around the empire, but Tuath had them in abundance because this was where the Fae camps were.

Just thinking about the iron encampments made a shiver slice down the length of her spine. Iron was deeply embedded into every city across every kingdom and she could taste it in the air. It made her eyes water and her breathing shallow, but like always, she plastered on a smile if only to pretend nothing bothered her at all.

Not even here, where it all began. Where she'd found Piriguini's Circus and had forged a new life for herself. She had to admit, there was a certain melancholy here. While there was excitement in the air and the people were happy that the circus served as a distraction against politics and everything else in the world, it still didn't help stray her attention from the WANTED posters that crinkled beneath her feet as she walked. Balled up parchment with sketched images of faces that hurt to look at. Slashing lines of Fae and Fae sympathizers in bold, charcoaled strokes.

Discreetly, she pushed one aside with her foot that the wind carried towards her. She barely caught a glimpse of the face on it and forced herself to look away. She knew what would be portrayed there.

Pointed ears and elongated canines that were a complete exaggeration. Fae were beautiful, but this artist had all but announced the pure hatred and fear with each dark line across the parchment. Whoever had drawn it had made this particular Fae look like an abomination.

A monster.

Shula barely heard Fanny and Wells engage in conversation around her. Her heart was pounding, and her lungs were aching. The day was taking a toll on her. Not just the dancing, but the pretending. She was tired, so tired of the world and her circumstances. But if she didn't keep up with the pretense, she would die. Or worse, her face would be etched onto posters just like the Fae beneath her sandaled foot.

A monster he may have looked like, but she could see the dark head of hair tied back in a knot. She wondered how much of a glimpse they'd gotten of him. How much of a likeness this portrait really was.

She wondered, if she was ever caught, would they make *her* look like a monster too?

"Shules!" Fanny wrenched her out of her thoughts by waving a pastry beneath her nose.

Shula's mouth watered instantly. "Oh, thank goodness." She yanked the confection from her friend's hands and all but inhaled it down her throat. Flakes of sugar clung to the sides of her mouth, and she dusted them off with the back of her hand.

"Your manners are despicable," Fanny teased, eating her pastry much more slowly.

Shula smirked, but inside anxiety rose to choke tightly at her chest. If she ate too fast, it was because Shula knew what it was to go hungry. She knew what it was to be rail thin, with skin clinging to bones like nothing more than a wraith or a living ghost.

The truth was, she could alter her appearance all she wanted. She could diminish her beauty, suppress her magic, pretend to be human rather than Fae.

But the phantom pain of stabbing hunger in her gut was something she would never forget.

"Can I have a chocolate covered one next?" Shula was already reaching for the confection.

Chocolate was a weakness. She remembered the first time she'd tasted it. It had been two years after she'd joined the traveling circus. She'd seen it, smelled it, craved it like she hadn't craved any other food before. She'd just never had the money to actually buy one for herself. And since she'd been a new hire, no one had wanted to give her anything. Not even the scraps. She'd been nothing more than a juggling orphan with stringy hair who danced and tossed rocks for meager coins. Eventually, she'd saved enough to buy herself a small piece of chocolate the size of her nail.

She hadn't been able to relish it. The taste had exploded over her tongue, and she couldn't stop her young mouth from devouring the whole thing as if it would disappear if she didn't.

Wells slapped her fingers away. "Get your ash covered fingers away from my pastries."

Shula smiled sweetly at him, and for a moment, he lost himself in her gaze.

Fuck.

She reeled back the dazzling smile, her heart pounding. For a second, he'd gotten lost in the haze of her glamor. Unfortunately, that seemed to be the one aspect of her magic she couldn't very well help. Next time she vowed to wear an iron bracelet. Even if it burned her skin, she needed to diminish her Fae allure.

"Let's go get some roasted sweet meats," Shula suggested, hoping her voice didn't betray her nervousness.

"No more dessert?" Fanny asked in a teasing tone.

Shula shook her head and tugged her friend away before tossing a coin to Wells. "I satisfied my craving." What she didn't say was that she needed to get away from him before he fell deeper into her thrall.

She couldn't say that to Fanny. Though they had been friends for years, being Fae was a secret Shula could entrust to no one. It wouldn't just put her life in danger, but Fanny's as well. Besides, she knew what everyone thought of her kind.

No one could know her secret.

No one.

"Give it a few minutes and you'll be craving sweets all over again. I swear, that sugar has something magical in it that keeps making us go back."

Shula just laughed, even though any talk of magic made her nervous. "Right? I wonder what it is."

"Fae drugs, probably." Fanny dropped her voice to a whisper. Like even muttering the word 'Fae' was somehow forbidden, even when they'd been called much worse. "Can you imagine if that were true? If he was putting Esses drugs in our food?"

Shula tried not to grit her teeth.

Esses was a derogatory term. One she'd heard far too often. It was human slang derived from the words 'Seelie Scum'. They'd shortened it to S.S. Eventually, Esses. But everyone knew what it meant, and it wasn't kind.

"Ugh, I would just die." Shula pulled her hair in place over her ears.

"Right? Gross!"

They skipped their way over to the sweet meats and bought two kabobs. Shula devoured those just as easily as she had the pastries, and when she finished, they tossed them into an overflowing garbage bin.

Circus goers were already stumbling away, back to their little homes, back to the reality of their world where they were protected by what they were and what blood ran through their veins.

"See you tomorrow, Fanny."

"Bye, Shules." Fanny, like always, wrapped her arms tightly around Shula's waist in a hug that spoke of caring and friendship. Shula held her back with a smile. It was in these moments, when she was held with no reservations, that she could pretend like everything was normal. Like she wasn't what the world despised and feared above all others. She could pretend that Fanny would never fear her, if she ever knew the truth.

Fanny extricated herself from Shula and skipped away. Their living tents were on opposite sides of the dry field, Shula's near the very back on the western end. She walked through the pitch-black field. Lights had already begun shutting off, candles and torches that had illuminated even the darkest of shadows had now died. Her feet didn't stumble against the uneven earth, because she could see well in the dark. She could make out the outline and details of every tent, every rock, and every hidden pebble.

So when a lone figure cloaked in shadows stepped from her tent, Shula did not cry out in surprise.

She probably should have, at least to keep up with the illusion that she was human, but there was no one around her that would witness this interaction. She hadn't heard footfalls or the deep rise and fall of breathing. No, the mask was not necessary at all when she came face to face with Davina.

"Shula Azzarh," the woman greeted, her voice a low, ominous sound in the dark.

Shula fought back a shiver. She hated the way her name sounded on the woman's mouth. The way she ended it on a low growl that could very well have been threatening.

"Madame Davina." Shula nodded and tried to sidestep the woman, but all she did was follow and block her path once again.

Shula frowned at the woman. Clad in purple drapery that hid the shape of her body and a turban that wrapped around the entirety of her head, covering her skin and the tips of her ears. There was an ethereal beauty about her. Pointed cheekbones and a sharp cutting chin. Her eyes were wide and knowing.

Knowing.

Because she *knew*. Davina knew exactly what Shula was, what flowed through her veins.

The same thing flowed through hers.

Davina was Fae, too.

Shula remembered the first time she'd ever laid eyes on Davina. The impact of seeing another Fae that made her stagger back. The shock that rippled through her. Electricity had cackled between their bodies. An awareness that sent her every nerve into haywire, made every hair on her body stand on end. It was like her blood had hummed, her heart beat faster in her chest. And when their eyes met, they knew deep down what the other was.

Shula had promptly fled afterwards. She ran and didn't stop until her lungs burned and begged for rest. Fae were rare. With them being hunted for years, they'd all but gone extinct. The emperor's soldiers still actively looked for any Fae they could find. So to see anther one of her kind at the circus had rocked Shula on her feet. Out of pure instinct, she'd avoided the other woman. It was better to separate herself from her. So she did. She stayed as far away from Davina as she possibly could.

And now they were face to face and something uncomfortable stirred in her stomach. The longer she stared at the woman, she could just make out the press of her pointed ears beneath the turban.

"You're nervous." Davina smiled, revealing the elongated state of her teeth, a sharp smile that reminded Shula of razor blades.

Canines emerged at will, or when feral instincts aroused. Teeth elongated into sharp points at the scent of blood or fear, only to slide back into the gums afterward. It was an instinct Shula had always tried to keep firmly at bay, especially in anger. One that Davina obviously had no qualms about hiding, even in the dark.

"I'm not." Shula kept her voice firm, even while her heart pounded in her ears. She tried to keep her emotions steady, her body still.

"Care for your fortune? A glimpse of your future?"

Shula's eyes flicked to the sign beside her small, purple tent.

Davina's Fortune and Tarot Readings, it read.

"You can't lure me in with promises of love." She started to walk away but Davina's hand snapped out and restrained her. As strong and as cold as iron, her fingers dug into Shula's wrist painfully.

"You are not like the humans who come running to me at the first sign of a broken heart. No, you are different." Her white teeth flashed. "Just one reading. I sense your future. I know what looms around the corner."

She knew what one reading would mean. It would lead to a second, and a third, and another, and another. It was the price seers paid for the magic of the future. It would make Shula crave another glimpse, another hint at what was to come. It created madness and rotted the mind entirely.

"You are afraid of being captured. You fear, but you cannot hide from your true nature, just like the moon cannot hide from the sky."

Davina was already smiling triumphantly, and Shula knew it was because she'd already seen the future, the seer already knew what her answer would be.

"Fine. One reading."

"One reading is all I need." Tugging on her wrist, Davina pulled her behind the dark flaps of her tent. "Come. Sit." She pushed on Shula's shoulders and Shula obeyed, letting herself be guided onto plush pillows.

The smallest of tables sat in front of her, covered in a silk cloth that depicted constellations, astrology, and other things that Shula couldn't really make much sense of. She watched warily as Davina took a seat at the table across from her.

"Bones or cards?" Her long fingers held up two little bags, presumably with the objects she said.

Shula shivered at the thought of bones. She wasn't afraid of them, for the dead could not harm her, but it seemed morbid, and she figured it would be best if she pretended to be human, anxious to get a reading on a long-lost love. It would keep the madness at bay.

"Cards."

Her sharp teeth flashed again, and Shula wondered why the woman even bothered asking her, if she had all the answers already. She drew open the drawstrings of the bag and pulled out a stack of cards. Shula watched as Davina methodically shuffled them with quick snaps of her wrists and fingers. When she finished, she slid the cards in front of Shula in a line.

"Choose your cards."

"Why? Aren't you supposed to do that?"

"We all forge our own destiny, Fire Dancer." Her voice was low and strict. "The cards you choose is the path you pave."

Sighing and deciding it was better to get this over with, she swept her hand down the line of cards, stopping and picking those her instinct told her to claim.

Davina slid the other cards away. Shula had chosen six total.

"Flip over the first one."

Shula did as she was told.

The Lovers.

"I thought you said this wouldn't be promises of love."

Davina ignored her. "Flip the rest."

So, she did. One by one, she turned the cards over.

The Lovers. The Fool. The Devil. Ten of Swords. Five of Wands.

And Death.

Before she could ask, Davina was already speaking. "You will accept your true self in the face of danger. Your future holds much darkness and difficult trials ahead. It holds..." She paused, cocking her head to the side.

"What?" Shula almost felt disinterested. This was the same drivel she likely tossed at clients to keep them on the edges of these plush seats.

Davina smiled sharply again. "I see love."

Shula couldn't hold back her eye roll. "Alright. You have my gratitude, Madame Davina, for such an interesting reading. I will be sure to consider all aspects of my future." She stood up and started to leave, only to find the only exit blocked.

Davina had moved, and Shula hadn't sensed it. In the blink of an eye, the Fae woman was in front of her, and the dark color of her eyes was gone. Pure white eyes glared at Shula, seeing but unseeing. She blindly reached for her, gripping Shula's wrists tightly and keeping her tethered in place.

"I see blood and fire." Her voice was hoarse with strain and fear. It was different. It was frightening. Shula tried to pull her hands away, but the woman didn't budge at all. It was like she wasn't even present in that moment. "I see robes of white and red and chains of iron. I see men cloaked in shadows and darkness. I hear the echoes of your screams, drowned out in the agony of burning water. I see twin flames carved in flesh... I see... I see pain and fire. A pattern of scars. I see..." She jerked back on a gasp and her whole body fell, crumpling to the ground.

Shula didn't have time to catch her as she hit the floor with a sickening thud. Her body convulsed a moment later, limbs thrashing out. A high-pitched keel sounded from her throat that was loud enough to wake the dead. Words were thrown from her tongue, leaked through with madness.

It was the price of her magic taking effect.

All magic came with a price, some prices were just higher than others.

Fortunately, soon after she'd screamed, Davina stopped thrashing as well. Her body stilled and Shula bent down to press two fingers to her pulse. She was still breathing. Thank Mana, she thought. If she would have screamed any louder and any longer, anyone could have come running, bursting into her tent.

It was dangerous to be here, but Shula couldn't bring herself to leave Davina on the ground. Digging into whatever well of strength she had, Shula hefted Davina up and all but dragged her over to her pillows where she gently laid her down.

She stared at the Fae woman a moment longer, at the beauty she tried to dim with makeup and drab clothing and costumes. Her turban had slipped in her fall, exposing the tops of her ears and the pointed aesthetic of them. Shula bent down, tugging at the edge of the turban to cover them up once more. When she stood up, it was almost instinct herself to pull her long, dark locks forward.

Davina's words burned and echoed in Shula's mind. Because she had the gift of prophecy, they rang strangely of a dark premonition, and Shula didn't like that one bit. These were dark times and danger hid in the shadows of every corner. She wished she could push them away. Wished she could somehow turn back time and not have gone into the tent to hear prophecies, fortunes, or futures. She'd known how dangerous it was, and still something had compelled her to enter. To go along with the madness and listen.

The problem with listening to madness was, it invaded your senses like a black plague. It spread through the mind like a contagion. Sometimes, the madness was easy to fight off. And other times, it was just easier to give in.

And in the rarest times, one could stare long and hard and find the madness looking back.

Cowardly Fae

The hardest part about being in Tuath was the camps. Though she'd traveled all over Illyk and knew that every kingdom across the lands had camps, Tuath was the worst. It was where the original had been built, and many more after that. Iron structures that rose into a permanently bleak, gray sky, looking like towers out of a nightmare-ish tale.

Because the camps were constantly burning, ash coated thickly through the air, polluting everything with the rotting stench of burnt flesh.

The smell wasn't as strong as it used to be.

Shula remembered when officials tore through the reservations, actively looking for Fae with magical abilities. When protective treaties failed and laws were changed, she remembered how the hatred for Fae with magic became hatred for Fae in general. Nowhere had been safe. *No one* had been safe. Children were ripped from their mother's arms or killed on sight.

Being killed was a mercy.

The camps were unforgiving; made of iron to debilitate magic and prevent them from fighting back. Numbers had already been low, too low to start the wars the emperor and council of kings claimed the Fae were capable of starting, but that didn't matter to the humans. All that mattered was their fear, irrational as it was.

Shula remembered the smoke emanating from the buildings, the putrid stench of burning flesh. She remembered looking up into the sky to find ash raining down over her skin and wondering if the flakes that stuck to her eyelashes were the remnants of the parents she had once loved.

She'd been a child then and had cried a thousand tears before she'd fled. She had nothing left now. The memories of them were practically a blur in her mind. All she knew now was survival, and tears had no place among the living.

Gray was the color of the sky now, but sometimes even the sunlight filtered through the clouds. She relished in it as much as she could, because she didn't know when the last time she'd see the sun would be.

She strolled around camp in the early morning, not daring to go outside of circus bounds. Every time they camped, they always did it near a river so everyone in the pilgrimage could have a place to bathe and wash their garments close. Shula walked near the edge of the river, kicking her toes across the surface of the shallow end before treading back over dirt and grass.

It was the perfect time to go over what had happened the night before. She hadn't gone in to check on Davina because she hadn't wanted to draw attention to herself. Even if she'd been worried about her wellbeing, her prophetic words had left Shula tossing and turning all night. By the time day broke through the fog, Shula was out of her tent and taking a walk. The fresh air wasn't fresh enough. She inhaled the iron-coated air into her lungs and pushed it out on a heavy breath.

It did no good to worry about the future, even when it came from a seer. The truth was, the future wasn't set. It had been given to her in shattered bits and pieces that didn't interconnect in any way. Nothing was certain, especially not her choppy premonition.

That didn't mean Shula was going to be letting down her guard. If anything, she would have to be even more vigilant and careful than usual, she thought as she walked back up towards the line of tents. The thoughts flew straight from her mind the moment she heard the voices. The shouts. She should've hid, but she'd stepped into everyone's line of vision and it was too late.

Uniforms, armor of steel was what she saw first. It was *all* she saw. Steel. Swords. Blood. Fire. Ash. Years' worth of memories came flooding back through her mind; the memories of her twelve-year-old self, and she tasted the fear so clearly on the back of her tongue like poison. A whimper threatened to rise, and Shula wasn't sure if it was in her mind or the sound had really come out of her. She bit her tongue so hard, she tasted blood.

Turmoil raged inside her and she could show none of it. Slowly, she blinked and stepped forward with careful steps. These soldiers weren't here for her. She knew that because they hadn't rushed to arrest her yet, even when she knew they'd already seen her. They were watching as she took careful steps towards them.

The emperor's soldiers weren't the only people in attendance. Shula's own people had emerged from their tents to watch the spectacle. Even Piriguini himself was in front of the officers. Among all the oddities, among two headed twins and secret Fae and men with reptilian skin, Piriguini was the oddest yet. At least, Shula thought so, and simply because he was a dwarf. Not an actual dwarf of the Fae race, but a human dwarf with a long beard that touched to his knobby knees.

A silk bathrobe covered his small body, and he looked little more than a child playing dress up with his mother's clothes. He made a comical sight with the sleeves dragging against the earth and his ruddy face reddened with anger. All humor was lost on Shula as she approached and a soldier stepped forward and asked, "Shula Azzarh?"

The soldier's face was visible as he wasn't wearing his helmet like the others. It was settled against his hip, held in his gauntleted grip. Hair cropped short in the typical soldier style, dark searching eyes, and a stance that was prepared to kill. A sharp iron sword was sheathed at his waist and Shula could feel the poisonous pulse of it from a foot away where she stopped to face him.

Her eyes didn't go to the weapon even while she felt it. It would be just a quick way to announce her guilt, to let everyone know what she was.

"Yes?" She cocked her head to the side. A strange sense of calmness settled over her. She had prepared for this day for years. Her heart didn't pound, her hands didn't shake. She had done nothing wrong because she wasn't Fae. Not in any way that counted. She was human now and they could prove nothing, could do nothing.

Or so she told herself.

"I am Captain Brannon of the Emperor's Royal Guard, battalion currently stationed under King Ernest of Tuath's rule. I am here because you have been suspected of being Fae."

Her heart didn't even give out. She just stared at the face of the human whose gaze pulsed with the vicious desire to condemn her.

Before she could reply though, Piriguini was stepping forward and waving his small, boney fist in the soldier's direction. "And I told you that whoever suspects a thing has sand for brains!"

Shula counted the soldiers. Ten soldiers. They'd overpower her easily enough with the iron.

The captain glared like he would be glad to run Piriguini through with little effort.

"Stand back, dwarf," he spat. "You're lucky we aren't investigating your bloodline for Fae taint."

Piriguini made a face and held up his silk clad arm. The material of his robe slid down to reveal a skeletal limb and a band of iron around his wrist. "Try again, soldier! I'm as human as they come, but I have a condition, you hear? A condition!"

"In the name of Emperor Robert Laurel and King Ernest, move aside before I move you myself." The soldier's voice was a sound of deadly calm like the spark of a fire before the wild blaze.

Shula bent and placed her hand on Piriguini's shoulder. It would do no good for him to get arrested as a sympathizer for defending her. Piriguini grumbled but waddled to the side and got out of the soldier's way. With the smaller man gone, the soldier's eyes flicked back up to her.

"A complaint was made known to us that Piriguini's Circus was harboring a fugitive from the law, a Fae woman known as the infamous Fire Dancer."

"A load of crock!"

The soldier replied to Piriguini's outburst with a calm threat. "The crime for hiding Fae is severe in the form of death. Do well to stay silent, dwarf, before we arrest you."

Piriguini was a rage-filled man who didn't know how to keep quiet. "I pay the emperor's taxes every year! I extensively and thoroughly test my performers before I allow them into my circus. I am frankly appalled—"

"It's alright, Piriguini," Shula interrupted. "Of course, I'll do whatever the soldiers ask of me. It is for the good of Illyk and in the name of Emperor Laurel, after all." Shula met the soldier's gaze and saw the briefest flash of surprise there. Whatever it was he thought she was, this wasn't the reaction he'd been expecting. Perhaps he'd hoped for resistance, denial, a chase. But his sword of iron would not taste Fae blood today. "How shall I assist you?"

"You will show us your ears."

Shula could feel everyone in the crowd still. She knew she always had the bad habit of hiding her hair over her face. She knew they wondered, knew they were holding her breath. Shula was beautiful, almost too beautiful. She held herself with grace and elegance, a confidence that they figured was too ethereal to be human. She was friends with all of these people, but for so long, she had read the suspicion in their eyes because of how careful she was to keep her ears covered.

Shula didn't waste time. She didn't delay. Everyone's eyes were glued on her as she lifted her hands and pushed aside her dark locks and tilted her head so they could see her ears.

And the perfect roundness of them.

The soldier blinked with what she was sure could only be surprise. She felt everyone around her relax as if the great mystery of her had finally been solved.

"Is that all you require of me, officer?" She dropped her hands to the side and made sure he could see the iron bracelet around her wrist. He would never know they were fake; they looked all too real.

But he didn't notice the bracelet. He was still staring at her ears. She didn't hide them with her hair; instead she'd tucked the strands behind her ears to leave them on display as if they were an artifact in a museum.

They almost panged with the phantom pain of the past, but she ignored it.

"How do you explain your act?" he all but demanded, an accusing note to his voice. "The fire?"

Humans always wanted an explanation for what they didn't understand. It was how this problem came to pass in the first place. Because the humans couldn't accept things that were out of their control. Like perhaps the god they worshipped wasn't real when it came to the race of the Fae. Because they couldn't accept that the magical life force of Mana lived within the Fae and connected them to the holy elements.

At least, that's what Shula's father had told her. It was one of the many lessons he'd imparted before he'd been taken. They were also lessons she struggled to forget in order to become as human as possible.

"Now wait a moment!" Piriguini stepped forward again, his robe trailing behind him like a royal cloak. "It's one thing to barge in here and question my performers without rightful cause, but to ask them to give up the secrets of their acts? I won't stand for it! I won't!" He stomped his little feet and kicked dust up.

"It's fine, Piriguini," Shula reassured. "It's for the emperor." She looked back up at the soldier. "If you'd please follow me?"

She had planned this as well, of course. When people would question how she was doing it. Even the simplest of human parlor tricks could be considered magic, if done right. All it took was the sleight of hand, one she would be revealing to the officers today.

She led them into the main tent and behind the velvet curtain where they kept all of their supplies. It was easier to let them sit there on hand for their acts instead of hauling them back and forth to their personal tents every night. Shula immediately went to her own pile and pulled out her things.

"The answer to your inquiries, good soldier, is gun powder, oil, and flame. Not particularly in that order, and not always together." She picked up a long piece of thin cord that had a ball attached at the bottom. She dipped it in oil and stepped back. "Let me give you a demonstration." Quicker than he could blink, she struck a hidden match and the ball lit in a small flame. "Sleight of the hand, soldier." Then she stepped back even further and began to move, going through the motions of her dance. "The trick for creating figures is to draw them in the air. I'm an artist, you see, and I have to move as fast as possible for the illusion to stick." She traced the image of a kitten in the air, moving so fast that sparks trailed wherever she moved the ball of fire, leaving behind works of art. "The cord is thin so the crowd can't see it." She stopped and dipped the fire in a bucket of sand to put it out.

The soldier still looked skeptical. "What about the fire dragon?"

"We have a backdrop for that. Thin, string-like structures that are dipped in oil and molded overnight. They harden and the backdrop is placed up just before my act. When I strike a match, the whole thing catches fire."

"See? And you all better keep your mouths shut about it, too! It's a secret!"

Piriguini, again, went ignored.

The captain nodded at his soldiers, and they began searching through the things in the tent and they weren't kind about it. They knocked stuff over, tore through Fanny's ribbons and ropes. They made a mess of the entire tent, all while keeping his deadly gaze locked tightly on Shula. She met it without fear. If anything, her expression appeared demurely innocent.

Finally, the soldiers all snapped back towards their leader, shaking their heads back and forth. Of course, he wouldn't find anything.

Shula had ensured that she would never be found out like her parents had been.

"Thank you for your cooperation, Shula Azzarh, and forgive us. You must understand the importance of tracking down any and all Fae." The captain bowed, but the suspicion never once left his eyes. She could still read the thirst for blood tensing his every movement.

Shula still smiled sweetly at him. "Of course, I understand. I hope you find what you're looking for."

When the words left her lips, she wasn't even sure if she believed them herself. Did she want the Fae found? If they did, then all of this would end. The fear, the bigotry. But if they were found, it would mean their death and how could she ever hope for that, even if it meant her own safety, even if it meant she would remain hidden from the emperor? How could she wish to condemn her own race to die for her own protection?

The truth was, her own had abandoned her long ago. The humans didn't protect her, and the Fae only brought with them death.

She could count on no one in this entire world. Not on humans, not on Fae. The only person she had to help her survive was herself. Humans wanted her dead, and the Fae were sparse.

And Shula Azzarh couldn't bring herself to put her faith in legends or cowards who hid in the shadows.

Even while that thought fluttered through her mind, she ignored the pang of guilt. Because if they were cowards, then that made her the biggest one of them all.

"Shula, are you okay? Are you harmed?" Fanny's hands slid over Shula's whole body, patting her down to check for injuries that weren't there. Shula grabbed Fanny's wrists and gently pushed them away.

"I'm fine, Fanny. They didn't hurt me."

Fanny expelled a breath of relief, her eyes closing as if sending out a quiet prayer to her god. When her eyes opened, there was a ferocity in them that moved Shula. "Good. The audacity of those soldiers! As if you'd ever be an Esses!" Shula held back her flinch at the word. "Really, the nerve! Shouldn't they know what those pointed ear abominations look like?" Even as she said the words, her eyes strayed over to Shula's ears, not visible beneath her dark waves of hair. "Although, I do admit I'd been curious for a while. You're always hiding your ears."

All Shula could do was wave her words away with a careless flicker of her hand, but her insides were rolling like clouds after a storm. "I'm self-conscious. My ears are too small." A lie. The real reason she hid them was so no one could ever see the scars, the proof of what she'd been forced to do to keep herself safe.

"You have nothing to be self-conscious about. All of you is lovely, I am sure your ears are too. As long as they aren't pointed, who cares what they look like?"

The words were like a small dagger to her heart. They hurt. They put a pressure on her chest that made it hard to breathe for a fraction of a second. If she needed any more proof that no one would ever accept her true nature, it was right here. While she'd known that, she couldn't believe that it still hurt to realize it, fully and completely.

She took a step away from the human. Her friend. Were they even friends? she questioned. Surely friends should know one another's darkest secrets. What did Fanny really know about Shula?

She knew all the things that mattered.

She recognized the lie for what it really was. And all she wanted right then was to get away. To go see someone who knew what she really was, what she kept inside. Someone who would understand.

She couldn't explain it, couldn't even understand it herself. This sudden, fierce need to be acknowledged when she never even acknowledged herself.

"I—I have to go," Shula said, her voice shaking with emotion.

Fanny's blonde brows pulled into a tight frown. "Are you okay? You look flushed." She pressed her palm against Shula's cheek and her frown deepened. "And a fever has set in."

Shula pulled away, not able to bear her friend's touch. She tried to explain away her abrupt behavior by forcing a smile to her lips. "Fine. Perfect. I think last night's sweet meat upset my stomach." That was too much information, but she didn't care. She just had to get away.

"Oh, okay. If you need a tea brewed let me know. I'm sure we could find something to ease the aches. Are you sure you don't want me to—"

But Shula was already turning and staggering away.

She couldn't help this pull she felt to find Davina. It was a bad idea, a terrible one, and yet her blood hummed. Her nerves were on edge and she felt like her blood was boiling beneath her skin. Her clothes clung uncomfortably to her skin and she tugged at the garments. They felt all too suffocating, causing her lungs to squeeze and her breath to come out in short pants.

She didn't know when she started running, just that her feet were pounding against the earth, rocks digging into the calloused skin. She couldn't feel the pain of it, couldn't break past the wall of her own tumultuous emotions rising, higher and hotter against her skin like they would break forth at any moment. Like something violent and wild lived beneath her skin, waiting to explode.

She didn't stop running until she saw the hand painted sign that read *Davina's Fortune and Tarot Readings.* She burst past the tent flaps only to find the place empty.

She didn't bother calling out to Davina. She could already sense she wasn't there. There were no sounds of breathing or the eerie, prickling sense she usually got at the back of her neck when others were near.

Shula tried to calm her breathing, but that sense of wrongness still climbed viscerally beneath her skin. The need to find Davina just grew stronger and stronger. She walked out of the tent. Everything seemed brighter, every noise louder in a way it had never been before. Not even when she'd been growing into her powers as a child had she felt this ill.

Shula was by no means a seer; she couldn't see the future in any capacity. Her own powers were more volatile than that, more unpredictable. Yet the strangest sense of premonition settled over her mind. The image flared in her mind as if she was seeing it through the eyes of someone else. Because she was. She was staring down at the rush of river water, a flash of bare skin, hands with long fingers and purple nails that looked like claws.

Davina.

She was seeing this from Davina's own eyes. It was a calling, like will-o'-the-wisps beckoning Fae to their fate, and Shula had to answer.

A moment later, the image faded, and she rushed across the circus grounds. She followed the river upwards, the sensation in her blood growing stronger with every step she took, each more grueling than the last.

And then she finally saw her.

Davina stood in the shallow end of the river, bare from head to toe. Water rolled off skin as smooth as porcelain. Her long hair was unbound and cascaded over her shoulder and down to her narrow hips. The lush locks left her ear bare on one side like a flaring sign of culpability, the tip elongated and pointed towards the sky.

"Fuck."

Her own pain forgotten, Shula rushed to Davina, the water soaking through the hem of her long skirts. Her legs tangled, but she kicked the material away with impatience as she reached the Fae, fingers already unwrapping the scarf from around her shoulders.

"Davina..." She wanted to chastise her for being so careless until she saw the goosebumps all over her naked skin, the way her whole body shivered as if she were standing in ice.

It wasn't particularly cold or warm out, but when Shula pressed her hand against Davina's shoulder it felt like she'd dipped her fingers in snow.

Shula looked at Davina's eyes, unseeing and rolled to the back of her head. Sympathy rose inside her. One couldn't very well help what powers they were born with, and they couldn't always help when the power looked for an outlet.

All magic needed to be released, otherwise it built inside a Fae's body. To suppress magic meant terrible consequences. Shula didn't want to think about what would happen to her for keeping her powers tightly leashed, or how she'd been able to keep them that way for so long. She wondered if it would be this bad or worse.

"Let's get you out of this cold water." She threw her wrap around Davina's shoulders. Even though the woman didn't reply, she was docile as Shula pulled her away from the river and up the little slope of dirt and grass. "Can I dry you off?"

Davina dipped her head in a nod. Even though her eyes were completely white, she was still capable of hearing. That was something, at least. Taking the scarf from her shoulders, Shula used it to pat down Davina's body as gently as she would for a child. Being out here in the open with Davina's ears exposed made Shula nervous, but her worry overrode that sentiment.

She briefly wondered if the reason the discomfort had swept over her body was because she was meant to find Davina, to help her. Now that they were so close, her own pain seemed really far away.

"Did you send that vision to me somehow?" Her ministrations didn't stop against Davina's body, but Shula's voice was quiet as she asked the question.

Davina's response was a mere rasp of breath. "Yes."

"Why?"

"Because the prophecy..."

A shiver slid against Shula's skin that made her hands shake. "What prophecy?"

Her eyes were blank and unseeing, but they focused on Shula with such an intensity that it made unease crawl over her. "Our destinies are already foretold." A deep breath. "Yours will change the world as we know it."

"Speak clearly," Shula snapped. She knew it was out of fear. Fear of those words, about the world changing. Everyone feared the unknown, and the Fire Dancer was no exception.

But Davina sounded far away. "I see robes of white and red. I see chains of iron and symbols carved on the ground. I see you, choking on water that burns like fire."

"Davina, what are you talking about?"

"Twin flames carved in flesh."

"Who's flesh?"

"Scars." Her whole body shuddered. "The eyes of the demon lead to freedom." Her every word was shaky and disjointed, and Shula couldn't make sense of a single word of it. "The resistance. Twin flames. Twin flames. Twinflamestwinflamestwinflames—" She broke off and crumbled.

Shula cried out and grabbed her before she could fall to the grass. The impact of their bodies colliding seemed to break Davina out of her stupor. She gasped, blinked, and her eyes went back to their normal dark hue. She pushed away from Shula and straightened, taking the scarf with her to wrap it around her body.

"It's awakening," Davina whispered.

Shula clenched her jaw. "What's awakening?" she gritted out from between clenched teeth.

And Davina met her eyes and there was something coherent and ominous in them. Her eyes spoke of warning and danger. "You."

Before Shula could ask what she meant, Davina turned and walked away.

"Wait!" Shula took a step and that's when the pain came. Her knees buckled and gave out under her. She dropped to the ground, a cry bursting past the barrier of her lips.

It was an all-consuming feeling that ripped through her every nerve. It burst past her bones and her head pounded like she'd been hit with a hammer. It spread over her every inch, rising. Her blood heated beneath her skin, and her body shivered even while she felt the heat like she was over a bonfire. It burst. It burned. It took her sanity and every sensation except the pain.

It was how she knew. Her magic; she'd suppressed it her whole life and now it was fighting back, retaliating and demanding exit.

No. Her fingers scraped over the earth, and her nails cracked and bled.

No.

She wouldn't let it. This couldn't be happening.

No. No!

A silent scream echoed through her mind. She wasn't sure if she voiced it or not. All she knew was the dizziness in her mind rising to fervent heights, bursting... bursting...

She screamed just as the fire consumed her.

She'd wondered on the day she would explode, wondered if it would be tranquil or if it would shake worlds.

This was worse than anything she could have imagined.

Her whole body lit up in flames. Fire, looking to wreak destruction. Everything she ever suppressed, every memory, every urge flicked out of her in blazing fingers that reached and searched.

A tingle spread down her spine, making her gasp. She thought she knew pain? She'd been wrong. It seared across her back like a burning blade against flesh, carving against her spine.

It felt like an eternity before the pain ebbed. Slowly, it spilled from her body like honey sliding from a glass jar, and the feeling it left in its wake was an aching throb that pulsed. And her back? That pain stayed.

Bile rose to the back of her throat. Her mouth opened and saliva slid out. She wanted to vomit; her stomach heaved but nothing came out.

"Ggnnh..." Her fingers dug into the dirt as she tried to haul herself up. She managed to get to her knees, which scraped across rocks and dirt. Her whole body was covered in ash. It coated over her lips and eyes, remnants of her clothes that the fire had burned off. Her hair curtained her face and she tossed it aside, but even the simple act of turning her head hurt. She heaved again and through the haze of agony, she heard a voice.

"Shules?"

Fuck, fuck, fuck!

Through her lashes, she saw Fanny, saw her expression, saw the disgust on it enough to know that she'd witnessed everything. She'd seen Shula go up in flames.

Shula had wanted a friend. A deep part of her had wanted Fanny to accept what she really was. But she saw the expression in her eyes, and she knew, without a doubt, that it would never happen.

"Fanny..." Shula's fingers struggled for purchase as she pushed herself upwards with painstaking slowness. She made it to her knees and began to crawl.

And Fanny... Fanny stepped back and tripped over her feet. She fell to the ground. "Stay away from me, Esses scum!"

Shula stopped, the impact of Fanny's words hitting painfully like a spear to the chest. "F-Fanny." She hated the weak sound of her own voice, the desperation in it, the hurt that leaked through every word. "Fanny, it's me..." She reached her hand out and Fanny flinched.

"Stay away from me, Fae scum!"

The denial came to Shula's lips, but she forced it back. What could she deny? Fanny had witnessed it; she'd watched as Shula's body had caught fire. And now everything Shula had ever worked to keep hidden crumbled into the ash beneath her knees.

"Fanny, please." Her voice cracked and she felt her lips bleeding. The fire hadn't burned her. The first time her magic had come out, all those years ago, she hadn't felt the heat of it touch her skin. She felt warmth and comfort of her elemental magic. She felt the life force inside her as bright as a star flicker to life. Only now, it hurt. She wondered if that was the price she had to pay for suppressing it for so long. The burns slicing down her back.

"Help me," Shula begged again. She didn't know who else had seen the flames or heard Fanny cry out. It wouldn't be long before the emperor's soldiers came running to chain her and take her to one of the camps. "They'll kill me."

And Shula didn't want to die.

"You're a Fae," Fanny argued. She still hadn't moved. She still hadn't run away shrieking. Shula wanted to hope that it was a sign her friend cared for her, that the initial shock was wearing off. That she could put aside her prejudice and help Shula, who had been her best friend for years. "But, your ears..."

"I can explain everything, but please help me." Her limbs still shook almost uncontrollably as she tried once again in vain to get to her feet. The pain down her back was too prominent. Her flesh felt carved up and she couldn't even move.

Fanny's eyes darted around, and she chewed at her bottom lip. Shula knew her well enough to know that she was contemplating it, that she was weakening Fanny's defenses. If there was one thing Fanny liked, it was helping the less fortunate.

"We're friends."

"You lied to me. You're a dangerous Fae."

"When have I ever harmed you? You have to believe me. I would never, ever do anything to put you in danger."

"But you are by asking me to help you."

"Because I don't have a choice."

Shula waited, counting the heartbeats that followed. Just when she started to lose all hope, Fanny pushed herself to her feet and walked cautiously towards her.

"You have a lot of explaining to do, Shula Azzarh."

Fanny's hands were firm as she gripped Shula's shoulders. Though she was small, she was strong. She had to be for her act, and she hoisted Shula up as if she weighed nothing, and all she gave was a tiny grunt.

Shula's every muscle screamed in protest as Fanny pulled her in that first step. Her knees shook and she tried as hard as she could, gritting as she placed one foot after the other.

At a slow and excruciating pace, Fanny helped slip her into Shula's tent. She was glad she decided to always keep apart from the others and even more grateful for her hindsight now.

"Do you think anyone heard or saw?" Shula asked as Fanny set her down on plush pillows. The moment her back hit the material, she hissed out her pain.

Fanny stood across from her at a protective distance. Though she'd brought her here, she was still staring warily, like Shula would lose control at any moment and attack. Her hands pressed against her hips. "I don't think so. You know they all sleep like the dead during the day."

A small blessing, really.

Shula sat up and winced as her back muscles pulled. "Fanny, can you hand me that mirror over there?" She needed to know what her back looked like, why it hurt.

Fanny frowned. "Aren't you going to explain things to me?"

"I will, I promise I will, but I have to see my back." She felt blood trickle down her wounds.

She sighed with exasperation but did as Shula obliged, hoisting up the full-length mirror and bringing it over to her.

As carefully as she could, Shula stood on wobbling knees and flicked her hair over her shoulder. Angling her body, she let her back face the mirror, and turned to look at the reflection.

Fanny gasped.

"What in god's name happened to your back? Is that some sort of Esses curse?"

Shula couldn't find offense at the word. Not at that moment.

Not when what she was looking at was far more surprising. It did look like someone had taken a blade to her back. It looked like they had embedded steel deep into her flesh and carved images. Two circles in a straight line starting just below her neck and down her spine with curving flames in the center.

Twin flames carved in flesh.

Davina's vision of the future… it had come true.

The wounds were little more than bleeding, mangled flesh, but Shula could still make out the design as if it had been carved with a talented hand. She didn't understand it. She didn't want to understand. She wanted it off. Bile rose to the back of her throat and she forced it down.

"What's that?" Fanny was staring at her back with open disgust marring her features.

"I don't know." Shula didn't have to lie about that. She didn't know if it was the price of suppressing her magic or something else, something more sinister.

Davina's words came back to her, prophecies and premonitions that had been too disjointed for her to make any sense of. Even when this had happened, she couldn't understand why.

Robes of white and red.

Chains of iron.

Demons and scars.

One thing was certain: there was still more to come. Shula didn't want to know what.

"Are you lying to me?" Murder laced through Fanny's words. It was the most violent Shula had ever seen her, her blue eyes flaring as she stared down her slightly large nose at Shula.

"I'm not." And she didn't want to talk about the markings on her back anymore. She would find Davina, and she would demand her answers. If she ever got that far. First, she had to speak to Fanny, to convince her not to turn her into the emperor's soldiers.

As quickly as her wounds would let her, Shula turned and grabbed a spare tunic thrown carelessly on the floor. Wincing as she put it on, she let it settle over her thighs, covering the worst of her nudity. Once she settled into her pillows, she gestured to Fanny to have a seat across from her.

She set the mirror aside and crossed her arms over her chest. "I'll stand, thanks."

Shula sighed and resisted the urge to rub her temples. She had to remind herself that she was the liar here, the Fae. Fanny had every right in the world to be wary of her because she'd lied.

"I don't know where to start." Or if she even wanted to, but she had no other choice. Fanny could go to the soldiers. As much as Shula wanted to keep this a secret, she couldn't. Not anymore. And she'd be lying if she said a deeper part of her didn't want Fanny's acceptance. But she was terrified of what the truth might bring.

"The beginning. Now. I'm losing patience, Fae."

A bitter laugh rumbled from Shula's throat and when she met Fanny's eyes, her own narrowed into thin slits. "That fucking word." She shook her head. "You say it with so much venom. And that is precisely why I could tell you nothing." Some of her Fae cadence had slipped between her words. They had a lilt to their speech that was refined, something she'd hid for so long. A little part of her Papa that she kept hidden within herself. All it had taken was for someone else to know the truth for her roots to slip between the cracks of her walls.

"Can you blame me? I don't even know what the truth is anymore! Are we even really friends or did you use your magic on me to trick me? To trick everyone?"

"I don't use glamor. I haven't used magic in years."

Her eyebrows rose in a condescending way. As if to ask what Shula called bursting into flames, then?

"Except for today. I don't know what that was or what happened. But I swear to you, I left the Fae life behind." *I don't even want to be Fae.* Those words went unsaid. Even thinking them felt like a betrayal, so she didn't. "I left that life behind ten years ago." The moment her parents were taken from her. The moment the old woman's blood coated her dirty legs and hem.

One look at Fanny's unconvinced expression, and Shula knew she was going to have to bare her heart, her soul. She would be forced to give up every secret she could, tear herself apart in a way that terrified her.

With a shaking hand, she shoved away the errant waves of hair that obstructed her view of Fanny. "What do you want to know?" Her voice was a broken, fearful sound.

"Everything."

And with a heavy breath shaking through her smoke-filled lungs, she began to speak.

Mana

Soul raw and aching more than her back, Shula slumped against the pillows. While her body looked relaxed, she was anything but. She was filled with fear as she waited for Fanny's reaction.

She had kept quiet for the most part, letting Shula speak her story. Shula hadn't held anything back. She gave every bit of herself, stuttering through the story of her life. She'd separated herself from it as best as she could, telling it like she was a mere spectator in her own life, if only so she wouldn't break down crying like she truly wanted to with every painful word that wrenched from her throat.

Her life had been one tragedy after another, and the only happiness she could find had been at Piriguini's Circus. And now even that was on shaking ground, threatening to crumble and destroy.

Shula stared at Fanny, taking in a deep breath. Fanny just stared right back. Her expression had softened every time the story progressed, but she was still hard lines and slashing glares.

It made Shula lose hope.

Just as she started to say goodbye to her life, for there was no possible way she was making it through the day alive, Fanny slowly took a seat across from her.

"Why didn't you tell me this before?"

Shula made a choked noise. "How could I? You're looking at me like I've changed right before your eyes. Like I am some type of monster."

"You're Fae."

As if that said everything, explained everything.

"I am still Shula Azzarh. I am still your Shules, your friend. That friendship? It was never a lie. I still care about you. I still love you, even if fire flows through my veins. Even if I have magic, I am still me. I still like dessert before dinner, I still am a talented dancer. We still laughed together, and those jokes weren't a lie. The only thing different is that now you know that we are different. Yet we are the same. Friends. At least, I pray that we still are."

It took a long moment before Fanny answered. "You don't like what you are, do you?"

Shula didn't want to say the words, but she forced them out anyway. Her cheeks heated with shame, and she could taste it like a visceral venom coated along her tongue. "If I could change what I am, I would."

Those words would seem rudimentary to a human, but they were a perilous betrayal to Shula's parents and to everything she'd ever known. But they were enough for Fanny.

Smiling, Fanny reached across the space that separated them and gripped Shula's hands in her own. "Then that is all that matters."

It was acceptance. Broken acceptance, but acceptance just the same. And hadn't Shula dreamt of this? Of a life with no barriers, with a friend who would know what she so deeply hid and who would take her hands anyway and smile like nothing had changed? They would never be the same now that Fanny knew the truth, but a monumental weight had shifted from her shoulders.

And shifted to her heart.

That, like everything else in her life, could be hidden behind unfeeling walls of lies and treachery. Nothing else mattered right then but Fanny's wide smile and her hands clutching Shula's, like she could ground their friendship to the earth with the strength of her grip.

Like, all things considered, she was just too afraid to let go.

"I need to go see Davina." Shula settled a new wrap over her shoulders. She'd changed into a simple white tunic, brown pants, and sensible boots. She usually didn't wear such practical clothing, as it took away from the illusion of the illustrious Fire Dancer, but all her stage outfits were revealing, and she didn't want anyone to see her scars bleed through the bandages on her back. She still kept the wrap, though. A sheer red material that made her feel pretty. Perhaps it was vain to want to feel that way, but with slashed flesh across her skin, it had her feeling some type of way.

Fanny looked at her warily. "Why?"

No more lies, Shula had promised only moments before. She would no longer lie about her life, but Davina's secret wasn't hers to tell. It was the one thing in her whole story she'd left out. She might have accidentally condemned herself and shared her secret, but she wouldn't do the same to Davina. It had been difficult enough getting Fanny to keep her secret without having to drag the seer into it.

"She makes poultices and remedies. I am going to ask her for something for my nerves and my back..."

That answer seemed to satisfy Fanny, though Shula did have to admit, the woman looked a bit distracted anyway. She supposed it was because of the shock of what she'd found out. So much information about Shula's troubled life would have upset anyone. To find out that your friend was on the run from the law couldn't have been easy.

"Alright," said Fanny. "I have to go get ready for my act."

Shula didn't comment on the fact that it was still daybreak outside and their acts didn't start until another four hours. Fanny was already walking out of the tent, and Shula just watched her go, feeling a strange sense of tightness in her chest. Unable to explain why the sudden wrongness slithered down her spine, she pushed it away and went out in search of Davina.

The camp was finally beginning to stir. Shula felt nervous walking among them. Everything felt different now that Fanny knew her secret. Her gaze darted everywhere, gauging the reactions of everyone around her, to see if they'd heard, if they'd witnessed. No one was looking at her any differently. They all were very cordial as she passed by. It seemed the only one changed was her. And Fanny.

She made it to Davina's tent and didn't bother announcing her presence. Why would she when the Fae had great hearing? She walked in and Davina was already waiting for her. Tea had been set out on her small table, the strong smell of incense and herbs clouding the confined space.

The Fae appeared more coherent and in her full senses, which was a relief. She smiled her razor-sharp smile, but there was no malice in it. Only a sad, soft sort of calmness.

"I have been expecting you. Please, sit."

Shula did as she bade, reaching for the teacup and saucer that had been set out for her across the table. She didn't take a sip.

"What's happening to me?" she demanded on a low voice.

Davina picked up her own teacup and sipped, giving her a pointed glance. Sighing, Shula picked up her cup and drank it all in one swallow. The bursting taste of herbs exploded on her tongue, and she regretted it immediately because the tea was scalding hot. Perhaps her own fire could never burn her, but other things could.

"Tea should be enjoyed." When Shula placed the cup back down, Davina was already topping it off again. "So, enjoy it."

This time, she did. She brought it to her lips and blew before taking a dainty sip.

Davina seemed pleased with this. She set her own cup on its saucer and interlaced her fingers together above the table. "What do you want to know?" Her words sounded mocking and strangely echoed what Shula had asked Fanny about an hour ago, but she ignored the seer's tone.

"What happened to me?"

"My dear, didn't your parents tell you anything at all?"

"No," Shula gritted out. "They died before they could get the chance."

Davina didn't look sorry at all that she'd asked. She didn't look moved, either. There was always a coldness about her. Most of the older Fae wore that same expression. As if nothing and no one, no emotion or anything could ever touch them. Shula had only ever met a few older Fae in her lifetime. Before the Fae registrations and reservations. Before the camps. Before death.

"My dear, you are an Elemental."

Shula blinked. "I know." That was the one thing her father had told her. Her parents had been normal Fae, neither of them with any powers beyond the typical ability to glamor. It was a talent all Fae were born with, and a talent that worked mostly on humans. A Fae could glamor themselves to look more beautiful, alter their own appearance, but they could not seduce another Fae with that magic. Not all Fae had an extension of powers beyond that.

"Then you must know how rare the Elementals are?"

Shula didn't know that.

"The markings on your back just prove you are the rarest. A fire Fae, yes?"

Smoke filled her lungs, but she didn't choke. She never could. Not on her own magic, but she could still feel the ash coating her body, still feel it in her hair, on her tongue. "Yes," she ground out.

Davina smiled and took another sip. "A rare gem. Do you know why you're so rare?"

"No."

"Of course not. You've been living as a human your whole life, suppressing what makes you integral to us." She said it with a disdain that bled into her tone and made Shula uncomfortable. Fanny had spat at her for being Fae, Davina for being too human. "It is a wonder you did not explode for keeping it tightly leashed inside."

"Can you skip to the part where you explain everything to me?"

Davina sighed and set her teacup down, the porcelain clattering against the saucer, echoing her annoyance. "Mana save me from ignorance. Fine. You are aware that all magic comes with a price?" Shula's answer was a barely perceptible nod. "It is a way to balance out things in the universe. If you use magic, you are taking and that requires a tithe. I see fragments of the future, the price of it is my sanity."

So she was aware of it. Shula looked at her with sympathy, which only seemed to amuse the seer.

"Some have it worse. Some seers have visions of death, and the price is that they can never witness their own."

That didn't seem so bad, all things considered.

"Because you are an Elemental, you draw your power straight from the universe, from Mana. You do know what Mana is, yes?"

Shula's eyes rolled. "Of course I know what Mana is." It was basic Fae knowledge. Mana was everything. It was the life force that flowed through the earth, the soul that connected the race of the Fae and kept them tethered to their magic and to nature.

"Since your magic is a fragment of Mana, it is raw power and, as such, requires no tithe. Because you are literally part of Mana itself. It is also why you were able to suppress your power so long without your well of magic becoming too great."

The bleeding wounds on her back argued otherwise. "Then what was that?" Shula demanded. "Why did my magic consume me? And why do I have the scars you predicted I'd have?"

"Things are changing, Fire Dancer. The Fae will fall beneath robes of white and red unless we do something."

"What does that mean?"

The darkness in Davina's eyes faded until her entire eyes were white.

No, not again.

"Things are changing, Fire Dancer," she repeated. "Will you rise to the occasion or diminish your own flame?"

"Davina."

But it was like Davina couldn't hear her, like she was too far gone. She stared and stared until her gaze became lost to an eternity only she could see, and no words elicited a reaction from her.

"Davina!"

She began to convulse, falling face first against the table. The teacup clattered and tea spilled all over the silky cloth. Her body shuddered in violent waves and words spilled from her mouth.

"You will be betrayed, Fire Dancer. Beware the robes of white and red. Remember, the eyes of the demon lead to freedom."

Her head hit the table. Hard. Then there was silence.

Shula sighed and walked around the table to pick her up and lean her back against the pillows. A giant knot had formed on her forehead where she'd slammed her face, and Shula didn't doubt she'd have a headache when she woke up.

Once she had Davina laying comfortably, she cleaned up the mess. Shula couldn't bear to leave her like this, so she waited, waited for hours and still Davina didn't stir. It would have worried her, had she not sought out the pulse at her neck and felt the steady, strumming beat of her heart. When the sun finally began to lower across the horizon, Shula knew she had to leave her and get ready for her show.

The words she'd spoken while convulsing tried to haunt Shula. She forced herself to shake them off as she exited the tent and tied the strings of the flaps together, letting customers know that Davina was currently out of business.

Even if one of her prophetic ramblings had come to pass, how accurate were the rest of them? She didn't understand the powers of a seer, but Davina had said it herself. The price was her sanity, and so her ramblings had sounded crazy, unpredictable, and unrealistic. Still, Shula wouldn't disregard the words. Robes of white and red. The eyes of the demon lead to freedom. It was the same ramblings over and over.

You will be betrayed...

That made her stumble as she walked towards her own tent. A dire, sick feeling climbed up her throat, but she shoved it down. Fanny wouldn't betray her.

Would she?

No. She had to believe that their years of friendship had counted for something. They *had* counted for something. She might have trouble accepting her at first, but Shula was desperate enough to believe that Fanny would come through for her.

All her life she'd been alone, had trusted and confided in no one but herself. She'd come from nothing, a poor orphan with blood on her hem and stolen pearls in her pocket. She'd turned that into a strength of her own; she'd become as human as she possibly could be. Life had been safe, and it had been lonely.

And then she'd met Fanny.

Fanny had been a brightness in the blight of Shula's soul. For the first time since she'd lost her parents, she'd felt a closeness to someone else. Even if all the puzzle pieces of truth weren't set in place, there was no faking that connection they shared. Best friends. Fanny did have her flaws, Shula wasn't blind to them, but Fanny was the one thing she couldn't give up. Because it was that closeness she craved, and it was that closeness she believed she wouldn't find with another.

She wondered if that made her weak. Perhaps what was happening went against everything she ever believed in. Had it been anyone else to discover her, Shula would have done whatever it took to keep her secret safe. She would have killed. But Fanny was different.

Friends. We are friends.

She had to keep repeating that to herself, because if she thought for even just a moment that Fanny would betray her, then Shula wouldn't hesitate to take a blade and plunge it into her friend's heart.

Into the Madness

Davina's eyes slowly blinked open, but it was her body that was faster to react. She shot up from her pillows and stared into the darkness of her tent. Night had fallen and already; she could hear the cries and shrieks of revelry.

Human revelry was vastly distant from the wild drumbeats of the Fae. There was no magic or passion in it, just dead laughter and eyes that were not fully open. Humans just did not see. At least, not like Davina saw. They did not live with the curse of catching fragments of memories that were not memories at all, but rather a future yet to pass.

It happened in flashes, like bright bursts of blinding light against the vision, and so often that sometimes she could not quite distinguish the differences between past, present, and future.

Sometimes memories of her own long life passed, of a time when her homeland of Tir na Faie, The Feylands, to the south, had been ripe with magic.

She remembered the elegance of the Seelie Court, and the savage madness of the Unseelie near the Black Ocean. Until the blight came upon the lands and everything changed.

No more faerie lights canopied over an endless expanse of trees. No more magic. No more selkies pushing through rivers and swamps, or pixies buzzing in hoards and streaking across the sky like clusters of falling stars.

For the first time, though, the future was clear. And at the center of madness not her own, was Shula Azzarh.

The time was coming, and all the pieces of the future were aligning, falling into place.

And for the first time, Davina felt a clarity deep in her bones.

Standing to her full height, she set to work, pulling a drab, brown cloak over her shoulders. She pulled the turban from her head, unwrapping it carefully. It was second nature now to hide her true self behind drab clothing, and yet what she did was nothing compared to what Shula had done to hide her nature.

What traumas she must have lived to have to hide so.

The thought broke her heart and pushed Davina to move faster. With her hair loose and cascading over her shoulders, she pulled the hood of her cloak up, concealing her features in shadows. Only then did she step from her tent, blending into the darkness and walking on steady, determined feet, leaving Piriguini's Circus behind.

The place had never felt like home. Not in the way the Obsidian Court in Tir na Faie was home. She had only come for Shula. Because Davina had known what she would be, what the fire Fae would mean to their entire race.

And Davina prayed to Mana that Shula find the fire inside herself before it was too late.

Stepping on human roads in the middle of the night was likely unwise, and yet Davina already knew that nothing would befall her. Not yet. Not at this hour tonight.

Fate would be kind to her as she walked through the semi-empty streets of Tuath, and it was the own power of her visions that guided her down dark, poor alleyways and led her to what looked like an abandoned building.

No fire lantern burned down these ways, and so nothing illuminated the run-down factory. Made of steel and crumbling brick, the entrance was a thin wooden door, held together by thicker wooden planks hammered down with iron nails.

Davina rapped her knuckles across the surface in a four-note pattern that she'd heard in her dreams. She held her breath, gripping the lapels that held her cloak together with one hand, the other hovering over the doorway.

Her heartbeats measured the seconds.

Ba-dump.

Ba-dump.

Ba-dump.

Slowly, the door creaked open and she stepped back, finding weapons staring down her nose threateningly.

"Show your face, stranger," a commanding voice ordered. Another sound she'd dreamt and recognized like the melodies of home.

Coherence was an affectation when all she knew was madness. So Davina was surprised, when she lifted her hands and slowly lowered her hood to reveal her face, that she did not tremble. Looking up into different sets of eyes, she offered up a razor-sharp smile that showed canines and all, like she was looking into the madness itself.

"Good evening," she purred. "I would ask your forgiveness for the interruption, but I have found the answer to all your problems."

Chains of Iron

"Another crush," Shula whispered as she peeked behind the curtain and out at the crowd. But the words felt hollow and empty leaving her lips.

Tonight made her more nervous than any other night had simply because the wounds on her back ached. They pulsed and burned, and every time she moved, she could feel blood drip down her spine.

She'd dressed carefully in silky clothes that draped across her body and covered the symbols etched onto her back. Golden bands wrapped around her throat, the black cloth tied on them flowed down her curves. She'd left her arms bare of everything except the golden bracelets.

She was going to go with her gentle routine tonight; slow, sinuous movements that wouldn't pull at her wounds. The black would hide the blood.

"Break a leg," Fanny replied absently.

Shula stared at her friend. Her eyes were wide and bright, and she was smiling too widely, as if nothing between them had changed. As if they were back to before she knew the truth about Shula. It was nice to not have her glaring at her with suspicion. It was nice to know that there was a bright side to all of this.

"Break yours first." Shula smiled and bent down to ruffle Fanny's hair like she usually did. Fanny didn't tense or pull away. She smirked as though all was right and well in the world.

And it was.

Those were Shula's thoughts as she stepped out and began her routine.

The night dragged on painfully, and Shula was exhausted by the end of it. She just wanted to crawl over her pillows and fall into a dreamless sleep, but the moment their acts ended, Fanny looped her arm through Shula's and smiled up at her.

"I'm exhausted. Dessert first?"

It was such a normal thing to say, that even feeling bone-deep tired, Shula couldn't deny her. They walked around, watching the circus goers stumble away, high on popped corn and sparkling drinks, with empty pockets, prizes, and a lifetime of memories. That's what the circus was; it's what it signified to others and specifically to Shula. It was new beginnings and memories and happiness.

Fanny drug her all around the stands and together they had their fill of caramel apples, chocolate-dipped bread, sweet meats and vegetables on kabobs, and sparkling cider that Fanny insisted on drinking, one heavy drink after another that made Shula dizzy on her feet.

Feeling full and ready to burst, they stumbled towards the back of the circus where their tents were set up. Shula nearly tripped. Her head felt dizzy, her vision groggy.

"I think I drank too much," she complained, wrapping an arm around her stomach. "I think my back is bleeding again." The material of her skirts clung to her soaked bandages, and she knew it would be painful to rip away. "I need Davina to look at the wounds..."

"I can do that for you," Fanny offered, her voice dropping to a whisper.

Heat pricked at the backs of Shula's eyelids, and she forced it away. "You'd do that?" The alcohol mixed into the cider was making her head swim, and she didn't like it. Shula didn't usually drink the fruity drinks because they messed her up worse than straight alcohol ever could. She liked fruity things, but in pastries, not in her alcohol. She could usually drink a lot and not feel the effects. Perhaps she'd drunk more than she realized?

"Of course," Fanny said. "We're friends, aren't we?"

The statement moved Shula. She threw her arm around her, Fanny's small body keeping her upright. "We are, aren't we?" While her feet wobbled, her voice didn't slur or come out distorted in any way. She tried to steer Fanny towards her own tent, but Fanny veered off the pathway and led them down towards the river.

"Let's just do it down here," she suggested. "I'll need water to clean your wounds and we can't carry buckets of it to your tent."

"Sounds like a plan."

They walked in silence after that, Shula's vision threatening to blur. She just wanted to sleep. It had been a difficult day and her body was protesting all over. Sleep was threatening to claim her mind, and she was trying very hard not to fall under.

"We've been walking for forever." Shula blinked rapidly, trying to clear the cobwebs from her mind. She looked around. They'd gone too far away from their encampment. "Wha—"

"Do you want others to see your scars?"

"No."

"We need privacy." Her grip tightened around Shula's waist to the point of pain. She let herself be guided without further comment until they finally stopped. "Here is good."

Shula pulled away and grabbed the hem of her skirt and slowly glided it up the length of her legs. "Can you see in the dark?" she asked Fanny. "Will you be able to see my wounds to clean them?"

"I don't want to see your stupid scars, fucking Esses. Demon blood!" she spat.

Shula paused, dropping her skirts. Her eyes were suddenly alert, the pain on her back momentarily forgotten as Fanny's words chased away any dizziness she might have been feeling. She sobered, straightening.

"Fanny?" Confusion sliced up her mind. Her eyes adjusted well in the dark, and she could make out the sudden distorted expression on her friend. An expression she'd never seen her wear before. One that spoke of hatred and revulsion.

And fear.

"Don't speak my name, Fae! Don't you dare speak my name!"

Shula's mind was too slow to catch up to what was happening. "Wh-what's going on?"

"You really thought I could be friends with you knowing what you are? Fae scum!"

"Fanny—"

Shula didn't get the rest out. Figures burst from the shadows on silent feet. Had she been sober, had she been paying the slightest bit of attention to her surroundings, she would have noticed them. But Shula had placed her trust in Fanny, and when the emperor's soldiers surrounded her, she knew she'd been betrayed.

They swarmed around her, blocking out Fanny's figure as she stepped away. Not before Shula caught the malicious smile curving her mouth.

You will be betrayed, Fire Dancer.

And she had been.

In the worst way possible.

Shula had fallen for the lies. She had really thought that Fanny would accept her Fae heritage. Before she could give into the hurt, survival instinct kicked in. Too late. She turned and ran, but her legs wobbled. As if... as if she'd been poisoned.

The soldiers blocked her path, but she fought. Limbs shot out, fists connecting to steel breastplates and helmets. They barely felt the pain as her mind panicked, and all she could think about was escape. Like an animal backed into a corner, her mind went savage with the thought of freedom. Her legs kicked out blindly and her arms were nearly yanked from their sockets as they hauled her back, restraining her.

And inside her body, deep down to her soul, something stirred to life and rose. Smoke swirled in her lungs, and she inhaled it like oxygen. Heat prickled beneath her skin; it boiled her blood.

"Shit! Restrain her! Now!"

The voices were far away when a roaring suddenly appeared in her ears, like the rushing blaze of a wildfire. Someone cursed, and the stench of singed flesh filled her nostrils.

The backhanded slap came next and her eyes shot open—when had she closed them?—just as Captain Brannon came forward.

Chains of iron dangling from his fingers.

Shula barely had time to scream as the manacles were clasped around her wrists. The pain came immediately. It was like nothing she'd ever felt before. Worse even than the marks down her back. It was like a shroud had been thrown over her body, dulling her senses, her magic. Something that had lived inside her for so long, that she herself had suppressed and hadn't realized had even been there at all changed in a single instant. It dimmed, left her feeling hollow and dead inside.

She crumpled in on herself as the energy inside depleted. She sagged in their hold, but their grips remained shackled around her arms. They hauled her up unkindly, even as her legs dangled uselessly beneath her. The smell of singed flesh reached her nostrils, and it took but a moment to realize that it was her own skin burning against the touch of iron.

"Please..." The word cracked out of her throat.

Through dark lashes, she stared up at Captain Brannon. She hadn't bothered to memorize his features before, because she'd known she'd make it out of the situation and never thought to see him again. She'd been cocky, too confident in her own humanity that she'd forgotten what she really was. She'd misplaced her trust and now everything she'd built had crumbled apart.

All because she'd wanted to keep Fanny's friendship. And Fanny had betrayed her.

The captain pulled his helmet off, holding it against his hip. He stared at Shula like she was a rare treasure. Like a spider studying the prey in its web. Dark eyes were bright with rancor and something darker, too.

Malevolence.

"A fire Fae," he breathed.

Shula cringed back at the inscrutable way he whispered the words.

He stepped forward and gripped her chin in his gauntleted fingers. Steel dug into her skin and she felt the first scratch of blood flow down her face. The thick interloping chains threatened to weigh her down, but his arm kept her upright so their eyes met.

"We have been searching for you for a long time."

Fear transcended into terror. After all this time? After ten years they'd still searched for her for what had happened? She opened her mouth to argue that it hadn't been her fault. It had been the emperor's own soldiers who'd killed that human woman. Shula had just happened to be there. It just happened to be her hem dirtied with blood, her pockets filled with stolen jewels.

She bit her tongue. It didn't matter what he said. She knew all words would fall on deaf ears anyway.

He pushed aside the hair that curtained her face and his eyes locked onto her curved ears. He stared at them, long and hard enough to make Shula jerk away.

The captain chuckled and dropped his hand.

"We have great plans for you, Fae."

"What will you do with her, Captain Brannon?" Fanny asked from behind them.

Captain Brannon turned with a flicker of annoyance, as if he'd forgotten she was there at all. Instead of answering, he gestured to one of his soldier's, who tossed him a sack that clinked as he caught it. He turned and with an impatient flick of wrist, tossed the sack at Fanny's feet.

"You've served your purpose. Take your pay and leave."

Shula watched with growing horror as Fanny bent and picked up the sack of coins, weighing it in the palm of her hand.

"Fanny." Shula's voice cracked.

But Fanny spared her one last, cold glance. As if all history they'd ever shared had been broken by one single truth. As if they hadn't known one another at all. As if all their laughs, cries, and friendship had vanished into little more than ash. And Fanny turned...

And she walked away.

"Fanny!"

But Shula couldn't struggle. She couldn't do anything, because at a quick signal from the captain, a sack was pulled over her face and darkness descended.

And Shula welcomed its embrace.

Robes of White and Red

It was the sickness that woke Shula up. A roiling sensation in her stomach that had saliva dribbling from her mouth. She heaved, gagging as her stomach lurched. She couldn't help that the vomit came soon after. She didn't notice where it landed with her eyes closed, and she didn't particularly care until her body collided onto solid ground, jostling her senses awake.

"Fucking bitch!"

She felt the blow a moment later, a fist to her face that had her seeing stars. Her body hugged the floor, her wrists tethered close together by iron manacles that had started bleeding into her skin. She curled into herself on the cold ground, as if being in the fetal position would somehow save her from the death she knew would come.

It was the pain that made her curse still being alive. She was Fae, she'd broken the law by hiding, why weren't they killing her yet? Why hadn't they shoved her face first into the iron camps? Where were they taking her? Even as she wondered, she was too cowardly to open her eyes and see.

Another blow came against her ribs and she winced, using her legs to push herself away from the presence of her attacker. With the iron around her wrists, it dulled her natural Fae senses. Her hearing, her smell...

"What are you doing, soldier?" Captain Brannon's voice clipped out, berating and firm.

It silenced everything else.

"I was carrying her and she vomited on me—"

"Her stomach couldn't handle the ashwood the circus freak slipped into her drink."

So Shula had been right. Fanny *had* slipped something into her drink. Ashwood was as poisonous to Fae as iron was.

"And yet that still doesn't explain why you are abusing her," the captain continued in deadly tones.

"She vomited on me!"

Shula peeked her eyes open in time to see the captain strike at the man who had spoken. Vomit was dripping from his shoulder, disappearing down to his back. The slap had him jerking back, surprise in his eyes.

"You fucking fool," the captain hissed. "We are meant to take her in unharmed. Do you not realize how important she is? She is the emperor's property now." The other man opened his mouth to answer, but the captain shoved him away. "Of course, you didn't realize. You know nothing except what you are told, and I recall I gave you specific orders not to harm her."

Then the captain turned to Shula and bent down. His eyes didn't soften into caring, not exactly. He looked at her not like she was a living being, but like he was staring at a prized possession he didn't want taken from him.

"Are you alright?"

Shula didn't have an answer for him. How could she even begin to answer that? She *wasn't* alright. She was chained, beaten, poisoned. Betrayed.

Just like Davina said she would be.

But he seemed like he was truly waiting for an answer, one that Shula couldn't give. Captain Brannon pulled her towards him by the chains and lifted her into his arms. His touch was careful, and yet it still burned; it didn't fit against her skin.

Cradling her to his chest, he walked along corridors and Shula finally took in her surroundings. High arched ceilings loomed above her, curved structures with stained glass windows and mosaic walls in bright colors and images. The place reminded Shula of the temples she'd seen in passing in the kingdom of Dana. All somber tones and echoing footsteps. Gas lanterns lit up the shadows, and a thousand flickering candles held up on bronze tapers lined along the walls.

It was like following will-o'-the-wisps, leading Shula to her fate, whatever that may be. She wasn't sure anymore. If they wanted her relatively unharmed, that had to mean something. Something worse than immediate death. He'd also called her 'the emperor's property'. That was worse.

She counted the corridors he turned, leading them all the way down a dark hall and a set of stairs. There were no candles here to illuminate their way, but the captain's footing was sure as he stepped down into the darkness. There was a door down there, one he knocked on. Shula knew that whatever was on the other side would change her life forever.

The door opened as if by its own volition and the captain stepped through. This room was different from what they'd wandered through upstairs. It was damp and not at all pretty; like catacombs beneath the temple, it wreaked of death and was decorated like a graveyard.

Ivory skulls lined the walls in clusters, a latticework of bones spread across the ceiling, as intricate as a spiderweb's design. In the center of the room there was a table of lit candles that cast buttery light across the marble floor and the designs carved there. It looked like the floor had taken a knife to it, thick slashing lines that curved into a circle, like a pentagram with six points around it.

It wasn't until the captain set her on her feet and shoved her forward, her feet giving out under her as she crashed onto the circle, that she realized what it was. Images cut into each point, and her knees had come crashing down onto the exact replica that now lived on her spine.

Twin flames.

Shula's heart began beating at an alarming rhythm. The chains clattered together as she pushed herself up from the circle. It felt wrong to be inside it, to touch the same design that mirrored in new wounds along her back. It was like touching poison, a blight.

She remembered looking at the wounds on her back earlier. They had hurt, they still did; they'd even been confusing, but they hadn't felt *wrong*. Not like this. She scrambled away from it until her back hit armor. She bit the inside of her cheek to keep from screaming at the jolt of pain. Tilting her head up, Shula met the eyes of Captain Brannon.

He stepped away, his voice echoing through the cavernous space. "Here is the fire Fae."

"That remains to be seen." The voice that answered was ominous, and it prickled the back of Shula's neck. She twisted her body, her skirts catching against her ankles as she tried to find the source of the voice.

"Let her go through the trials. Let us see if she is the one we've been seeking."

The clattering of the captain's armor began to fade as he walked from the room. Other footsteps joined and then the door closed.

Shula instinctively knew that she was alone.

She stood to her feet, knees wobbling. The iron was taking a toll on her body, and the ashwood in her veins made her stomach roil. But it was the fear that was the worst of it. Sweeping her gaze across the room, she tried to gauge the situation. It all seemed ceremonial somehow, and she didn't know what to make of it.

She was still bound in her chains and they dragged across the floor, weighing her arms down as she studied the circle on the ground.

Each point of the circle was decorated with different designs. A single circle in the shape of the cresting waves of an ocean was across from the twin flames. Shula's feet grazed the edge of the circle and she followed the curve, staring down next at the three small circles with whorls and curves that looked suspiciously like clouds. Across from that, four circles with curving lines and leaves etched through it; the fifth point looked like glass shards broken into the center of five circles. The final point in the circle didn't show a design at all, but a single, bold line that cut across the whole pentagram like a crack splitting the earth.

Shula couldn't make much sense of it even if she wanted to, because at that moment the doors opened. She whipped around so fast her head spun.

Women filed in. Women in drab, brown dresses that touched pale ankles. Their heads were fully shaved, and rods of metal gauged through their noses. In their boney hands, they carried steaming bowls, heaps of folded cloths, and bottled oils. They didn't speak as they walked plaintively into the catacombs and got to work.

There was a methodical way about them as they moved, and they looked almost subdued. When they were close enough, Shula caught the sight of the sides of their heads. Where their ears should have been.

They had none.

As if they'd been cut off, nothing but curving stumps lay there. It twisted Shula's insides, but they didn't seem to notice she was staring. Their eyes were downcast as they set to work, setting the steaming bowls down. There were four women total, and Shula wondered if they were Fae as they poured oils into the water and unfolded a cloth to dip it in.

One of the women came close to Shula, cautiously like one would a wild animal.

Shula waited until she was close enough and then she lashed out. Using the chains, she whipped them out at the woman. She should have felt guilty when the woman had done nothing to her, but Shula didn't care. All she wanted was escape.

The moment her chains connected against the woman's arm, flesh hissed and smoke rose in tiny plumes.

So they were Fae. Shula's eyes narrowed and upon closer inspection, she noticed that the bars and piercings on their faces were made entirely of iron. It distracted her from escape to realize that these Fae women were slaves, tortured with iron through their skin and their ears cut off.

She felt even worse about the way she'd reacted, but Shula could see her own future so clearly. She could see her own head shaved just like theirs, see the iron protruding from her nose, forced to wear brown cotton and no shoes, a dead look in her eyes.

She wouldn't become that.

She refused to.

She tried bolting for the door, but the Fae women were faster and stronger than they looked. They quickly subdued her, grabbing her by the arms. The one she'd harmed loomed in front of her, pulling out a knife. Shula screamed and fought, but the knife came towards her and slashed her garments down the middle. Cold air touched her skin as they began peeling away the leftovers of her Fire Dancer costume, taking away the final bits that tied her to Piriguini's Circus.

She fought them every step of the way. Even as they took the oil and water-soaked cloth and began rubbing her body down until she was slick and shining. Even when they tied a garment over her body toga style, sheer material that showed her every curve and left absolutely nothing to the imagination. It wasn't brown and drab, but she felt dirty despite having just been cleaned.

Jewelry was draped around her neck, a single red ruby stone that looked like it contained flames within it. They brushed out her hair and braided it over her scalp and down her back, managing despite her kicking and screaming and clawing.

She fought to bring out whatever strength she had left within her. Even trapped as she was, she would not stop. She would fight until she took her last, smoking breath. She would fight until her death. Like her parents had fought when they were taken from her, so would she.

When they finished primping her, she was held down while two of the Fae grabbed the end of her chain and tugged, placing it on the ground right over the symbol of two flames. They procured a hammer and iron nail from their pile of things and began striking the nail through a loop in the chain, tethering her to the ground with a few strikes.

She looked up at the Fae she'd burned, holding the hammer in her hands with dead eyes. Well, Shula felt the fire in her own, she felt it rippling like never before, felt it rise and threaten, choked down by iron but lying in wait just the same.

I'll kill you, Shula's eyes said. Fae or not, slave or not, she would kill her. Shula had betrayed her own kind many times over by denying her heritage, but never like this. She would never tie a Fae down with iron, would never primp them up like this to await their detestable fate.

She'd sooner take a dagger to her own chest.

I'll kill you, her eyes repeated. And there, she caught the flash of something. Something perhaps still alive in the other woman's vacant eyes. No sooner had she seen it did it disappear.

Shula watched as the women picked up their things and filed out the door, one by one, closing it behind them. Only when they were gone, did she slump to the floor, hunching her back, promising herself she wouldn't cry.

She was stronger than her tears. She hadn't cried since she was twelve, when she'd watched her parents ushered into the camps or when the emperor's soldiers chased her. When she hid in a human's attic, only to be found and taken care of. When the soldiers had barged in and killed her for treason.

That was the last night she'd ever cried, and she had vowed then that she'd never be weak again. Yet here she was. Helpless to get out of this.

No. She shook her head vehemently and tugged on the chain. She had to get out of this. She had to. She tugged again, getting on her feet and finding as much purchase as she could with oiled skin, she tugged. And tugged. And tugged.

And when the iron nail began to slowly slide up, Shula held her breath and her joy inside.

That flash in the Fae's eyes, had it been a message? That she wasn't so far gone, that she wouldn't condemn Shula to die?

She pulled again, and again, and with a final tug and all of her might, the nail came undone. She wanted to turn and run, but she heard the sound of voices, of footsteps, and she knew her time was up.

As quickly as she could, she slipped the nail back into the hole, angling it just right so it didn't appear loose and she sat against the floor just as the doors flew open.

She didn't turn around to meet her captor's eyes, and she didn't hear the clanking footfalls of steel, so she knew it wasn't the soldiers, but someone else.

She held her breath, counting at least three different sets of feet. Eyes downcast, her whole body shook when the fluttering of white cloth snagged her attention. Her gaze darted up discreetly, and her throat tightened at what she saw.

Six figures encircled around her. Six human figures, males with bald heads that shone in the flickering candlelight. They were visible from the neck up.

Because from the neck down, they each wore long robes.

Robes in white and red.

Shula swallowed as they moved, the ends of their robes rustling like parchment. She could feel their gazes on her body, felt the demand in their intensity. It frightened her.

"The Brotherhood welcomes you, Fae."

Shula couldn't bring herself to look him in the eye.

"I am Brother Bastien. These are Brother Lara, Brother Sarahias, Brother Lincoln, Brother Mathew, and Brother Malcolm." He was silent a moment as he let her process this. "Let us begin."

Before Shula even had a chance to react, they surrounded her from all sides, just like the Fae women had. But these men, they pulled her head back so she was glaring at the ceiling. Tears prickled the backs of her eyelids and she tried to shove them away, she tried to focus on anything else other than the pain they were causing.

Another man stepped before her, his robes drowning her in a sea of blinding white. Spots of crimson besmeared the cloth of his robes, and it took Shula but a moment to realize it was blood.

Bile burned in the back of her throat as he gripped her chin and shoved his thumb past her closed lips. She gagged as he forced her mouth open. She tried to bite down, but his grip was forceful and demanding. Another one of the human priest's went forward, a vial full of clear liquid in his hand. Shula struggled then as he uncorked it, but she wasn't strong enough to pull away as he forced the contents down her throat.

A calloused hand covered her nose and mouth, making her swallow the contents. They burned on the way down, choking her with fire down her throat.

I see you, choking on water that burns like fire.

Just another one of Davina's predictions that had come true. Shula thought that as whatever unholy liquid burned and scraped down her throat. She gurgled, feeling her stomach lurch. It tasted like poison and felt like death. Sweeter than candy and hotter than fire. It closed her airway entirely until she couldn't suck in breaths, couldn't breathe.

Her knees slammed onto marble, pain ricocheted up her body as she writhed, convulsing while at the same time trying to keep herself upright.

Voices sounded around her, but she couldn't make out the words when her choking drowned out everything else. When it finally, slowly, abated, she wanted to lower herself to the ground, but felt the slightest jerk of her restricting chains.

Weakly, she lifted her head. The movement made her neck hurt, everything ached, but she managed to look up into Brother Bastien's eyes. He held the end of her chain in his long, wrinkled fingers and tugged again, harder so her hands slid across marble and she fell forward.

Right onto the symbol of flames carved into the floor.

"Stay," he ordered in a voice bereft of warmth. "The trials have not concluded."

Her palms scraped over the carved symbol, chipped edges of marble digging into her skin. She let that pain ground her. She wanted to move from the symbol, just because he'd ordered her to stay like a dog, but she couldn't bring herself to. Not when tremors tried to take over from the inside. Her teeth clattered together, jarring her pounding skull. The pain was prevalent throughout her body, that all she wanted to do was vomit.

Each brother stepped back, taking a point on the circle, with Brother Bastien in the center. Captivated by their movements, Shula could do little more than whimper as they lifted their hands in unison and chanted. They were words she didn't understand, words in some ancient language, and yet she felt the magic in them as they rose to crescendos like a dangerous song. Humans couldn't wield magic, and yet this moment was magical. It leaked through the words, more ancient it seemed than the Fae themselves. She didn't know how she knew, but the language tugged something inside her. Her own magic, the thick threads of Mana that made her what she was.

The circle lit up. A soft glow that spread like glittering wine dripping down the creases in a table, sliding like the flow of a river. It slipped through the cracks and spread until it was beneath her, and the symbols of flames lit up, brightly, blindingly. Red flared beneath her fingertips and roared, enveloping her in preternatural light.

The ominous chanting stopped, and the echoes of gasps rang out.

"So it is true," one of the brother's said, she wasn't sure which. "She is an Elemental."

Her nails cracked as she dug them into the floor.

"The circle confirms it. Look at how it glows."

The light pulsed brightly like the flickering orange and red of an inferno. Something that no man-made fire could ever be. Ethereal.

She wondered why it was so important, there was so much she didn't understand.

"The emperor will wish to see her."

"We must take her to him."

Her whole body tensed. The emperor? The Emperor of Illyk wanted to see her? A damning fate, she knew, for all who were presented before His Majesty never returned. His hatred for Fae was legendary. Rumors said he kept the remnants of Fae preserved in his throne room, mounted on his opulent walls.

Remnants that could soon belong to Shula. Her ears. Her hands. She gulped... Her head.

She needed to get out of there.

The need of survival hit her and pierced past any pain she felt. The pain was miniscule compared to what could come. The emperor? He would do much worse than these brothers ever could. Instinctively, she knew it, and she wouldn't be victim to it.

She'd been victim to a lot of things in her life. To death, to fear, to pain. She didn't want to live that way. Didn't want her head mounted above Emperor Laurel's throne, something for him to stare at when he was feeling particularly conflagrated.

She'd built her life around Piriguini's Circus, and she knew she could do it again. Somewhere else. She'd done it when she was twelve, and she could it now that she was twenty-two. But first, she had to get out.

Just a tug would pull the chain from the floor where it was lightly embedded. But how would she get away from them? Her mind began spinning as she tried to plot.

All her bravado fled when she realized there wasn't a way she could escape. Not without magic, not bound in iron, with ashwood poison still in her veins, and that water still burning the back of her throat. Her magic was useless, but she'd survived years without magic, armed with nothing but her wits. She may have been overpowered, one against six, but there was something she'd learned from the circus that was integral in tricking humans.

Sleight of hand.

And humans were creatures that were easily fooled.

She was sure they would be, too.

If there was one thing she gauged in the few moments of contact with them, it was that they wanted her unharmed. While they'd shoved that liquid down her throat and it burned like never before, she was sure it wouldn't do her any damage beyond her current discomfort. Not when she was the emperor's property. The bindings were likely more for their sake, so she wouldn't use her powers on them.

Within moments, she'd formed a plan.

Taking a deep breath, she groaned, loud enough to break through the plans they made about her life, her body as if she weren't there. She groaned a second time, affectively silencing them. They turned to her and the now pained expression she wore. She didn't look, but when she felt every single eye on her, she slumped forward. Hard. Hard enough to crack her face against the glowing marble beneath her. Hard enough for her nose to crack and blood to spill. She let it slide down into her mouth and stain her teeth. Only then did she get back up and let them see the stains.

Once they caught a glimpse of her bleeding face, she slammed herself back down against the ground again and this time, she convulsed. She let her body wrack with shivers so hard, her eyes rolled to the back of her head. Blood heaved from her mouth and she gurgled on it, choking.

She'd seen her fair share of death throughout her years. She knew how to convince them.

She knew that it worked.

Their panic was palpable. Beyond the coppery taste of her own blood coating her tongue, she could taste their fear. Fear that they might have inadvertently harmed what the emperor desperately desired.

"Go get a healer! Now!" Three sets of footsteps retreated. The door to the catacombs opened and closed.

With every convulsion of her body, she propelled herself forward, closer to where the chain was embedded into the ground. Shula rolled onto it, hiding her hands with the position of her body so she could pull the nail from the ground. She grasped it tightly in her hands and when one of the brother's bent to check on her, she moved on instinct and fear, her own need for survival.

She brought the nail swinging up against his throat. Skin tore open and blood poured from Brother Lara's neck. It stained the pristine, parchment robes, blooming red across the material.

Robes of white and red, indeed.

Demon Eyes

Brother Lara made a choked noise and staggered back. The two remaining brothers stared in confusion, and Shula took advantage of the moment. She pushed herself to her feet and ran for the door. Her muscles screamed every step of the way, her chains were heavy, and blood dripped down to her elbows.

She'd never killed anyone before. She'd been to blame for deaths, but it wasn't the same as actually taking a life. It didn't feel good; she felt no happiness, only the desperate pounding need of her heart, begging her to survive. So she listened to the heavy thumping like it was the song of a siren.

By the time the brothers gained their wits, she was nearing the door. But she'd been abused, her body weakened. They were faster.

Fingers grasped her hair and tugged her back. A cry of pain pushed past her lips as her neck was jerked back. The action caused the necklace at her throat to break and clatter to the ground. She whirled on her captor, swiping the iron nail out. It snagged against his robes, so she swiped again, tearing against the material of his arm and to the skin underneath.

Manic, angry eyes stared back at her as she struggled. She wanted to believe she was getting out of this alive, but she could feel the second brother creeping around her, threatening to close her in.

Panic seized and she whirled, using as much strength as her body possessed and more. The suddenness of it had the hairs from her scalp pulled. She bit back the agonizing cry that wanted to slip from her throat. She pulled herself from the brother's grasp and charged at the one sneaking up on her.

His eyes went wide at the feral madness she felt deep in her soul. Her grip against the iron burned, but she didn't drop it as she forced the tip straight into the brother's chest. She pushed with all her might, just scratching the surface of his skin. Just enough to make him *bleed.*

He gasped as she yanked the nail out and dodged his falling body.

She didn't think about the blood coating the spaces between her fingers. She fumbled with the door and threw it open, pushing herself up the stairs. Her chest was on fire, the sensation rising to the back of her throat. Every heaving breath she took, she feared would be her last. That the one brother she'd left standing was right at her heels.

Still, she ran.

The chains threatened to pull her back to the bottom of the steps, but she mustered all the strength she had left in her body. Feet slamming up, up, up... She broke past another door and into dim candlelit hallways.

She could hear the brother behind her, and in her panic, she couldn't remember which way to go, so she turned down a hallway at random.

Death rode at her heels, she was sure of it. Just like she was sure she'd lead a pathway straight to her if she wasn't careful. Pressing the nail to her chest and ignoring the burning sting it brought to her flesh, she wiped it down the thin material of the garment. Turning and skidding across marble floors, she ran.

Faster and faster.

And Shula did not look back.

She knew they would find her if she stopped, so she didn't. Even when she felt like she'd vomit, keel over, when her feet begged for rest, she couldn't. It didn't matter how many turns she took, how many exits she frantically searched for in passing and failed to find, she still didn't stop.

When tapered candles disappeared and made way to complete darkness, she forced herself to slow.

A flash of bright yellow caught her attention in the shadows. A flash of searching, evil eyes. She blinked, sure she'd imagined it, but when her eyes opened once again, she was positive she hadn't.

Floating in the darkness, like the faerie lights from her dreams, were two eerie yellow eyes. Something about them seemed sinister, like the slashing eyes of a demon in the night.

Shula sucked in a breath, remembering Davina's ominous words.

The eyes of a demon lead to freedom.

Heart pounding up to her throat, she dared to take a step closer.

Those twin eyes blinked at her and came closer as well, stepping into her line of vision to reveal itself.

It was a cat. A sleek, black coat covered it, and it stared at her with a rather superior expression. It was a single moment of connection before the feline turned and stalked back into the shadows.

The eyes of a demon lead to freedom.

Every word Davina had spoken had come to pass. Shula had been a fool to ignore it before. She wouldn't make the same mistake twice. So she dug deep inside herself to find her bravery, and she followed the cat.

Her feet shuffled quickly along the marble floors to catch up with the feline. The chains held up by her aching arms so they wouldn't drag across the floor.

After a moment of adjusting her eyes to the darkness, she caught sight of the beast.

It moved quickly, turning back in flashes so she could follow at its paws. It ran and so did she, panting to keep up, skidding as it turned hallways and led her down an ominous staircase. She should have feared running into the unknown with so much left to lose. But Davina had said, the eyes of the demon led to freedom. She had to believe it would come true.

She had to.

Or else she would be trapped in this Fae-hating temple. They would catch her, and they'd take her to the Emperor of Illyk.

It couldn't happen.

She refused to let it.

The cat led her to the end of a hallway; a door was propped open, and the night sky greeted her beyond. It stepped out, disappearing from her line of sight and Shula's breathing grew labored as she realized how close she was to freedom. Just like Davina had said.

She rushed out blindly, the taste of her freedom on her tongue, overriding the sweet, bitter taste of ashwood and burning water. The outside air chilled her skin, making goosebumps crawl along her body, but she didn't care about the cold. She didn't care that she felt it through the sheer shift. All she felt was the open air, the familiar press of fog, the lack of walls enclosing her body in their confines.

And the collision into a solid wall of flesh.

She startled back, dropping the iron chains to the ground, but gripping the nail tightly in her palms until they sliced along her flesh. She didn't wince because she was too busy staring up at the mammoth of a person she ran into.

Features hidden beneath the shadows of an old, dark cloak, he was obviously male. It was in the width of the shoulders and the gruff grunt he'd emitted when she'd rammed into his wall of a chest.

Fear closed her throat tightly, and for a moment, she didn't know what to do. Had it all been a trap? A lie? Had the demon-eyed cat not led her to freedom at all, but something worse?

She swung the iron nail out at the man. She didn't make it within inches of him. Faster than she could blink, his hand shot out and shackled her palms. His grip tightened painfully until she was crying out and felt like her fingers would break. The nail clattered from her fingers to the ground.

She couldn't possibly beat a man his size, but she had to try. Her feet kicked out, connecting with his body. She rammed her shoulder into his chest, her nails gripping at his cloak and in their struggle, she yanked the hood from his head...

...and froze.

"I—you—"

No coherent words came out.

How could they?

Perhaps she was dreaming. Perhaps all of this was nothing more than a nightmare she couldn't escape from. Her worst fears come alive to haunt her.

Because she was staring at a monster.

A Fae monster.

It was the scars she noticed first. Dozens of them, raised over olive flesh that bisected across his entire face like the designs on a spiderweb. They slashed over his left eye, seeming to cut through the pupil, making it look white like a ghost's. The other eye looked normal. Black and glaring. But the scars... His thick beard seemed to hide the worst of them, but they were still visible as they spread over his cheeks, stopping at his hairline.

Dark tufts of hair trailed down his shoulders in thinly braided strands that parted like a curtain, showing off his smooth, pointed ears.

Fae ears.

She didn't know where to lock her attention on. If on the scars or his ears, if that single white eye or the black one.

Shula staggered a step back. "You're a Fae." That wasn't what she meant to say, but it still stumbled out of her mouth.

The massive man grunted out something that sounded eerily like a snort, but he didn't reply. He didn't say anything at all. His white eye seemed to glow in the darkness, and she wondered if he could see her out of it, thinking that perhaps he could when it flicked over her body. Assessing. Dangerous.

It was a stare she felt deep in the marrow of her bones, a stare that stirred the magic inside of her despite the iron locked around her wrists, weighing her arms down. Despite it repressing her magic, she felt something implode within her. Something akin to her fire blazing.

Oblivious to her inner thoughts, the large Fae man blinked down at her. They stared. And stared.

And when Shula felt a touch against her legs, she let out a small shriek and jumped, nearly stepping on the demon-eyed cat.

It wrapped its lithe body around her legs and purred before turning towards the hulking figure. A cry of surprise left Shula's lips as the cat gave a jump and climbed his tree trunk of a body, perching itself on the Fae's shoulder.

It was a surprising night.

"Who are you?" she demanded. Her nerves frazzled with each passing second. Staying here was dangerous and she wanted to get away, but the Fae stood across from her as if he had no plans whatsoever of moving out of her way. "You know what... scratch that, I don't care who you are. Move! I have to leave." To get out of these confines. To start a new life.

She started past him, fighting back a shiver as their bodies grazed. There was something about him, though she couldn't quite place what, that made her uncomfortable. It had nothing to do with the scars and everything to do with his silence.

The moment she stepped past him, she felt a yank on her dragging chains, and she fell back against him again, drowning her in the splintering fragrance of his body. Rosemary and chamomile and something darker, intoxicating. She tried to pull away, but he held her firmly in his thick arms.

Like he didn't want to let her go.

She struggled against him, but he only tightened his hold, and then a voice cut through the night.

"Fuck, Ryker, let her go."

Like magic, his hold on her loosened and she stumbled, righting herself in time to see men in cloaks step into the alleyway.

The one who'd spoken brought up the front of the two-man procession. His hood was lowered enough so she could make out his features in the dark.

He was the most beautiful man Shula had ever seen in her life.

Bright eyes shone with what could have been equal parts mischief and flirtation. Shula wasn't sure, because she was lost in his smile for the briefest of moments before she shook herself out of whatever glamor he wore. She blinked, realizing that it wasn't a glamor at all. He was just that gorgeous. But she wouldn't let his beauty distract her. He was like a parlor trick. Bright and flashy to hide the secret mischief underneath.

It made her instantly alert.

"That's not how you treat a lady." The new Fae man stepped forward and Shula stepped back. She was surrounded at all sides.

It was one thing to escape from humans and another entirely to escape from Fae. And she had no doubt that the one still cloaked behind the beautiful one was a Fae, too. She caught glimpses of him, flashes of a feral-looking face and wide, sharp smiles that looked more malicious than friendly.

"It's okay, Fire Dancer. We aren't here to harm you." The beautiful one held his palms up, a gesture of surrender that Shula didn't buy into. He was Fae, after all. He could have powers of any kind that he could use against her. "My name is Clay."

"We don't have time for this." Another Fae stepped forward, lowering his cloak with an annoyed flick of his wrists. Silky dark hair cascaded over his shoulder, grazing his cheekbones. He was all sharp angles with a razor-pointed chin, straight prominent nose and glaring, dark eyes. He looked familiar to

Shula, though she couldn't place where she'd seen him before. "We have to go. Now. Humans lurk in the shadows." He stared intently at Shula. "Let's go." He turned, his cloak a swish of dark fabric against a lighter night.

It was as he was turning that Shula realized what he was, where she knew him from. "You're from the *wanted* posters. You're the wanted Fae." She remembered stepping on the portrait of his face. The angry, slashing lines of a monster. "You're a criminal."

His body went taut at her declaration, as still as a predator hunting for prey. He didn't turn around as he answered, but his voice carried malignance. "So are you."

She jolted. Of course, she'd known she was a criminal just by being Fae, by hiding her true nature. She'd lived all of her life on the edge, wondering if she woke up, would it be her last day? But something about him saying it made an ache build in her chest. It dropped her from the perch of adrenaline she'd found herself on earlier. She suddenly felt exhausted and a thousand years old.

"We're all criminals, pretty little Fire Dancer," the Fae named Clay said, a sad but understanding smile curving his mouth. "That's why we have to stick together. Let's go." He held out his hand.

Shula didn't want to take it.

Despite her exhaustion, despite feeling like her head was lolling where she stood and her arms dragging nearly to the floor, she tilted her chin up and stared Clay in the eyes. "No."

He blinked. "No?"

She knew what would happen if she went with them. The dark haired one was on a WANTED poster, for Mana's sake. If she went with them, that would be the end of her peaceful life. She wouldn't be able to start fresh. She would be living on the verge of danger and death, hunted at every turn.

She wondered if Clay could read minds, because he seemed to understand every flicker of emotion she'd tried to keep hidden behind a mask of furious indifference. "They know your face now too, Fire Dancer. They'll find you, regardless of where you hide."

A distant bark sounded, and the hiss of the demon-eyed cat followed. She didn't even have time to absorb Clay's words like the blow they were because everything after happened very quickly.

"They're coming," the Fae from the poster spat. "We are out of time. Let's go."

"I—I'm not going with you!" Stubbornness was something she knew well. Only the stubborn survived, and while Davina had said that the demon eyes led to freedom, Shula wasn't sure anymore if this was what she meant. How could she go with complete strangers? What if the Fae were worse than humans? "I don't even know who you are!"

Perhaps she'd been living as a human too long, that she'd let herself fear the Fae, too. And she was scared. She was terrified that her parents' fates would befall her.

The one name Clay puffed up his chest with obvious pride. "We are the Resistance."

"Stop calling us that." The *wanted* Fae sighed impatiently from behind him. "We are wasting time. We must leave."

The Resistance. Those words rang no bells through Shula's mind, but it didn't matter what they were. They could have been sent directly from the Fae courts and she would not go.

"No," she repeated. "I'm not going."

She stepped back and rammed into Ryker's chest. Scarred palms came down on her shoulders and she shivered.

"I'm sorry, Fire Dancer," Clay looked at her apologetically. "But you don't have a choice."

Shula's scream was lost in her throat.

And a moment later, her body gave in to its exhaustion and lethargy.

And she welcomed the darkness.

Pathways of the Future

The Fire Dancer's body went slack as if she was too weak to hold herself up at all, like she had shut down and given up.

Clay darted forward to catch her, but Ryker was already there. He moved so quickly; in a second her legs were already under his arms, and he had her body cradled to his chest. His familiar dug her sharp claws into his shoulder at the disturbance but otherwise remained perched where she was.

The manacles and chains around the Fire Dancer's wrists made her feel heavy, but Ryker could tell she had a delicacy about her. Not that she was thin. Curves spread through her body in all the right places, *not* that Ryker particularly cared. He was more preoccupied with leaving this place at the moment. The close proximity to the iron made his head pound and the magic inside him sputter.

"Let's go," Valerio snapped with impatience.

He wasn't usually irritable, but these were dark times, and this was a strange situation.

When the seer had knocked upon the door of their safe house, demanding they come to the temple and rescue one of their own, Valerio had scoffed in her face.

"Risk my men to save one female?" He spoke those words in a tone that said, 'Now, why the fuck would I do that?' But Valerio would not say such a thing, for he was not a vulgar man.

The seer—Davina, she said she was called—had then given Valerio a glimpse of the future. A prophecy that claimed this Fire Dancer would help save their race.

They'd debated, had spent the better part of a few hours arguing the pros and cons. They almost hadn't come.

Ryker wished they hadn't.

It was obvious she didn't want to go with them. She was terrified and trembling, and Ryker didn't have the patience to deal with someone who didn't want to be saved, not when there were hundreds of Fae begging to be rescued. He much rather would have spent his time finding them instead of this fearful thing.

"Heal her," Clay ordered. His eyes raked over her body in the darkness. As they could see in the dark, Ryker knew Clay was inhaling every curve that the sheer material draped over her could not hide.

Prick.

"No." Ryker shouldered past the other Fae and they began walking, then running, trying to get as far away from this place as possible.

The emperor's soldiers would send the hounds out next; trained bitches that could make out the scent of a Fae from a mile away.

As he ran, the sudden jostling had his familiar digging her claws tightly into his shoulder for purchase. He didn't wince. He hardly felt much pain anymore unless he was using his magic.

They moved quickly through the night, faster than they'd ever run before.

"Whose genius idea was it to leave Uric behind?" Clay complained, his arms pumping at his sides. He wasn't even winded as he ran, but the thrill of danger delighted him. It shone in his eyes. He was a mischievous little fucker and relished in a good fight.

Ryker itched to break that pretty boy nose of his.

They were a blur through the dark streets of Tuath. Any humans peering out of their windows at this time would merely glance and see fog blurring across the grounds.

Better for them. Better for them all.

Yet, the dogs were following.

"Shit." Valerio skidded to a halt near an alleyway.

Ryker shifted the Fire Dancer in his arms and glared at the figure who had appeared before them.

Her hair was unbound, the hood of her cloak around her shoulders. A vacant look was in her eyes, but when she spoke there was nothing but clarity in her words. "She will fight you."

Wind whipped at her dress and cloak. Her hair pushed away from her face to show her ears.

"What are you doing, Davina?" Valerio demanded. He shoved his own hood down. Half of his dark hair was pulled back into a knot and the other half spread down his back, disappearing into the black cloak. The sides of his head were shaved; all the better to show his ears.

It was a sense of pride for them. They were warriors, after all. Humans would have them hide what they were, so showing off what made them different in appearance was imperative.

"Protect her at all costs." Davina stepped forward and bowed low before Valerio. "And may the Ashera of the Seelie rule again... my prince." She straightened and stepped around them, walking away in the opposite direction.

Clay cursed and his hand shot out to grab her arm. "Where the fuck are you going? Uric is waiting that way!"

She smiled at him and gently pried his fingers from her arm. "I know my destiny, Clay Valentino. Do you know yours?"

Clay tugged at his hair with impatience.

Ryker didn't blame him. The seer was frustrating, infuriating. Yet she was hypnotizing just the same. Ryker knew how dangerous promises of the future were, what type of seduction they held. It was why they found themselves in this position in the first place. The promise of a better future for the Fae had been too tempting to pass up, at least Valerio thought so.

Ryker had yet to be convinced.

"We have to go." A note of impatience slipped in Clay's words. He rarely lost his temper or shouted, but he clenched his teeth as if he were on the verge of losing it.

"Would you like to know your future?"

Clay hissed out a breath. "No, I would like to leave before the emperor's soldiers catch us. We're on thin ice as is."

"Ice? No, no ice is not your future. Ice is for Julius. Water for you."

Ryker rolled his eyes and adjusted the Fire Dancer in his arms again. The close proximity to iron was starting to tire him.

"What are you talking about?"

"I've seen my future. I have seen my ears cut and mounted."

Every single one of them stilled.

Because that was the signature of Emperor Laurel. He hunted down the Fae and those that weren't tossed into camps suffered a fate worse than death. They were dismembered piece by fucking piece and stuffed like dolls to hang over his throne.

If she'd seen that in her future, then that meant the emperor would capture her.

They couldn't let that happen.

Not just because she knew the location to their safe house, but because she knew their faces, their futures. Even the bravest of men could crack under torture.

"Then we have to leave so that it doesn't happen to you." Clay tried tugging her to him again, but she sidestepped away from his grasp.

"The future ahead has many pathways," she said eerily. "Many paths, and I have seen them all. It does not matter which I take, my end shall be the same. My ears will be sheared and mounted. I will die with your secrets safe. But fear not; even after I am gone, I will help the Fae." She started to walk away.

Valerio pushed his way past Clay and Ryker, his sharp jaw clenched tightly. "Where are you going?"

Her voice trailed behind her even as she walked away. "To buy you time. For I have seen the future and what comes of you if I do not do this. Death is unbecoming for a Seelie prince. Now go."

Ryker grinded his teeth together and fought back the urge to clench his hands into fists. Not that he could with the Fire Dancer in his arms, but he wanted to step forward and stop this madness.

If they let her go, they would be no more barbaric than the humans. It was in their nature to protect one another, to save each other from the clutches of monsters. So to watch Davina walk away and buy them time killed him inside.

He wanted to hand the Fire Dancer off to Clay and run after her. Sacrifice himself instead. But he knew there was no other like him within their ranks. His prince needed him. And he couldn't seem to move. He held the Fire Dancer, as if he could draw strength from her prone form. Strength he would need to live with the fact that he let one of his own walk to her death.

Instead, he felt a tugging pull of raw magic spark from his chest to hers, a sensation that had his hands curling against her form.

Valerio let out a slow breath. "We have to go. Let her sacrifice not be in vain." He lifted the hood of his cloak and turned.

Clay followed.

But it was Ryker who stayed a moment longer than either of them. The steady breathing of the Fire Dancer's chest pressed against his own.

Everything in the world had a price.

And the price of their lives, of the Fire Dancer's life, had been Davina's.

Ryker only prayed that she was worth it.

"Ryker!" Clay hissed. "Let's go!"

Ryker forced his feet to move. He turned and ran to catch up with his brethren.

And in the distance, he could make out the shrill bark of a hound who had found its prey.

The Seer's Sacrifice

Davina showed no fear, for she had lived a long time and had experienced many things, and nothing would ever be as terrifying as the madness that crawled through the remnants of her mind.

It was not the future she feared or even the unknown, but that her own madness would betray the Fae, would betray herself.

She'd seen glimpses of her future. A bloodied tongue stuck between teeth that refused to talk.

If she could do something for her kind, it would be this. Her only regret would be that she would cause Shula Azzarh heartbreak.

They had not been close, yet the call of Mana within their blood was too hard to ignore. They had not spoken, but they had been friends. And Davina's death would be a mere chip away from Shula's heart that she would need to lose in order to become who she was meant to be.

So Davina would sacrifice herself this night, and the next, and the next. She would submit her body to the emperor's torture and when she died, her spirit would carry on.

This she knew with clarity.

The hounds were closing in on her. She could hear their paws pounding against the pavement as they picked up her scent. By the time they caught up to her, the Fae would be long gone. They'd make it to Uric and to the portal. To a new safe house.

And the Resistance would rise, and the Fae would be strong again.

Only if Shula accepted her fate.

The hounds were closer now, so she stopped just beneath the burning light of an oil lamp. With firm fingers, she twisted her hair back so they could see her ears. For she was Fae, and she had hidden them for far too long.

No more.

Barks permeated the air around her. Their beasts were hungry; they had not been fed in days. But she would not run from their teeth.

They burst from the darkness and circled around her. Futile, since she would not run.

The soldiers came a moment later. At the head of them, the Captain Brannon of the Emperor's Royal Guard.

He held up a hand, stopping his soldiers from advancing, but not from pointing their iron-made weapons at her.

She could feel the buzzing from the weapons overtake her senses. Iron tended to do that to a Fae. Soon, she would be useless.

"Fae," the captain spat as he stepped forward, pulling the helm from his head. "Where are the others?"

She inclined her head in his direction. "Captain Brannon."

If he was surprised that she knew his name, he did not show it. "Where are the others?" he repeated, with far less patience than the first time.

Cruelty lived deep within this man. Davina had seen it; had seen the blood tainting his fingers and the joy he would get from it.

"Others who?" She cocked her head to the side, but they all knew she was not as ignorant as she appeared.

The captain unsheathed his sword and pointed it in her direction. The tip searing her neck with its proximity. A single swipe, and she'd be dead. But she knew she would not die here.

"You see my hounds?" The captain's gaze swept across the beasts, snarling and growling at her. "I have not fed them for days. They are hungry for the flesh of a Fae."

"Would you like to know your future, captain?"

Of course he did. They always did.

The future was too tempting to ignore.

Without waiting to hear his answer, she proceeded, "I see you in a forest. Sword in hand and blood on your face. You are quite the fighter, are you not?"

"Silence, witch! And tell us where the others are!"

"Oh, captain, I am just getting to the best part, don't you see? Your own arrogance will be your downfall. And that which you have hunted your entire life will be the death of you."

She could see him pale beneath the light even as he tried to hide it.

No one wanted to hear about their own death, and yet they all did. Little did they know that the harder they tried to prevent it, the more it would come to pass. That was the future and the price they had to pay.

And the captain's price was steep.

And it was one he would not accept.

"Hounds!" he snapped. The mutts snapped their ears at attention. Of course, Davina knew what would come next. "Attack."

So as they lunged for her, she didn't even scream.

The Resistance

Uric waited right where he was supposed to, looking bored with the entire night as he leaned one shoulder against a crumbling brick wall. The moment they approached, Valerio at the head of them, Uric snapped his fingers and the air shimmered behind him.

It was always eerie to watch the portal come to life. To watch particles shimmer into being, to watch lights and shadows coalesce into a rounded doorway. A mirror shone on the surface, rippling and distorting their images.

"The safe house in the mountains?" Valerio asked without preamble.

Uric shot the prince a look of impatience that Valerio ignored.

"See you on the other side."

Valerio stepped through first. It was like watching someone step through a waterfall and into another world. One minute the prince was there, and the next he was gone.

Uric nodded at Clay. Already, the price of his magic was taking a toll on him. Because he manipulated time and space, the price to pay for the portal was his youth. It never lasted long. Sometimes the price lasted weeks, but it depended on how long he kept the portal opened for. Clay had made fun of him for sporting bald patches of skin on his scalp and sagging, wrinkled skin for a week. Even now, his long strands of silver-white hair drifted from his head to his chest.

He squinted at the figure in Ryker's arms. "That the Fae, then?"

Ryker snorted. "Hardly a Fae," he grumbled.

It caused Clay to roll his eyes. Ryker was all about Fae pride, and sometimes he took it to the extremes. He didn't say anything though. Not when his mind was still distracted with thoughts of Davina and the sacrifice she made.

In a rare moment of seriousness, he clapped Ryker in the back. "Best get going. You first, big guy. We need to get those chains off her as quickly as possible."

She already appeared to be paling like a corpse.

Ever silently, Ryker stomped over to the portal and stepped through.

"Hurry up," Uric urged. "I'd prefer not to have to suffer through ulcers and varicose veins for the next few hours."

Clay flipped his friend the finger but still hurried to step through. It was like being sucked in through a pool of honey. The shimmering liquid clung to his skin and tugged, pulling him through brightness and darkness at the same time. It was instinct to hold his breath as if he were wading through water, but he didn't need to.

His eyes opened as the portal pushed him out on the other side. His feet collided with solid ground and the quiet rustling of a forest greeted him. He turned just in time to see Uric burst through the portal. A moment later, it disappeared.

Clay smirked. "How you feeling, old man?" He clapped his hand against Uric's shoulder. He felt frail and wrinkled. It was a rare sight to see an old Fae. Old as in wrinkled with age. The truth was, Fae were immortal, so every time Clay saw Uric with imperfections on his skin, he snorted out his laughter. "The arthritis treating you okay?"

Uric flipped him a vulgar gesture and wobbled away after Valerio and Ryker, who were already storming through the cluster of trees and towards the run-down safe house beyond.

The Resistance, as Clay liked to call it, much to everyone's annoyance, had safe houses scattered throughout all of Illyk. In the human lands, at least.

It was too dangerous to travel across the Ley Line that separated human soil from what had once been the Tir na Faie. What once had been thriving, magical lands were nothing but desolate, dangerous grounds now which the Fae avoided at all costs.

They instead hid out as much as they could. In human safe houses, their numbers depleting thanks to the tyrant Emperor of Illyk.

It was the Resistance who helped find Fae of all kinds and protected them from the emperor's soldiers. Without the Resistance, the Fae would surely perish.

Clay swaggered after his friends in confident steps, untying the deplorable, smelly cloak as he went. He hated wearing the damn thing, but it was necessary on stealth missions like the one they'd just gone on. It was imperative that they hide their identities. The more the humans knew of them, the more danger they were in.

They already had Prince Valerio's mug slashed all over WANTED posters as a result of an incident that *hadn't* been Clay's fault.

He would deny culpability until he drew his last breath, no matter what anyone else said.

The little cabin was sequestered in the woods. A broken-down thing with a shabby roof and broken-down door, vines clung up the sides of it, wrapping around the rotting wood like a lover's caress. It was scarcely inhabited at the moment, with only a few members of the Resistance and Fae they'd saved in the past month. They would move locations soon, and he knew even now they were all getting ready.

Valerio stepped up to the door and knocked a four-note pattern that had it opening to him immediately. It was their secret code.

Valerio strode through first and Ryker followed, the giant mammoth of a man growling for the blacksmith as he strode inside. The cat that had been perched on his shoulder jumped down and disappeared down a hallway. Uric left; not to rest, but to follow Ryker, and so Clay did the same.

He couldn't hold back his curiosity.

It wasn't every day they rescued a beautiful woman from the clutches of humans, and at a temple no less. Even rarer for her to be an Elemental Fae like Davina had claimed she was.

Of course, they had yet to see her power when she was bound in iron, but the blacksmith could get that off of her quickly.

Ryker went into one of the few rooms he used as an infirmary. It smelt moldy, making Clay wrinkle his nose upon entering, but that couldn't be helped.

It wasn't as if they had many options lately. They couldn't stroll up to a hostel out in Dana and demand their best room to allow her to rest.

Still, Clay winced as Ryker gently lowered the Fire Dancer to a thin, torn up pallet on the ground. The chains clanked as they fell into a pile on the ground. When Ryker stood back up, it was to unclasp the cloak from his body and toss it into the corner.

The four of them, Valerio, Ryker, Uric, and Clay surrounded her. Clay cocked his head to the side, a smirk on his mouth. "She's kinda pretty."

Valerio scoffed without humor. "Mana's sake, Clay. Have you no shame? She's fainted."

"Yeah, at least wait until she wakes up before you shower her with your infamous charm," Uric added.

Clay shrugged. "Hey, it's not my fault women flock to me." And he didn't doubt that she would too. He knew very well what he looked like; more handsome than this sorry lot, at least. Although Prince Valerio did rival him in beauty, no one really looked twice at the Prince of Seelie because he wore such a grave expression all the time that frightened them.

Clay, however, exuded sex and charm.

He'd caught the way this Fae had looked at him when she realized his beauty wasn't glamor.

Every woman looked at him like that. He relished in it, honestly.

"Where's the fucking blacksmith?" Ryker growled. "I can't heal her with all that iron..."

Huh. That was the most Ryker had spoken today.

"Someone's already gone to fetch him, don't worry."

On cue, the softest knock came on the walls. They turned and the blacksmith entered. The little human man looked nervously around the room until his eyes settled on the Fire Dancer, his expressive eyes taking in the manacles on her hands.

"So?" Valerio asked imperiously, causing the blacksmith to flinch. "Can you do it or not?" He didn't even have to ask what it was he wanted. The answer was obvious.

"Of course, but she's sleeping and—"

"And what?"

"You'd have to hold her down so she doesn't wake. If she wakes while I'm in the process, I could accidentally hurt her—"

"I'll do it." Ryker bent and pulled the still woman into his arms, her back to his chest. His scarred hands gripped at her wrists, holding them tightly in place so that if she jerked awake, she wouldn't hurt herself or others. Ryker slashed a glare the blacksmith's way. "Hurry up."

The urgency in his voice caused Clay to chuckle, though he couldn't be sure why. Ryker was a hard ass. He hardly touched anyone and hardly ever let anyone touch him. He was the group's healer because he was damn good and, while he wouldn't admit it, he cared about every single life he saved, regardless of the frown constantly marring his face.

The blacksmith set to work, taking out his tools as he began hammering away with firm, strong gentleness.

Ryker held her tightly and she barely even stirred as the tools dug into her skin. It made Clay wonder what all they'd done to her. Who, and why?

Davina hadn't given them specifics when she'd gone knocking on the safe house door. She'd mentioned an Elemental Fae, the Fire Dancer; chunky, chopped bits of a prophecy that surrounded this Elemental; and a future that had convinced Prince Valerio to go after her.

No one else had heard what Davina whispered to the prince, and they knew better than to ask, to question his authority.

He was their leader, not just of the long-forgotten Seelie Court, but of the Resistance as well. If he believed this Fae could help tip things in their favor, well, who was Clay to disagree?

They'd all been curious about her. They'd all wanted to go to the temple and get her out, but when they'd arrived, she'd already saved herself. From what? Humans. Obviously. But it ran deeper than that, and Clay couldn't wait until she woke up to tell them.

Once her manacles had been forced off, Ryker slid her body back onto the pallet. A single glare dismissed the blacksmith, sending him all but running from the room with his tools in hand.

Clay rolled his eyes. "That's why Fae have a bad rep, big guy."

He snorted, which showed how little he cared what humans or anyone else thought of him, and he hovered his hands over her body.

With the iron gone, he could heal her now.

Ryker's eyes closed and his palms began to glow with the gentle press of his healing magic.

"There's ashwood in her blood," he declared with a guttural groan.

Clay tensed. Someone had poisoned her. No wonder she'd passed out on them.

Silence followed as Ryker got to work. His hands passed over her whole body, and the golden brown color appeared over her skin again, making her look less like a corpse and more like a healthy Fae.

Ryker's brows pulled together. "Something isn't healing..."

Clay's own brows rose up to his hairline. "What do you mean something isn't healing? Your magic depleted or something?"

He let out a growl that was meant to silence Clay and it did. Letting out a frustrated breath, Ryker's eyes opened and he grasped the Fire Dancer's body, turning her gently to the side. His hand gripped the hem of the sheer material adorning her and slowly slid it up.

"What the fuck are you doing?" Clay demanded, feeling heat rise to his face.

As much as he joked, he didn't want her privacy violated like this. Ryker ignored him and pulled the material up over the rounded globes of her ass and exposed her back.

What they saw silenced Clay and had everyone reeling back.

"What is that?" Valerio demanded, bending to get a better look.

It looked as though her back had taken a knife to it. Carved in her flesh were two circles, one starting just under her neck and a second that followed just beneath that. In the center of the circles were whirls of flames.

The skin was puckered, the wounds fresh, and it looked like they were just beginning to crust over at the edges. Blood still seeped from it. They looked deep enough to be painful as fuck, Clay thought.

Ryker ran his hand over the wound and golden light glowed from his palm, but her skin did not heal.

"This has never happened before," Uric pointed out.

"Yeah, no shit." Clay bent so he was staring at the wounds. "Do you think they did this to her in that temple?"

"We can't be sure until she wakes." Valerio stroked his chin, contemplating the wounds. "You can't heal it at all?"

Ryker tried again, and Clay could tell he was giving it all he had. His whole body vibrated, and golden light enveloped his skin. Clay watched as her skin started to knit closed in the tiniest of fractions. When Ryker couldn't take anymore, he grunted and nearly doubled over from the pain of using his magic.

Uric was there immediately, his semi-wrinkled fingers holding the big guy up before he fell face first over the Fire Dancer's exposed body.

"You good?" Uric asked.

Ryker waved him away and stood on shaking legs. "Fine," he ground out. But he was staring down at the woman like she was poison to this earth. "Her back..." He broke off on a growl and bent to adjust the material of the dress and accommodate her body onto the cot.

"Put a poultice on it. And clean her hands. She's covered in blood."

Ryker didn't seem to hear Valerio. He was still staring down at her, with disgust suddenly marring his features. "Her *ears*..."

Clay hadn't noticed before, but now that Ryker had pointed them out, disgust roiled uncomfortably in his stomach. Where pointed ears should have been, rounded human ears sat instead.

Ryker snorted with disgust and started to walk away.

Valerio stopped him with his cutting voice. "Ryker, after you clean her up, I'll need you to stay with her."

Ryker's whole body pulled taut. His movements were forced as he turned his scarred expression to face the prince. "What?" he demanded darkly.

Valerio's eyebrows rose. "You will stay with her and heal her if need be. Will that be a problem?"

It was a test. Clay knew it was a test, and that Ryker had no choice but to obey. So it was no surprise when he gritted out, "No. No problem." But his fists were tightened at his sides, making it obvious that it *was* a problem, but Clay couldn't figure out why.

"Good." Valerio turned to the rest of them. "The moment she wakes, we leave for the mountains. We will rendezvous with Julius and his group of rescued Fae and head to the mountains to meet with my father." His sharp gaze went to Clay. "Stay with Ryker. When she wakes up, help explain things to her."

A smirk spread across Clay's mouth, and he crossed his arms over his chest. "Tall, dark, and silent over here doesn't know how to explain?"

Valerio's eyes rolled. "We all know how that will go."

Disastrous, to say the least. Where Clay drew women to him like magic, Ryker repelled them.

"Uric, come with me. We need to prepare the survivors for all possibilities."

Uric nodded, his silver hair grazing his cheeks. "Yes, my prince."

The two of them filed out of the room, leaving Ryker and Clay alone with the Fire Dancer. They both stared at her long and hard.

Dark, thick lashes fanned out against her curved cheeks, dark hair spread beneath her, and plump lips opened with dreamy sighs.

She had a body that was perfect for fucking, Clay thought humorously. A body he wouldn't mind sinking his cock into—

"Don't," Ryker growled, snapping Clay from his thoughts.

He stared at the scarred man. "Don't what?"

"Keep your dirty fucking thoughts to yourself."

"Well, shit, it wasn't as if I was saying them out loud." He paused, observing Ryker. The man usually showed very little emotion, but there was something completely tense about him that Clay couldn't quite place. His scarred fingers twitched along the side of his pants, and Clay found himself smiling. "Aw, Ryker, do you want her for yourself?"

Ryker's head snapped so hard it was a miracle it didn't fall off his shoulders. He glared at Clay with an intensity that was near blinding.

"No."

And then he was storming past Clay, slamming the thin door behind him so hard, it broke and crumbled in little bits and pieces.

Clay chuckled. *Well, I'll be damned,* he thought as he took a seat and kept his watchful eye on the pretty little Fire Dancer. The one woman who may have gone and caught Ryker Valda's attention.

Safe House

Shula awoke with a gasp. Nightmares had plagued her. Images of blood and iron and scorched skin, of poison being shoved down her throat. Nightmares that weren't dreams at all, but memories haunting her subconscious.

She took a moment so assess the state of her body, surprised to find she no longer felt as weak as before, but there was a bad taste in her mouth and her throat felt dry and gross. The side of her face and ribs where the soldier had hit her no longer hurt, and her chafed, bleeding wrists were healed, free of iron manacles. The only pain she felt was the burning sensation along her back, and she could almost trace the images of her scarring wounds with every pulsing beat of agony.

She let out a husky groan as her palms pushed herself up from the floor. Her eyes opened and panic set in when she didn't recognize her surroundings.

Then a voice broke through her confusion, making her look up into a face she recognized.

Brilliant green eyes stared at her; dazzlingly white teeth smiled at her. The Fae man from before—how long ago had it been?—Clay, he'd introduced himself as. He was sitting in a rickety chair that creaked under his weight. His legs were spread wide and he leaned forward, resting his forearms against his thighs as he took her in. A head of light brown hair was moussed above his head. He looked like someone who didn't take care with their appearance, because the ruffled look made him all the more beautiful.

And he *was* beautiful.

Plump lips that looked like they were made for sin, lithe muscles that pressed against a tightly belted tunic that was opened at the neck to reveal the smooth panes of his chest. He wore simple, dirty clothes that did nothing to tarnish his beauty, but enhanced it somehow.

His smile didn't falter, and Shula immediately distrusted him. Why was he smiling so much? It made no sense. What was there to smile about? And why was he staring at her as if he meant to make her his next meal?

"The beautiful Fire Dancer awakens at last."

She frowned at the compliment and looked down at herself, just to make sure she hadn't woken up naked. When she found she still had on the garment the brothers had dressed her in, she breathed a sigh of relief. Not that her relief mattered an ounce, since the cloth was see-through anyway.

"The blacksmith did a wonderful job at taking those off you." Clay nodded at her wrists.

Shula stared at him warily. "Then I will make sure to thank the blacksmith."

"Sure, I think he'll like that." Then he smirked. "And maybe thank Ryker for your lack of wounds, too." Before she could say anything in response to that, he stood up and the chair beneath him groaned. "If you want, I can find you something more comfortable to wear. I'm sure we have something in your size. You'll have to hurry, though. We're leaving and Valerio doesn't like to be kept waiting." Before she could say anything, *ask* anything, he winked and went out the only door in the room, a cracked thing with broken bits on the floor.

She waited a few moments, counting the heartbeats and listening to his retreating footsteps. When he was a safe distance away, she jumped up to her bare feet. There was no dizziness, which she was thankful for. Shula ran for the door, yanking it open. Her strength had seemed to come back to her tenfold. Either that or the door was incredibly fragile. The moment she pulled it open, bits of the wood crumbled off.

She didn't care. She wouldn't be here long. She started off at a sprint. Of course, she had no idea where she was going, where she was, or how she'd escape. And it was just her luck that, for the second time within the day, if it even was the same day, she'd run straight into a solid body of flesh.

She yelped and jumped back, once again finding herself staring up into the eyes of the monstrous Fae from before. He was glaring down at her, one eye white and the other black.

In the light of day, he looked different. Not obscured by shadows, he didn't look as sinister. The scars spread across his face like the broken edges of a mysterious puzzle piece she couldn't decipher. Without his cloak, she could see them run down his neck and into the collar of his buttoned-up tunic. Shula wondered what had happened to him. Some of the wounds looked fresher than others. Even though he wore a long sleeve that strained against his bulging, thick muscles, she could make out the pressed pattern of scars. Some looked like burn marks, others like stab wounds carved through his flesh. It made the wounds on her own back ache.

He was glaring down at her with little remorse in his gaze. It made her regret her startled yelp, made her cross her arms against her chest and glare right back.

Perhaps the night before she'd been frightened of him, but she'd been running for her life, scared and betrayed, aching and filled with ashwood poison and bound in iron. This was a new day and all of her aches and pains were behind her. She would fight if she had to. She would fight to get past him and make it to her freedom. Finally.

"Move," she ordered.

His massive, hulking body took up the entire hallway. She would have to squeeze herself very thin to make it past him.

He snorted though his expression didn't change.

"Either move or I move you myself." She felt the vehemence in her own words, even if she had no idea how she would even begin moving him. Shula wasn't on the short side, though neither was she tall. And this Fae man towered over six feet. Maybe seven? She couldn't be sure, but he packed stone upon stone of solid muscle that made him look like a beast.

He could take her out if he really wanted to, but Shula wouldn't go down without a fight.

Her temperature flared and with it, she could taste ash and smoke in her lungs. She exhaled a breath and smoke clouded before her.

Finally, she got a reaction out of him. His eyebrow rose and then he spoke, and the gravely sound of his voice did something to her insides she couldn't explain. Just like before, she felt her magic stir to life at his nearness. "What are you going to do? Burn me?"

She pushed her confusion away and held up her palm. It had been so long since she last used her magic, but she dug deep inside herself to bring forth a glimmer of sparks to her fingertips. They popped and sizzled like the remnants of a campfire.

"If that's what it takes," she threatened.

The male stepped forward, close enough so that his chest brushed across Shula's. She was suddenly too aware of what she was wearing, of the thin shift that was see-through, but his eyes never strayed below her own.

"Try it," he dared. There wasn't a whisper of the thrill, of mischief. No, this man's voice held all the dangerous promise of death. And of a male who wasn't afraid to impart it.

"Ryker, big guy, what the fuck are you doing?"

The man—Ryker—took a single step back as Clay came jogging towards them. Ryker angled his body so Clay could get through, and Shula didn't miss the glare Clay shot Ryker, or the surreptitious glance he shot the little sparks on her fingers.

She smothered them in her fist.

"She was trying to escape." Ryker's big arms crossed against his chest.

Clay shot her a glance. "Aww, already? You haven't even let me kiss you yet."

Shula felt her cheeks heat at that, but all it did was cause Clay to laugh. He thrust a pile of clothes and boots into her arms.

"These should fit. Orna loaned them to you, so you might have to give them back once we can find you your own set."

Ryker snorted at that and turned to stalk away now that Shula was with Clay.

"Then I'll have to thank Orna *and* the blacksmith," she replied reverently, hugging the clothes to her chest. She didn't mention that she wouldn't be thanking Ryker at all, and Clay didn't mention it again.

"Yup. Now go get dressed. Valerio wants to speak with you, and I'm sure you're hungry, right?"

In response, her stomach emitted a soft growl.

"I could eat." Her cheeks heated again.

Clay nodded in understanding. "Go change. I'll wait right here."

As she turned, Shula couldn't help but feel like those words weren't just spoken lightly like his tone implied.

They'd been a warning.

She went back into the room, closing the door behind her, though it seemed futile at this point since there were gaping holes in them. Thankfully, she could make out Clay's figure on the other side turn his back to her.

She breathed a sigh of relief and began to strip. If she were being honest, she was glad to get rid of the sheer dress the Fae servants had forced on her. It felt tainted, like poison against her skin and burned as badly as their touch had.

She yanked it off and tossed it aside, making quick work of putting on the clothes from the mysterious Orna. There were no undergarments, but that didn't worry Shula too much. She slid a pair of drab, brown pants over her legs, shimmying into them. They were tight against her ass, but fit perfectly around the waist. Then, she pulled on the long-sleeved white tunic and belt. It was short and tight as well, constricting against her chest. Lastly, she pulled on a warm pair of socks and snug leather boots.

She wished she had a mirror to look at herself, but under the circumstances she supposed it didn't matter. Her heart clenched tight as she realized that she would never see the inside of her tent again. Never step foot within the circus again. She would never see the place she'd called home for years. No more silks and fluffy, comfortable pillows. She'd no longer hold her jeweled combs, look at her reflection in the full length, obsidian-rimmed mirror.

She wasn't sure why the tears threatened to come at the thought. She hadn't cried when her best friend betrayed her, but the fact that she'd never see her things again brought tears to her eyes. She was just now processing everything that had happened. The way her life had suddenly, irrevocably changed.

Taking a deep breath, she tried to keep the tears at bay by running her fingers through her tangled hair. When she finished with the knots, she felt calmer. A part of her still felt dirty, covered in the oils the Fae slaves had slathered her with. She hoped she could find a stream or a tub or something soon so she could wash the taint of their touch off.

When she was as presentable as she could be, she went back out into the hall to meet Clay.

He turned to her and offered his arm like a proper gentleman. Strange when there was Fae wildness in his smile. "Shall we, Fire Dancer?"

She found herself slipping her hand into the crook of his arm. "My name is Shula," she corrected him. "Shula Azzarh." She wasn't the infamous Fire Dancer. Not anymore. She never would be again.

The thought broke her heart.

"And I'm Clay Valentino." He flashed her a dazzlingly blinding smile. "At your service."

He guided her down a series of hallways with broken structures for walls and rooms without doors, until they made it to what seemed like the back of the semi-destroyed cabin.

"You slept all night and Valerio is eager to speak with you," Clay explained as he pushed open the back door. "You don't have to be afraid of him, though. He looks much more dangerous than he is, but don't tell him I told you that or he'll cut my head off."

Shula didn't question how he could not be dangerous and then threaten to chop his head off in the same moment. It wasn't her business. Soon, she'd be away from them.

Clay led her outside, and Shula was surprised about the warm splash of sunlight that wafted over her face. She was so used to the fog and smog of the city that when she stepped onto clumpy bits of grass, dirt, and rocks, she nearly tripped. Inhaling deep, she relished in the fresh air, her eyes darting around the open expanse of space and the forest beyond. Thick leaves clustered together, so close that the trees formed an umbrella over their own trunks and the grass below.

Even more surprising still were the people wandering along the backyard like this was some type of... camp.

There weren't that many people, about ten or eleven or so, and they were a mix of humans and Fae both, of all ages, working together to shove things into packs and wagons tethered to mules and horses.

"Where are we?" she asked, hoping to keep the bit of awe she felt from her voice.

Clay tugged her along the camp. Curious stares followed her, but no one said anything. The humans didn't rush at her to kill her, but they seemed to all nod respectfully at Clay. It was something she never thought she'd see in her lifetime.

"We're at one of our safe houses." He cast her a side glance. "Don't worry about the place being shabby. We won't be staying here indefinitely. It's not safe to keep to one place for too long."

She knew that all too well. It was another reason why she'd joined the circus. Movement meant survival.

"Come. Valerio is just over here." He pulled her near the edge of the forest and her booted feet skidded along the dirt.

She knew what going into the woods with someone like him meant...

He cast her a glance and sighed. He released his hold on her, and she watched cautiously as he pushed aside the hem of his tunic to reveal a weapon's belt wrapped around his waist. He whipped out a dagger that had her flinching back.

"Geez! Put the fire out! I'm not going to hurt you! Shit..."

She hadn't realized her palms had caught fire or that the fire had spread up her arms. She'd always been so controlled before, so careful to keep her powers repressed. She wondered if it had anything to do with those brothers and the liquid they'd shoved down her throat. If it had awakened something within her that she'd always kept tightly locked. Or maybe it hadn't even been them at all. Maybe it was the scars on her back. After all, it had all started with Davina's predictions and the flames carved into her flesh.

She blinked, but the flames were still there. It had been so long, she realized she didn't even know how to control it in this quantity anymore. She tried picturing how to smother it, and it felt like it took forever before the flames disappeared back inside her, settling right next to her frantic heartbeat.

"Shit, little Fire Dancer. You could've fucking killed me. I guess you won't even need this, huh?" He thrust the knife towards her, hilt first.

She eyed the weapon warily and he rolled his eyes, stepping forward to slam it down onto her palm.

"There, since you seem so inclined to be protected around us. I hope this makes you realize that we aren't going to hurt you. You're safe with us, little Fire Dancer."

Shula's palm closed over the hilt. The weapon did make her feel safer. Just holding the simple blade in her hand made her feel like she had her power back. Like she wasn't helpless among these mysterious Fae who had taken her.

"Now can we go see Valerio? I really don't want to piss him off again."

"You have a lot of experience with pissing him off?" she asked as she shoved the blade into her pants pocket. She kept her hand plastered to it, feeling the weight of it bounce against her thigh and dig into her palm.

He walked into the copse of trees and she followed before answering. "I piss him off enough, which means I'm on thin ice. I don't want to piss him off again."

"Is he just a really angry person—Fae—uh—" She wasn't exactly sure how to direct herself towards them. Fae weren't people. Not exactly. They were living beings, but they were so vastly different from humans that they had their own category.

Clay chuckled. "You can call us people, Fire Dancer. It's fine. We're all alive and breathing, aren't we? We all bleed, we all live, and we all die. Well, the Fae die slower than mortals, but you get what I mean."

She supposed he made a fair argument.

"So what did you do?"

"Hm?" Clay sounded distracted as he pushed aside a thick branch and held it aside for her to pass through.

"What did you do to piss him off?"

"I don't think you're ready for that story yet."

A million scenarios, each wilder than the last, played through her mind. What could this man have possibly done to piss off Valerio? And why was he so frightened of him? Obviously, he was a powerful Fae, so she made a mental note not to piss him off, either. But if he tried anything, she would try right back. Anything to save herself.

"Besides, we're here." He stepped into a small clearing where three other Fae men were standing. Among them, Ryker, the other one from last night, and another Fae male she didn't recognize.

In the light of day, she made out their features clearly. All of them were tall, the four of them. Clay went to stand beside them, and she realized that while he was still average height, the others towered over him, but no one towered over Ryker.

She avoided looking at him, and instead studied the other two Fae males.

One of them had pale skin and long silver-white hair that brushed over his shoulders. Some of the strands were braided and pulled away from the hard, angry angles of his face. There was something brutal about him, something grave and deadly about his demeanor as well as his scent.

But not as deadly as the other Fae at his side. This male was all sharp, cutting angles and black, bleeding eyes that were trained on Shula with no remorse. The sides of his head were shaved bald, but dark, long hair covered the top in an elegant knot. She remembered him from the night before and the posters scattered around Tuath.

These two Fae weren't as muscular as Ryker, but they still had a foreboding bearing. Their arms bulged as they flexed, and she could make out the shadow of muscles against their tightly pressed tunics.

Seriously, she thought, *what is with these Fae and the tight shirts?*

"Shula Azzarh." Her name leaving the dark-haired Fae's lips made her still. His glance was cutting, the kind that threatened to tear through her whole soul.

"Shit, Valerio, you're scaring her," Clay snapped.

Despite him being the one who'd told her she hadn't had a choice but to come with them the night before, she felt like she now had an ally in him. He was staring angrily at Valerio.

So he was Valerio?

No wonder Clay was frightened of him.

He looked more formidable than Ryker even and emitted a fragrance that was too sweet and unrecognizable.

"I do not care," Valerio replied impatiently. "We do not have time to coddle her. We need answers."

Clay clamped his mouth shut. Shula grew annoyed. She didn't like the fact that he was bullying Clay or her. She didn't appreciate the way he was treating her, kidnapping her and forcing her into this safe house.

She pressed her palm against the blade, drawing strength from it. "I'm not going to give you anything until you give me answers, too."

Valerio's jaw clenched tightly, and she wondered if he was contemplating striking at her.

You can try, her gaze said.

"Fine."

Keeping her satisfied smile to herself, she demanded, "Who are you?"

"You've already met Ryker Valda." He nodded towards the scarred man, who she refused to acknowledge. "And Clay Valentino." Clay gave her a finger wave. "This is Uric Adriel Nova." The silver-white haired Fae glared at her. "And I am Valerio Ashera."

"And we are the Resistance," Clay added.

Valerio closed his eyes and let out a breath of exasperation. "Stop calling us that." When he opened his eyes again, he looked straight at Shula. "We travel Illyk looking for Fae in need of help and offer them sanctuary."

She swallowed. To think there were more. Shula had all but written them off as extinct.

"Why were you being held at the temple?" Valerio asked.

Memories came flooding back at the mention of that horrid place. Not that they'd ever been far away, but just mentioning them out loud made the air escape her lungs. Shula saw black spots behind her vision, and when she opened her mouth to reply, nothing came out. Panic set in her gut and she remembered the pain of water burning a pathway down her throat. The symbols on the ground, the iron nail driving into Brother Lara's throat, blood coating her fingers...

She suddenly felt suffocated, like she was drowning, like she needed air and she couldn't get any... She was dying. She was...

A strong hand gripped her chin, hauling her gaze up into a scarred face. "Breathe," Ryker whispered. Magic glowed from his hand and spread over her. She wanted to jerk away, but she was hypnotized in his bicolored gaze and the intensity there. He wasn't showing emotion, not exactly, but there were a million words and sentiments in the depths of those two-colored eyes.

Suddenly, she felt revitalized. She gasped, inhaling a sharp breath. The moment her lungs opened and her panic abated, Ryker dropped his hand and staggered backwards, clutching a big hand to his chest. He let out an animalistic growl and barreled past Shula and away from the clearing, panting as he went.

"I—is he okay?"

Clay waved her concern off with a flick of his fingers. "He's fine. You were saying?"

She stared at the spot where Ryker had stood, wondering what that had all been about. His magic filling her body...

"Today, Fire Dancer," Valerio snapped.

Shula took a breath. "The emperor's soldiers captured me and took me to the temple. They took me downstairs to catacombs. They had me bound in iron..."

"There was ashwood in your blood," Valerio cut in.

"H-how did you know that?" She didn't want to talk about that. She could tell them what went down in those dungeons, she could tell them about the brothers, the Fae slaves, all of it. But she couldn't tell them about Fanny's betrayal. She wasn't ready to rip her soul out to these people just yet.

"Let's just say Ryker has many talents in his repertoire. Continue."

She grinded her teeth together. "They left me alone with Fae slaves and they were ceremonial about washing my body, combing my hair, and dressing me." She swallowed and looked at the ground.

"What?" Valerio demanded with impatience.

Shula took a breath. She was braver than this, so she met his eyes. "The Fae women... their ears had been cut off."

Clay made a sound of disgust. "The emperor's work, no doubt. Fucking bastard."

Shula was inclined to agree.

"They chained me to the ground, but I think... I think the women tried to help me, because they didn't hammer the nail in all the way. Once they left, I tugged it out. I would have run, but they came in."

"The emperor's soldiers?" Clay's voice was sympathetic.

Shula shook her head, her hair grazing along her cheeks "No, the Brotherhood."

The three of them shared an indecipherable look and when Clay turned back, his brows were furrowed together. "What the fuck is the Brotherhood?"

"That's what I'd like to know." Shula's hands tightened into fists. "Because the moment they arrived, they shoved something down my throat..."

"Ashwood," Clay commented. Shula didn't correct him.

"It burned. Then they chanted above a pentagram on the floor, and the symbols I was kneeling on lit up." Talking about it now made her angry. It made her want vengeance, but she shoved those feelings away. It was better to forget any of it had happened. It was better to move on with her life and build herself anew where they would never find her again.

"What were these symbols?" Valerio asked.

So Shula explained. She explained each circle and the symbol within, the slashing line across the floor. Just talking about it made the wounds on her back ache, but she left that part out of her story. As she explained, she noticed the Fae men look to one another with a conspiratorial look. She wondered at that but continued to force her way through the story of the six brothers, how she'd slashed out and killed one and harmed the other before her escape.

"Why would the emperor want you alive and unharmed?" Valerio stroked his chin, his gaze assessing as it flicked over her body.

"To torture me himself, probably." She'd heard the stories of what he was like. A hero to humans, a menace to Fae.

"No, this seems like a lot of trouble to go through for a simple fire Fae."

The wounds on her back burned, but she didn't mention them. They seemed personal, and if she told them, they'd want her to strip so they could see, and she wouldn't be reduced even lower than she already had been.

"My turn to ask a question. How did you find me? I find it hard to believe it was a coincidence that you were all there at the same time as I was."

"You're right, it wasn't a coincidence. A seer sent us. I am sure you know her. Davina?"

"Davina's here?" Shula's spine straightened and she twirled, looking through the trees as if she could somehow find Davina hiding among them. She couldn't explain her relief. She and Davina hadn't been close, but she'd shared a connection with the other Fae. She'd worried for a moment that the emperor's soldiers had caught her as well, but if she was here with the Fae, that meant she was safe. Shula turned back to them. "Where is she?"

The three of them shared another look that sent a bad feeling coiling in her gut. "Where is she?" Shula repeated.

Clay took a step forward. "Maybe you should sit down, Fire Dancer..."

She jerked away. "No. I want you to tell me where Davina is! What have you done with her?!" Her shout echoed through the woods, startling birds from their perches.

"We have done nothing," Valerio said. Something in his voice now was far more patient than it had been before. "Davina came to us last night with a request. She told us an Elemental had been taken to that temple. She begged us to help you. She said you were important, though she conveniently left out the *important* details."

"What did she say?"

"*'Twin flames carved in flesh'*, and a lot of other dribble about Fae Elementals, prophecies, and saving our race. Ramblings of a madwoman."

Shula couldn't hear anymore. She whipped out the knife from her pocket and stalked over towards Valerio. "Do not speak about Davina that way!" Even though Shula had done it. Many times over. She couldn't stand to hear it come from his mouth. To hear her own ugly thoughts voiced.

Before she even reached Valerio, though, Uric was there and a blade was pressed to her own throat, digging into her skin.

"Come at the Prince of Seelie with a knife and expect a swift death."

Shula swallowed, her throat working against the sharp edge of the blade as she absorbed the words. His cutting scent was overwhelming, as cutting as the weapon pressed to her throat. Like ice and mint and something else that was piercingly intense.

"Uric," Valerio commanded. It was all he needed to say. Uric pulled the blade away from her skin and took his place next to Valerio once again.

Chest heaving, Shula slammed her palm against her neck, narrowing her gaze at him. "Prince?"

Uric stared at her with pride-filled eyes. "You are in the presence of Prince Valerio Ashera, son to King Amos Ashera of Tir na Faie, the lands beyond the Ley Line and the Seelie Court."

Shula had thought that the Fae courts had fallen. At least, that's what she'd been told. As the old war had progressed and humans gained more power, they'd invaded the lands of the Fae and murdered the court nobility. No one had been left alive.

She wanted to be impressed, but how could she be? This whole situation seemed bigger than even her. So instead of bowing to the prince of her race, she snorted, shoving the blade into her pocket, and muttered, "Sounds fucking pretentious."

Clay barked out a laugh.

"Anyway, if you thought Davina was such a madwoman, why come to my aid?"

Valerio's—Prince Valerio's, she corrected—eyes narrowed. "Because, she gave me a glimpse of the future, and I believed her. But when it came to the important stuff, they were nothing but ramblings. So, enlighten us, Fire Dancer, Shula Azzarh. Of what prophecy does she speak? Why did the Brotherhood take care with you?"

"I don't know," she hissed. "And that's the truth. You think Davina gave me any clues either when we were at the circus? She told me the Fae would fall beneath robes of white and red unless I came to my powers. What colors were the Brotherhood's robes? You guessed it. White and red. Now tell me, what happened to Davina?"

"The emperor's soldiers got her." Valerio's voice was clipped and without remorse. "They sent the hounds, and she sacrificed her life so we could get you away. Now we must leave. It is time to move to the next safe house."

Shula staggered back, clasping her palms over her ears. No. She didn't want to believe his words, didn't want them to be true.

Davina couldn't be dead, much less because she'd sacrificed herself for Shula.

Not again.

Not *again.*

She was cursed, cursed so that all who helped her died, and if there was one thing she knew she couldn't do, it was go with them.

Because if she did, she would surely bring death upon their camp.

And their so-called Resistance?

It would be the death of her.

The Fae's Captive

A suffocating pain nearly drowned Ryker in darkness. Spots of white lights and shadows blinked behind his closed eyelids as he struggled for breath. Shit. This was always the worst part of his magic: the price he had to pay. It had been instinct to heal her, even if everything in him told him to let it be.

He shouldn't feel any sympathy for her, but in that moment he had. He felt sympathy for the Fae who was more human than not, and so he'd taken her suffering.

Fuck, he should have just let her suffer. He rubbed his hand across his chest to ease the ache. Taking deep breaths, it was minutes before the pain finally passed. When it did, he pushed himself off the bark of the tree he was leaning against and started towards the sound of shouting voices.

He would have stayed to hear the entire conversation, but he loathed to show this weakness in front of her. The others had already seen him at his lowest. They'd known him from before, before he'd been this monstrous thing he was now. He hadn't always had the scars, and he wasn't ashamed to look in the mirror now that he had them, even when he knew how others cringed upon first seeing him.

Many wore the scars of battle proudly, and while Ryker hadn't been in many great wars, living in the present day Illyk was war enough. The raised flesh along his skin were his own proof of valor.

Not that he expected her to understand. He noticed the way her eyes traced the pattern of his scars, the questions burning in her eyes. He knew he repulsed her as much as she repulsed him.

It was a mutual feeling.

Leaves crunched under his boots as he stomped back into the small clearing. He'd gathered bits and pieces of the conversation, but the closer he got, the more he gauged what was happening. So when he stepped forward, it was just in time to catch the Fire Dancer as she tried running away.

She rammed straight into his chest and staggered back. His hands shot out to hold her in place. To keep her from falling or to keep her from leaving, he couldn't be sure. But he kept his palms on her arms and glared down in her face.

He could see the tears glossing over her eyes. Tears she was too stubborn and furious to let fall.

"You again?" she demanded. As if he'd been the one to run into *her*. "Get out of my way!" She pressed her delicate palms to his chest and shoved.

He didn't move an inch.

"Prince," she sneered over her shoulder. "Tell your brute of a bodyguard to stand down!"

Bodyguard?

Gods, he missed her sleeping form. It had been quiet then.

"No," Valerio replied coolly. "We are not finished here."

She jerked out of Ryker's hold and whirled around so quickly the ends of her hair slapped across Ryker's skin. "I am finished here. I'm leaving."

"The Brotherhood is out there searching for you. If you leave, you will not get very far."

"And if I stay, I'm as good as dead with you people," she spat. "You claim to be helping the Fae, but you're just going to get them killed. All of them."

Valerio's eyebrows rose, and Ryker could tell he was battling to keep his expression stoic, to keep the laughter from there. "And why is that?"

"You think the emperor won't realize what you're doing? Your face is plastered all over the *most wanted* posters, for Mana's sake! The more you gather, the easier you all will be to detect. You will lead them straight to you."

Ryker could hear the fear trembling through her words. He glared at her back.

"Fear is no excuse for cowardice," he muttered, low enough for only her to hear, but he knew Valerio, Uric, and Clay were paying attention, so they heard it, too.

The Fire Dancer whipped around, her chest straining against the tight restrictions of her shirt. For a moment, he swore he caught the flare of fire in the depths of her brown eyes.

"Call me a coward, then," she gritted out from between clenched teeth. "But all I want is to stay alive."

Ryker snorted. "You think hiding among those who would turn you to the authorities the moment they find out what you are is life?"

She flinched at his words, and in the back of his mind, he wondered if that's what had happened. If that was how she'd been caught?

"It's surviving."

"But it's not living." Ryker took a step forward, so close that he could feel the heat emanating from her body, as warm as a bonfire, this little Fae. He lifted his hand and pushed aside her hair, exposing her rounded ears.

Just looking at them offended him.

She jolted away, but they'd already caught sight of her treachery. The ultimate betrayal to their race.

"Do not think we haven't noticed what you've done to your ears."

Her hands trembled as she set her hair over them again. Out of habit, or because she didn't want them to see the scars?

It made him smirk cruelly at her. He knew when he smiled, the scars twisted on his cheeks and made him look grotesque. It was why he'd grown out his beard, because it made him look somewhat normal. He was glad for the insanity of his features right then, though.

"I've heard of Fae like you," he sneered. "You go to surgeons so they can alter your true nature, distort your features so you look more human. That's what you did, isn't it? Because you are ashamed of what you are?"

He heard the hitch in her breath, heard her heart pounding, faster and faster.

"Yes," she hissed. "Yes, I altered my ears. I did it to survive, because I was alone." There was such heartbreak in her voice, but it failed to touch Ryker. Because all he could see was the shame that burned inside her, brighter than any fire, brighter than any star.

"You won't be alone here," Clay cut in. His voice was soft and gentle. Caring.

It made Ryker want to scoff.

"Regardless of what you did in the past, we protect our own." Valerio stepped forward. There was finality in the gesture as well in the expression he wore. "The Brotherhood wants you. The *emperor* wants you, and so we will not let him have you. We will protect you now."

"So you're going to keep me prisoner here?"

Valerio shrugged. "Call it what you will, Shula Azzarh. But we will not let you go."

"You can't keep me here against my will!"

"If it means protecting the race of the Fae, then I will do whatever it fucking takes."

"No." The word was but a breath leaving her lips, and yet he could feel the heat, the vehemence in it clearly.

Clay shifted uncomfortably. It was unwise to deny the Prince of Seelie. No Fae would dream of it, and yet she did. *Because she's more human than Fae*, Ryker thought bitterly. That was the only reason she defied him.

Valerio's lips pressed into a thin line. "Then I will keep you here by force." He blinked.

And the air around them was consumed with the prince's magic.

It wasn't something that Ryker could see, but he could feel its intensity like a blow to the chest. He sucked in a breath and watched as Valerio used his magic against the Fire Dancer.

Her body tensed, pulling as taut as a bow string. She gasped, her head darting around the clearing, looking at things that weren't really there. Because that's what his magic was. It was glamor and illusions.

It was temporary insanity.

The Fire Dancer began to scream. "No! You aren't real! You can't get me! No!" The panicked sound of her voice built an ache in his chest that he forced himself to ignore because it was an ache that didn't make sense.

Perhaps they were not real, whatever it was she was seeing, but it always felt like it was. She swatted at the air and cringed back so far and so fast, she hit Ryker's chest.

He wanted to push her away, but something seared straight through his chest, so he didn't. It was her scent, all warm campfires and confections. Her nails reached back blindly, digging into the skin of his arm.

His heart pounded against her back but he doubted she could feel it. But he could taste her fear. It was sharp in the air and coated along his taste buds.

It made Ryker wonder what Valerio was making her see? Her worst nightmare? The Brotherhood?

She gripped Ryker tightly and whimpered.

Just like Ryker felt the power of Valerio's magic, he felt it slipping away as well until nothing of it was left. He cast a glance at his prince wondering how soon the toll would fall upon him.

The moment the magic dissipated, the Fire Dancer extricated her nails from his arms. He felt the abrasions give off the slightest burn and he knew that if he looked down, he'd find her markings against him like a claim. A brand.

The Fire Dancer stumbled forward a step; she tripped and promptly vomited all over the forest floor.

The putrid stench hit Ryker's nose, but he'd smelt worse in healing rooms. Vomit, piss and shit, burnt flesh, festered wounds, puss, infections... He recognized it all.

Clay was suddenly there, his palm rubbing gentle circles around her back, but she jerked away from him, falling into a pile of leaves.

"Don't fucking touch me! Don't!"

Clay's expression flashed with hurt, and Ryker fought not to grunt and roll his eyes. The Fae would do whatever it took to get laid, even wade through her fucking vomit.

Slowly, the Fire Dancer pushed herself to her feet, groaning as she went. She sent Valerio a glare and stumbled away without another word. This time, they let her go.

Ryker listened to her retreating steps, lethargic, unsteady. She stopped to vomit again.

"What the fuck was that?" Clay accused Valerio angrily. He was one of the only ones to speak to their prince in such a manner. Perhaps because they were cousins and Clay was royalty in his own right. "Instead of drawing her to our side, you're pushing her away and fucking traumatizing her!"

Valerio's eyes were blown wide. Feral, almost.

Since he played with the sanity of others, the price he paid was with the fragile pieces of his own mind. Sometimes he became violent, though his violence was nothing compared to Julius'.

"I don't care. She needs to get her shit together. For the good of us all."

"Haven't you heard of tact?"

Valerio's nostrils flared. It was obvious he was fighting to keep hold of his sanity, of not falling into wild, crazed instincts. He was a prince above all and comported himself as such.

"I don't give a *fuck* what I have to do. If saving our race means keeping her here against her will, then so fucking be it." He growled and his hand reached up to tug at his hair. Uric hovered behind him, ever the worried guard. Valerio took a breath and fought for his composure. "Still, it would be... beneficial... if she were to stay here willingly."

Beyond, Ryker could hear the Fire Dancer stand and stumble through the woods.

"Follow her, Clay. Convince her. Make her want to stay. Whatever means necessary."

There was so much implication in those words that Ryker fought back the gritting of his teeth. Was his prince really suggesting Clay fuck her into submission?

Clay looked uncomfortable at the idea, which Ryker found odd. When was he not willing and able? Where there was a beautiful woman, Clay followed, no matter her race. Because of that golden dick of his, he'd gotten them *all* into a lot of trouble. More than any of the women had ever been worth.

"Fine," Clay conceded and turned to follow after the Fire Dancer.

"Ryker." His name was the snap of a whip off of Valerio's tongue.

Ryker looked up at his prince in time to see his sanity slipping.

"You will watch over her."

His answer was immediate. "No."

Even Uric looked at him as if he'd lost his damned mind. Maybe he had, for Ryker had never disobeyed an order from his prince before. But he didn't want to waste his time babysitting someone who didn't even want to be here. Someone who hated her own race.

"No?" Valerio, in a clear moment of lucidity, cocked his head to the side.

"I have Fae to heal."

"And an Elemental to watch over."

Ryker's temper flared. He had better things to do, like give help to those who really needed it.

"I won't be her babysitter."

And before his prince could say anther word, Ryker whirled and stormed off. He didn't take the time to contemplate his disrespect. He knew it was disrespectful, that Uric should have been shoving a blade between his shoulder blades for it, but he wasn't thinking clearly.

She was invading everything, and it infuriated him. All he knew was that he wanted nothing to do with the infamous Fire Dancer.

As he stepped through the leaves, he heard his prince's voice follow him back to the cabin.

"Uric... let him go."

So the Fae had been planning on shoving a dagger into him?

Perhaps that would have been preferable. Preferable to feel the pain of a blade, rather than that of her presence.

Shula's every step pained her. It wasn't an ache in her body, but in her mind. Her head pounded, and she felt like with every grueling step, she was going to be sick. Again.

Her stomach roiled and she gagged, stopping to bend over with her palms against her thighs as she heaved.

That fucking bastard prince, she thought viciously. He'd glamored her, made her see terrors that weren't really there. While she'd known it was all part of some trick, her mind had been unable to separate fantasy from reality.

Once the sensation in her stomach ebbed, Shula stood up and wiped her sweaty brow. Footsteps sounded behind her, and she knew who it was based on the lightness in foot alone.

"Go away," she growled to Clay.

"Not a chance, Fire Dancer."

Shula straightened and began walking away. He followed closely at her heels, giving her the smallest illusion of distance, but she felt him close.

"What do you want from me?" She hated how weak she sounded, how small they'd made her voice. They were going to keep her here against her will. And really, did that make them any better than the Brotherhood that had taken her? They claimed they were protecting her, going to save her. But she was just their prisoner.

"That's a loaded question, isn't it?" Clay asked. He sauntered next to her, his hands shoved into his pockets as if nothing had happened. As if her mind and sanity hadn't just been thoroughly violated. "We want you to stay here, Shula. Is it so wrong for us to want to be together?"

Was it? Was it wrong?

Her answer came with complete honesty. "No, it's not wrong." Everyone needed someone. For as much as Shula professed to be alone, it was Fanny who got her through the loneliness. Which made her betrayal hurt all the worse. "What's wrong is that you're no better than the emperor's soldiers."

Clay's feet skidded against the ground. He tumbled and then rushed to catch up to her again. "Why would you say that?" He sounded genuinely offended. "We are in no way the same."

"Aren't you?" Her palm went to touch the knife pressed against her pocket. This time, the blade didn't bring her comfort. These Fae were obviously powerful. At least, the prince was. She still wasn't sure what powers the others had, and she wasn't sure she wanted to find out. "They stole me away and kept me prisoner. You all did the same."

"We wouldn't hurt you!"

All Shula did was give him a pointed look, but she remained silent. She didn't want to speak anymore. She wanted to be free of this place, of them.

Beside her, Clay raked a hand through his hair and sighed. "Look, Valerio is—" He broke off with a soft curse, as if his mind couldn't quite conjure up the words to describe exactly what Valerio was. The old myth about how the Fae couldn't lie? It held no standing with the Seelie. It was complete shit, and yet it seemed to apply with Clay.

"Don't," she warned quietly. Her fingers dug into the side of her pocket. She wanted to feel the blade dig into her skin so she could feel something other than the tumultuous storm inside her. Instead of betrayal and panic, she wanted pain so it would ground her. So she could focus. "Don't sing his praises. I don't need to hear them."

Clay sighed again and stopped her, his hand tugging gently at her upper arm. He turned her to face him and his features were smoothed over with regret and sadness. "Shula, I am sorry. The truth is, we didn't expect this either. We don't want any of this to happen. We just want to go back home."

Home.

To Tir na Faie.

He said it with such longing, she wondered if he'd been there himself, but couldn't bring herself to ask. Her parents hadn't told her stories of the Feylands, of the magic beyond the borders of the Ley Line. They hadn't been born there.

They'd been born on human lands in the midst of a war and had lived through the eradication of Fae rights.

They hadn't taught her about the wild, fun stories of the Unseelie, but stories of fear. They hadn't taught her to use her magic, but they'd taught her to hide. They'd taught her the most important lesson in life: survival.

If Clay knew what a home was, if he knew the magic of Tir na Faie, it meant he was old. Older, even, than her parents would be, had they survived.

"If there's a chance that you can help us have our home back... Valerio is going to take it. He's a bastard. A fucking bastard, but he cares about our race. Our future is on his shoulders."

She admired Clay for a moment, she really did, but he was trying to excuse his prince's abhorrent behavior as if that could make a single difference. It didn't.

"What... what did he make you see?"

Horrors. Absolute horrors.

Shula extricated her arm from his hold and turned to look out at the trees. They canopied over their heads, soft buttery sunlight filtering through the leaves and casting golden colors on the dry earth. Soon, winter would come. The evidence of the change of seasons lived in the array of reds, oranges, and browns scattered across the floor. It was still the beginnings of fall, so not everything looked dead. Green still burst vibrantly above them.

There was something melancholy about the change of seasons, but Shula liked the fall the most. Even though it reminded her of a far more complicated time. Even though the bursting of red and orange leaves reminded her of fire. Even though the crumbling, dried earth reminded her of ash.

Even though everything reminded her of death.

It also reminded her why she had to live.

"I'm sorry, Fire Dancer." Clay brought her back to reality. "Please, please give us all a chance. We will protect each other; we will protect you."

"I can protect myself."

Storming footsteps came up behind them. Shula didn't have to turn to know it was Ryker. Her body instinctively tensed up.

"Evidently, you can't," he growled angrily, shoving past Clay. Ryker stopped, hesitation breathing over his movements. He half turned to glare at Shula with that single white eye.

It was eerie, unnerving.

"You were captured by the Brotherhood. Now that they know what you look like and have your scent, they will never stop hunting you. And they *will* find you if you're out there on your own. And if you even think about escaping, Valerio will be worse to deal with than the humans ever were."

Fear sliced straight down Shula's body.

Clay let out a hissed curse under his breath. "Great going, Ryker," he admonished. "Because *that's* going to make her want to stay."

Ryker didn't look apologetic. "You are a wanted criminal now. Why? The seer didn't say, so we can't know. But we are the lesser of two evils, Fire Dancer." He turned from her, but his voice hung in the air like thick, dense smoke as he walked away. "You need protection, and we will give it to you."

As he stalked away, Clay glared at his wide back. "Jackass," he muttered, not concealing his annoyance. Then he turned back to Shula and offered her his arm again, only this time, she didn't take it. "You hungry?" He lowered his arm back to his side. "Let's go get you some food. The journey ahead is long. You'll need your strength."

So Shula followed him. Because, what other choice did she have? She didn't want to contemplate that what Ryker had said was right.

Evil lived at every turn.

But whether or not the Fae were a lesser evil still remained to be seen.

"Yeah," she murmured. "I'm pretty hungry."

Plan of Escape

They'd given her a meal of dried meat, fruit, and cheese. It was a bland meal that made her miss the kabobs at the circus rather fiercely. While she chewed on the tough meat outside, she watched with detached attention as everyone packed up their things into the wooden cart.

She was careful to keep her expression guarded, focusing on eating while her mind whirled like a storm. She could feel eyes on her, though she couldn't discern whose. Ryker's? Clay's? Worse, Valerio's?

She'd caught a glimpse of the Fae prince again, wearing his stoic expression as he hauled heavy packs onto the cart without even breaking a sweat. He didn't look at her, but Shula didn't doubt that he knew she was there.

That was the only reason she didn't look towards the line of trees and contemplate her freedom.

She couldn't escape with all of them near. They would easily follow Valerio's orders to retrieve her and then she would be truly fucked.

She needed a better opportunity to escape, one where they weren't close, where they weren't near her at all.

She nibbled on a bit of cheese as she thought things over. They wanted her to stay with them, but they didn't trust her. It wasn't like she hadn't noticed how closely Clay was hanging around her. Like a babysitter.

She almost sneered but stopped herself by shoving the whole piece of cheese into her mouth.

If they had Clay following her, it was because they didn't trust her. That was fine; she didn't trust them either. The only problem with this was that it made escaping difficult.

Shula knew they wouldn't leave her alone. Not unless they trusted her.

So quickly she found her solution.

She had to get them to trust her. The more they trusted her, the quicker she could be left alone to make her escape. But she couldn't be obvious about wanting to earn their trust. They wouldn't believe her if she suddenly threw herself into their fold and acted friendly.

This wouldn't be believable unless she actually attempted an escape.

Swallowing down the last of her food, she stood up and dusted off her borrowed clothes. She still hadn't gotten an opportunity to thank Orna or the blacksmith for what they'd done for her. She didn't like to seem ungrateful, but she'd had more pressing matters to worry about.

She walked casually over to the line of trees, trying to be as inconspicuous as possible, but she was intercepted before she could even walk into the forest by Clay.

His smiling face looked down at her and she couldn't tell if the expression was fake or not. "Careful there, Fire Dancer," he said pleasantly, though there was a note like something of a warning in his voice. "The woods are dangerous. There are all sorts of creatures there."

"I have to relieve myself," she lied.

Clay's nose scrunched up. "I'll take you."

Had she really expected him to let her go off alone? Perhaps she had hoped, because Clay seemed to be the most pleasant of all of them. She couldn't let herself forget that he was her captor as well, no matter how nice he was being. He would betray her at the first order from his prince and wouldn't think twice about it.

She cleared her throat. "Never mind." As she turned away from him, she caught Valerio's gaze and the dangerous glimmer there. Like he knew what she was up to, and the promise of consequence laid in that single, cutting glare.

She forced herself to look away and walk back to where she'd been sitting.

After a few minutes, she grew bored and restless. Being a captive hadn't prepared her for this. She squirmed in her seat, having the sudden urge to get up and help everyone pack up, but that would make her seem like she was submitting, and while she wanted to gain their trust, they wouldn't believe her if she helped just then. So Shula sat where she was and glared as they put the last of their belongings into the cart.

Clay came over then and offered her his arm. "Time to go, Fire Dancer."

Ignoring him, Shula stood up. "Where are we going?" It would be better if she actually knew where they were and where they were headed. She couldn't blindly walk through the forest without a sense of direction.

"Into the mountains of Tuath to meet up with Julius." He led her away. A soft groan sounded as the mule and horse tethered to the cart started forward, and the small procession of Fae began to follow behind slowly, falling into easy chatter.

"Who's Julius?" Her strides were long but unhurried. She and Clay were at the very back, with Valerio and Uric leading the front. Ryker was in the middle, walking among the others. She tried not to look at him.

"You'd like him." Clay smiled widely in a way that made Shula think Julius was special to him. "He's nothing like these brooding assholes here. He's the definition of a good time."

"Uh huh." Shula was only half listening. Her gaze kept darting everywhere, feeling suddenly nervous. As if there were humans lurking behind trees and in the branches.

She'd always traveled in procession before, but never like this. Not with Fae who showed their ears so openly.

It was a recipe for chaos.

"And why are we going there?" she whispered, hoping that talking could calm her rapidly beating heart and her nerves.

"We have safe houses all over," he explained. "It's not exactly safe for us to stay in one place too long, but the mountains are safest. There's a lot of wildlife and it's easy for humans to get lost, so that's where our main strong hold is."

"But why in Tuath?"

He knew what she was really asking. Why the most dangerous Fae hating capital of the world?

He smirked. "Because that's where they'd least expect us to be."

Her nerves dissipated a fraction as she chuckled low. "That's either really brilliant or really stupid."

Clay chuckled back at her. "Why can't it be both?"

She rolled her eyes again.

"Seriously, we've used these mountains before. We're always finding Fae who need homes, so we've traveled these woods before. They're safe, as safe as they can be. Even if we come across humans, Valerio and I could get rid of them easily."

Shula was burning to ask about their powers. Her fingers twitched at her side, going again to her pocket and pressing against the bulge of the knife.

Clay's voice held humor. "Go ahead and ask, I can see you're dying to know."

"What powers do you all have?" She'd never known many more Fae besides her parents and Davina. Davina's power had been obvious, but her parents had been powerless. Was it rude to ask about powers?

She stared at Clay, but he didn't seem offended.

He shoved his hands into his pockets. "Well, you know Valerio can glamor the mind, create illusions."

She knew all too well. She still felt the spectral images buzzing around her mind, like they were shadows ready to spring to life at the most opportune moment.

"Uric can open portals through time and space."

At that, Shula blinked. "If that's true, why do we have to walk through the mountains? Why can't he just portal us there?"

"*'Why can't he just portal us there?'*" Clay mimicked then laughed. "Because, Fire Dancer, using that much power can take a toll on his body. The price of his magic is his age. He could become as frail and weak as an ancient human male and it could last for days. To use his power on so many Fae at once isn't a good idea, and he likes to save his strength in case of emergencies."

Shula supposed that made sense. She didn't have experience with her own powers. Now she knew that there was no price to her magic, she wondered how far her own well of power could go and how she would feel after she used it. As soon as the thought came to her mind, she shoved it away.

She didn't want to use her powers, even among the Fae. The more she gave into those urges, the more she'd want to stay. And to stay could mean death.

"And you?" she asked curiously.

"Oh, this and that." He smiled demurely, and a single dimple quirked the side of his mouth.

This man was kind of perfect, Shula thought. He held himself so carelessly in a way that made him absolutely beautiful. Perhaps the only imperfection in him was the slightest indent on his chin, but even that looked endearing.

Shula wondered how much of it was a façade, and how much of it was real.

"I'm sure you'll get the opportunity to see me in action, Fire Dancer."

His vague answers only made her more curious and more nervous. If he wasn't telling her, could it be he was powerful? Or could it be that he was messing with her and had no power at all?

Shula thought about that in silence when Clay chuckled again.

She shot him a glare. "What?"

"I just noticed you didn't ask about Ryker's powers..."

She'd done so deliberately, but she hated that there was insinuation in his tone. "That's because I don't give a fuck about Ryker." Even as she said this, her gaze was fiercely on the Fae in question. His broad back tensed suddenly, as if he possibly could have heard her. Maybe he could with his Fae hearing.

She didn't care.

"Aw, what did he ever do to you?"

He'd helped kidnapped her. Shit, he hadn't done anything that Clay hadn't, but she still liked Clay more than the brooding asshole of a Fae. It was his tone, his growling, biting words. The way he acted like he was better than her.

He was infuriating.

She ignored Clay's question and he didn't elaborate either, probably sensing that she really didn't care or want to know what Ryker's power was. That was probably her being petty and stupid. She knew that she needed to know everything, down to the price of their magic, but she couldn't bring herself to think much more about the scarred man. He'd made it abundantly clear what he thought of her. He was cruel and rude, and the easiest way to deal with him was to ignore him.

Yet her eyes strayed to his back again.

Almost as if he could sense her watching, Ryker turned, his dark eye breathing her in.

And, damn her, she couldn't bring herself to look away.

Because he was dangerous, deadly, more than any of the others. She didn't know how yet or why, but she didn't trust him as far as she could throw him.

And by the murderous look in his eyes, she knew that he felt the same.

Orna

They walked for hours without stopping. Until the sun drifted high into the sky and the heat beat down on them in the late afternoon.

Throughout it all, Clay tried making inconsequential conversation that Shula couldn't bring herself to follow. She knew what he was doing. Knew he was trying to appeal to her better nature, to bring her into the fold. She should've taken the bait, gotten him to trust her, but her heart felt too heavy, and she couldn't.

Eventually, he gave up and gently pulled her deeper into the crowd of Fae, depositing her next to a Fae woman and giving her a glance before stalking forward to go whisper in Valerio's ear.

Unfortunately she couldn't hear what was being said, which she knew was deliberate.

"Hello," the Fae woman next to her said with a smile.

Shula almost startled and looked down at her. She was a few inches shorter than Shula and a bit thinner, too. Her expression was open and friendly, her dark hair was braided down her back, and she wore dirty clothes; pants, boots, tunic, and jacket.

"I'm Orna." She held her hand out and Shula shook it.

"Shula Azzarh. You lent me your clothes."

Orna's smile widened as she dropped her hand back to her side. "I'm glad they fit! I wasn't sure they would. Your body is curvier than mine."

Shula's face heated.

Orna gave her a pat on the shoulder. "I'd kill to have curves like yours. But I know that if I had them, my husband wouldn't keep his hands off me. He already has trouble enough as is."

"Oh, you're married?"

Orna's smile brightened and as it did, something in the air around her shimmered. Shula's eyes narrowed and she stared harder.

"He's over there."

Shula forced herself to look away from the strange magic that surrounded Orna to where she was pointing and Shula jolted.

"He—he's human..." The sight baffled her. He was a human man. Without pointed ears, without canines, or the fierce elegance the Fae possessed. He was... normal.

She turned back to Orna, her head whipping so fast that the air that surrounded the little Fae woman shimmered and was torn away like a curtain being ripped down.

All that smooth white skin turned blue, a bright color that seemed to shimmer with glowing specks, and the dark tumbling hair was a light shade of periwinkle. Eyes were midnight black like marbles, and her teeth were sharp points.

Shula's heart beat faster and faster.

She'd never seen a Fae like Orna before, and the survival instinct she had deep inside her made her want to recoil, but she managed to blink away the surprise.

Not fast enough, because Orna frowned. "Oh, shoot, my glamor fell." She closed her eyes, brows pulled together with fierce concentration. A moment later, the air shimmered once again, and she looked human. Fae, but normal.

"Why use a glamor at all?" Shula found herself asking, "I mean, if you're among trusted Fae..."

The glamor dropped and Orna's blue skin glowed purple, making Shula wonder if it was a blush. "It's nothing like that. It's just... I'm learning to better control my powers, and I need as much practice as I can get."

"So your powers are glamor?" She immediately thought of Valerio and inside, she recoiled in fear.

Orna's head whipped back and forth. "No. It's basic Fae glamor. Hiding your appearance doesn't come with a price. The High Fae like you and the others look more beautiful, so you don't have to use it often. We Unseelie are, you know, *this*." She waved a hand down at her body and she said it with such sadness that something in Shula ached.

She knew what it was to be ashamed of what she looked like. Of what she was. "What are you talking about? You're beautiful."

She flushed a deeper shade of purple. "Thank you," she whispered demurely.

"So, you're an Unseelie?"

Orna bit her bottom lip between her teeth and nodded.

"What does that mean exactly?" At Orna's incredulous look, her face heated and she elaborated, "I was raised in human lands on the reservations and my parents died. Since then I've been blending in..."

The reservations were where the hierarchy threw the Fae after running them out of their homes. A "safe" space on human lands where they could be themselves in a controlled environment. The reality of it was that they kept them locked up, controlled, not because they respected the Fae and their culture, but because it was easier to access them that way. Easier to pull them out of the fenced land and take them away.

Orna stared at her with fierce understanding but didn't comment to degrade her like Ryker had. It made Shula grateful not to know her true thoughts on the matter. "The High Fae are from the Seelie Courts. Before the war and before Tir na Faie became uninhabitable, the courts were ruled over by the High Fae nobility while the Seelie Court was ruled by the Ashera bloodline.

"Deeper to the south lived the Unseelie. Fae, but different from the High Fae. Goblins, pixies, mermaids, banshees..." She held up her hands, her black, depthless eyes raking over her blue skin. "I'm part pixie. That's why my skin is blue."

"And do the Unseelie have... powers?"

"The Unseelie are tricksters and are considered savage by the High Fae. Some have glamor, some have song, some tails and such things. We don't have powers like you." She looked straight at Shula's chest, as if she could see the flames inside her soul. "You're an Elemental. The power of Mana lives within you. You're special."

Shula was really starting to hate that word. She sighed and focused her gaze forward. "So I keep hearing."

Shula felt the slip of Orna's arm loop through her own. When she looked at the other Fae, there was nothing but friendly understanding in her eyes. She didn't speak, but then again, she didn't need to. Shula got it just the same. This was an understanding between the two.

Shame, and not being happy within their own skin. It was quick and inarguably what Shula needed.

Someone who knew what she felt inside and who wouldn't judge.

A friend.

Thoughts of Fanny tightened her throat. She tried not to give into her emotions, tried not to think about that betrayal. It was still a raw wound against her chest that she knew was festering, yet she didn't want it healed. It was a sharp reminder that nothing was safe. Nowhere was safe. No one was safe.

She wanted to pull her arm from Orna's and wallow in her own self-piteous thoughts, but the Fae kept them tightly tethered together, pulling them behind the cart and other Fae.

They walked together in comfortable silence and not once did Orna's hold slip from Shula's. It wasn't until night descended along the horizon that the procession finally came to a stop.

Valerio started barking out orders and everyone quickly got to work.

Orna pulled on Shula's arm. "Come. You can help me hand out the food to the others."

Shula didn't want to; she didn't want anything to do with this, but her stomach rumbled loudly. She hadn't eaten since that morning; none of them had. Plus, Orna's expression was hopeful. Like she wanted a friend as much as Shula wanted to push her away. But Shula couldn't give in to the urge.

Orna had done nothing wrong. She couldn't possibly know that Fanny had betrayed her and that Shula was still hurting. It wasn't anyone's fault but Shula's. Deep down she knew that her friendship with Fanny had been doomed from the start. That's why she'd never told her the truth. But the moment Fanny had found out, Shula had hoped...

A fool, she'd been.

But Orna was Fae herself, and the friendships weren't the same. If this could even be considered a friendship.

Orna had seemed to know that Shula had wanted silence, so she hadn't pressed the entire way. That had to count for something.

"We feed the children, elderly, and women first," Orna explained as she hauled down a box from the cart. Shula rushed to help her, taking one end so they could carry it together. "The men take up their positions for the watch. If Valerio deems everything safe, sometimes we can build a fire and the men can hunt so we all have fresh meat." She took the lid off the wooden box and began pulling out little scraps of wrapped food. Dried meat and cheeses. "Here, take these around. When we're finished we can take them to the men."

Shula was quiet as she did what she was told. It gave her a small sense of purpose as she placed the bundles of food into the Fae's awaiting hands. They thanked her, and Shula's heart twisted as she recognized the hunger in their eyes.

She knew what it was to starve, and it made her wonder exactly what these Fae had been doing before Valerio had supposedly saved them. Where had they lived? What had their lives been like? How similar had it been to her own?

"Now, we have to take this to the men. Since I know where they typically keep watch, I'll take it to those on guard duty. You stay here and give it to the others."

Shula handed food out to the human men first, where she met the blacksmith.

He was a scraggly man, with shaggy hair and a robust belly and big arms, but he looked timid as he'd ducked his head while she thanked him for removing her shackles.

Then she moved on to the Fae men, going around in a circle until the last ones left were her captors. She gritted her teeth, hating that she would have to serve them like some maid, but she sucked it up and walked over to where they were convened in a semi-circle.

She handed a bundle to Clay first, the lesser of four evils.

"Aw, thank you, little Fire Dancer." He unwrapped the cheese and stuffed it into his mouth, chewing delicately.

She turned and gave Uric his next, who took it wordlessly without looking at her or even saying thanks.

Prince Valerio was eyeing her as if she would whip out her knife and plunge it into his ribs at any moment. The thought was tempting, but she placed the bundle into his awaiting palm, and he surprised her by saying, "Thank you."

She nodded in response and turned to Ryker next. He was pointedly ignoring her, favoring the attention of the cat on his shoulder, and she was tempted to just throw the food at his face when Clay nudged his elbow into the other man's side so hard Ryker's head snapped over to her.

She held out the food, and he took it quickly and grunted. She wondered if that was his way of saying thank you.

"I see you've found a friend in Orna," Clay said conversationally as he munched on the tough, dry meat.

Shula wanted to leave and not have this conversation. "I suppose."

"Orna is nice."

There was a flirtatious note in his voice that had Shula instantly narrowing her eyes. "She's *married.*" She put enough emphasis on the word so he knew to back off.

"I know that. Geez, what do you take me for? I don't sleep with married women. Especially not mated women."

The word 'mated' seemed to shiver down Shula's body, making her swallow past a sudden tightness in her throat.

She may not have known much about the Fae, but everyone knew about mates. Her parents had been mates. Their love transcended what humans thought the word meant into something else entirely. It went beyond basic love. It was... it was everything. A bond that could not be broken except by death. It joined two souls together and kept them tethered wholly from one to the other.

"They're mates?" Shula asked.

Clay smirked. "Couldn't you tell?"

No. She hadn't really been paying attention.

"They're always sneaking off together, and they're insanely in love." Clay shuddered with mock horror.

Shula arched a brow at him, staying glued to her spot. Her arms crossed against her chest and she pursed her lips. "You have something against love?"

At this, Valerio snorted and for the first time since she met him, Shula saw a flicker of amusement in his gaze. "Clay wouldn't know love if it smacked him in the face."

Uric chuckled.

Ryker, of course, glared.

"I am the king of love," Clay declared, offense over his expression.

"The king of lust," Uric corrected, dark eyes shining.

"Same thing. Look, Fire Dancer, I love women. Fae women, human women, I love them all."

"Slept with them all, too," Valerio muttered.

"Except the innocent, the mated, and the married..."

"Yeah, right, remember that female in Teg? Her husband chased you out the—"

"I don't think the Fire Dancer needs to hear this story," Clay interrupted.

Shula could see the flush crawling up his neck. It must have been a really bad story if Clay was blushing. Now she *had* to hear it.

"Oh, I think I do." A smile twisted her mouth.

"Trust me, you don't. Now, don't you have things to do?" Clay dismissed her, turning his head away. Uric and Valerio burst into laughter.

Shula startled. It was so odd to see them like this... Laughing, bantering. They'd been stoic before, glaring. She knew what they were doing now, though. They were trying to include her, make her feel welcome. Make her forget she was anything more than their captive.

The remembrance hit her square in the chest. Her feet skidded across the ground as she jerked back. She knew for a split second, her expression betrayed what she was feeling, and she schooled it a second too late.

Clay's smile fell and he reached out for her, but Shula was already turning away. It was hard, she thought. It was too difficult to pretend like she could be friends with these Fae; she'd barely even tried.

But she couldn't. How could she be friends with those who were keeping her prisoner?

She couldn't be. That was the answer.

She couldn't and wouldn't.

Whether they were Fae or not, Fanny had broken something inside her. Torn her soul beyond repair so she couldn't accept anyone else into her life, her heart.

She'd been a fool to try.

She wouldn't do it again.

A Dream

"She will not accept us so easily."

Clay tore his gaze from where Shula walked away. She all but stumbled in her rush to flee from them, and he didn't want to admit it was... confusing. Usually women were running to him, not from him, and he was a bit offended that he couldn't convince her to even be his friend, no matter how hard he tried.

He didn't even want to get between her thighs. Which was odd. But he had a feeling that—

"You aren't even trying, are you?" Clay was torn out of his thoughts by Uric's angry accusation.

Clay's temper flared as wildly as his nostrils. "Do you want to try it, then?" His gaze flicked to Valerio, to Ryker, and there they stayed on the scarred Fae's face. His gut roiled about what Valerio was proposing. It just didn't sit right with him.

He wasn't a piece of shit, and he wouldn't take advantage of her. Because despite what she felt about him, he was starting to consider her his friend.

"You kidnapped her then used your powers on her," Clay went on. "How do you expect her to feel? She feels fucking violated. We took away her free will, so what makes us different from that fucking Brotherhood? From the emperor?"

Clay saw Uric coming in moments. Protecting himself was instinct. He dodged the blow aimed for his throat, slapping the dagger from Uric's hand with a strike to the wrist. Uric retaliated by swinging another knife towards him.

Clay jerked back, his hand snatching out to pull Uric with him. Soon, they were little more than a scuffle of fists and dodging bodies and flailing limbs.

Clay was a good warrior. He hailed from the Sapphire Court, powerful Seelie warriors.

But Uric was from the land of Obsidian, and he was better.

A knife pressed against Clay's throat and Uric loomed over him. His nostrils flared, and those black eyes were like a demon's, holding in them the promise and whisper of death.

"How dare you make such a comparison?"

Clay smiled widely at him, and he knew he looked a little manic. "You know it's true. We might have saved her life, but we took away her free will. No wonder she's eager to get away from us."

Uric snarled, snapping his canines close to Clay's face.

"Uric. Stop."

At a single command from Valerio, Uric shoved Clay away with a snarl.

Clay scoffed and straightened his tunic, spreading his palms across the front. His glare didn't falter, and he didn't look away from Uric even as Valerio spoke.

"Clay is right. She won't trust us."

"So what do we do?" Uric asked.

"There's nothing we can do," Ryker supplied, speaking for the first time.

Valerio sighed. "Ryker's right. We can do nothing but wait and hope she eventually trusts us." He snapped his gaze from between Ryker and Clay. "Watch over her. We already committed this mistake. We cannot afford to make any more."

The bonfire blazed and crackled, meat roasting over the licking flames. A single, skinned rabbit, whose pieces would have to be rationed. Shula knew she wouldn't take any when the others in camp were truly hungry, their skin clinging to their bones.

The flames called to her, hypnotizing in their entirety. It was like a calling to her blood and she wondered if that's what her own blood looked like. If her heart pumped fire through her body and her veins. If the evidence was in the disruptive force burning her chest, the smoke in her lungs, her fiery temper that wanted to do nothing but wreak destruction.

She swallowed the lump in her throat.

Idle talk sounded around her, and she tuned out most of it. Orna still hadn't come back from feeding those on guard duty, so she figured she had gone to have a tryst with her mate in the woods like Clay had insinuated.

It felt rather lonely. But loneliness was something she was familiar with and always would be. Because loneliness was a prominent, recognizable feeling. Once it sunk its claws into you, there was nothing more you desired than to eradicate it in any way you could. It's why some people fell. Why they tied themselves down to people who hurt them.

Because anything was better than being alone.

She was so lost in her thoughts that she startled when two figures sat next to her.

"Sorry," Orna breathed. A full smile pulled at her mouth, and in her arm she held her husband close. They both radiated a happy glow that suggested they'd been doing... things. Their clothes seemed immaculate, but it was their hair that was ruffled, their lips plump. Even Orna's shimmering blue skin seemed to sparkle like she was sprinkled with star dust. "I left you with all the work."

Shula smiled knowingly at her. "It's fine."

Orna snuggled close to her husband, a dark-skinned man with a radiant smile, her eyes closing in marital bliss. This? It was something more than just that. It was mates. The bond was a vibrant thing between them.

"How long have the two of you been together?" Shula couldn't help but ask.

"Six months," they answered in unison.

Shula's eyes widened. "So little." She hadn't meant to say that out loud. She would have guessed they'd been together for longer. "It just seems like you've known each other forever."

Orna couldn't have possibly been more charming, but she somehow was with every passing second as her smile got wider and wider. "It *feels* like we've been together for a lifetime."

"And even then that doesn't feel like enough." Her husband patted her hand.

Shula found it surprising that a human could look upon a Fae without anything other than hate. There was obvious adoration in his eyes, like the sun rose and set on Orna, like her skin shimmered with the golden dust of shooting stars and he meant to worship every single one.

For a single moment, Shula wished for that. It gripped her chest tightly, made her crave that type of acceptance. She had to look away from them and into the flames of the fire.

They held her attention for a moment, but when her eyes followed the licking tips, her eyes caught Ryker's and her breath stuck in the back of her throat.

He was cold and unfeeling and just staring at him made something brittle and dangerous stir inside her chest. Shadows danced across his rough features, making that single white eye glow and the black eye flicker with golden specks.

He didn't tear his gaze away, like he wasn't embarrassed to be caught staring. Like he didn't care at all that her own eyes traced the rigid lines of his scars like one would trace the rivers on a map. She wondered how he'd gotten them, and when the scowl formed on his face, she decided that she didn't care.

Shula forced herself to turn back to Orna and her husband. They seemed to be in their own little world that she dared to interrupt. She despised the bitter edge in her voice, the questioning of it. "How did a human and Fae meet?" Her eyes narrowed on the husband. "You weren't... disgusted... with her being Fae? Or do you not see her as Fae?"

Like all the other humans were.

Like Fanny had been.

Her question set a melancholy tone around them. Shula was aware that everything had gone quiet, save for the cackling flames. All the eyes were on her; she felt them, judging her harsh, bitter tone. Judging her for asking that question.

"I think the fact that Orna *is* Fae is what makes her beautiful. She wouldn't be Orna without it." Her husband's hand smoothed over her arm, which shimmered brightly as if pleased by the compliment. "Of course when I look at her I see her for what she really is. I know she's different from me, but different doesn't mean bad." He looked at Shula with a ferocity in his eyes that was intense for a human. "I accept her fully, wholly. Because I love her. Always and no matter what."

Shula bit her bottom lip and forced herself to look away from him. Since *when* had Shula become so bitter? Had she always been this way? Was that what death and fear did? Was Fanny's betrayal affecting her more than she realized?

Shula rubbed at her eyes with the heels of her hands, willing away the stress and shadows from her mind but they clung sharply to her.

"It's okay, Shula, I don't mind the questions." Orna's palm settled over Shula's shoulder. She dropped her hands and turned to Orna. Her skin hadn't lessened its shine. She still sparkled like the sky. "I know our relationship might be odd for you..." *Since you've only ever known cruelty.* Those words went unsaid, but Shula felt them just the same. "But I have a dream that one day, the Fae will rise again. One day, we'll walk among the humans again, and there won't be fear in their hearts or ours and all will be as it once was."

She smiled radiantly, like she was so sure of this outcome. Of her own dream.

But Shula stared, and all she could do was muster up a tight smile that didn't reach her eyes.

That dream shone brightly around Orna. It shone against her very skin, and Shula wondered if she wished on the glitter that streaked across her flesh all because the smog covered the sky. She wondered how many hopes and dreams could possibly live within one tiny, young Fae woman in a world so cruel and full of darkness.

Betrayal was everywhere, and yet Orna and her husband had hope. For a better world. A better future.

And Shula turned away from them again to stare into the fire in silence, biting down on her tongue until she tasted the copper of her own blood. It was better this way, she thought. It was better if she didn't say anything at all.

Because Orna's dream?

That's all it was.

Just a dream.

Death, Lust, and Love

They traveled for days at a slow, grueling pace. Woods hollowed out into mountains and caves, which diverged into more forests. The routine remained the same for the three days they walked. Tirelessly and without rest in the mornings, and they only settled down late into the afternoon.

Every night, Shula helped Orna pass food along to the others. When they finished, Orna disappeared into the woods, likely to steal a moment alone with her husband.

If only things could have been so simple for Shula.

She'd tried wandering into the woods on her own, but before her feet even touched the inside of the forest, Clay would appear, wrapping his arm tightly around her shoulders and steering her away with idle chatter in her ear. As if it wasn't obvious what he was doing. Sometimes even Ryker stopped her from wandering, moving so fast he was a blur to appear in front of her. Every time, she rammed into his chest. It was becoming habit now, for her to slam into his solid body and glare up at his scowling face.

How someone so large could walk as quietly as the cat that usually remained perched on his shoulder, she didn't know. It defied all logic.

But she was annoyed that she kept running into him and even more annoyed with herself for turning and wandering meekly back to the campfire like a good little captive.

They didn't own her, and she had the right to wander and do whatever the hell she wanted. She'd grown too complacent to their wishes. So that night, when her feet walked towards the line of trees and Ryker appeared before her, she side stepped him and swept past his towering form only to be yanked back once again.

She whirled and brought her fist up in an arc, but Ryker caught it in his massive palm, enclosing her hand entirely and squeezing gently. It was like a sharp reminder that if he put just a bit more pressure on it, he'd crush her fingers in his grip and wouldn't be afraid to do so.

"Where the fuck do you think you're going?"

Shula still wasn't used to the dark timbre of his voice. It did something dangerous to her insides and made her body tremble with something she was sure was fear.

Her lip pulled back from her teeth in a sneer. "I have to take a shit," she spat. "Want to watch?"

His frown only deepened. "You cannot wander off alone."

Her sneer curled into a smile that was just as vicious. "Why?" she demanded, yanked her fist and arm from his hold. He let her go easily. "Afraid I'll escape?"

He growled low in warning which she ignored and turned back around to walk into the woods.

She hoped with everything he would ignore her, but much to her annoyance, he followed close behind. Not close enough to touch within arm's length, and yet she still felt his heat as if his body were pressed tightly against hers. There was an awareness that sizzled between them, and it pulsed like currents of electricity in a storm.

On impulse, she skidded to a halt, just to give him a taste of his own medicine. But when *he* rammed into *her*, his bulking body nearly sent her flying forward.

She swore she heard him chuckle behind her.

Huffing an embarrassed breath, she kept forward, wandering with no purpose.

"Hurry up," he growled.

She didn't have to shit. Not really. She'd just hoped the words would deter him from following her. What kind of a sick, weird person watched another take a shit anyway? That seemed more like a Clay thing to do. Then again, she didn't really know Ryker, so she couldn't say what he liked to do and didn't.

The snapping of a twig caught her attention. The sound cracked like thunder. Close. So close.

Before Shula could even breathe, Ryker's big arms were wrapped around her and he was yanking her to his chest.

Her back collided against him, and she felt the steady rise and fall of his breathing. She was too surprised to admonish him for the action. She couldn't speak, could barely breathe.

His body was warm, pressed against her own so tightly that she swore she could feel the latticework of scars through the material of his shirt. He moved so quickly, her feet lifted from the ground as he hid them behind a bush and ducked.

In that position, Shula found herself bent over slightly, with every tight ridge and bump of his body pressed against hers. Her heart pounded against her chest at the proximity, at the steady heat of his breath near her ear.

She wanted to move, desperately wanted to yank herself out of his hold, but the snapping grew closer and closer. She knew this was a precarious moment. That they shouldn't make noise, but she feared the beating of her heart gave her away.

Her eyes widened, and her whole body relaxed when she saw Orna step through the trees, skipping and laughing lightly. Her body gave off the softest of glows, dark blue skin that shimmered with stardust. She was a single light in the darkness streaking between the trees, her tinkling laughter a thing of stories and seduction. Behind her, her husband caught up, catching her around the waist to pull her against his chest in a position that mimicked Shula and Ryker's, with Orna's body bent over slightly.

Shula watched, enraptured as he pressed a kiss to Orna's neck. The echoes of her sighs reached Shula's ears, making her face heat.

She wanted to look away; this moment was too intimate for their eyes, and yet she and Ryker both held still and watched as Orna's husband slipped his hand beneath the waist of her pants.

Her moan was loud, the sound causing Shula's own core to tighten with need.

Ryker breathed in deeply and she knew. She knew he could smell her desire, something she'd scarcely felt in all her life. It was just... witnessing it, seeing the way the human brought Orna to breathless whispers and desperate moans... It made Shula crave that closeness with someone else.

And it made the male prominently pressed to her back sense it.

She was suddenly ashamed. Of herself and of him with his body wrapped tightly around her. Because she couldn't find that release in him, in any of them. It left her feeling frustrated, it left her craving, and it made her *angry*.

Because a human would have been oblivious to what she was feeling. But Ryker was Fae and she could hear his nostrils flaring, could hear him inhaling even while he made no further movements to ease her aches.

She suddenly didn't want him touching her, this Fae who despised her with every fiber of his being. Well, she despised him too.

She jerked out of his hold quietly and stepped back, one stumbling step after another. He straightened and turned, and the noises of desire beyond them paused.

Shula couldn't handle it. Not when Ryker turned and stared at her with something unreadable in his gaze. It wasn't desire. It wasn't affection. It was hatred, and she had absolutely no idea why.

Just like she didn't know why her heart felt like it was breaking.

Shula whirled, choking on her own breaths.

And she ran away from the woods.

Away from Ryker.

Away from the sound of lust and love.

Two things she knew she would never have.

Shula lay on the dry earth, her palms pillowing her cheeks as she stared into the flames. They grounded her, brought her back to the present. They made her forget.

She smelled Orna before the Fae laid down next to her. She smelt musky like the earth, with an underlying tone of something sweet and floral.

And she smelt like sex.

Shula held her breath and closed her eyes, hoping Orna wouldn't speak.

"I know you aren't sleeping."

Damn it.

Shula's eyes opened and she took a breath, but she didn't turn around.

"You and Ryker saw us."

Heat that had nothing to do with the bonfire suffused Shula's whole body. Still, she didn't speak.

"That's okay. I'm not shy. The revelries in the Unseelie Court were rife with orgies. Not that I'd know, since I'm too young to remember, but that kind of exhibitionism and wildness lives in my blood, you know." She sounded breathless, as breathless as Shula felt. "Des doesn't mind either. It was kind of exciting. But then you ran away." She went quiet again, and Shula didn't have it in her to fill the spaces of silence with her own words. "Why did you run away?"

Shula turned so she lay flat on her back. She stared up at the sky for so long that she traced the patterns the stars made and compared them to Orna's shimmering skin. Everything in Shula's body vibrated because she could still hear the whispered caress of Orna's sighs in her ears, the way the sound spread over her own body like the slippery slide of phantom fingers heightening her desire. It was followed by a searing jealousy and embarrassment.

Her face heated at the emotions that rolled through her, one after the other. She tried to rein them in, shoving them down where they belonged. And in the darkness beside the crackling fire, with all those emotions swirling inside her and Orna beside her, it seemed safe to give up a confession, the tiniest bit of herself.

"Because I'll never have what you have, and I can't imagine what it's like."

"You've never...?" The question was implied in the silence.

"No. Never."

"I didn't either. Not until I met Des." Her hand reached out and squeezed Shula's. "Maybe someday soon, you'll meet your mate."

"I don't want a mate." Shula pulled her hand from Orna's and turned back to face the flames.

What she didn't say was why she didn't want one.

Because everyone she loved was doomed to die or betray her. It was why she didn't want to get close to Orna. The Fae was pure hearted and kind, and there didn't seem to be a drop of malice in her body. Not a single one.

Shula knew now that Orna wouldn't betray her.

Which meant the only other option was death.

And if Orna died because of Shula, just like everyone else in her life had died, Shula didn't know how she'd ever live with herself.

She wouldn't be able to.

If she allowed herself to care for Orna and Orna died, then Shula would wish for death, too.

The wind rustled the leaves and swayed the branches from side to side. Ryker's ears twitched as he took the sounds into his system. This was second nature to him by now; breathing in the life of the mountains that wasn't polluted with iron and human industrialization.

There was none of that here, though. The mountains of Tuath had always been a peaceful place, but it could never compare to home.

Twigs snapping caught his attention, but because he recognized the footsteps and the sweet scent, he didn't whip around quickly this time. Not like earlier.

He grunted noncommittally as Valerio stood next to him. Ryker didn't speak because there was nothing to say and he hated wasting words when actions were so much louder.

"It's not your watch, Ryker," Valerio said.

Ryker didn't take his gaze away from the darkness. His prince didn't either.

"I know," Ryker replied softly.

"You should sleep, rest up."

"Orna and Des went for a tryst in the forest again."

"Oh?" He could hear the amusement in Valerio's voice. He didn't turn to look at the prince, but he knew he'd find his lips pressed into a thin line and his eyebrows up to his hairline.

"I could have easily mistaken their footsteps for someone else's. The next time they wander the forest, they might not be so lucky."

"Hmm, I'll have Clay or Uric speak with them."

Ryker grunted once again. His eyes darted through the darkness, but he felt distracted, his mind restless... his body aching.

"The Fire Dancer—"

Ryker snorted, interrupting his prince.

"You despise her so. Why?"

Ryker shifted slightly as if by moving he could expel the discomfort the question brought from his body. "I have my reasons," he muttered. Reasons he didn't want to talk about. But Valerio knew them anyway.

"Ryker, is this about Mairin? It was a hundred years ago."

And yet the pain felt like it had been yesterday.

Ryker didn't reply. He didn't need to. Valerio, though was his prince, knew better than to pry into Ryker's mind, his past, or his feelings.

Fucking feelings.

All he'd ever felt for years had been rage, grief, sorrow. He'd become familiar with such things like all Fae had. Yet when he felt, he felt profoundly, wholly. It consumed him like a blight that spread through his soul and blackened his heart.

He couldn't remember what love tasted like. What *lust* tasted like.

Until today.

The fact enraged him. It haunted him enough to push him from slumber. It had led him here, to keeping watch at ungodly hours so he didn't have to face the truth of his own dreams.

"Ryker..."

"Hmm?" He couldn't turn to meet his prince's eyes. He'd never been frightened before, but he was afraid the truth would be read from his own eyes. That Valerio would look at him and know what had happened. The way he'd held the Fire Dancer to his chest and watched Orna and Des with a pounding heart and an aching cock.

There had been something taboo about what they'd done, watching a scene that hadn't been meant for their eyes.

He should have tugged her away the moment he saw Orna step from between the trees. The only reason he'd even pulled her behind that bush was because he hadn't recognized the footsteps. That just went to show how much the fire Fae distracted him.

Something he'd never admit to anyone. Something he didn't even want to admit to himself.

"I think it's time you moved on from the pain."

He didn't say anything, even as Valerio waited. When Ryker didn't open his mouth, Valerio clapped him on the shoulder.

"Get some rest," he said, and then he was walking away.

But all Ryker could do was stare off into the distance and grit his teeth. There were words on the tip of his tongue that he could never say.

It was the pain that helped him move on.

The pain, the grief, the sorrow. He held onto those and let them blacken his soul.

A part of him barely remembered what everything else felt like.

But maybe there was no difference between death, lust, and love at all.

Julius

The mountains were clustered close together, forming a maze of pathways and trees and rocky caves. It was a place that would be easy to get lost in no matter how hard Shula tried to memorize their steps and surroundings. She knew there would be no chance of escape until they reached civilization.

The next two days of their journey, Shula spent them ignoring everyone. Her every movement was mechanical, like she was sleepwalking every step of the way. Orna tried to speak with her and make the load of emotions lighter, but Shula just wasn't in the mood and eventually the blue-skinned Fae backed off.

Shula should have felt guilty for the way she was treating Orna, but she tried to tell herself it was for the Fae's own good. Shula's as well. She couldn't afford to get attached to anyone when she was planning on escaping anyway.

She didn't want to have a reason to stay.

Even though she knew she should have been making friends, getting them to trust her, her own stubbornness was holding her back from doing just that. It was hard to look past the fact that these Fae had kidnapped her and were keeping her here.

Regardless of what she was or what the Emperor of Illyk wanted with her, she refused to be used by either of them.

So she kept to herself as best as she could, moving when they told her to move and glaring all the while.

It was the middle of the day, and darkness was only a few hours away. Shula walked behind the cart as usual, Orna by her side and Clay and Ryker at her back. As the days passed, she was getting more annoyed with her bodyguards and the way their gazes followed her around everywhere.

Mainly Ryker's.

He hadn't spoken to her, though that was no shocker, even after what they'd witnessed together in the forest. She didn't want to acknowledge what she'd felt in that moment, so she'd shoved it to the back of her mind. That didn't stop Ryker from awakening those thoughts with a single, heated glance.

He still stared at her like he wanted to kill her.

It was easier to hate him than to feel that desire she'd felt in the forest. If she were going to sate her need, it would be with Clay, not with the big brute of a Fae. At least Clay pretended he liked her, and she almost tolerated him.

Captor or not, there was something likeable about Clay that she would deny until her last dying breath.

The front of their procession suddenly stopped, jerking Shula from her thoughts. Her feet skidded to a halt, and she leaned on the tips of her toes and looked to the front.

Valerio stood with his fist in the air. Uric's body was tense, his hand on the hilt of his sword. His pointed ears twitched, silver hair grazing along the cutting tip of his chin as his gaze darted back and forth through the copse of trees.

Shula felt her heart pound in her chest like it meant to burst free. Something was wrong. Something was here. She tried to strain her ears to listen, but she could hear nothing beyond the rustle of leaves...

And then twigs began cracking.

A gasp rose and she nearly choked on it.

She couldn't tell what it was, but by the defensive stance of Uric, her mind took a wild guess.

Humans.

No. No. No.

She took a fearful step back and rammed into a solid chest. Her eyes closed as she felt strong hands grip her elbows for a single second before dropping. She knew who was behind her without even having to turn around.

Ryker's presence was even more frightening than the situation, and yet she felt the smallest bit of comfort by it. Clay stepped beside her, and she could already see the weapon he brandished in his fist.

Everyone shuffled nervously, and she could feel the tension in the air. No one dared breathe or speak.

Panic began to settle in her chest. What was going on? She tried to listen, tried to hear, but there were no more twigs snapping. There was nothing but the eerie echo of silence, too still to be natural.

Then Valerio stepped forward. He was a hard Fae to read, but he seemed confident in his stance. He turned in a slow circle, and his voice projected out loudly. "I know you are out there," he said confidently. "Show yourself!"

There was silence.

Minutes passed and just when Shula's body wanted to relax, just when her mind started to tell her that perhaps it hadn't been anything at all...

An arrow shot out from between the trees.

Someone screamed, but the panic was far away now. Shula watched with a detached sort of numbness as the arrow flew its way towards Valerio's face.

It was going to kill the Prince of the Fae.

But in the blink of an eye, Uric was there, hand closing around the arrow just centimeters from Valerio's face. He crushed it in his grip and the wood snapped in half.

Shula almost expected the Fae to brandish their weapons and prepare for battle. For cries to ring out and for the earth's floor to be covered in blood and bodies.

But that didn't happen.

Uric backed away from his prince, and Valerio smirked, staring up from where the arrow had appeared from.

"Your aim is shit."

And then the trees ruffled. Everyone seemed to huddle together, step back, as an enormous figure stomped out of the shadows.

He was huge, bigger even than Ryker, with muscles that looked like boulders and white sleeves rolled up to the elbows. The Fae man was formidable in size. Orange hair was slicked back into a ponytail, and a ginger beard peppered along a strong, square jaw.

He would have seemed frightening, if he hadn't been smiling wide.

Or maybe that's what made him terrifying.

That he could smile like that after shooting at Valerio and with a notched arrow and a bow in his hands as he descended the slope.

He made it a few feet in front of Valerio and spoke.

"Your tracking is worse." His voice was surprisingly pleasant and held traces of humor. "We've been following you for hours."

"I know. I could hear you panting from the exertion miles away."

They stayed silent and stared at one another in what seemed to be a deadly face off.

Then the ginger haired man burst into laughter and slung his weapon over his shoulder, dropped the arrow into the quiver at his back and stomped forward, pulling Valerio into a hug.

The two embraced like long lost friends, meanwhile Shula could only stare in confusion.

"What—?"

Clay laughed. "Julius, you fucker!" He cupped his hands around his mouth and cried out. It drew the ginger's—Julius'—attention towards them. "I'm a little disappointed to see you!"

Julius laughed. "Keep holding your breath, little dick. No humans are killing me yet!"

Clay threw his arm around Shula's shoulders and tugged her forward, even as she tried to dig her heels into the earth.

Once they were close to the front, he let go of her and threw his arms around Julius and they clapped each other on the back. "How'd everything go?" Clay asked once they separated.

"Check for yourself." Julius brought his fingers up to his mouth and let out a shrill whistle that echoed across the mountains. A moment later, dozens of people, Fae and human alike, came out of hiding from the trees and shadows, carrying heavy-looking bags and leading a few horses.

Julius' procession was relatively larger than Valerio's, and Julius wore a smug expression as if it were some competition.

Valerio just smiled at his friend and clapped him on the back. "You did good," he complimented.

Julius soaked up the compliment. Shula could tell by the single interaction that the man loved the attention. He seemed to be like Clay in that regard.

Julius' gaze strayed over to where she was standing awkwardly, and his bright green eyes seemed to pierce her.

"And who is this lovely thing?" His tone was flirtatious, bordering on the edge of dangerous.

She wanted to retreat from the whole situation. Mainly because she knew by looking at him that she and Julius could be friends in another lifetime, one where she wasn't their prisoner. Then again, he hadn't been the one to kidnap her, but he was good friends with those who had.

Before she could bolt, Clay clamped his hand on her shoulder and pulled her forward. "Julius Darah, meet the lovely Fire Dancer of Piriguini's Circus, Shula Azzarh."

Julius' eyes widened. "No shit." His eyes flicked to her ears, but she knew they were safely hidden beneath her long hair. Besides, she didn't need him judging her decision like Ryker had.

Just his eyes straying there made her self-conscious.

She tried not to look away.

"I've heard about you," Julius went on. "Heard your act is the best there is to see."

Shula's throat tightened at the compliment, and something like longing surged through her. She had worked hard to gain a reputation for herself. A reputation, it seemed, that even this Fae had heard about. Pride pressed around her, followed by immeasurable sadness. She would never be able to dance again, never feel the gaze of the crowd as she hypnotized them with the movements of her body.

Dancing was all she'd ever loved. It was her solace, and now she didn't even have that.

Julius was still staring at her, and she wondered just how much they could read from her expression.

"Shula's an Elemental Fae," Clay explained. "Fire."

Julius' eyes widened. "Elemental, huh?" He took a step towards her. He used the same stance Ryker usually did. Shula always shied away from Ryker because of his overbearing presence. This man was different. She didn't fear him. Perhaps it was his attitude, or perhaps she was just a good judge of character and knew he wouldn't harm her. Okay, maybe she wasn't the *best* judge of character, but there was something kind shining in Julius' eyes. It was the same kindness that shone in Clay's, bright and blinding.

"Welcome to the Resistance, Shula." Julius wrapped his arms around her and lifted her feet off the ground to twirl her in a circle. Her hands scrambled for purchase on his shoulders, and her nails dug into his skin. A moment later, he settled her back down on her feet and she swayed backwards. "We're excited to have you on our side."

Smoothing her hair down over her ears and shoulders, she sent him a glare. "I'm not on your side," she snapped. "I'm not on anybody's side."

She regretted the venomous way she spoke when Julius' expression fell. He looked from face to face and uttered, "Seems like you all have a story to tell."

Valerio nodded. "We do. Let's set up camp and we can catch up." That cold gaze slid over to Shula, and she met it with one of her own. Two could play at that glare, she thought vehemently. Valerio just quirked his lip up in amusement. "I believe Orna needs you."

A dismissal.

One she was glad and willing to take.

She turned on her heel and stomped over to where Orna was helping tether their horse and mule to a tree, not caring if they talked about her behind her back. Already she was mingling with the new people with a smile on her face. She cast one look at Shula's expression and a frown creased her brows.

"What's wrong?" she asked.

"Insufferable Fae bastards," Shula grumbled, yanking the ropes from Orna's hands and tying the knot to the tree herself. She needed to give her hands something to do, lest she find them wrapped around Valerio's skinny little neck. "Arrogant pricks," she mumbled.

"Alright, it sounds like they did something to make you mad again, didn't they?"

Shula grunted in response.

It was at times like these when she desperately wanted a friend. Someone she could vent her emotions to. And Orna was looking at her with such trust in her gaze, and Shula knew instinctively they were the eyes of a friend. That she could confide in her and the trust wouldn't be broken.

Anytime she'd ever thought about entrusting Fanny with the truth of her heritage, Shula's stomach had roiled and lurched painfully. Like her gut was telling her that Fanny couldn't be trusted. It had happened every time. But as she looked at Orna, she didn't feel that dizzying need to hide herself. Not in her gut or in her mind. Rather, her own heart was afraid, even when her instinct said that Orna wasn't Fanny and would not betray her.

Shula sighed, and the words that came out of her mouth were the words she'd hidden deep in her heart. "I miss the circus."

Just saying the words made a fierce longing ripple through her chest. Mana, how she missed it, and she hadn't even realized it. She missed the scents of popped corn and candied apples, of sweet meats and pastries, she missed the sounds of humans running, but most of all, she missed dancing.

"You were the Fire Dancer, right?" Orna smoothed a hand down the mule's flank. "You did fire tricks and danced while you did it?"

Shula smiled, the first real smile she'd given in what felt like weeks, even if it *was* laced with a bit of sadness. "Yes."

"What was it like?" Orna whispered.

"It was the best feeling in the world." Stepping out on stage, controlling her body, her movements, hypnotizing and moving to the beat of drums. Shula had lost control of everything in her life. She couldn't control the world or how they saw her kind, but she could control her body in dance. And that was a beautiful thing. "I miss dancing the most."

Orna was quiet for the longest time, and Shula didn't realize she was still gripping the cord so tightly until Orna's small, blue hand settled over hers.

"I have an idea," she whispered.

Fae Wine

"How many?" Valerio inquired.

"Thirty." Julius leaned against the inside of a cave wall and used a dagger to pick at his nails. Uric stood at the entrance of the cave, guarding to make sure no one came too close to listen to their plans.

"A good number," Valerio replied. "My father will be pleased." He'd found twelve refugees. Forty-two was despicable compared to the numbers their race had before the war, but they would have to make do with anyone loyal they could find. "Supplies?"

Julius broke out into a smile. "Pelts, dried goods, clothes, instruments, *and...*" He let the word trail off and he looked up from his task to meet everyone's gazes. "Fae wine."

Clay nearly fell over in his surprise. "Fae what now?" he demanded, his bright eyes wide.

Valerio felt shocked himself. Fae wine was a delicacy they hadn't had in years.

Julius flashed them all a shit-eating grin. "Found a High Fae and his little goblin who produce the stuff together. I had a sip of it and, shit, it took me back." His eyes glowed in the shadows, likely remembering the past when they celebrated openly, when there hadn't been strife with humans and they could afford fermented, magical wine.

Now they were reduced to little more than scavengers, criminals on the run, hiding from the laws of humans. Laws that dictated how a once proud race should live in fear.

Something in Valerio's blood boiled and he couldn't hide his deadly stare.

He feared for his kind; feared that there were so little of them left, that they had no home but safe house to safe house. He wanted more for the Fae, Seelie and Unseelie alike. He didn't know how to go about that. They didn't have the armies to spare.

The seer's, *Davina's*, words rang in his mind about Shula Azzarh and the salvation she was.

For years he had watched his people diminish into practically nothing, so he didn't feel guilty that he'd taken away her choices. He would do whatever it took to save his race. Whether she liked it or not.

"What's the deal with the Fire Dancer?" Julius asked cautiously, as if he'd been in tune to Valerio's thoughts.

Valerio brought his attention back to the present and noted everyone was staring at him, waiting for him to answer. He relaxed his angry expression into a serious one that didn't breathe a whisper of murder.

Clay snorted before Valerio could open his mouth. "Princey here thought it a good idea to kidnap her."

Julius just opened his mouth. "Ah," he murmured.

Valerio glared at Clay. "You conveniently left out the part where we rescued her from a deranged Brotherhood of humans who kept her chained to an altar."

Julius' eyes widened then. "Ah," he said again.

"Yeah, ah." Then Valerio proceeded to explain what had happened. He told Julius about the seer, Davina, and her request—he left out the prophecy she'd whispered in his ear like a dark temptation—about going to the temple and finding Shula. They relayed what Shula had told them and what the Brotherhood had done to her, about how she could be the savior of the Fae, about how they were keeping her there against her will because as long as they had her, it meant the Emperor of Illyk wouldn't.

By the end of the story Julius had stopped picking at his nails to stare. "Well, it makes sense. It's fucked up, but it makes sense." He shrugged and went back to cleaning his cuticles. "If she's meant to be some sort of savior, maybe Emperor Dickface knows about it and wants to kill her before she can save us all? It makes sense to keep her in our care."

Clay groaned.

"But," Julius continued, dragging emphasis out on the word. "It doesn't sit well with me that she's here unwillingly. She's a Fae too."

At those words, Ryker snorted. "Fae don't butcher their fucking ears."

Clay rolled his eyes. "Again with that? Have you even asked her why she did it before you start judging her?"

"You seem mighty defensive of her," Julius joked, his mouth pulled up in what could only be described as mischief.

Valerio always thought Julius was a descendent of the people of the wood. They were mischievous Fae who liked to stir shit and play practical jokes.

If he didn't know Clay's own heritage, he would have assumed the same thing about him.

"Because I like her," Clay admitted, shoving his hands into his pockets.

Everyone stilled.

Even Valerio.

None glared at him fiercer than Ryker.

"It's no secret. And I don't mean like her like that. She's my friend. I care about her like friends should."

"Are you sure it's only that?" Uric asked dangerously from the entrance of the cave. "Are you sure she is not your mate?"

Clay's whole body froze at the accusing tone in Uric's voice.

"If she was my mate," Clay began slowly and through clenched teeth, "you would all know that by now."

Uric turned to him then, and there was a deadly expression on his gaze. Valerio knew there was animosity between them and at that moment, he felt it deep in his bones. "You never know. She could be. Mating bonds don't always snap into place immediately."

"Yeah, well," Clay waved him off with a flick of his hand. "If she were my mate, I would know. But she's not. Moving on now, what are we going to do?"

They all looked to Valerio and he didn't cower under the weight of their expectations. He was born to lead, born to follow in his father's footsteps and protect the Fae. He was used to dealing with all sorts of predicaments, used to making difficult decisions.

His mind began stirring.

"Set up camp," he finally decided. "Make sure you post guards all around the area to take up watch. Our people deserve a break." Valerio felt a smile touch his mouth. "And I deserve some Fae wine."

Julius pushed himself off the cave wall and sheathed his dagger. "Hell yeah." He pumped his fist in the air. "Party time!"

"Tame," Valerio reminded him. "And quiet. We still aren't clear yet. Danger is around every corner." They all nodded and exited the cave, Julius and Clay joking as they went, Ryker following much more somberly with his arms crossed against his chest.

Only Uric stayed and Valerio went to stand beside him as they looked out over the camp that was already being set up.

"Why party at all?" Uric scrutinized. Valerio knew his second didn't agree with the decision, but he wouldn't voice such a disagreement outright. Rather, he'd ask the question veiled with the slightest bit of disgust in his tone.

"The people have been traveling for days. They are restless and afraid, and they need something to look forward to." His gaze snagged on the Fire Dancer as the blue skinned Unseelie gripped her wrist and dragged her across the crowded camp. They stopped in front of a thin, tall human woman and gestured at her bag. "And," he added, "I want Shula Azzarh to see what she's missing."

He needed her on their side. Desperately. He could see her eyes working every day as she searched for possible ways to escape.

He couldn't afford to lose her. She was vital in the war that was brewing. He didn't know how or why, but once he got back to his father, he was going to find out.

In the meantime, he needed her to cooperate.

And everybody loved Fae wine.

Perhaps if she saw that they weren't a threat, she could ease towards a friendship with them all and stay. Because through her, he would not only achieve a fighting chance at saving the entire Fae race, but the one thing he'd always wanted above all others.

"Let's go." Valerio patted Uric on the back. "I have a craving for wine."

Like Flames

"Are you sure about this?" Shula hid behind the bushes and toed her boots off. Even as she questioned Orna's decision, her fingers worked by their own volition, thumbs hooking into the waistband of her borrowed pants as she pulled them off. Her shirt went next in the pile of garments.

"Positive." Shula could hear the smile in Orna's voice. "Look, we're setting up camp; night is falling, they have a fire going, and I can smell them passing out wine."

Shula stopped her movements and took her bottom lip between her teeth. "Are we sure it's safe to have a party?" she asked, trepidation sliding through her every word and heartbeat.

Orna scoffed. "It's not a party. We're setting camp. Besides, you're already naked and putting on the clothes. Why are you hesitating now?"

Shula wasn't sure. Maybe it was because she'd only ever performed for humans, or maybe because even through her giddy excitement, she still felt like she was among enemies.

She heard Orna sigh on the other side of the bush, and then her blue hands poked through the greenery and parted them so she could peek in at Shula's naked form.

Shula yelped and covered her arms over her body. It didn't seem to matter though, because Orna's gaze barely flicked over her figure. "You miss dancing, right?"

"Yes," Shula answered honestly.

"Then put on the clothes that Lila so graciously let you borrow, get your Fire Dancing ass out here, and *dance* for us."

Mana, Shula must have been crazy for even considering this.

To be honest, if she thought about it, she had been prepared to give up dancing forever. That part of her life had nearly died with her old job and her old life. She would have escaped, disguised herself, and found something new to hide. Giving up dancing? She enjoyed what she did. That was part of the reason she had found it so difficult to accept the end of that cycle.

But Orna was giving her another opportunity. Did the crowd really matter? After all, Shula couldn't control that they were keeping her hostage, but Shula could control this. Her own innate talent, her movements.

She took in a breath. "Fine," she conceded.

Orna made a giddy noise in the back of her throat. "Okay, okay, this is so exciting. Let me go find you some of that wine they keep passing out. Wait here and get dressed, quickly." Then she disappeared.

Shula chuckled but bent and pulled on the clothes Lila had lent.

It had been Orna's idea.

She'd noticed one of the humans dressed in a loose skirt and flowing scarf. They'd been outfits similar to what Shula wore during her acts, but in dull, faded colors. Orna had asked to borrow a flowing skirt and a top that covered only her breasts and dangled little jewels. She'd lent them a head wrap that Shula lifted and tied over the lower half of her face. She opted to go barefoot because Lila's shoes wouldn't have fit Shula's much bigger feet.

Once she was finished getting dressed, Orna poked her head through the bush again and took her in. "Oooh, you look so different!" She pushed her way through the leaves and emerged on the other side wielding a goblet of something that smelt like sour grapes and magic; if magic had a scent, it would be fizzling and sharp. "Fae wine," Orna offered, handing Shula a cup. "Packs more of a punch than human wine because it's infused with magic. Bottoms up."

Shula went with the flow and tipped the contents back. It burned a path down her throat that she welcomed. When she finished, she handed the cup back to Orna.

The sun had already begun to set, and everyone had settled in for the night of relaxation. Orna pulled Shula out of the bushes and shoved her forward between the shoulder blades.

"Hey, Fire Dancer—woah—" Clay nearly tumbled as he took Shula's appearance in. His eyes went wide, looking her from the toes, up to her midriff, and stopping at the swells of her breasts in the top. Even in the dimness of the night and the light casted by the flickering fire, she could make out his flush. "What are you doing?"

Orna looped her arm through Shula's and shot Clay a smug grin. "She's going to dance!" She yelled the words, and Shula felt many eyes stray over in their direction.

She swallowed her nerves.

"Dancing?" Clay echoed, as if he hadn't quite heard correctly.

"Dancing," Orna confirmed. "Look, there's Paulo with his drums now." She slipped her arm from Shula's and all but ran in Paulo's direction.

Shula watched her go, feeling her face heat. "Seriously, the others have been here all but five minutes and she's already friends with everyone."

Clay chuckled. "That's Orna for you..." His eyes roamed over her body once again and stopped on her eyes. "You look good, Fire Dancer. I can feel Ryker burning holes in my back just at the sight of me talking to you."

Shula rolled her eyes and resisted to the urge to confirm if it was true or not. "Whatever." She shoved him lightly on the shoulder. It felt natural, and she realized the Fae wine might have loosened her whole body a bit. She no longer felt like she was wound tightly, so on edge.

Even Clay seemed surprised by the action.

Shula cleared her throat and tried not to look shy. She steeled herself and remembered why she danced. Because it gave her power, control over her own body and her own actions. She couldn't control the world, but she could control herself through movements. She could tell her own story. She could tell others. She could be vulnerable without anyone ever knowing.

And she desperately needed that just then.

She needed to stop being so angry, needed an outlet, and if not with her magic, then through dance.

Just then, the soft beating of the drums sounded around them. A hush fell over the crowd as music began to strum out through the night. It was a song that Shula recognized, as old as her soul.

She closed her eyes and swayed slightly, and when she opened them again, Clay was smiling at her. "Break a leg," he whispered.

The reply was at the edge of her tongue. *Break yours first.* But Clay wasn't Fanny, and that part of her life seemed so far away now.

She let her eyes fall closed. Shula didn't need her sight when she felt the beatings of the drums vibrate through her body. When she felt the earth beneath her feet. When she heard and felt down to her very soul. Her feet began to move, tip-toeing closer to the crackling flames of the fire.

The hush seemed all the more profound now, and she instinctively knew that she'd captured everyone's attention.

She felt eyes on her, and it fueled her ire; it fueled every single emotion she'd kept locked so tightly inside. She hadn't been able to express it before except in bouts of anger and threats of escape, but now she could display every vulnerable emotion she wished.

So she did.

Her body moved in time with the beat, her feet pounding against the earth as she stomped and twirled. Her body undulated, her arms moved like waves. No, not like waves.

Like flames.

She gave herself up to the music, to her feelings. She controlled every single aspect of herself, she let her anger be heard. The beads on the top slid jangled together with every roll of her chest. Every movement was a breath released. It was letting go. It was accepting that her friendship with Fanny had been a doomed thing from the start. Every movement was her heartbreak given words. It was her sorrow crying out the tears she refused to let fall.

It was her hatred for the Brotherhood and the vulnerability they made her feel. It was her hatred for the Fae that held her captive—no, that wasn't quite right. It wasn't hatred exactly. It was something else, something more that she couldn't describe with words but with the undulations of her body. It was the word *special* ringing over and over again in her mind without pause. Because she *was* special, even if she couldn't accept it yet.

She was the Fire Dancer, and that life was now behind her but, in this moment, it didn't have to be.

Her eyes flashed open as she twirled, and she caught sight of Orna cuddled close to her husband, watching Shula dance around the fire.

Shula closed her eyes again and opened her palms. She was so used to shoving her magic away, but there was no need to do that now. She wasn't amongst human haters. She wasn't near Fanny. She was near those who cared against all odds, even while everyone else shunned them, she was with people who worked together as a single unit of love and respect in a world where only hate existed.

Shula took a deep breath and summoned the flames.

They burst against her fingertips and rose high. She wasn't deaf to the gasps that rang out around her. The flames engulfed her hands and spread along her arms. She kept them contained as best as she could, but she wasn't used to using her magic. She wasn't used to having to control it instead of repressing it. But those faltering movements of her feet and arms only added to the allure of her hands. She pulled the fire deep back inside herself and skidded to a stop just as the drumbeats rose to a deafening, roaring crescendo. Her heart was beating rapidly in tune with the rhythm. Her chest heaved, and when the beating of the instrument died, she was sure everyone could hear her harsh breathing and knew there were tears she was refusing to cry.

After a moment, she opened her eyes and realized she stopped right in front of Ryker by the end of the dance. Like a string that kept pulling them towards one another that she wanted severed. He was staring intensely at her, with no expression other than contempt on his features.

The silence pressed for minutes and she stayed where she was, staring, glaring at one of her captors, making sure he could read every emotion in her gaze.

But then an arm wrapped around her shoulders and Julius shouted near her ear, "Now that's how we start a party!" He raised his glass and laughed before swallowing all of the contents in one go.

It broke the spell she'd cast over them, and everyone began laughing and mingling.

Meanwhile, Shula felt the somberness in her heart.

"Here, Shula Azzarh, it looks like you could use a drink." Julius tugged her away, breaking her gaze with Ryker and she went willingly. "That's what I call dancing. You're amazing." He all but stumbled his way over to where a High Fae man was sitting near a rocky lump. "Top it off." Julius shoved his goblet to the High Fae. "And one for the lady, please."

Then, much to Shula's surprise, the lump of a rock moved. It seemed to unfurl from itself, and she blinked at a creature she'd never seen before. It was about two feet in height, with wrinkled, gray skin and green cloth that hung in scraps from a twisted, ugly body. Black beady eyes stared up at her from behind a long, crooked nose covered in moles. A lipless mouth pulled back in a sneer, and she couldn't stop herself from shuddering.

"Goblin," Julius explained as two goblets were filled to the rim with more Fae wine. Julius removed his arm from her body and took both goblets, turning to hand one to her. After she took it, he clinked the glasses together. "Cheers." And then he downed the whole thing in one swallow. "Chug it or you're weak," he dared.

Shula felt her eyebrows raise. "That's the kind of daring behavior I expect from Clay."

Julius laughed. It was hearty and full of soul. "Clay is the bigger daredevil than I am. He's just being somber lately. Fuck if I know why. Come on, let's go dance."

He tugged her around the fire again. No more passionate music played, but music that was upbeat and fun. Several people were already pairing up and doing a jig with their feet and moving around the fire. She caught sight of Orna tugging her husband to his feet, and the two of them slipped out into the copse of trees to steal their moment together as usual.

Julius pulled her into the fray, and she had no choice but to follow on quick feet. She had to hurry and down her drink as she went, wincing while it burned her throat. The effect was instantaneous. It loosened her body, and soon she was getting into the groove with Julius.

He was such a boisterous, fun Fae who let his hair down. The orange strands danced around his ruddy cheeks like flames, and his face reddened as the night went on, though Shula couldn't tell if it was because of drunkenness or the dancing.

He didn't let her go unless it was to spin her over to Clay. Back and forth they shared her for the dancing, and she found herself throwing her head back and laughing. She couldn't help it. The dancing she'd done earlier had helped expel her of her emotions, and Julius had an infectious personality.

"Clay! Catch!" He twirled Shula in Clay's direction, but he wasn't fast enough, and she twirled too hard. That and the laughter mixed with the drinks had her losing her footing and falling. A gasp left Shula's lips as she sprawled straight onto Ryker's lap.

Her whole body froze against his as he glared down at her. He didn't speak, and she knew he was about three seconds away from pushing her off his body and maybe kicking her in the face.

She took a breath and blurted, "I have to take a piss."

Ryker's eyebrows rose, and it wasn't in amusement.

"You're my bodyguard, aren't you? Guard my body," she teased. She wasn't sure what was wrong with her. It was the wine. The bubbly effect of it had migrated to her brain and she couldn't think clearly. Her hands reached up and stroked along the strands of his beard, and just as soon as she realized what she was doing, she yanked her hand away. "Don't bite my arm off," she pleaded breathlessly.

His thick brows pulled together. "Why... would I do that?"

"For touching you."

They both kept quiet, and she was a bit amazed that he still hadn't roughly shoved her away from him.

"You hate me," she observed.

Shut up, shut up, shut up! She willed her mind, but it wasn't listening. Words just kept pouring out of her.

"Is it because of my ears?"

His lips pressed together in a thin line, and he tried to look away, but she reached her palms up and brought his gaze back to hers.

"Listen here, asshole." The anger suddenly rose. She hated the way he looked at her, the way he judged her for what she had to do to survive. "We were staying in the reservations. I don't know if you're familiar with the rules, but they only allowed magicless Fae. Anyone caught with magic was taken. The emperor's soldiers took my parents because of *me*. Because of this stupid fucking magic inside. I let it loose, and it destroyed everyone there. I watched them take my parents away into the camp..." Shula broke off. Ryker tried to look away, but she forced his gaze on hers, keeping his face pressed tightly between her hands. "I ran. I had no idea where to go. Then this old human lady found me and hid me in her attic."

Shula remembered vividly what she looked like. The pearls around her neck. The kind eyes and graying hair. Just as vividly as she remembered the floors stained crimson with her blood.

"She took me to a surgeon. Said she would keep me and protect me, but I had to look normal to survive. I was just a kid and I trusted her, so I let them change my ears. But then a day later she fucking died."

"Shula..." Clay's voice sounded behind, past the music, past her own pounding heart, but she ignored it. She focused on Ryker and the hatred in his eyes that she was tired of feeling keenly around her.

"Soldiers found us. Again. They murdered her in front of me." Tears prickled behind her eyelids, and she tried to blink them away, but they slid down her temples. "I tried to stop them, but they came after me, and I burned them with my fire." She still remembered their expressions of panic as the fire spread against their arms. "I took her jewelry and ran straight to the circus. The only place where they wouldn't find me, because that's where all the freaks live. So think about *that* next time you look at me with those judgmental fucking eyes of yours, you big bastard."

Shula let go of his face and slid from his lap, falling into the dust. She forced herself to her feet, brushing herself off with her palms. She turned and found Julius and Clay staring at her. Ignoring the pity in their eyes, she stormed away, hating herself for everything the wine made her confess.

Maybe she'd hoped that by talking about it, she'd feel some type of closure, maybe become closer to someone, anyone.

Yet Ryker had still looked at her like she was scum of the earth.

The worst part about it was, he was probably right.

"Fuck." Clay raked a hand through his hair as he stared after Shula.

Julius echoed the sentiment. "Fuck."

"I'll go talk to her." Clay started forward, but Ryker felt his legs pushing up until he was standing.

"No," he stated, cutting Clay off mid-step.

He couldn't explain it. He didn't feel particularly closer to her after that confession. He didn't even fucking like her any more than he had before. All he knew was that it was a confession meant for him and no one else. She'd been trying to prove a point. That she wasn't a coward? That she was Fae, too? Ryker wasn't sure, and he didn't give a fuck.

The story had been meant for him and so he would go after her and drag her back.

Ignoring Clay's gaping mouth and Julius' annoying smirk, he stepped past the revelers and followed the Fire Dancer's stumbling footsteps into the woods.

She was quite loud in her drunkenness, so he followed. She wandered deep into the woods and when she stopped, he tilted his head to the side. The sudden trickle of dripping reached his ears along with the smell of urine.

His eyes rolled.

She really *had* needed to take a piss. He'd assumed she was making up more excuses to try and escape.

It wasn't as if she was fooling anyone with that. They all knew what she was doing every time she made her way to the trees. She was hoping they'd get distracted enough so she could go away and make a new life for herself.

What she didn't understand was that there *was* no life beyond this. She would always run and always hide. If what the seer said was true and the Fire Dancer really was a key point in the war, then she had to realize that they needed her. They needed her to restore the balance, to win their lives back so they didn't have to live in fear. So they could thrive once again. So there could be no more death or betrayal.

Once the sounds stopped and he heard the rustle of her clothes, he started forward again. He could see her slumped against a tree trunk, her head lolling, and he briefly wondered if she was going to puke and gritted his teeth together.

When Valerio had assigned him babysitting duty, holding her hair back while she puked her guts out wasn't in the description. It wasn't even something he wanted to do.

Silently, he made his way to her side, but she didn't look up.

"You'll have to carry me back because I'm not fucking moving," she slurred quietly.

Ryker rolled his eyes. Stubborn wench.

"Come on." He gripped her arm. "Let's go."

Her knees shook as she stood up, and then she suddenly slid off to the side and promptly fell to the ground. He just let her go with a sigh.

"Ew..." she groaned. "It's sticky."

That's when the smell hit him. His nostrils flared and his ears twitched.

Shula pushed herself up and froze, her gaze going straight to what she'd fallen in.

Ryker didn't know how he hadn't noticed sooner. He was distracted, and the smell of her urine had been sharp enough to mask the smell of blood.

The copper scent hit him then, and both he and Shula found the puddle of it and followed the trail...

...straight to the dead body on the ground.

Like Blood

There were some things a Fae could note even in the darkness. Like how orange and red leaves could look bright like spilled rubies.

Like flames.

Like blood.

Her palms met the stickiness of it, and it took her mind but a moment later to capture the scent. It was so sharp, it permeated in her lungs and made her want to gag. It was a sobering moment, to realize she was lying in blood.

Even more sobering to follow the trail left behind towards the dead body mere feet away.

Shula opened her mouth, her wine-filled brain preparing to scream, but Ryker was there, clamping a big hand against her mouth to silence the sound.

He hauled her up to his chest and darted behind a thick tree.

This position felt familiar, only there was no desire here. There was the urgent pounding of his heart against her back. There was just the heart-pounding fear, the acrid scent of blood, and a dead body a few feet away that she realized too late who it belonged to.

And then there were footsteps. Several pairs and cruel, cold laughter.

She tensed and Ryker pulled her closer, wrapping his arms around her mid-section to keep her pressed tightly to his body. She wondered if he did it to ground himself or to protect her.

It didn't matter.

She tried to silence her breathing, but her heart was pounding so hard she swore the people could hear it.

Their voices flittered over to them. Human, cruel.

"Blue-skinned bitch put up a fight," one of them tittered.

Shula choked on her sob and Ryker tightened his grip on her to keep her steady.

"Once the captain's done with her, she'll wish she'd never been born." She heard one of them spit. "Esses scum!"

Four different sets of footsteps. They all stopped a few feet away.

"Poor bloke would have been spared, but he decided to wet his cock in Fae pussy."

The crude words had Shula slamming her eyes closed. She felt the beginning of a growl rumble in Ryker's chest, but he tamped the sound down immediately. The words pissed him off as much as they did Shula.

"Let's take his body back to camp and nail it to a pike. The captain's going to make us come back and finish the rest of them off anyway."

"Shit luck we came across this."

There was a grunt and a rustle, and Shula knew they were hoisting the body up.

"The Fae aren't gonna know what the fuck hit them."

And then their footsteps retreated and left only silence in its wake. Silence and blood.

Ryker's hold on her loosened and she whirled around, tears in her eyes.

"They have Orna." Her voice broke. They took her. They took her and killed her husband. All of Shula's worst fears came to life in that single moment. That the humans would find them and kill them.

Here they were, partying around a bonfire while Orna had been suffering in the woods.

"Let's go," Ryker growled. His fingers threaded through the spaces between hers and he tugged her. They ran through the woods at a speed that was blinding. Shula's feet skidded and tripped, but Ryker kept her upright, pulling her so hard she felt the strain on her arm.

She tried to keep up, tried to breathe.

Her thoughts kept going back to Orna, though.

They burst into their camp and Ryker growled, "Valerio!"

The prince and Uric were in front of him in a second.

Ryker began filling them in with quiet, clipped tones. Shula felt her breathing become uneven. Dark spots danced behind her eyelids. This was everything she feared. It was everything she told them would happen. And Orna was the victim. All because she'd snuck away to have a moment alone with her husband.

Orna. *Orna.* Her thoughts filled with the blue skinned Fae, making her dizzy. She swayed where she stood, swallowing down the bile that rose behind her throat.

Ryker yanked her close. "Focus!" His voice cut through her senses. It was then that she realized he was still holding her hand tightly.

He hadn't let go.

Valerio looked gravely at Ryker and turned to Uric. Uric's jaw was set tightly. "Which way did they go?" he asked.

"East."

Uric nodded and waved a hand. A moment later, the air around them shimmered as a portal was created. Uric stepped through. He was gone for a few moments before he came back and the portal disappeared.

The Fae gasped a bit between words. "Not far. Their camp is surrounded by a shit ton of iron. It could be why we missed them..."

"How many?" Valerio barked.

"Fifty, maybe more," he answered gravely.

Valerio cursed and ran a hand across the shaved side of his head.

Clay and Julius pushed forward. "What's going on?" Julius hissed. He looked suddenly sober and aware. The same way Shula felt.

"Orders, prince?" Uric sked.

He knew what they wanted to know. If they should flee or go and save Orna.

Shula felt her tongue weighing heavily in her mouth. She didn't know what she'd do if the prince ordered them to leave Orna behind.

Valerio shook his head and sighed. "We go after her and end the humans who dared touch one of our own."

Uric's jaw clenched. "The needs of the many—"

"I am doing this for everyone in this camp," Valerio interrupted, snapping out the words. "They are too close and could catch up to all of us. We end this now. Tonight. Julius! Grab every able-bodied person, Fae or human, and suit them up. Uric, prepare to portal us all there. Can you handle it?" At Uric's stiff nod, he turned to Clay. "You're with me when we go through the portal." Clay nodded. "Ryker, we'll need you in case..."

He didn't finish the sentence.

Finally, Valerio turned to Shula. "We need you Fire Dancer. Orna needs you."

The weight of those words settled over her. Orna needed her. Not to be a coward, but to be brave. Not to run, but to fight. Shula hadn't wanted to get close to her and even as she pushed Orna away, the Unseelie Fae managed to somehow wedge herself into Shula's heart. She'd become her friend when Shula didn't even know she'd needed it.

Now it was time to return the favor.

She nodded firmly.

"Get everyone together and ready to leave. When we come back, we'll need to make a hasty retreat."

Shula's heart dropped along with her mouth.

"I can help fight." There was a sudden violence in her heart. A thirst for blood. Orna was out there and she needed Shula's help. She wouldn't stay behind twiddling her thumbs and packing bags into the carts.

"You have no training," Ryker said. When he spoke, she realized he still hadn't let go and seemed reluctant to pull away. She did, slowly prying her fingers from his grasp, one by one, but even then, she still felt the whisper of his touch like a brand.

Shula glared at him. "I can fight. I want to. I need to help save Orna."

Ryker growled and snapped his attention to Valerio, dismissing her entirely. "We don't have time for this. We have to leave now."

Valerio still didn't take his gaze from Shula. "He's right, Shula. You have no training. We cannot afford for anything to happen to you. You will stay here and help the women and children. Control their fear and be prepared to leave."

Shula opened her mouth, prepared to argue, but Valerio interrupted with a cutting voice.

"That's an order."

She clamped her mouth closed, rage rising in her. She was being tossed aside like she was nothing, like she wasn't valuable in this fight against the humans. Was it because of her ears? Did their prejudice run so deeply that they thought she would betray them? She'd given them no indication that she was on their side and she wasn't. She wasn't on anyone's side but her own. But Orna was her friend.

And for her she would fight.

Valerio turned from her and nodded to Uric. A moment later, a portal opened. "Time to go," Valerio announced. Julius showed up then with both human and Fae men brandishing an array of weapons; swords, lances, shields, looking ready yet a bit fearful.

"Let's go." Julius led them into the portal in single file. One by one they stepped through to the other side and disappeared from view. Ryker went next, followed by Clay and Valerio.

In a split second, Shula had made her decision.

The rage inside her swelled to impossible heights until she was shaking. The realization hit her straight in the chest. The realization that she'd been a coward. A coward for pushing Orna's friendship away, for ever comparing her to Fanny. And now she was out there, afraid, hurt, captured by humans.

Humans who had stolen Shula's parents from her.

Humans who had killed the old woman.

Humans who had forced her into hiding, into fear.

Yes, she decided. She would save Orna, and in turn, she would make those humans pay for everything she'd suffered as well.

Shula watched Uric step into his own portal. She knew she only had a single, split second to act. So she jumped in after him, ramming into Uric's body and propelling him forward. Then she was falling, a scream catching in her throat as the world behind her disappeared.

Burn

She fell with a painful thump straight onto Uric. The Fae man groaned and when he shoved her off, his whole body was trembling. He rolled on the ground while Shula sat up on her knees and stared down at him.

Gone was the Fae elegance; he looked like an aged human, wrinkles spreading around the corners of his eyes.

He glared up at her with old, soulful eyes and his voice was raspy when he said, "What the fuck, Fire Dancer?"

Shula pushed herself up from the ground. "Shut up, old man," she snapped with impatience, feeling a brief flare of satisfaction at the sight of his wrinkled scowl. She held her hand out to him, sweeping her gaze around. She noted that Uric had transported them on the outskirts of what seemed to be a human encampment. She could see it beyond. Bonfires blazed and people in uniforms milled about, laughing and shouting. She stilled and felt the hot press of iron almost immediately. It seemed to settle over her bones, and she felt the weakness immediately.

Uric knocked her wrist to the side and hopped to his feet himself. He glared at her. "What the fuck?" he repeated on a low growl.

Shula ignored him. "So what's the plan?"

Uric shoved a hand through his hair in a move that spoke entirely of frustration. "Prince Valerio gave you an order."

"Valerio is not my prince. Now let's go. They need us."

Uric looked like he wouldn't have any problem with strangling her to death. Instead he sighed and gestured with his chin. "The only reason I'm not sending you back ass first through a portal is because I need to reserve my strength for my prince. Now, let's go save your friend."

Shula swept her gaze across the darkness. They'd landed about half a yard away from the human camp. Close enough so they could see, but far enough to not be heard. The shadows cloaked them as Uric gestured her to follow him behind shrubbery.

Her footsteps were silent, but it was her top that jingled with each step she took. She was still wearing the outfit she'd danced in, made for flashy show. Uric shot her a glare and she tried to step even softer to avoid making noise.

They'd been right about the iron. Even from their position, she could feel the slightest pulse of it, but given that they were far enough away, she couldn't feel the effects just yet. So she still had use of her hearing and other senses. That meant she heard the steady thumping of his heart.

Ryker met them halfway, his glare prominent in the darkness.

"What the fuck?" he hissed, glaring between Shula and Uric.

"She stowed away." Uric's palm pressed against her shoulder and he shoved her forward. Not expecting it, she slipped and fell against Ryker. He caught her with ease against the hardness of his body. "She's your problem now." And then he slipped away into the darkness.

Shula's heart pounded as she listened to him walk away in near silence like a feline.

With him gone, Ryker shoved her lightly away. "Stay here," he commanded and started to turn around.

Shula caught him, her palm connecting to his arm before he could turn away from her. "I'm here to help."

He gave her a look of impatience. "In that outfit? They'll hear you from a mile away. No."

Her fingers tightened against his arm, but he didn't flinch. He barely even moved. "I want to help. I have to. Orna—"

"You'll get yourself killed," he interjected.

"What do you care?"

His jaw clamped down and he gritted out, "I don't."

"Then let me fucking help."

He looked like he wanted to tie her up against a tree. He looked like he was debating doing just that, but eventually he shrugged out of her hold and raked a hand through his long hair. "Fine," he conceded. Then his hand placed against her hip, and he tugged her forward.

Her breath caught in her throat when they collided, and she felt her heart pound up to her throat as his hand slipped between them. She audibly gasped as his fingers tugged at the beaded strings of her top. A few snips of his knife later and the beads were slipping between them, falling to the ground. She couldn't take her eyes off his even though she knew it wasn't wise to let Ryker get this close to her with a weapon.

He sawed through strings, his hands dangerously close to her breasts.

"Turn," he ordered.

She obeyed, turning around. He continued to cut at the top until all the beads were gone and she could move as silently as possible.

When he finished, she turned, and he pressed the knife into her hand.

It was like she was receiving his silent permission to fight, to prove herself to him somehow. She swallowed the rising lump in her throat. She had nothing to prove to him, but she was grateful anyway for the weapon. Hers had been stuck in the pocket of her borrowed pants, which she'd left behind at the camp.

Her palm closed around the hilt, but before she could thank him, Ryker was walking away.

She didn't know what she should do, if she should go after him or go her own way? She contemplated it, chewing against her bottom lip but eventually decided it would be better to see what the plan was to get Orna out of there. So she followed after him as quietly as she could, ducking beneath branches, avoiding twigs.

Her feet hurt. She stepped over rocks, feeling the pain of the ground scrape against the soles of her feet. She gritted her teeth and bared with it, because nothing that was happening to her then could have been worse than what Orna was likely suffering right now.

They made it to the edge of camp, so close she could smell the meat burning over their campfires.

It was hard to believe that only moments before, she'd been dancing around their own fire, with Orna watching on, a dreamy look in her eyes. That they'd been together. That she'd felt *content* and now Orna was in there somewhere.

She crept up next to Ryker, staring intently at the humans wandering about. She felt a bloodlust rise up in her like never before and whispered to him, "What are we waiting for?"

He shot her a glare and for a moment she thought he wouldn't answer but then whispered, "They're taking care of the guards."

She was itching to edge closer but forced herself to be patient. She knew this moment was precarious. They needed to be careful, because it could mean life or death.

She focused on her thoughts of finding Orna and getting her out of there alive when she felt a squeeze on her arm. Snapping her attention to Ryker, he gave her a slight nod. It was all the gesture she needed.

They started forward, closer to the camp.

With every step forward, a feeling of dread weighed heavily at the pit of her stomach. It hit her so suddenly like a sixth sense, an instinct she didn't understand.

Not until they stepped closer to the entrance and the sight there stopped her cold.

Bile rose in the back of her throat. The Fae wine in her stomach churned and rose, but she swallowed it down and forced herself to stare.

An anguished cry threatened, but she bit down so hard on her tongue that she tasted blood.

Ryker's touch steadied her, but she still couldn't take her gaze away.

Iron spikes were hammered into the ground. Tall and rusted, dark red liquid slid down the poles that Shula immediately knew was blood. And on top of the pike? A severed head was impaled through it. Mouth opened in a scream with a missing tongue, she recognized the terrified lines of the face, the hair, the brown skin.

Des' body had been brutally butchered, pieces of him scattered and skewered against iron like a warning or an expression of cruelty.

Once the horror and urge to vomit washed away, Shula's vision went red. She was blinded by the rage and fire inside her. The images of Des' kind face and what he'd become blurred together in her vision.

He hadn't deserved this. *None* of the Fae deserved this cruel treatment. They didn't deserve to be butchered, to have their bodies disrespected, their remains mounted like trophies.

Shula inhaled and tasted smoke, and she *knew.*

Today, the humans would burn.

A Light in the Dark

Ryker unsheathed his sword from his waist and held it tightly in his grip. His heart was pumping wildly and his teeth grinding hard. He was barely hanging on by a thread, ready to throw himself into the camp and tear every human there limb from limb.

The sight of Des' body hammered into iron took him back to memories of the past and of Mairin. He kept his gaze trained forward to the camp. They'd already stayed too long to stare at the body.

His hand went to the Fire Dancer's, and he gently touched her wrist, drawing her attention towards him. With a jerk of his chin to indicate she should follow, he started forward, and she did what he asked.

He was glad she was obeying his silent commands, but he should have known it wouldn't last.

At the first shout and sound of clashing battle, she broke away from him and ran into the camp.

He knew his prince would want him to follow her, but Ryker wasn't her fucking babysitter. If she wanted to disobey orders and get herself killed, that was her own fucking problem. Not his. His problem was making the humans pay for what they did. To Des. To Orna. To Mairin. They would all taste the rage of his vengeance and his sword would mete out punishment in swift, agonizing blows. And when he found Orna, he would heal her and take on pain as a penance for all he'd done and all he would do.

Not out of guilt for the lives he took. He would never feel guilty for taking a human life. Not again. Not after all they'd done. Because once their souls were reaped by their devil and the blood cleaned off his sword, he remembered Mairin and the guilt hit him. He mourned her and the deaths of his own people, and he took the pain that came with his magic, because if the price to pay was his own agony in order to save one more life, then he would accept his punishment tenfold.

So as Shula ran away and met the violence head on, Ryker forced himself away from her and with a growl that shook the ground, charged towards a soldier and swiped the blade across his throat.

Blood ran red and slid against his leathers. Ryker didn't watch as his dead body tumbled to the ground because he was already turning away to meet the next human. The iron debilitated him, slowing what would have been otherwise quick, blurred movements. It didn't matter, though. He was still a warrior at heart. Still strong, and he took down the humans. One after another, they fell to their deaths.

Iron met steel, and the pulse of the substance made him grit his teeth with discomfort. He tried to ignore it. Tried to push past it, but it was strong.

Beyond the fray he could make out the bodies of his own people. Uric slashed his way through the darkness like a demon of legends, the steel glinting against his black eyes. Clay battled next to Valerio. Whatever flaws Clay had, like that big fucking mouth of his, he was a fighter.

His gaze darted around, frantically searching for any sign of Orna among the chaos. What he saw instead made him freeze.

"Clay!" he shouted.

The Fae in question jerked his head up in time to see Ryker gesture across the camp. He turned and cried out Shula's name.

Ryker let out a roar and started towards her, and in that moment, he made a mistake. He let down his guard and a moment later, felt the sting of iron slash through his side.

Shula had never experienced the chaos of a battle. At least, not like this. This was brutal. It was watching bodies skewered with steel and fall in a spray of blood and earth. Shula stayed out of the battle, sticking to the shadows and keeping her eyes out for Orna. As much as she wanted blood and vengeance, Orna was more important and she had to find her.

She weaved her way past tents and tried to remain as inconspicuous as possible, but a human caught sight of her and charged.

Shula had never fought before. She was a dancer, not a warrior, and the one time she'd seen blood had been at the hands of an emperor's soldier, a human who wore leathers just like the one charging after her. As he charged, her mind flashed back to that moment. So similar to this. Only then, the old human woman had placed herself before Shula.

But Shula wasn't a little girl anymore and she reacted on instinct. She cried out her rage as she ducked away from him. Her knife could never be a match for his sword, but she had to try. She lifted her weapon and slashed out at him. He dodged and slapped the side of his sword against her wrist.

Agony radiated up her arm and the dagger clattered from her grip. She dropped to the ground at the swing of his sword and scrambled for her knife when she felt a yank on her ankle haul her backwards. She screamed and kicked out her feet but was tossed to her back.

The human loomed over her, pointing his iron weapon against her throat. An evil sneer marred his face as he lowered himself to the ground to straddle her waist.

"I'll kill you, you Fae bitch." She felt the press of iron against her throat sting and draw blood.

No!

She bucked against him and threw her hands up, scratching his face.

The taste of smoke pressed through her lungs, rising until she nearly choked. Something stirred inside of her, like dying embers suddenly sparking to life. Her palm slapped up and connected to his cheek and in a moment, all the rage and fire inside flared at the tips of her fingers.

The human screamed as she scorched his face. The stench of charred flesh reached her nostrils, but she didn't care. All she could think through was her own rage, to make him pay. For what they did to her parents. For what they did to her.

A scream erupted from her lips as the power surged through her veins and all over her body, so hot, so unimaginably hot that the iron pointed at her neck suddenly erupted into flames and slowly began to melt. She didn't feel the sweltering drip of it slide onto her body. She was already on fire. Her entire body combusted, covering her from head to toe.

She saw the moment the human's eyes widened and fear consumed him.

It consumed him just before the fire did.

She pushed herself to her feet, looming over his body as he incinerated within seconds. She pulled away and when the flames died down, all that was left of the human was marred flesh, charred remains.

She heard the distant shout of her name, but the roar of flames in her ears was louder than any voice. She turned full circle. Humans were rushing towards her, wielding iron in their hands.

They reminded her of the soldiers that rushed at her parents and took them from her forever.

She screamed and the flames responded. They shot out and caught against every human near her. The sparks of the flames jumped and caught against the tents, causing the night to blaze up.

The humans were burning, just like she'd promised they would, and yet she still didn't see Orna.

Shula ran, leaving a blazing trail behind her. The night ignited, and she ran and ran until she came upon an iron cage.

Her feet skidded to a stop as she beheld what was inside.

Orna lay in the corner of the cage, curled into a ball and unmoving. Naked, her blue skin had lost its star dust shine. Her body looked bloody and bruised over every inch.

The sight broke Shula.

She stumbled forward and wrapped her fiery hands around the bars and they began to glow. Slow and steadily at first. The first touch of iron brought the smallest twinges of pain, but it didn't matter. Nothing did except for getting Orna out of her prison.

And in doing so, it felt like Shula was breaking out of her own prison as well. That's what fueled her. The violence and cruelty she'd known for years now. The need to protect her friend... To protect herself.

She dug deep into her well of power and ripped it out with all her might. She'd never used so much fire and didn't care that it suddenly made her weak in the knees or that her whole body trembled. All she could think about was getting Orna out.

She didn't stop the rising swell of power. Even when she felt those first drops of blood drip from her nose to her mouth. Even when her limbs eventually gave out and she dropped to the ground, still gripping tightly to the bars.

They began to melt into pools at Shula's feet until the bars disintegrated completely, leaving a gaping hole in the cage. Shula fell back to the ground with a gasp, her chest heaving as she rasped in painful breaths. Like a cord snipped inside her, the fire rushed back inside, and the stench of smoke settled in her lungs again.

She coughed, feeling blood and spit spew from her tongue. With lethargic movements and shaking limbs, she got up to her knees and crawled through the hole, her fingers grazing Orna's skin.

She was cold to the touch.

"Orna..." Shula's voice wavered, and her friend did not stir. "Orna, wake up." Her fingers fumbled against the slick blood on blue skin, but she gripped Orna's arm and tugged. Cold. She was so damn *cold.*

With aching muscles and using all the strength she had, Shula reached for her friend and tugged, feeling the muscles on her neck strain as she pulled Orna's body out of the cage.

Perhaps it was just the iron, she thought desperately as she rolled her onto the charred ground. Her body rolled to her back, and Shula couldn't hold back her sob at the sight of Orna's lifeless, black eyes, staring up at the night sky.

"Orna..." Shula's fingers trembled against her body. "Orna!"

But the Unseelie Fae did not respond.

It was in that defining moment that Shula's heart cracked into a million pieces. She'd thought losing Fanny had been bad? This... this was worse. Orna couldn't be gone, she tried to deny. The Unseelie Fae was a force of nature, a light in the dark, stars streaking across the sky to provide hope to those who had none. And to see the dark, lifeless way she lay on the ground broke something inside Shula.

She searched for the fire inside herself, but she felt drained, hollow, with nothing but smoke where her magic should be.

She growled in frustration, screaming Orna's name over and over again.

This couldn't be happening. Another person Shula cared about couldn't be dead.

Flashbacks plagued her, meshing in with this moment until Shula couldn't tell them apart. The grief of the past became the grief of the present, and a sob wedged in her throat, threatening release.

So caught up in her grief, Shula didn't hear the footsteps until it was too late. Until the cold press of the iron blade was against her throat.

She felt a slight sting against her skin and gasped as a hand snatched up her long hair and yanked her to her feet.

She complied, too weak to fight back. An armored arm snaked around her bare waist and tugged her close, but the sword didn't lower from her neck.

"Elemental bitch," a voice in her ear spat. "I'd kill you now except the Emperor of Illyk has ordered to keep you alive."

Her blood went cold at the words. The Emperor of Illyk still wanted her? Of course he did, she chastised herself. He wouldn't give up easily on what he considered his property.

She struggled against him, but he only dug the blade in deeper and pulled her away. Away from Orna's body and towards the copse of trees.

"Let me go, you bastard!" She struggled harder, but it was futile. She was burnt out. Had this been the price of her magic? She didn't know.

She only wished she had more of it.

If only to burn one last human to the ground.

Her eyes stayed on Orna's lifeless body as he pulled her away. She forced herself to stare at her friend.

This is your fault, her mind screamed irrationally. It was always her fault. Perhaps it'd be better if they just gave her to the emperor—No! Her thoughts halted that direction.

The emperor despised the Fae, despised *her,* and he wanted her for a reason. The emperor was responsible for this, for this death and destruction.

And it was looking into the dark eyes of her friend that Shula realized that she could not give up so easily.

That there was still revenge to wreak.

She kicked out vigorously, ignoring the screaming pain in her limbs. She cried out, screaming for anyone who would hear. For anyone who could come. And she prayed like hell they would.

The blade pierced his flesh, and agony ricocheted up his entire body. Ryker grunted, the only sign he'd show that he was in pain. His whole body burned like the fires Shula trailed behind her as she ran away, obliterating every human in her wake.

Ryker wrapped his hand around the blade stuck in his side and pulled, shoving the human back as he did so. The human looked determined and afraid in equal measure. He should be afraid. He should be afraid because Ryker was a warrior before he was a healer, which meant that he had no qualms about taking a life.

He raised the sword in his own arm, metal clashing against iron. He gritted his teeth and nearly doubled over. The iron must have left traces inside him; Ryker knew he only had moments before he was completely weakened. But he couldn't afford to let himself fall. Shula had rushed away and somehow his gut told him that the Fire Dancer would find Orna. And he had to get to them both.

With a fierce cry, he pushed the human backwards, but didn't get the chance to end his life himself, because Clay appeared behind the human and held his hand up.

And when the human next opened his mouth, he crumbled to the ground as Clay drained him of his life force.

Clay opened his mouth and blood spilled from it, from his nose, and his eyes went bloodshot from the use of his power. Using the back of his hand to wipe his nose with impatience, he gestured at Ryker.

"Let's go," he demanded. "Shula went that way!"

Ryker's booted feet pounded against the warm ground as he followed Clay through dying embers of fire and Shula's madness. He ignored the wince of pain every step had him grinding his teeth and breathing through his nose. He knew he was losing blood and fast, but he had to push his discomfort aside.

They followed the trail of fire until they reached a cage. The first thing that hit Ryker was the stench of melted iron, followed by death. Death smelled cold and sweet. There was no other way to describe it. It was the lack of warmth, complete stillness that made the hairs over his arms stand on end.

It was then he knew they'd been too late for Orna.

But just in time to see a soldier holding the Fire Dancer to his chest with a sword pressed to her neck as he tried pulling her towards the copse of trees.

The human caught sight of them and pressed the blade tighter.

Blood dripped down her neck, and the sight of it had Ryker growling in a rage that was so sudden it surprised him. Her body sagged against him, and Ryker was old enough now to recognize the sight of a Fae with depleted power.

"Let her go," Clay ordered. His hand tightened around the sword in his hand as he took a step forward but stopped when the Fire Dancer cried out in pain.

"Clay!" Ryker's voice barked out in warning. A warning his friend read all too clearly in the sharp tone of his voice.

He's mine.

Ryker saw this man with his knife against a Fae, and his blood boiled and thirsted for vengeance.

He wanted to be the one to kill him.

"That's it," the human purred. "Stay right where you are. If any of you get close, I'll slit her fucking throat."

Ryker saw the moment fear flashed in the Fire Dancer's eyes. He let his eyes lock on hers and held her stare.

"Eyes on me," he growled low. Low enough that she could pick up the words, but they were oblivious to the human.

She hitched in a breath and understanding flashed through her golden-brown depths.

"He's taking me to the emperor!" Shula shouted, her voice firm. "He's not going to hurt me!"

"Shut up!" he hissed, jerking her back. In doing so, he sliced at her skin and she whimpered.

Ryker knew then that if the emperor wanted her, this human wasn't going to kill her. That didn't mean he wouldn't hurt her to get what he wanted, to save his own ass and get the both of them out of there.

Ryker didn't have any powers to save her, and Clay... He was staring at Ryker as if waiting for direction.

"We need him," Ryker whispered so only Clay could hear.

It was a command to stand down. Ryker's rule didn't supersede Clay's, and yet Clay listened and took a step back.

"Why does the emperor want her?" Clay demanded.

The human scoffed. "Wouldn't *you* like to know? Now fuck off. I'm taking her or she loses body parts."

Shula tried leaning away from the blade, but he held her too tightly. "No!" she screamed. Despite everything, she fought. Her legs kicked out, flailing as hard as her weakened body would allow her. "Let go of me, you bastard!"

But he was already pulling her away. Back further and further until he reached the line of trees.

The air behind the human shimmered and another step back had him ramming straight into Uric's chest.

The human barely had time to react. Uric was already wrapping his forearm around the human's throat and Julius appeared next to him, yanking at his arm to pull the sword away. With a single squeeze, Julius broke the human's wrist.

His cries rang out through the camp, and the minute his hold on the Fire Dancer loosened, her bare feet hit the ground in a wobbly sprint and Ryker was running, meeting her half way. Not once did her gaze stray from his as she collided against his chest. Like he was her protection. Like she somehow felt safe near him.

He couldn't fathom it, and the move shocked him. His fingers grabbed her chin and tilted her head up.

"Orna..." Her voice trembled.

"I know."

Tears swelled in her eyes, and Ryker pressed his palm to her chest. Her clothes were mere scraps, hanging on by simple, charred threads and she didn't even realize it. He laid his palm against her collarbones, his skin smearing the blood from her wound.

"Do not move, Fire Dancer," he barked.

And he let his magic heal her.

A warm tingle spread through Shula's neck, and the stinging pain and lethargy that had pulled at her whole body suddenly was gone.

Having his hand pressed to her skin spread heat through her that had nothing to do with his magic. Like a key falling into its corresponding lock, their eyes held. For a single second, everything faded away, including the pain.

A moment later it was gone as Ryker jerked away with a growl and stared down at her with such anger and hatred burning in his eyes. As if this had all been her fault. It was a look she was already growing accustomed to, but she still couldn't fathom how his expression could change so instantaneously.

With the spell broken, she turned away from him and all the sorrow came rushing back. Her legs gave out from beneath her, and she dropped to her knees next to Orna's body.

All the heartbreak came crashing back into her body. The impact had her gasping as sobs wracked through her. Her ash-and-blood covered hand trembled as she reached out to cup her friend's cold face.

"I'm sorry, Orna..."

A strangled sound escaped her lips, and the tears fell down her cheeks. It had been so long she felt since she last cried, and they spilled freely now. Her sorrow and heartbreak trailed down her cheeks, and at her knees lay the evidence of the emperor's cruelty and fear.

Death and blood.

Shula tried not to look at her battered body, at the blood covering her paling blue skin, the fingers twisted at odd angles, the burns of iron pressed to her skin in the shape of the bars of her cage.

Shula wanted to burn the whole thing to the ground. The whole camp, she wanted them to *burn.*

Her hair grazed across Orna's body, and she knew her friend could no longer feel it.

She was dead.

Just like everyone else in Shula's life ended up dead.

And perhaps this time hadn't been her fault, but if there were any survivors in this camp, they'd tell the emperor that Shula was with them, and she would bring death upon them. That would be on her hands.

Pushing that aside, Shula bent and lifted Orna into her arms, cradling her to her chest. She was so still, so quiet that Shula could almost convince herself that she was sleeping, but that wasn't the case.

The press of a hand against her shoulder tore her out of her sorrow. She turned and looked up into Valerio's dark eyes.

He wasn't staring at her with anger for disobeying his orders, but there was an infinite amount of sadness.

It broke her heart more.

"Let us leave this place," he urged quietly. "Let us put your friend to rest."

"What should we do with him, Prince?"

Valerio pulled his attention from Ryker and Shula with great reluctance. The two were a conundrum, and while now was not the time to think about it, he did. Magic appeared in the subtlest of shapes and forms. It lived in Mana, in the Fae, and even in the bonds they made.

He would never tell his men this, but there had been a reason he agreed to rescue Shula Azzarh from the temple. A promise the seer had whispered into his ear that ran through his bones and touched the very edges of his tattered soul. Of bonds as ancient and powerful as Mana itself.

Like the seer had known exactly how to seduce him. Like she could see the desires of his heart, see what went beyond protection of the Fae, of saving his race from extinction. She didn't just gently push past the surface but jumped into those darker parts with promises of forever.

But one look at Shula Azzarh and Valerio knew the seer had been lying to him. Now, Valerio had to contend with the fact that he'd lied to his comrades, even to Uric, who knew everything about him.

If they knew the real reason why he'd gone for her hadn't been some selfless desire to save his race at all but something else, they would have him stripped of his imaginary crown and banished from what was left of their scattered court forever.

He'd not let that happen.

Lucky for him, the Emperor of Illyk wanted the Fire Dancer this badly, and so as long as *they* had her, the emperor would not. Unlucky for him, the emperor wanted her, and they had no idea why.

This soldier was the perfect way to finally find out.

Valerio turned to acknowledge Julius' words. The big ginger Fae was now restraining the human with very little effort. He'd relieved Uric of that duty. Uric appeared to be struggling with the darker aspects of using his magic.

Flicking his gaze back to the human, Valerio strode up in confident, angry strides until he was face to face with the soldier.

The human was either exceptionally stupid or brave. He did not recoil in fear at the sight of Valerio, but the Seelie Prince did not mind. After all, he had schooled his expression into neutrality so that no one could see what really lay beneath.

The soldier was rather unimpressive. Tall as far as humans went, but not as tall as the Fae. The armor he wore gave him bulk, and the helmet on his head hid most of his features. With viscerally controlled movements, Valerio reached his hands out and plucked the helmet off the man's head. The sting of iron brought with it a modicum of discomfort that he ignored.

The sound of the helmet hitting the earth at their feet made the man wince.

"What is your name?" Valerio's fingers wrapped through those blond strands of hair to yank his head back uncomfortably. Hatred burned in this man's eyes that didn't even make Valerio flinch.

You didn't live in this day and age without getting used to the humans' vehemence towards the Fae. But unlike Ryker, Valerio didn't let it cloud his judgment. He was perfectly aware that there were good humans just like there were evil Fae. No one was innately one thing or the other, but this man reeked of sin and blood.

He spat in Valerio's face. A glob of vile spit clung to his cheekbone and dripped down. "Fuck you, Esses bastard," he growled.

Uric's body jerked forward and Valerio held up a hand to stop him. If he gave the word, Uric would have his blade striking from the asshole up to his skull.

Valerio smiled and dropped his hand from the human's hair. A single swipe was all it took to clean his face and then he was staring up at Julius.

"He won't talk now, but perhaps we can persuade him to give us the answers we seek."

A laugh rumbled out of Julius' chest that couldn't be described as anything but deadly.

Horror washed over the man's features as he realized what was in store for him. "No," he begged. "Please!"

Shula's soft sobs of heartache reached him. He'd gotten a glimpse of Orna's body. Broken, bloodied, abused.

He let the glimmer of death shine through his expression and knew the taste of it permeated the human's tongue. The stench of fear and urine came next, and Valerio knew he was going to have fun breaking this man.

He didn't relish in cruelty, but it was a necessary evil. One he wouldn't mind imparting in this instance.

"Everything you gave to my people, you will find returned to you tenfold." With that, Valerio nodded at Uric who opened the portal back to camp where they would keep this scum for interrogation.

And avenge the deaths of his friends.

A Star in the Sky

Back at the camp, everything happened so slowly, it was as if time had stopped completely. They stepped from Uric's portal and were met with a crowd of crying, fear-filled eyes. Shula couldn't bring herself to meet a single one of them. She stared at nothing but Orna's body cradled against Valerio's chest.

The Seelie Prince had bent down only moments before, his hands gentle and firm as he pried Shula's fingers off of Orna's body, one by one.

"It is time to let go," he whispered. For a moment, he hadn't been the Seelie asshole who'd abducted her, but a friend sharing her grief.

It was with that in mind that she allowed Orna to be tugged away from her. He'd hoisted her up into his arms and walked in long legged strides right through the portal.

She looked so small and fragile against him, and she was so unmoving that there could be no mistaking she was dead.

Some of the men who'd gone to help hadn't returned either, and what bodies they could find were passed through the portal and laid on the ground. The humans' death count had been higher, but this hurt more.

Cries of sorrow and heartbreak rang out like a somber dirge. There would be no music to lead their souls back to Mana, though. There would be no funeral rights, no words to declare how much they would be missed.

Valerio stepped towards the center of the camp and laid Orna's body gently on the ground. Clay came beside him and laid down a bag. They'd gathered what body parts they could of Des; they'd died together and should be burned together.

Then came the rest of the bodies. One by one they were laid out next to one another. Soft cries filled the night, and then Valerio's voice echoed.

"Fire Dancer," he declared. Shula snapped her gaze up. "Put them to rest."

She knew what she was asking, and Shula searched inside herself to find the same strength as before, but she felt hollow. No more rage lived inside her, just emptiness left behind. She thought if she'd stayed away that there wouldn't be pain when the inevitable happened. Shula had only known Orna a handful of days, but the blow of her death felt like a lifetime of friendship yanked away in a single, bloody instant.

And it left her hollow inside.

Yet for Orna, she *needed* to do this. It was an ache that would never be healed, guilt that she would probably never assuage, but Orna deserved a funeral. She deserved to be sent off with the love of her life, her mate, into the beyond. So, Shula pulled whatever scraps she had left and shot her hand out to the bodies.

They caught fire quickly, the flames charring their flesh. It was the only goodbye they'd get. The closest thing to a funeral they could afford to have.

"Let's go," Valerio announced. "It is no longer safe here."

And they wouldn't even stay to watch their bodies drift back to Mana.

Shula sucked in a breath as she watched the flames flicker. In them, she wore she could hear the laughter of her friend. Like her soul was rising happily through the fire.

To give Shula one last goodbye.

And watching Orna's body burn was like watching a sunrise chase away the darkness until there was nothing left of it, winking out every light until not a single star was left in the sky.

Castle Aileach

They packed quickly and in silence. The whole camp's mood was vastly different now from the way it had been hours ago. Even Shula felt drained.

They hadn't yet tended to the wounded, because Valerio didn't want to waste any more time where they were. If the humans had found them, then more might come after. They couldn't go on foot, either. They'd have to portal.

Uric looked beyond exhausted, more so than the rest of them.

Valerio stared at his friend and whispered words that Shula caught in passing. "Are you sure you can do it?"

They discussed things silently for a few moments before Uric spread his arms wide and the air behind him shimmered as a portal was opened.

Where they wanted to go, Shula wasn't sure, but she didn't have a choice, and she felt like she'd lost the fight in her anyway. It wasn't like she had anywhere else to go. It wasn't like anyone was coming to save her.

So when the portal completely opened, she helped them usher everyone through. It was the least she could do. Grief rushed through her chest and clogged her throat, making it hard to breathe. It was made worse by the sad smiles Clay threw her way or Ryker's glares.

She could read between the lines of the glares far easier than she could the smiles.

It was like Ryker blamed her and let it be known through the expression on his face. Like he thought her sorrow wasn't genuine. Or maybe his anger stemmed from something—somewhere—else. Whatever it was, he didn't stop frowning in her direction, but she ignored the feelings he twisted within her gut and focused on what needed to be done.

One by one, they walked through the portal. The longer it was held open, the more Uric gasped. She watched the transformation settle over him with the smallest bit of fascination. Smooth skin wrinkled, and it was like watching parchment crumble in a slow grip. His silver hair began falling in wisps over his shoulders. Liver spots appeared on his hands.

"Hurry along," Valerio snapped impatiently, his worried eyes on his friend.

Once everyone had gone through, all that was left was Julius, who held tightly to the bound and gagged human prisoner, Ryker, Clay, Valerio, Uric, and Shula.

Clay settled a hand against her lower back, drawing her attention to his bright green eyes.

"Ready, Fire Dancer?" he asked in gentle tones.

She wasn't. But she didn't have a choice. She had nowhere else to go, and with the humans hot on their heels, she wouldn't risk leaving.

Nodding once, he urged her towards the portal, passing by Ryker who glared between them, a sight that went ignored by both her and Clay.

With a deep breath, Shula and Clay stepped through the shimmering air and arrived on the other side.

She wasn't sure what she'd been expecting, but she was sure it hadn't been to land on the top of a soft blanket of white. Her body sank into it, the sensation of cold assaulting her like the sharp ends of a thousand knives. The pervasive sense of cold had her shivering instantly. Shula wasn't used to freezing climates since the circus always migrated away from cities before the snow could hit, especially in the north of Illyk.

Pushing herself up to her bare feet, she kept her footing only to realize she was still in the charred remnants of her outfit from before. In their haste to leave camp, she'd left her garments behind. Perhaps the last bits of Orna she'd ever come to possess, and she'd left them behind.

The thought settled worse than the cold somehow.

Brisk wind slapped against her skin, hauling her from treacherous thoughts. Eyes squinting, she looked through the blurry maelstrom of snow and ice. Footsteps scrunched around her, but she focused instead on the darkness of her surroundings and not the people.

They were in the mountains, at the very tip of them where the peaks touched the sky and the frost reigned like its own special hell. She felt the torture of it against her body, numbing her senses.

"Shit, Shula!"

Warm arms wrapped around her body, but she hardly felt them. The cold hit fast, and she was all but naked. Wind whistled like a constant horn, so Clay had to scream to be heard above the noise.

"Let's get you out of this cold!"

He moved, and she twisted her head slowly to catch a glimpse of him shrugging out of his tunic and pulling it over her stiff arms. It brought little warmth, but it left him naked from the waist up.

He didn't appear annoyed by this, though. The wind tousled his blond strands of hair against his forehead and cheeks. Her gaze skimmed over his bare body. It definitely wasn't the time or place to ogle him, but seeing the rigid set of muscles that tapered down to a thin V line of his waist made her eyes almost bug out of her head.

She tore her gaze away to his face, only to catch him staring at her. He winked and her face heated, but he immediately threw his arm around her shoulders and tugged her close.

"Come on," he urged. "The stronghold isn't far from here."

Questions burned at the tip of her tongue, but they froze with the biting cold. She decided to keep quiet until she was near a roaring fire, hoping they'd come to one soon.

Clay guided her along, rubbing his palm up and down her arm to get her blood circulating. She wondered what would happen if she let a sliver of her power loose, but then decided against it. She was still feeling a bit depleted from before. All her superficial wounds had healed the moment Ryker had placed his palms against her collarbones. She'd felt a bit of her energy come back to her as well, but that fight had been brutal. Her power had exploded, and it left her body feeling odd in the aftermath. She couldn't quite describe it.

Magic felt like... like a soul inside her. Like some separate part of her soul that clung inside her, down to the marrow of her bones. As essential to her body as the blood flowing through her veins, and yet she could *feel* it like it was its own being. Right then, it felt *tired.* Overworked like sore muscles after dancing for a week straight.

They trudged through snow, her feet and toes numbing more and more after each step. Shula wasn't the only one. Everyone in the procession shivered as though unaccustomed to the cold, or perhaps it was because it was unexpected.

"We're almost there, Fire Dancer," Clay whispered, his lips against her ear.

Her teeth chattered. She couldn't feel her feet anymore and it made walking difficult. She stumbled, snow kicking up to her knees. She felt the cold down to her bones, and her magic was so dormant, there was absolutely no hope at all that she could access it.

"Shit," Clay cursed.

A moment later, she felt warm hands wrap around her and lift her from the snow. She went, burrowing close to the thick wall of muscle that held her and inhaled the scent. Like herbs and spice and blood...

Her eyes snapped up to look into the familiar scarred face of Ryker. He grunted with each step he took and ignored her. Shula frowned. She hadn't even realized he was the one to pick her up. It was surprising, to say the least, especially with those glares and growls he gave her constantly.

"You should've given her your shoes instead, dumbass," he growled, but this time it wasn't directed at her, but at Clay. "Her toes are frozen."

"W-what d-d-do you c-c-care?" she chattered.

His arms flexed around her, and the scowl on his face deepened until a crater damn near appeared between his eyebrows. "I don't."

Of course he didn't.

But sometimes it felt like he did.

Sometimes it felt like he used these moments to his advantage just to put his hands on her. Just so the others wouldn't suspect he actually gave a shit about Shula. Maybe she was just delusional, because despite the strange pull both Shula and Ryker seemed to have that made them gravitate towards one another, she hated him. He hated her. It was the way it should be.

He was too big, too frowny, too *mean.* And she saw the way he stared at her ears with disgust. As if he could ever know what she had to do to survive, the things she had to give up, the feelings she had to betray to live. She'd watched her parents get taken, and she had no doubt they were dead. Those who entered the iron camps never came out. She only wondered if they suffered and prayed that they hadn't.

Ryker couldn't possibly understand her feelings, her fears, her own culpability. He didn't deserve to know. Whatever she'd confessed under the allure of Fae wine didn't matter, so she doubted he'd want to swallow the rest of her history.

At some point, Shula must have dozed off with those angry thoughts in mind. She awoke with a start as Ryker jostled her awake. He barely took the time to wake her up fully before he was placing her on her feet. She stumbled, groaning at the pins and needles sensation creeping up her legs.

After straightening, it took all but a moment for her to take in her surroundings. They were no longer in the snow, but she could still feel the breeze flittering ice through the massive arched doorways behind her. She turned and watched as two Fae pushed it closed with a squeak.

Her feet were pressed on stone floors that matched the drab, crumbling walls. A fire roared in a nearby massive hearth, and the people's footsteps milling about echoed up to the cavernous ceiling. Candles tapered across walls and provided dull illumination.

It was a castle, that much was obvious, with broken, boarded up windows that the cold snuck through. Shula's gaze wandered around the space with curiosity. Fae and humans bustled around; newcomers she didn't recognize walked up to their little group with blankets and furs. They proceeded to wrap them around the wet and shivering people.

A small female Fae with green skin and twisting horns that protruded from her forehead came towards Shula and threw the blanket around her shoulders. Enveloped in instant warmth, she pulled the ends of the blanket together, wrapping herself tighter in it.

Wings snapped out from behind the female's back, clear and shimmering; they buzzed at a rapid pace, and she flittered in a circle around Shula's body, not asking permission before she pulled her hair out and began wringing it out and letting the water splatter on the ground.

She chattered rapidly in a voice that sounded like fluttering insects, and Shula didn't understand a bit of it.

"She'll be showing you to your quarters," Clay explained, appearing suddenly beside her.

"Where are we?" Shula was glad her teeth had stopped chattering.

"This is our Fae stronghold, Castle Aileach. We bring Fae and human alike here to protect them from the Emperor of Illyk."

She turned in a slow circle, gazing up at the place. It was... drab. Yet it had a warm feel to it despite the dull tones.

A sharp, piercing cry echoed through the castle, capturing Shula's attention. A Fae man dropped to his knees, face scrutinized in pain. He grasped for his midsection, where blood seeped through the material of his jacket and stained his hands.

"Fuck!" Ryker growled, pushing his way over to the fallen Fae. He laid him back on the ground and, in a careful move, ripped his jacket and shirt, tearing at the material to display his gaping wounds. "Fuck!" Ryker turned his grave eyes towards Clay. "There's a chunk of iron in the wound. I can't heal him with it stuck in there." Then he got up and snapped at the serving Fae who had all come to help. "Get him to a room. Put all the sick together so I can tend to them. Now!" They rushed to obey his brusque command. Shula watched with barely veiled fascination as he stopped another fluttering Unseelie. "I'll need water and cloth, things to dress and change wounds. Herbs, boiled water, ice, and all the helping hands I can get."

Movements became blurred as everyone rushed to do Ryker's bidding. The injured were carted away up a staircase and down a hall, while those who were fine were pulled near the hearth to warm up.

Shula stared after Ryker, watching him take hulking strides up the stairs. She was staring so intently, she noticed he was walking with the slightest limp.

"Miss, are you hurt? Miss?" The fluttering green Fae was suddenly there in Shula's line of vision. Black, worried eyes glided down the length of her body, as if trying to assess the damage.

"I'm fine," Shula croaked. "Ryker—"

"His power is healing," Clay supplied, the smirk evident in his tone. "In case you didn't realize that yet."

"We should help him." She couldn't get the image of him limping out of her mind, or the image of the Fae man dropping to his knees. Of blood. Of Orna's bruised and beaten body. So much death, so much blood. And she was helpless to do anything about it.

"Nah, he doesn't like us in his space. Growly asshole."

"Come, come." The green Fae tugged at Shula, edging her towards the direction of the fire. "Let us warm you, miss."

All her life she'd been helpless. She did nothing but watch as they carted her parents away, just like she did nothing but watch when that old human had died for her, and the same went for Orna and Des. She always felt controlled through her movements, but this was something that wouldn't be solved with a dance. And Shula didn't just want to sit around by the fire and not do something.

Who cared if Ryker got upset? Help was help, and there were so many injured. What if the Fae with the iron in his body died? Iron was poisonous in direct quantities; it could kill him before they got a chance to operate.

Decided, Shula tossed the blanket from her shoulders and darted towards the staircase. She barely heard Clay's shout behind her. Her feet pounded, the pain jarring up to her knees. She didn't care. Shula followed the retreating footsteps and caught up in time to see them being laid down on thin cots on the floor.

"What the fuck are you doing here? Get out!" Ryker was on his knees by the Fae with the iron inside him. His hands were covered in blood, the panic evident in his dark expression. But it wasn't to him Shula looked at. It was at the Fae male, twisting in agony.

His cries set Shula into motion. She rolled the sleeves of Clay's borrowed tunic up to the elbows. "Where do you want me?" she asked, grim determination set in her stance.

Ryker looked inclined to argue, but the male let out another wail. Ryker jerked his head to the side. "Wash your hands with warm water and rub alcohol over them as disinfectant. Bring my forceps and alcohol. Now."

Shula dodged past the helping Fae and the injured on the floor, rushing to do what Ryker had ordered. There was a station in the back of the dry room with a table and all the instruments on top of it. She quickly went to a basin of warm water and scrubbed from her hands up to her elbows before rubbing them with alcohol. She grabbed the forceps and stared at them for a moment before decided to disinfect those too, just in case. After bundling everything in her arms, she ran back to Ryker and dropped to her knees beside him.

He let out a curse. "I need fucking light!" Immediately following his request, a bright cluster of floating lights that emitted buzzing noises hovered over them, illuminating the Fae.

His wound was grotesque and fleshy, and blood oozed from it onto Ryker's hands.

"Forceps," he ordered.

Shula's fingers trembled as she dropped them into his awaiting hand.

"Alcohol."

As she handed that to him, she said, "I already disinfected them."

He grunted in response then tipped the bottle over directly onto the Fae's wound. He screamed. Shula winced. "Warn a Fae next time," she mumbled.

Ryker had no comment. His entire focus was on the task at hand. For the next few moments, they worked in silence until the iron and any remaining shards were out of the Fae's body. Only then did Ryker place his palm over the wound. Then the room was filled with light. Glowing, white-golden light that rivaled what emitted from the twinkling Fae floating above them.

And it felt like the softest sting, like a drifting cold breeze in the summer heat. It was an all-consuming calm that had tears prickling behind Shula's eyes.

The light shimmered and slowly died. When it did, Ryker doubled over gasping, a sound he immediately sucked in and held. And the wound? It was completely gone. Unmarred skin lay where gaping flesh had once been. Not even a scar was left behind.

Ryker pushed himself to his feet, and Shula noticed how he wobbled slightly. But he didn't stop to breathe or to rest. For the next hour, he barked orders that she obeyed. Getting cloth, washing patients, disinfecting tools and wounds, and all the while Ryker healed.

It was a fascinating transformation, to see wounded flesh mend itself with the power of his magic, the way it wove together like string in a tapestry.

By the time Ryker got around to tending to the last patient, Shula was exhausted. She wanted to fall asleep on her feet, and it took everything she had to drag herself towards the entrance of the room and stand there. She was hypnotized by Ryker. He was such a big man; it was hard to imagine how he could be so gentle with others. It was so at odds with his scowling demeanor.

Every time he healed, he gritted his jaw in what looked like pain. As if...

"Pain is the price of his magic."

Shula startled at the voice and turned to see Clay who propped his shoulder against the doorway. He didn't meet her gaze, but he stared at Ryker like he was a fascinating, rare creature.

"To heal them and restore the balance, he takes their pain onto himself," Clay continued. "The pain and the—"

"The scars," Shula finished for him, her eyes widening with realization.

Of course.

Of course.

That's why he had the scars.

"So many of them..." At least that she could see. There were probably more, too. More she couldn't see. The wound from the first Fae he'd healed alone would leave a scar the size of her fist on his abdomen, she was sure of it.

"He is kind. Some would say too kind."

Shula wanted to snort at that but stopped herself. As much as she wanted to poke fun at the notion, she couldn't. Because it was true. Or at least, it had to be. Only a kind Fae would look out for others, would constantly heal them despite the pain it brought himself and the twisted deformities it left behind.

And her injuries? He'd healed those too. Of that she had no doubt. Was that what the tingling sensation had been when his palms explored her collarbones? And what about the injuries when they'd dragged her unconscious body through a portal and to that first safe house?

Ryker had healed her, even though he obviously hated her.

If that wasn't selfless, she didn't know what was.

Ryker stood up. Most of those who had been sick were sleeping, but those who were awake called out their gratitude. He didn't stop to accept their good graces or wishes. He all but stumbled passed their forms.

He barreled his way towards the door where both Shula and Clay stood and stopped.

"Move!" The word was a growl of rage.

Shula started to take a step back but froze when she saw his shirt dripping crimson. "You're hurt." She reached for him without realizing what she was doing. It was instinct, she supposed, after spending the better part of an hour dealing with wounds, to want to see this one as well. Before she could even touch him, however, Ryker shouldered past her quickly.

The action caused her to ram into Clay, whose arms shot out to hold her steady. Ryker growled and stormed down the hall like a hulking brute.

"The downside to his power is that he cannot heal himself."

"Shit."

What must Ryker be feeling? He'd healed her and every single person, Fae and human both, in this room, depleting his own energy, absorbing their pain and scars, all while holding in his own. But he didn't have to go through the pain alone. She could help. All he had to do was guide her through the process.

Fae were quick healers; quicker than humans, anyway. But they could still be wounded, could still be hurt, killed.

Her feet moved after him. Even injured, he was fast, turning down the castle hallways at a rapid pace that had her panting to keep up with. With harrowing speed, she burst towards him. He turned just before she reached him, and she slammed into his chest.

Grunting from the pain of the impact, Ryker took a step away from her. His hand cradled his wound, and she could see the blood flowing between his fingers.

"Let me look at th—"

"Fuck off!"

Shula reared back at his shout, but somehow it was the angry look in his eyes that hurt worse than the words. It was a look he hadn't hid from her before but somehow seemed amplified all of a sudden. Disgust. It was the same look Fanny had given her when she found out what Shula really was.

That look seared her soul in half and she didn't even know why.

She thought they'd shared a sort of camaraderie in that room. Healing together. More the fool she then to think that she could ever be close to one of her captors. She was a fool for forgetting who they were. That the only reason everyone in there had been hurt was because of them in the first place.

The only reason Orna was dead was because they wanted to play heroes instead of accept the hand the world had dealt them.

"I'm just trying to help." She hated that her voice quivered. That she felt weakened by his outburst when, really, she should feel angry instead.

"I do not need your fucking help, Fire Dancer," he spat. "Nor do I want your filthy hands on me."

Her rage shot up, mind flashing back to Fanny, to the reaction *she'd* had when Shula extended a hand for help. Shula had felt it like a blow and *cowered* instead of giving herself the time to feel the rage she rightfully deserved.

Suddenly Ryker's gaze became Fanny's. They blurred together in an angry mesh. Either she was too human for one or too Fae for the other, and it wasn't fair that she was receiving this treatment.

"You know what." She stepped close to him and shoved her palms against his broad chest, and he staggered back. "I am so fucking sick and *tired* of you treating me like shit, asshole!"

His eyes narrowed. "Treating you like shit?" He stepped closer. "You mean the way you've treated the entire Fae race by degrading yourself?" Ryker shook his head and snorted, a sound of wry amusement pushing past his lips.

"You hate me because of something I had no control over." Shula could barely hear her own words over the rapid pounding of her heart and her sharp inhalations. "I was a *child*! The decision was taken from me. My parents were murdered and this..." She pushed her hair out of her face to expose her ears. "This was done for my own survival. I don't know how you can't understand that!"

"I can understand perfectly fine. But you are no longer a child and still you hide that which should make you proud. You'd whore yourself out to the humans if it meant saving your life."

Her hand shot out before she could stop it, connecting to his face. The slap resonated through the castle, sounding louder than it actually had been. Her palm ached but she ignored the pain.

There were no words in her vocabulary to describe to him what she was feeling, and yet she tried anyway. "You're disgusted with me because I did what I had to do to survive. I had no one. Unlike you and your little Resistance. I've been on my own since I was *twelve*, Ryker. I'm not ashamed of what I've done because it means I'm alive." She sucked in a ragged breath, tasting salt on her lips.

Fuck.

She hadn't even realized she was crying.

She hadn't cried in years, and yet the exhaustion had taken its toll and the tears came uninhibited, unabashed, and Ryker stared at them like they were foreign and disgusting.

"No, Fire Dancer. I am disgusted with you because you are a coward. Perhaps you were a frightened child then, but you aren't any longer. You aren't *alone* any longer, either. You are surrounded by Fae and human alike who are willing to risk their lives for a better future while you'd rather stick your head in the sand and go back to a mediocre life on the run, with mediocre friends who would betray you for a sack of gold." He stepped closer and closer, until their chests bumped together, until she felt the blood from his body seep onto her shirt. "*That* is why you disgust me."

It hurt. Every word he spoke hurt because she couldn't deny their truth. Because wasn't that exactly what had happened? She'd survived and once it was discovered what she really was, she'd been tossed to the emperor's soldiers in exchange for money. Like she was property, like she had little value. Years of friendship gone. Just like that.

Fanny had betrayed her; the others at Piriguini's Circus would have, too. Deep down she knew that. Because every day all she heard were jokes at the expense of Esses, of Fae scum. And she'd laughed along right with them even when she died inside a little more each time.

But here among Fae? They protected her. Clay protected her, Ryker healed her, Julius laughed with her, and Orna had befriended her. She knew they'd rather die than hand her over to the Emperor of Illyk.

But Shula couldn't think of them in that positive light. Just because she'd made friends, shared Fae wine, and had a few laughs didn't mean they were completely innocent. It didn't mean they even saw her as a friend. She was their captive, a weapon that they didn't want the emperor to have.

So really, what was her purpose here? What was her purpose anywhere? She didn't have one. And that left her mind spinning. It left her more lost than she could ever be in foreign kingdoms. That she was nothing to no one, that she would always be labeled as everything other than what she really was.

Shula had nothing left. No words she could say to Ryker. He was adamant in his hatred, and while it stung her pride, there was nothing she could do to change it. Not even spend hours with him mending the sick. Not burning Orna's body. Not even offering to help his own wounds.

Fine.

She was too tired to continue this back and forth anyway, too resigned, too worn out. If he wanted to bleed out on the floors of Castle Aileach, then so be it. That was his business.

And she was a fool for even trying.

The Taste of Victory is Bitter

Ryker's heart was pounding. His side was aching, his magic depleted, and he could feel the traces of iron still in his blood.

And all he wanted to do was harm the Fire Dancer in every imaginable way. To keep her away from him, to get her to stop looking at him with varying degrees of severity in her expression.

Mostly, he wanted a fucking drink.

The Fire Dancer was a rather expressive female and easy to read. He saw her hatred for him burning clearly in her eyes, so he noticed when all emotion fell away. She hardened her features, tightened her jaw, and spun on her heel and stormed off.

She took all the warmth in the hallway with her and all the heat from his emotions, leaving nothing but a cold hollowness behind. He suddenly felt very tired and weak. Staggering a few steps, his back collided against the stone wall and he slumped against it, inhaling sharply.

Fuck, his whole body hurt. He felt like he was dying, but then that wasn't right either. He'd witnessed plenty of death in his lifetime. He knew exactly what it was like. Sometimes it was loud and painful, screaming agony that haunted dreams. Other times it was silent, a soul drifting in the shadows.

And death and pain weren't the same anyway.

But they did hurt a hell of a lot.

"Fuck," he groaned, pulling his palm from his abdomen. Blood stained his fingers and he grunted. That human had got him good. It was unfortunate his magic didn't extend to himself. But this? This was nothing compared to what others went through. He'd felt it all, had agonized through so many wounds that weren't his own and bared the scars so they wouldn't have to.

This was no different.

He took a steadying breath and pushed himself off the wall, slowly making his way to the room he used as his whenever he was in the castle. After cleaning and sewing his wound closed, knowing it'd heal in just a few days, he changed and went in search of a drink.

Things at the castle were quiet, somber. It was how he knew Valerio's father, the King of the Seelie, was not here. Had he been, they all would have been ushered into a meeting room as quickly as they could, sick and bleeding be damned.

King Ashera wasn't cruel. Not exactly. But he and Valerio both had a heavy weight on their shoulders. They needed armies, and the king meant to get them in whatever way he could. That meant the sick could wait but plans of battle could not.

Ryker made his way to the makeshift bar near the hearth where a blazing fire burned. He avoided looking too hard into the flames, because the dramatic flickering reminded him of Shula and her explosive magic.

He took a seat at a stool that groaned under his heavy weight and flagged down the Unseelie Fae behind the counter; a satyr named Ram who knew his order by heart. Without having to utter a word, a bottle and a glass were placed in front of Ryker.

He grunted his thanks and uncapped it to pour himself a generous amount. He brought the glass to his lips and felt the burn of the amber liquid down his throat.

Ryker was alone for all of a minute before the empty seat next to him became occupied with Julius' much bigger frame. After flagging down Ram and having an empty glass placed in front of him, Julius helped himself to Ryker's bottle.

"King will be here tomorrow." Julius brought the rim of his glass up to his nose for a sniff that left his face scrunched in a disgusted expression. "Valerio got word from Weylyn." He snorted. "Fucking Weylyn."

Fucking Weylyn, indeed. Ryker grunted his agreement and took another burning sip.

"They want us to wait on interrogating the human until after King Ashera gets here." He downed the contents in his glass and hissed. "Tastes like piss." And still, he poured himself a second. "So, how's your wound?"

Another sip. Another burn. "How'd you know about that?"

"Fire Dancer."

His reply was so casual and so filled with *something* that Ryker slammed his glass down on the table with a growl. Fuck. It was like he couldn't escape her. She was everywhere.

"Shit, Ryk, had I known she was such a sore subject I would've kept my mouth shut." Unlikely. But Ryker didn't say so. "She came up to Clay while we were talking, said someone should take a look at your wounds. All worried and shit even while she was frowning. Fuck you do to her, anyway?"

"Mind your damn business," Ryker snapped. He downed the rest of his drink and served another. He didn't usually indulge himself in more than one glass, but it had been a hard week.

"Would you clear that look off your face? We fucking won. A small battle, but we fucking won it."

But we lost Orna and Des. Ryker didn't have to say those words. They crept out in the spaces between the silence anyway. Any life lost in Ryker's opinion was a life wasted. Especially when they hadn't deserved it. Orna and Des were good, kind. He wouldn't admit this to anyone else, but he liked them.

He downed his drink.

Fuck this world. Fuck what Illyk had become. It was fear, violence, and death. As it had been for the past two hundred years in a war that was never ending. Many battles had been fought, and the humans had won. The Emperor of Illyk had driven the Fae into hiding, into camps, and to death. Now the Fae fought from the shadows.

So if fighting the humans in the shadows of the woods was a victory, then it tasted pretty fucking bitter on Ryker's tongue.

"All I gotta say is that your head is in your ass, brother." Julius pushed his glass away with the backs of his knuckles and rapped them against the surface of the bar. "She's here to stay whether you like it or not. Might as well make nice." And then he was walking away, leaving Ryker in his melancholy thoughts.

Of the Fire Dancer and of what the world had become.

Of Mairin.

He hated thinking about Mairin because thoughts of her dragged him into depths he didn't want to be in.

Sighing, he pushed the bottle away just as a dark blur hopped up onto the table next to him. He smiled at his familiar.

"Hey cat, where you been?"

His fingers stroked down the slick fur of her back. He hadn't named her; it didn't feel right to treat her like a pet. She was her own being and, while she was his bonded beast, he had no control over her or what she did.

The Fae valued animals as much as they valued nature, and bonding with one was as rare as finding a mate. Rarer, even. The connections were obviously vastly different. Bonding with a familiar was a friendly connection, a subtle magic that allowed a Fae and its animal to communicate sometimes mind-to-mind. A gift freely given by Mana.

While a connection to a fated mate was...

Ryker didn't know what it was, but he'd heard rumors that it was phenomenal. It was an explosion of sensations and emotions. It was finding your other half. Instant love. Instant attraction.

Like Orna and Des.

Ryker had met few fated mates in his time, and they'd appeared happy.

He didn't want to think about that, though.

He wanted to go back to his room and sleep because the day left him feeling dead inside. It had gifted him with memories of Mairin. Of her laughter, her smile, and everything in between.

Thinking about her was hell.

Perhaps Valerio was right and it was time to let go of the pain. But as long as that Fire Dancer was around, he'd never be able to let it go. Because she reminded him of a different time. A time when the war was just beginning.

And the Fae betrayed their own.

Shula spent the rest of the night in a shared room with other Fae from the procession. It made it hard to sleep, and when she could no longer stave off exhaustion, she fell into a nightmare-filled slumber that had her jolting awake the next morning in a cold sweat with the single sheet entangled around her legs.

Digging the heels of her hands into her closed eyes, she groaned, trying to push away the images she'd seen in her dreams. Orna's broken body, her horrific screams, chains of iron, robes of white and red...

She sat up in bed and dared to look around. Her room companions still slept; the quiet was almost a peaceful sound, were it not for her rolling thoughts.

After she left Ryker in the hall, she'd stupidly dared to go find Clay and let him know of his stubborn friend's wound. Clay had then led her to her room, where a change of clothes had been waiting for her. Once alone, she'd changed and slipped into the single cot that served as a bed and stared at the blank wall, lost in her thoughts.

Everything had spiraled out of control, and it had all started when those markings had appeared on her back. They still ached, but the pain seemed far away now, miniscule compared to everything else that was happening around her.

Her life had irrevocably changed, and she wasn't sure where to go from here. She was in the snowy mountains of Tuath, and it wasn't like she was an expert navigator. She wasn't even an expert at hiding. All her life she'd relied on hiding in plain sight, but if the Emperor of Illyk so desperately wanted her like everyone claimed, then she had no doubt her face was now plastered against every WANTED sign around Illyk. Now, if she wanted to hide, she'd have to become a solitary nomad.

The problem was escaping her captors, a feat she knew was almost impossible. They had her and didn't plan on letting her go. It seemed hopeless to want her freedom now.

A weak part of herself said that she should just give in to their demands. To stay. They were in the mountains, far away from the humans that wanted them dead. She was among her own kind. She could be safe here.

Safe?

She didn't know the meaning of the word.

A soft purring had her ripping herself from those thoughts. She looked down to find Ryker's cat sitting on her feet and staring at her with those bright eyes.

"Hey, little cat." Her voice was gruff with sleep. "What are you doing in here?"

Meow.

Shula chuckled and ran her fingers across the creature's head. It purred harder, angling its body so it was closer to Shula. It was calming, to be on the receiving end of affection and of giving it, too.

Meow.

"What's wrong, girl?"

She hopped out of Shula's reach and prowled to the doorway, which was opened a crack. She stopped and turned, her demon eyes demanding.

"I guess you want me to follow you."

Meow.

"I'll take that as a yes."

Throwing the sheet off the rest of the way, Shula slipped into the boots that had been waiting for her last night. They were made of some type of animal hide and lined along the edges with fur. The clothes were warm as well; soft on the inside, her shirt and fur-lined jacket kept out the harsh wind that seemed to breeze through the glassless windows of the castle. Her pants were regular workman's pants, a little tight around her ass and thighs, but she wouldn't complain.

She followed after the cat down the cold hallways of the castle, her attention snagging. It was rather empty, and she felt it deep in her bones, the lack of warmth. Like this wasn't really home but a space to settle in, and it showed.

The cat led her down a set of winding stairs down to the foyer they were received in the previous night and towards the opened front doors.

Breeze and snow filtered through. The cat stopped as if that was as far as she meant to go and wouldn't get her paws filthy with snow.

"So you won't go out there, but you want me to?" Shula cocked her head to the side.

She swore she could see the cat roll her eyes.

Fine, she'd go. But she felt it strange that she hadn't found one of her guards trailing after her at all yet. Perhaps they knew she wasn't idiot enough to escape through snowy mountains she knew nothing about. Because she knew they definitely didn't trust her.

Taking a breath, Shula stepped outside and into the cold.

The tip of her nose tingled at the assault. It was light out, everything made brighter by several feet of thick snow that expanded all across the landscape. She could hear voices outside, more than there were at the camp, but these sounded far away, and she couldn't make out what they were saying. In front of her, however, standing in a line side by side were Julius, Clay, Uric, Valerio, and Ryker.

Ugh. Shula turned to glare at the cat, only to find she was no longer there. *Traitor.*

"Morning, Fire Dancer."

She turned to find Clay smiling at her. She'd captured everyone's attention and it made her heart pound because she could feel Ryker's hateful gaze drilling holes into her skull.

She bit the inside of her cheek to avoid snapping at him, then forced a smile to her face that couldn't be considered anything but fake. "Good morning, Clay."

The beautiful Fae held his hand out to her. She hesitated; he saw it but still kept his palm up, waiting patiently.

When Shula finally decided to go to him, she tentatively placed her palm on his. Clay turned her hand over, and his lips skimmed across her knuckles. It was a gesture that was flirtatious, if the smirk on his mouth was anything to go by, as well as the wink he sent her way.

She rolled her eyes and pulled her hand from his. Almost without wanting to, her eyes found Ryker down the line of Fae males, and her face heated. He was staring at her with thick brows pulled together and his jaw clenched tightly. Like something about her interaction with Clay upset him.

She forced her gaze away from him to Clay's amused, glittering eyes. "What are you all doing out here?" she asked quietly.

"Waiting for the king."

Her body stiffened, and her lips pressed into a thin line. Fear beat a rapid pattern in her heart and her fingers trembled.

"The king?" She somehow managed to get the words out.

"Valerio's father. King Ashera. Uric's going to portal him here. He should be arriving in—"

His words were interrupted as Uric stepped forward and waved a hand around the air. It shimmered and the portal opened. Almost immediately, Fae stepped through it, bundled in dark, hooded cloaks.

"The king has arrived." Clay's lips pressed against her ear, and she jolted away from the contact.

Clay chuckled and pulled away.

The portal behind the newly arrived Fae closed. There were five of them, two on either side of the tallest who stood in the middle. They all lowered their hoods simultaneously, and it was the tallest who held Shula captivated.

He was an older Fae. Even with smooth skin and not a wrinkle in sight, that much was obvious. It was in the way he carried himself, his presence commanding respect. Long, dark brown hair curtained around a beautifully sharp face that looked similar to Valerio's. Everything about them was similar, and Shula knew he had to be the King of the Seelie Court. Except the king was broader than his son, with muscles that were more prominent and pressed against the material of his cloak.

And he looked meaner, if that were somehow even possible, his expression graver than Valerio's could ever be.

His black eyes flicked along the line of Fae males, who suddenly stood as rigidly as soldiers.

Valerio took a step forward first and bowed low to the waist. "Welcome back, Your Majesty."

"Rise." His voice was deep and as grave as his expression.

Valerio rose and met his father's gaze.

"How many lost?" the king asked.

"Only two."

The king's lips pressed together. "Prisoners?"

"One."

"Good." Then he turned and stared right at Shula.

She felt her whole body go rigid. It was like staring at a legend come to life and she had no idea how to react. She'd heard stories of Emperor Laurel of Illyk, but the King of Seelie had been little more than a myth until she met this group of Fae. She had no stories to base her assumption of him on. Was he cruel or kind? She had no idea. He cut a cruel and imposing figure, and it made a sliver of unease slide down her back.

"Shula Azzarh, I presume?" She swore she heard amusement in his voice.

"Yes."

She heard one of the Fae growl, though she couldn't be sure which one.

The king's brows pulled together, and his lips pressed into the thinnest of lines. "I may be a king without a crown or a throne, but I would think even you would know that I deserve a modicum of respect."

Her face heated.

Of course. He wanted her to bow to him. The thing was, Shula didn't want to. Why should she?

"All due respect, you were little more than a myth until a few weeks ago, so forgive me if I'm reluctant in your presence."

Why should she bow to someone who had done nothing for her? She harbored as much respect to him as she did the human royals, and she knew it showed in her disdainful features.

She had no respect for those who condoned the kidnapping of innocents. And if it would be the death of her, then so be it. After all, she wasn't safe anywhere.

For a moment, the only sounds that could be heard was the whistling of the wind and her own thumping heartbeat. She wondered what was running through the king's mind as he looked down at her with his cutting gaze.

He grunted. "Quite right." Then he turned away, dismissing her easily enough. "Let us feast in the war room. I'd have a word with you and yours, Valerio." And then the king was walking towards the castle, his entourage following behind him, save one.

Golden eyes stared at her intently, and the Fae man remained unmoving. He appeared to be paralyzed; his chest didn't even seem to be rising and falling with inhalations. His attention made Shula uncomfortable. Like he could see something inside of her that the others couldn't.

"Weylyn, this is Shula." Clay slapped a hand of the Fae's—Weylyn's—shoulder. The Fae didn't move.

He was tall, like most Fae males seemed to be in this group, but not muscular like them. He was lithe with brown skin and even darker hair that was in a long, loose braid hanging over his shoulder, revealing a single pierced ear with a gold hoop. Stubble darkened in a goatee around his mouth that was set in an unexpressive line.

"Um..." Shula felt his golden eyes piercing her soul. "Hello?"

Clay's eyes rolled. "Greaaaat..."

"Is he okay?" Shula asked. He still hadn't moved, and it was starting to make tingles to slide over her skin.

"Fine, just being an asshole." Clay grabbed his arm. "Come on, the king wants to talk to us." He tugged, hard, and that seemed to pull Weylyn out of his stupor. His eyes rolled, he blinked, and shook his head back and forth.

"You good?" Clay asked him with what seemed like amusement, but it also tasted a bit like a warning, though Shula didn't understand it.

Weylyn nodded but otherwise didn't speak.

"Great." Clay clapped him on the back again. "Let's go. King Ashera needs us." And he guided him in the same direction the king had gone.

Shula watched them go, questioning what the hell all that had been about. It had been an odd encounter, and she swore Clay had been slightly wary around him.

Too tired to guess, Shula filed inside after them.

Now that the king was here, her fate would be made clearer. Perhaps she could demand he release her. She had no idea where she'd go, what she'd do, but she knew she at least had to try.

Freedom Comes with a Price

The feast was set out before Valerio's father on the rickety table of their meeting room. Roasted boar, potatoes, and onions dripping in gravy made it a simple affair. Black eyes scanned the meager meal without much reaction, but Valerio knew his father well enough and could see the disgust shimmering behind the mask.

This was only a fraction of what they could have had. Of what they once had so long ago when the courts had still been intact and the Ashera family bathed in riches. This meager meal would have been much different two hundred years ago.

Besides roast pig, there would have been fish bathed in the richest cherry sauce, oysters, soups, desserts filled with chocolate and fruits, sweet tarts, and an abundance of Fae wine.

Now they were forced to survive on scraps.

The resentment in his father ran deep. Valerio could feel it every time they spoke. Sometimes Valerio felt the very real, very heavy weight of their future upon his shoulders, and sometimes, he felt as though his father was merely looking for the scattered Fae, not because he particularly cared that they were going extinct, but because he missed the richness of the life they'd had before and needed them to help get it back.

Of course, Valerio never said that. They were thoughts that were purely his and his alone. He lifted his head and caught Weylyn's gaze from across the table. The Fae male was as still as a marble statue, his golden eyes looking but unseeing in a way that made Valerio grit his teeth together.

Fuck.

He needed to remember to guard his thoughts better because now, surely everything he thought would be repeated to his father.

Careful to keep his mind blank, he faced his father again. After the king was served a hefty amount of food, he picked up an onion between his thumb and forefinger. The gravy slid down to his wrist, but he ignored the subtle lack of decorum as he plopped it into his mouth and crunched.

When he finished chewing, he faced his only son. "Speak," he ordered.

As if he didn't already know what had happened.

The night before when they'd arrived, Weylyn had contacted Valerio with his mind-linking magic, asking for all the details. So Valerio gave them. Now, he would give them again.

When he finished recounting the events, he waited with bated breath to see what his father would say. He could never gauge the mood the king would be in. Sometimes he was volatile, explosive, and those were tiring days.

"The human is in the dungeons?"

Valerio grit his teeth together. "Yes, father."

"Hmm..." He was quiet another moment, chewing and contemplating in silence. Finally, he swallowed and stroked his chin.

Valerio held his breath the entire time, too afraid to interrupt his father's musings yet too impatient to hear what he had to say. He adjusted his posture.

"Find out what he knows." The king turned to Ryker. "Keep him conscious enough to find the truth and take Weylyn with you."

Valerio swore he could hear Julius groaning.

Weylyn wasn't their favorite Fae simply because none of their secrets were safe with him around. He knew too much. But in this instant, he'd be perfect to help interrogate the human. Any secrets he held, Weylyn would be able to pull them out of his mind.

"Excuse me, Your Majesty?" Shula's voice piped up from down the length of the table.

Every single eye in the room turned towards the Fire Dancer. Valerio held his breath. She hadn't interrupted the king, but she was an outsider. Everyone currently in the room was a part of King Ashera's inner circle. She was their hostage; however well they treated her, she wasn't a part of this. The only reason she was in the room was because his father was intrigued, because the Emperor of Illyk wanted her. Valerio's father wanted to know why.

"Yes?" the king asked.

"You have to let me leave."

Valerio sucked in a quiet breath and looked at his father, waiting to see what he would do for that blatant order a commoner was giving him.

Slowly, he shoved the plates aside and pressed his knuckles into the surface of the table and pushed himself to a standing position. His entire expression morphed into something deadly. "Oh, I *have* to, do I?"

"You do." Her voice didn't so much as waver. She portrayed self-confidence, more so than she'd shown against Valerio himself. "I am not your prisoner. You have to let me leave."

Then Valerio's father did something strange.

He laughed.

A loud belly laugh. He pushed himself away from the table and lowered himself back into his chair. He wiped at his eyes with the back of his hand.

"Ah, the hilarity." He sighed, composing himself. "Shula Azzarh, can you tell me why the human emperor wants you?"

Valerio looked at Shula then. He could tell she was chewing on the inside of her cheek. "I have no idea."

"No?" Valerio's father tapped his fingers against the table. "There are so many possibilities... Here are a few..." He held up one finger. "He wants to keep you as his personal Fae whore."

Valerio closed his eyes and sighed. Shula gasped.

The king held up a second finger. "He wants to kill you and mount your body parts above his throne." He held up a third. "He and this mysterious Brotherhood plan to use you in their catacombs and keep you chained there for their own sinister plans." He smirked. "Do any of those options sound at all appealing to you?"

Shula's voice trembled. "No."

"No. Because what you would suffer at the hands of that Fae-hating lunatic is worse than what you could ever suffer here. So the answer is no, I do not have to let you leave. Because keeping you here means the humans cannot have you. Would you rather be used and killed by the human emperor or safe and protected by us?"

Shula didn't answer, but she didn't have to. Everyone present in the room knew what the better option was. Despite his father's cruel way of phrasing things, Valerio knew it was for Shula's own good. She'd be safer in their clutches. She just couldn't see it yet.

"Now, if no one else wishes to disrespect their king, I believe you have human scum to interrogate."

Valerio stood and bowed to his father. "Of course, Your Majesty."

They all stood to make their exit, Shula slower than the rest. "Your Majesty?" she began in a much more subdued tone, though Valerio could hear the anger beneath it.

"Yes, Shula?" King Ashera's eyes were shining with begrudging humor.

"I ask that I be present during his interrogation. If... if he knows why the Emperor of Illyk wants me, I think I deserve to know why."

Everyone held their breath once again. It wasn't every day Valerio encountered someone brave enough to demand things of his father.

"That you do. Very well, bear witness to it. We will find out what the human wants with you soon enough."

And just like that, they were all dismissed. Valerio could have told Shula she would have just been wasting her breath. His father bent to the will of no one, not even to the will of his own son. He was ruthless and unkind, and he more than anyone knew that all freedom came with a price.

He would not grant Shula's so easily.

If he even granted it at all.

For the first time since they found her, Valerio started to feel a modicum of guilt for keeping her tethered to them. Not because she was their well-kept prisoner, but because she'd been forced to endure this.

The sarcastic wrath of his father.

And Shula Azzarh might not know it yet, but that was the worst punishment of all.

Torture in a Touch

The dungeons of the castle were dark, dank, and cold. Not cold enough to kill the human from hypothermia, but cold enough to have his teeth chattering incessantly.

Bare-chested and in nothing but his pants, the human's arms were bound in chains that hung him from the ceiling. Every time his body shivered, the chains holding him up rattled.

They dismissed the guards watching him, leaving Clay to open the door. He let it swing wide open, and one by one they filed in. Valerio strode through first, followed by Julius, Weylyn, Ryker, and the Fire Dancer.

Ryker knew having so many in a single cell was overkill, but it drove fear into enemies' hearts. That's what mattered. Nothing else, and he couldn't let dark thoughts consume him. Not now, and not in here where anyone could see.

"Wakey, wakey, little soldier," Julius chirped, his voice echoing through the cavernous, cold space. His big hand slapped against the human's cheek. There was a hint of cruel amusement in his every move. Ryker knew that Julius enjoyed this. He enjoyed making people like this soldier suffer, and it never mattered what Julius did to the enemies of the Fae, because what the humans did to the Fae was always worse.

Ryker just had to picture Orna's body and what was left of Des'.

It was those images that would get him through what they had to do next.

The human jolted awake at the contact, though Ryker doubted he'd really been sleeping. Not with this cold.

Julius smiled at him. "Aww, did I wake you from your beauty sleep? Sorry about that. Prince wants to talk to you."

The human shivered, because the way Julius said *talk* implied something much more sinister than a mere conversation. And it was.

Once the human's gaze was riveted on Valerio, Julius stepped back, though not before making a show of pulling his dagger from his holster and picking at his nails with it.

"I assume you know why we are here?" Valerio began unbuttoning his jacket, his movements controlled and careful. The human watched his fingers go down the line. One by one. Valerio shrugged out of the garment and tossed it to Clay, who folded it over his arm.

This was like a dance, done so many times that they all knew their roles, their steps. It was all in perfect memorization, although the Fire Dancer had no idea what to expect. She stayed behind them, her breath clouding in little pants in front of her as she took it all in.

"If you do not know, then I will tell you." Valerio folded the sleeve of his shirt up to his elbow on one arm, then the other. The prince had to be cold, but he showed nothing except a hard, deadly exterior. "We are here because we have questions. Questions you are going to answer."

"N-n-n-no..." The human's teeth chattered loudly.

Valerio's eyes narrowed into thin slits. "Let us get this one thing straight. I ask a question, you answer, otherwise that mouth of yours stays shut. If you cannot remember that, then... well..."

On cue, Julius stepped forward and swiped his dagger across the human's flesh. He gasped as a slow stream of blood pooled down his stomach.

Ryker swore he could hear the Fire Dancer whimper.

As if she didn't know cruelty. Perhaps she didn't. Perhaps she was new to this type of treatment, but she better get used to it because this was how their world worked. They had to be cruel or die. There was no other way.

Julius stepped back, cleaning the blood across the hem of his jacket.

"Am I understood?" Valerio asked calmly.

The human nodded. "Y-y-yes."

"Good. Now, start by telling us your name."

"P-P-Philip O'Hare."

Valerio smiled. "Good. Were you following us in the woods or was that purely coincidental? And do not presume to lie to me. Weylyn here will know."

The human whimpered once. "W-w-we were under orders to scope out the w-w-woods."

"Why?"

"Our c-c-captain s-said he b-believed there were Fae s-safe houses. We caught wind of you instead."

"We covered our tracks."

It wasn't a question, but the human answered anyway. "W-w-we c-caught the Fae woman and the human man together. They traveled far from your c-camp. That's how we knew..."

Ryker tried not to give his prince a pointed look. He'd told him to speak with Orna and Des. Because they decided to get romantic in the woods, they'd died.

Rage surged up inside him. On their behalf, but also at them. How could they have been so stupid? Mated couples had no sense.

He dared not turn his gaze on Shula to see how she was reacting to all of this.

"Who killed the Fae woman?" Valerio asked.

That question seemed to suck all the air from the room.

The human took too long to answer because Valerio's fist shot out, landing a punch straight into the human's side. Ryker heard the ribs crack, heard one of them pierce a lung.

"How did you kill the Fae woman?"

These weren't standard questions. Ryker knew this was getting personal for Valerio. Because Orna and Des had been under his protection. A young couple in love that he *should've* spoken to about wandering off. But he hadn't, and now they were dead. As much as Ryker wanted to blame Valerio for it, he couldn't bring himself to do that. He wasn't the one who'd killed them. That had been the humans. And for that they would pay.

"I—I d-d-don't—"

Valerio's fist struck against his cheekbone, and it shattered.

Fuck. Ryker tensed, already anticipating the pain.

"Did you take a shot at her?" Valerio's eyes almost looked manic now. "Did you slice her up? Put her in the cage? Do not lie to me. A pretty Fae woman, I bet all you little soldiers wanted a shot at roughing her up. What. Did. You. Do?" Each word was accentuated with a punch over his body.

The human jerked, hanging his head.

"Valerio!" Ryker snapped.

The prince whipped around to glare at Ryker. He hated interrupting his prince, especially when this scum deserved everything that was dished out to him, but... The Fire Dancer was present, and Ryker didn't think she needed to know the sordid details of what had happened to Orna.

Ryker didn't even want to know them. Unfortunately, he *did.* Because he'd felt the pain of the wounds left behind on her lifeless body.

But Valerio nodded in understanding and stepped away, letting Ryker step forward. He held out his hand and let his magic loose. He was still a bit sore from the wound he'd received, though after a night's sleep, it was already healing.

All at once, Ryker absorbed the human's pain into himself. He gritted his teeth against it, but it was an overwhelming force. Pain exploded on his cheekbone as he took in the shattering, the slice of the knife, the scars.

He couldn't remember a day when he hadn't been covered in scars. Small ones, at first. Tiny, silver, they crisscrossed against his tan skin until the war. Until Mairin. He'd made it his mission to save every Fae he could, as if that could distract him from the fact that he couldn't save the one Fae woman in his life who really mattered.

So, he took the scars so others didn't have to wear them, and he didn't complain. Even when it weakened his body and he felt his knees wobble. He was already tired, his magic already weak, but he had a duty to his people, and he'd do it even if it killed him.

He dared to lift his gaze, and like an addictive force, his eyes went to her, and it was the look in her eyes that crippled him. It caught him off guard and he almost fell. But then she was moving towards him, like her body was just as addicted to him as his eyes seemed to be of hers. He couldn't fathom why it was so hard to stay away from her when he despised everything she stood for.

Then she was next to him, and he felt the strength in her touch. Heard the softest of gasps push from her lips. He knew what the sound was for. He felt it, too. Felt the rush of her skin against his like something foreign and forbidden.

Her strong arms held him up, one wrapping around his waist and the other gripping his wrist. Their pulses pressed together, and it felt as intimate as a kiss, and more painful than anything he could ever absorb.

The torture of her touch was too much. The compassion in her eyes was too much. *She* was too much. Like she was in his system, tattooing herself into his soul whether he wanted her there or not. And while his body told him that this was right, that she was right where she was supposed to be, he knew how wrong it really was.

Because him and Shula Azzarh?

They didn't fit. They couldn't possibly.

They were too different, too far apart on the spectrum that made them Fae.

But despite all that, his body leaned closer towards her, and Ryker found himself relishing in the warmth of her skin, in the way her body seemed to mold to his side.

Like she truly did belong.

He didn't push her away. Not like she'd expected him to do. *Why wasn't he pushing her away?* Her mind warred with the notion, and she repeated that question to herself over and over again as he healed the human slowly.

More importantly, why had she reached out to him? He was a magnetic force, and she knew she would regret this, but for now, she held him up as his body weakened. She knew it couldn't have been easy to use his magic when only the night before he'd been suffering from what was likely an iron inflicted injury.

It felt like hours, though in reality she knew it had only been a few minutes. When Ryker finished, she felt his entire body slacken, and she gritted her teeth to hold his heavy weight up.

The human had stopped his chattering as if, along with healing his wounds, Ryker had given him energy. In exchange, Ryker's whole body felt cold. Beneath the heavy weight of his clothes, she felt his tense muscles trembling in the most discreet manner. Like he didn't want others to see his weakness.

His head lolled slightly, and the sharpness of his beard scraped her cheek. She turned a fraction, and their eyes met. Something shone in the bicolored depths, something she hadn't witnessed before.

It was gone in a flash, and he grunted as he pushed himself up, pulling away from her grasp to stand on his own two feet.

Shula's face heated, and she forced her attention away from him only to catch Weylyn's golden gaze from across the small prison cell. An intense stare in place, his mouth pursed like a cat staring at a mouse he meant to toy with.

It was unnerving.

"Let's talk about the Elemental." Valerio's voice cut her out of her thoughts and had her focusing back on the interrogation.

The human trembled and his gaze went to where Shula stood.

Ryker growled, but it was Valerio's hand that struck out against the human's cheek. The slap resonated loudly. "Do not fucking look at her. Look at me. Why did you want to take her?"

He didn't answer right away, and that unwillingness seemed to anger Valerio. He leaned back and at a subtle gesture towards Julius, the massive man unleashed his fists against the human. Bones cracked under the Fae's ministrations that left the human whimpering.

"Let's try that again," Valerio said once Julius stepped back. "Why did you want to take the Elemental?"

"We were under orders!"

"Whose orders?"

"Emperor Laurel's, the Kings of Illyk's major cities, fucking *everyone...*"

Silence ensued after those words. They made Shula still. Her hands tingled with nerves, so she tightened them into fists and forced herself to focus.

"Why does he care so much about Elementals?" Valerio demanded.

The human was silent. As if he didn't know by now what his silence brought on. Only this time, Valerio didn't look to Julius. This time, he snatched the dagger straight from Julius' hand and brought it to Philip's face. He traced the tip of the dagger against his skin, over the ridge of his cheekbone slowly enough to be deadly.

Philip whimpered. "I—I don't know!"

Valerio acted like he hadn't heard. He gripped the human's ear and pressed the edge of the knife against it.

"W—what are you doing! I answered you! I told you I don't know!"

Valerio's dark eyes darkened further. Shula shivered, a sick feeling twisting at her gut. Was this the true nature that lived beneath the prince's skin? This cruel demon that could press a knife to a human with little remorse?

"You humans love to take our ears," he murmured softly.

Another whimper escaped the human.

"I do not really understand your obsession." The knife dug in and blood bloomed. The human began struggling in earnest, but Valerio's other hand shot out, gripping his head tightly to keep him in place. "I wonder what would happen if I..." He trailed off, and with a violent flick of his wrist, Valerio sliced the ear clean off.

A guttural cry of pain echoed through the prison. The human jerked against his bonds as blood spurted from the place where his ear had been. Valerio held the small piece of his body part up for examination and discarded it, tossing it against Philip's chest.

"Yeah, I still do not understand the obsession."

"Fuck you, Esses!" the human spat. "I gave you what you wanted!" Tears began streaming down his face. "I fucking told you I don't know shit!"

"That's a shame," Valerio purred. "Tell me what you *do* know."

"Emperor Laurel put an order out to all the noble families and his soldiers." He gasped and sobbed, heaving in breaths that sounded like they grated against his lungs. "He's doubling his efforts to find the Fae. He wants them all. But he wants the Elementals unharmed."

Shula tensed. She felt eyes on her, but she couldn't bring herself to meet them.

"Why?" Valerio asked.

"I don't know! All I know is he wants them. Badly. Any and all Elementals we can find, we are to turn them over to our captains so they can get them to either the emperor or the kings. We've been combing through Illyk for weeks to try and find the damn Elementals and any other Fae we can!" He started to cry. "That's all I know! I swear, that's all I know!"

Valerio smiled and patted his palm against the human's cheek. "I believe you, Philip."

Through his pain, Philip trembled and breathed a sigh of relief. "You—you do?"

The Seelie Prince's smile was a chilling thing. Humans had stories of hell, of demons, and Shula could picture it so vividly then. The legends they were so afraid of, they reflected on the prince's deadly expression.

"Of course, I do."

A hand clamped on Shula's arm, drawing her attention away from the sniveling human. She looked up and met Ryker's grave expression. Bicolored eyes flickered across her face in silent communication. She didn't know how she knew, but she felt what he was telling her, deep in her bones.

Eyes on me.

"No! No, please, what are you doing? I told you everything I know! Please!"

She started to look back to the human, but Ryker's hand shot out and gripped her chin, holding their eyes together.

Eyes on me.

He angled her so she couldn't even see out of her periphery. So that all she could focus on was the two different colors that were his eyes. One white, one black. One like the heavens, one as dark as hell.

And in them, she found a modicum of comfort, even as she heard the swipe of a blade being unsheathed from its resting place.

Eyes on me.

Because whatever animosity existed between them, he was still trying to protect her. She could see that truth at least in the intensity of his demeanor. It burned, hotter than her own fire. He was commanding, his presence consuming. He confused her, she hated him, they hated each other.

Yet she couldn't look away because he was equally hypnotizing.

"No! Please!" There was the sound of steel meeting flesh. Of gurgled cries, choking on blood.

She wanted to wince but couldn't.

Perhaps later the sound would haunt her dreams. But for now, she could focus on him and forget her fear. Forget, for a moment, that the Emperor of Illyk was sending armies out to find her and bring her to him.

Looking at him, she could forget for a moment that she wasn't safe, and she probably wouldn't be again. But at the moment, it didn't matter. Nothing did because it was his gaze and the hand that still gripped her chin, strong yet gentle, that made her feel safe.

It drowned out the sound of fear.

It drowned out the sound of the dying.

The Truth in Prophecies

"This means something." Valerio slapped his palm against the surface of the table. The dishes clattered together with the force of his distress.

The king merely raised an eyebrow, stroking his stubbled chin in thought.

As soon as the last dying cries of the human faded from the prison, they'd all ushered out of there and to the meeting room with the king, to tell him exactly what the human had said.

About Emperor Laurel, the Kings of Illyk, and the Elementals. About how badly the emperor wanted Shula.

All while Shula watched with detached emotion.

She'd just witnessed the Fae *torture* a man. They were supposedly kinder than humans, or so they said. But that hadn't been a kindness. It had been violent, brutal, *shocking*. They claimed to be different, but they used the same torturous methods the humans did.

Shula knew she should be afraid, be wary because of that.

Yet she didn't feel a thing.

Well, she did feel something, but it wasn't fear and it wasn't disgust. She didn't particularly care that they'd killed him because of what he'd done to Orna. Not that it had been said, though Valerio had asked. She didn't doubt that the human had taken part in brutalizing Orna's body.

That alone was enough for her to not give a single shit.

In the moment, the actual torture had threatened to unnerve her a little bit. The only thing to keep her mind from it had been Ryker's steady fingers on her chin and his eyes reaching down into her soul.

But the moment the human had died, it was like the spell had broken and Ryker and Shula were back to being enemies. He'd dropped his hand as if her body burned him, and he'd turned and strode away. Like he had to rush to get away from her. Like he couldn't stand to be in her presence anymore.

"Weylyn?" The king nodded once in the Fae male's direction.

Weylyn stepped forward. He'd taken off his dark jacket, wearing nothing but a long-sleeved, belted tunic despite the small chill. His dark, long braid hung over his shoulder, and his golden eyes glittered.

"He was telling the truth. The nobles want the Elementals, Majesty." Weylyn's eyes went to Shula, and his lips pursed briefly. "We do not know why. But if he's combing through Illyk to find them, then it must be for an important reason."

"Hmm." The king stroked his chin once more. "What are your theories?" This question he directed to all of them. All of those Shula suspected were in his inner circle. Valerio, Clay, Uric, Weylyn, Ryker, Julius, and a few others that Shula hadn't been introduced to yet.

"Maybe he just wants to kill them?" someone suggested.

Valerio's nostrils flared. "Why would he see to that? We are nearly extinct, and he has not cared about us before. For years, his soldiers find the Fae and escort them to camps. Never before a Brotherhood. Never to the kings or the emperor."

"Yes, he cannot possibly sit through every execution, can he?" the king mused.

As if anything about this was amusing.

Shula let in a steady breath.

"We need to take into account the seer's prophecy," Valerio continued. He made sure to meet everyone's gaze unflinchingly.

For a moment, Shula admired him. He was made of tough stuff, of leadership. It was in the way he held himself, the way he stood, the way he *stared.*

"Davina said that *she*—" He pointed at Shula, who stiffened, tightening her hands on her knees. "—would help save the Fae. If that is to be believed, then perhaps the emperor knows this and wants to take away our chances at victory."

One of the Fae that stood behind the king snorted and stared Shula up and down. She prickled at the assessment, the obvious disdain in his expression. "And what is so special about her? You, girl, what magic do you have?"

As if he didn't know. "Fire."

Another snort. "And can you control it? Have you ever been in battle? Have you saved any lives?"

Shula grit her teeth before answering. "No."

The Fae snorted again. "Exactly. No. Your Majesty, she's no one special. Look, she does not even have her ears. Disgraceful."

Shula's face heated with embarrassment and anger that she tried to tamp down when she felt the smoke in her lungs. It wouldn't do good to incinerate the meeting room or the Fae asshole who was looking down at her. As if he knew who and what she was.

Was this going to be the norm here?

Discretely, she lifted her hand and covered her ears with her hair.

"She's an Elemental," Valerio argued. "Those are rare creatures in and of themselves and you all know it. Their magic is different from ours. We have no idea *what* she's capable of."

Shula's heart warmed at the assessment from the prince. And here she thought he hated her.

"If I may?" Weylyn interjected. Something, Shula guessed, he didn't do often by the way everyone stared at him with startled expressions.

The king waved a hand. "Proceed."

"From what I have gathered, the seer's—Davina's—predictions were scattered in pieces. Though, some of what she said does lead us to believe that something else is afoot. Perhaps... if we find another seer to give us an accurate prediction..." He trailed off. "Davina is dead and cannot give us answers, so we must find them elsewhere."

No one spoke after that as they waited to see what the king would say. He appeared lost in thought.

"Where would we find another seer?" he asked calmly.

A throat cleared.

Shula looked up at a Fae man who stepped from the shadows of the room. She hadn't noticed him before, and she probably should have. He looked like a half breed. Half High Fae and half Unseelie. He was tall, beautiful, elegant, yet his skin was purple, his hair white and slicked back into a low knot.

"I know of a seer." His voice was melodic and dreamy.

The king spread his palms against the surface of the table. "Then by all means, speak."

The Fae cleared his throat again. "Not just any seer. *The Seer.* One who does not just see the future in flashes, but who sees all."

Quiet murmurs rang around the room. Shula could feel the tension suddenly ratchet up, and she wondered at that, wondered who this mysterious seer was. The Seer. There was reverence in the words he spoke, and most of the Fae present shuffled uneasily.

"The Seer," the king repeated drolly. "That is your solution?"

"Seers are rare, Your Majesty. We keep a record of every Fae we harbor here and what their abilities are. We do not have one. They are as rare as Elementals because Mana does not want to gift so many with prophecies. So, the solution is easy. You want answers to your questions? The Seer."

"It's suicide," someone spat. "You cannot just find The Seer."

Shula shifted in her seat from side to side, chewing at the inside of her mouth. Her mouth opened, closed, until she decided, *fuck it,* and asked, "Who's The Seer?"

All eyes went straight to her. As if she'd asked a ridiculous question. Perhaps she had, because she hadn't grown into the same culture they had, and it showed just how much she disgusted them for it.

She tried not to blush and failed.

"The Seer is rumored to be as old as time," Valerio answered her, his tone gentle yet firm. "She—or he—is a Fae with the gift of prophecy. You heard Davina's prophecies? The Seer's are nothing like hers. She—or he—knows all, sees all. Past, present, and future."

Then The Seer must have been incredibly powerful and, judging by the looks on their faces, fearsome as well.

Shula had seen what the power of prophecy could do to a Fae. It had slowly drove Davina mad until her ramblings resembled that of a madwoman.

"Why would finding The Seer be suicide?" Shula asked.

"Because, Shula, The Seer lives beyond the Ley Line."

Shula froze. The Ley Line. The line of magic that separated the kingdom of Orknie from Tir na Faie. That separated the human lands from the Feylands.

A place that used to be guarded by fearsome warriors to protect the secrets of the south. A place that Fae dared never to venture towards anymore. Because it had been infected, poisoned, a blight placed upon the land by the humans.

A kingdom now filled with iron.

"Because of the iron, not even Uric could portal us there. We would have to travel on foot. A month's worth of a journey, maybe more." Valerio turned to his father. "Please, father, let us go find The Seer and bring you answers." He dipped his head and lowered his voice. "Let us help the Fae thrive once again. I know it is what you want, and this might be the only opportunity we have at discovering the truth."

King Ashera sighed. "Fine," he conceded. "You may go. The six of you."

Valerio stiffened. "Six?"

"Yes. Six. You, Clay, Uric, Julius, Ryker, and Weylyn. You will need him to communicate with me. I want daily updates regarding the journey."

Valerio looked like he wanted to groan but held it back by biting the inside of his cheek. Clay did openly roll his eyes.

Shula wondered why they were so averse to Weylyn but brushed it off when she realized what the king had said.

"Your Majesty, I would like to go with them as well, please." She tried to phrase it as respectfully as possible but feared it came out like a command.

The king shot her a look. "Looking to escape, Shula Azzarh?"

"No." Her gaze darted up and down and she sighed, forcing herself to meet his eyes. "I will not run away, but I think if they are traveling to discover my own importance, then I have a right to go as well. I demand to know the truth about myself."

Collective gasps rang out and Shula cringed. She hadn't meant to snap out the last bit, but she was desperate and tired. Tired of being kept in the back like their chained slave. If they wouldn't let her walk away, then fine. It didn't matter right then, not when all of Illyk was looking for Elementals. But at least she had to know why it was happening. What did Emperor Laurel want with her? Why was she so important to him?

Shula refused to take no for an answer.

The king stared her down, giving her a glare that she was sure shriveled lesser men. Admittedly, it made her feel anxious, but she stood her ground, meeting him glare for glare until he dipped his head in a small nod.

"Fine. Take the Fire Dancer with you, but you stay with them at all times. No running. No escaping. Understood?"

Shula bit back her grin of triumph by bowing low. "Thank you, Your Majesty."

"Now go. Eat and rest, for you will leave tomorrow morning. The sooner we find out what we need to know, the better. The sooner we find out exactly what kind of weapon she is, the sooner we can take back our lands." The king dismissed them with a clap of his palms together. "All of you get out! Leave my sight at once."

It was all Shula needed to hear to rush from the room.

Tomorrow they set out on a mission that they deemed suicidal, deadly, dangerous. It didn't matter what they called it or how they tried to frighten her.

Shula was just glad she'd finally get to know the truth.

Little People of the Wood

Fire crackled, the noise somehow louder than the soft revelry that was happening around her. Voices laughed, music played, bodies swayed. But Shula couldn't bring herself to participate.

The last time she had, things had ended in disaster and there was no happiness in the situation at all.

Shula was going to the Feylands.

Her parents had rarely told her stories about the courts, because they hadn't been born in pleasant times, so they hadn't known what should have been their homelands.

Still, all the stories were handed down. Tales her grandparents had given her parents and that they in turn gifted Shula.

She used to imagine what it would be like. To be surrounded by the magic of Mana every day. To see magic unabashed and unrelenting.

It was dangerous to go there now. Even she'd heard the stories of how iron now eroded the soil, rendering what had once been a sanctuary for the Fae completely useless land.

A body curling around her legs snapped Shula out of her thoughts. She looked down to find Ryker's cat rubbing against her, demanding attention. Shifting her goblet to one hand, she reached the other down and ran her fingers against the cat's head.

"Hey, kitty," she greeted. "You coming with us tomorrow?"

Shula startled at the voice that replied. "Yes. Familiars do not like being away from their Fae."

She turned as Ryker helped himself to the empty seat beside her, the chair groaning under his heavy weight. He braced his forearms against his thick thighs and leaned forward, staring into the hearth fire.

Shula took a moment to study the left side of his face and that white eye facing her. Her eyes traced the pattern of scars against his skin like the roads on a map or jagged edges of puzzle pieces that fit together on this giant of a male.

Puzzle pieces she couldn't seem to piece together herself.

"She's your familiar?" She felt breathless, and as soon as the words left her lips, she already knew the answer. Of course, she was his familiar. There was a reason she was always perched on his shoulders.

"For a few years now." He still didn't take his eyes off the fire. A tankard was dwarfed between his massive hands.

The silence that ensued was uncomfortable at best. A strange tension filled the air, thicker than smoke. Silence encircled them that Shula couldn't read. She couldn't read between his growls, his glares, or the way his hands pressed gently and firmly against her chin, the soft way he commanded, "Eyes on me."

He was confounding.

But she didn't want to think about him and his mood swings. There were more important things at stake and on her mind. Like what tomorrow would bring, and what truth they'd discover on the road to Tir na Faie.

"Did you live in Tir na Faie?" she asked quietly. "Before..."

"Yes."

That was it. No explanation, no elaboration. Just his seething glare into the flames. Flames that cast a wicked blue reflection in that white eye.

"What was it like?"

She didn't know why she was engaging in conversation with him. Perhaps because he was there. Perhaps because out of all of the Fae she'd met so far, Ryker seemed... he seemed *real.* He didn't hide what he was. He didn't try to manipulate her into befriending him. He hated wholly, entirely, and unabashedly.

She could respect it, even when it infuriated her more than being kidnapped did.

He brought his tankard up to his lips and took a giant swallow. For a moment she thought he wouldn't answer her. Maybe it had been too much of a personal question for him? But she thought it'd be nice to hear about the land they would travel to. What it had been before the wars and hatred consumed the earth.

"It was home." His voice thickened with longing.

"I don't know what that means." Shula hadn't meant to say that out loud, but the words had already escaped her lips. They were true, though. She didn't know what a true home was. She'd lived a nomadic life for twenty-two years. Home was one place, not many. The circus hadn't been a home. It had been a means for survival and, deep down, she always knew she wouldn't be wholly safe there.

"The Crimson Court was my home," Ryker surprised her by saying. "But that was a long time ago."

"How old *are* you?"

He took another drink. "Old enough to have witnessed the start of this war. Old enough to witness death. Old enough to witness the humans go mad with hatred. And old enough to see Fae succumb to treachery."

And there it was.

He couldn't go a moment without jabbing at her. She didn't know why she kept trying, or why he even bothered on coming near her if he hated her so much. Maybe he just liked to annoy her on purpose...

Shula sighed and set her cup down on the floor between her legs. "Good night, Ryker."

He grunted in response as she stood and stalked back to her room. It was better if she went to bed anyway. Tomorrow was going to be a long day of travel and she needed to preserve her strength for the journey ahead.

She didn't need to waste any more time thinking about things she could never have. Like freedom. Like a home.

Like a gentle word from a hateful giant.

Ryker watched her until she climbed up the stairs and disappeared around the corner.

Meow.

He grunted. "Don't start with me."

Meow.

He imagined the cat rolling her damn eyes.

He couldn't help himself. Venom was churning in his gut, threatening to eat him alive. Any time he looked at the Fire Dancer, he remembered Mairin, her face pale in death, and the fact that he'd been too slow to save her. To take her scars and live with the pain of a betrayal that cut too deep.

He sighed and ran a hand over his face. The next moment when he opened his eyes, Weylyn was next to him, standing, staring at the path where the Fire Dancer had walked towards her room.

Ryker tried not to growl.

He hated Weylyn. Everyone fucking did. Nothing was private with him around, and the fucker relished in digging out their most intimate thoughts.

It was because of this bastard right here that everyone knew of Mairin, a secret he'd wished to conceal but had been ripped right out of his mind the moment he'd joined forces with the Seelie King.

"The fuck you want, lapdog?" Ryker growled.

"Her thoughts are scattered," he answered with an amused tone. "So many memories and thoughts all swirling together. It is hard to pick out just one."

"I don't care."

"No?" Now the bastard sounded openly amused. "Then you would not care that the one thought that is easiest to grasp, the one that sits between every scattered, painful memory are thoughts of you?"

Ryker stilled at the confession. He wanted to deny that claim, tell Weylyn he was a fucking liar, but he knew by now that Weylyn didn't lie.

"Why would she think so often of you when your hatred is so palpable?"

"I don't care," Ryker repeated through gritted teeth.

"Don't you? Some bonds are just too difficult to ignore."

Ryker shot to his feet, the chair he was sitting in skidding across the ground and falling. He didn't have to stay and listen to Weylyn spout his nonsense. He didn't want to. "Fuck off," he demanded and walked away.

He felt Weylyn smiling behind him like he'd won some sort of contest. Well, let the fucker bathe in his victory.

Ryker didn't fucking care.

He had better things to worry about. Like the arduous journey that would begin tomorrow. That was what he would focus on rather than whispers of bonds that didn't exist.

The next morning, they didn't waste any time leaving. Packed with all the essentials, the seven Fae stood in a line as the Seelie King wished them farewell.

"Daily updates," he told Valerio, though his eyes were on Weylyn as he said it.

"Yes, father."

"May Mana protect you all." Then the king turned to Shula, and she held her breath at the cruel disposition. "Do not attempt to escape, Shula Azzarh." That was all he needed to say to her. The tone of his voice worked better than any threat ever could.

She swallowed past the lump in her throat and nodded. "Yes, Your Majesty." She didn't like speaking to him with reverence, but it was better than being outright disrespectful. After all, he was giving her what she wanted, even when she'd been so rude upon asking for it.

Uric opened a portal, and they stepped through it. Shula didn't turn to look at the castle. She didn't feel particularly sad about leaving the melancholy place. It hadn't been a home. Just another safe house among many.

The portal sucked her in and spit her out in an entirely different location. One that wasn't covered in snow, but still had a cool, gentle breeze. Trees surrounded them from all sides, and there was no roaring wind or freeze. It made Shula feel overdressed in her coat and fur-lined boots.

Once the portal closed behind them, she turned to look at all six of her companions. They were assessing their surroundings while Uric caught his breath in the aftereffects of using his magic.

"Where are we?" Shula asked, the first to break the quiet.

"South of Tuath mountains, near the Arcana."

The Arcana was a wide rush of a river that spread down the middle of Illyk, from the north in Vellm and ending in Dana. It divided half of the human lands down the middle.

"We cannot travel by river," Valerio said. "Soldiers are stationed at major docks and checkpoints, checking papers and registration numbers." He looked around the woods, his gaze quiet and assessing. "We'll stick to the woods. Stealth is important. We cannot afford to be caught. We make our way to Dana, and then we will cross the river in a place we know there won't be soldiers."

Shula tried to pay attention to their plans, but her mind wandered, gaze scraping over the landscape. She listened intently to the sounds of birds chirping, deer roaming, and beyond that, the rapid rush of the Arcana.

She'd seen the river before. Dark and as deep as an ocean; on good days, it was still and gentle, but on worse days, it was rapid, deadly. Today seemed like a worse day.

"We're too close to the river," Shula chimed in, causing everyone to halt their planning and turn to her.

Clay smirked, the dimple in his cheek prominent, flirtatious. "Why do you say that, Fire Dancer?"

"I can hear the water. When I used to travel with the circus, we would walk along these pathways. They were always populated. Further that way will take us away from people and soldiers."

"Of course." Valerio's lips pressed into a thin line, and Shula swore it was to keep himself from laughing.

"So smart." Clay sauntered over to her and threw his arm around her shoulder, the sword sheathed at his waist bumping against her hip. They'd brought a pretty heavy artillery for the journey. It made her feel more nervous than safe, though. "Though we already knew that, it's nice to see you aren't clueless, Fire Dancer."

Shula rolled her eyes and shoved him away. "Then we should get moving." She began walking past their little huddle. "The sooner we move, the quicker we make it to The Seer."

What she didn't say was that she wanted answers. Desperately. But she didn't have to. Because she could tell they were just as desperate for them as her.

Shula shed her jacket as they walked, feeling suffocated in its girth. She paused merely to shove it into the pack she carried and continued walking.

For a moment, she felt all eyes on her, watching as she walked further and further from them. This could have been her chance to run, to *flee.* But it wasn't King Ashera's warning that echoed in her ears preventing her from doing just that. Rather, it was her own doubts and desires for the truth that made her stop and look over her shoulder.

Brow raised, she smirked at the group of Fae men. "Well?" she demanded. "What are you waiting for?"

They moved quickly then, swallowing up the distance with long strides until they were next to her and walking as a unit.

They walked for hours in the silence, everyone lost in their own thoughts and paying attention to their surroundings. They didn't stop once, not to rest or take in a breath. By the time night fell, Shula's feet ached almost painfully, and the muscles in her legs and shoulders were screaming.

Valerio and Uric led them at the front, veering into the smallest clearing in the woods surrounded by a cluster of thick trees that dripped with sap. Stones had been placed around the space in a circle, and it looked like something out of a Fae story Papa used to tell her. Stone circles were magical and could transport anyone who walked through them to other worlds entirely, only to never return.

They were placed there by trickster Fae who liked to lure humans into the Feylands, make them drink the sap from magical trees, and keep them there, suspended in time forever.

"The little people of the wood," Shula breathed, her chest hitching with memories and stories of her Papa's voice.

Valerio pierced her with an indecipherable look. "We'll camp here tonight." The bag he carried slid from his shoulders. "Weylyn and Ryker, take first watch."

Weylyn, after setting his bag off to the side, prowled away, disappearing through the trees without a word. Shula found herself staring at him as he walked. He was strange, eerie in a way that rivaled the silent and deadly Uric.

Not that any of these Fae seemed to have much personality.

Shula was used to the boisterous. While she had always been more reserved and quiet due to her Fae heritage, she enjoyed being around the humans at Piriguini's Circus because they were everything she *wasn't.* Their personalities were over the top, loud, *fun.*

The Fae were serious, brooding.

Assholes.

She knew it was because of their situation. That was why she was the way she was as well. She couldn't fault them for being cautious. The only two of the group who were fun were Julius and Clay. Weylyn always looked like his head was in the clouds, Uric like he wanted nothing more than to snap Shula's neck, Valerio like she was a conundrum he wanted to solve, and Ryker...

Ryker looked at her with heat in his gaze. It was searing, blistering to the point where she didn't know if he wanted to murder her or... fuck her.

She shoved that thought aside.

There was no way in the human's hell that he wanted to fuck her.

She ignored the tingling between her thighs as she thought of it. No, no, no. She didn't need to feel the sharp sting of desire. Not when he was so close. Not when he could *smell it.*

She avoided Ryker's gaze, looking everywhere but him while she got settled and as he prowled silently into the woods in a different direction than Weylyn.

Once he was gone, she breathed a little easier.

"I see you, Fire Dancer."

Shula startled, dropping the blanket she'd just pulled from her bag. She snapped her glare to Clay, who wore a smug, knowing expression. Though what he thought he knew was beyond her. "Taking out... my blanket?"

His shoulder bumped her. "I see you *not* looking at Ryker."

Her face flushed. "So?"

He blew out an exasperated breath. "*Sooo*, I also saw him pointedly *not* looking at you." His whole body vibrated like a child hyped up on sugared candy.

"Again, I ask: so?"

His eyebrows waggled suggestively. "*Sooo*, I can expect some fuckage in your future?"

Shula blanched. "What did you just say?"

"The both of you need to get laid." He clapped his hands together. "You're uptight, dancing around each other, acting like you hate each other—"

"We *do* hate each other," Shula interrupted. "I don't understand what you're trying to get at here."

"Do you hate each other though? Or are the flames just burning too hotly?" Clay pressed the tip of his finger to his tongue then to her shoulder, mimicking a sizzling noise.

Shula's eyes rolled as she spread the blanket out on the ground. "I still don't know what you mean."

The gravitas in her tone had Clay pausing and observing her. She felt his judging gaze keenly, only it didn't send her spine shivering like Ryker's did. It didn't make her skin break out in gooseflesh, and it definitely didn't make her thighs pulse or her mind swirl with confusion and frustration.

Ryker was an enigma, one she didn't have the time to understand, even if her mind had the desire. Her self-respect and pride were at war with his blatant dislike of her. It was the only reason there seemed to be anything between them at all. It was nothing but animosity due to their difference in circumstances and very different lifestyles.

He had Fae pride in an abundance that was almost as toxic as human pride. So much so that he shunned her when all she wanted to do was survive.

"I think—"

"Fuck off, Clay," she interrupted, plopping herself onto the blanket. She didn't bother taking off her boots because she didn't know what terrors the night held and if they'd be forced to make a quick escape. "Stop imagining things that aren't there." Then she closed her eyes.

She could feel him staring at her, but she chose to ignore the questions that pulsed silently and thickly in her direction. She didn't allow her eyes to flutter closed until he walked away, and as soon as she did, she fell into a dreamless sleep.

Survival

Steel clanging against steel echoed throughout the woods, startling birds from their perches on the high ends of branches. Shula herself sat propped against a rock, soaking up the early morning sun. Dew beaded against sharp blades of grass, and she ran her fingers through them.

It was an anxious gesture, the only one she'd show. An insignificant movement of her fingers so no one could tell that her heart was beating in her throat or that she felt nervous and perhaps even the smallest of thrills in her blood.

They'd been traveling for days now, falling into a simple routine. They walked until night fell, they slept in scheduled shifts, and by morning they trained while Shula watched.

She never particularly liked violence before. After witnessing death and killing someone—several someone's since meeting the Fae—herself, she shied away from such things. However, watching Clay and Julius shirtless and clashing weapons in the small clearing gave her a new appreciation for the primal, masculine energy the two radiated.

It wasn't just because they were shirtless, sunlight glittering off their sweating forms. Or even the stacks upon stacks of muscles that Julius sported, curly ginger hair spanning across his massive chest. Clay was thinner, yet no slouch. His arms were muscular, and his abs tapered down to a slim waist.

They were both extremely beautiful specimens, especially Clay. Though Clay's features were softer than Julius', who was rugged with rougher edges and a chin thick with a beard. While Julius was gruff, and radiated pure, masculine energy, Clay looked more feminine in his soft curves and panes. Clay was staggering, completely overwhelming in his countenance. *Pretty,* Shula thought.

What held Shula fascinated the most were their movements. Every turn of their bodies and gliding of their feet seemed like an impromptu dance. It was brutal, the force of their collisions, and it left them soaked in sweat and dripping blood.

Shula dug her fingers into the grass to avoid flinching as Julius landed a perfectly placed blow to Clay's face. Blood bloomed from his nose and he cursed, holding up a hand.

"My nose, you asshole!"

Julius twirled his wrist and sword, an impetuous smile curling his mouth. "Stop worrying about your pretty boy face and focus on your footwork."

Clay swiped the back of his hand against his nose and flipped Julius a vulgar gesture. "You're built bigger than a fucking ox. My footwork isn't the problem here."

Julius snorted and advanced, causing Clay to stumble back and hold up his hand. "Fuck, give me a second."

"I win, then." Julius dismissed Clay by turning towards the rest of them. "Who's next?" His eyes landed on Valerio. "Prince?" They swept over to Weylyn and the wide smile he wore suddenly turned malicious as he took in the quietest of the Fae. "How about you?"

In the few days they'd been traveling, Shula noticed the animosity between the others and Weylyn. With each other, they laughed and joked; even quiet Uric was included. Weylyn, however, was treated with outright hostility. Like he didn't quite belong.

It made Shula feel the strangest sort of kinship with him, because she felt as equally discarded as he was. Like she was little more than a burden to them when she wasn't even here by choice, at least she hadn't been at first. Neither was Weylyn. The king had ordered him to come, and he took their hatred without a word or single expression to hint at any discomfort.

Their relentless teasing was starting to grate on Shula's nerves. Every time they slew their words at him, it felt like a personal attack against herself. She'd been observing Weylyn. Despite being withdrawn, she could feel the press of pride that surrounded him. He wouldn't back down from such an open challenge, just like he always did their bidding.

Slowly, Shula unfurled her fingers from the grass and pushed herself to her feet.

"I want to go," she declared. She swore, everyone held their breath at the declaration. Six heads turned towards her direction, six mouths gaping open.

She didn't fidget under the judging stares but tilted her head higher and walked towards the clearing with a confidence her pounding heart didn't mirror.

"Fire Dancer, this isn't a joke. These are real weapons." Clay looked at her like she lost her mind. But she hadn't. Her thoughts were clear as a summer day.

"I want to learn." The obstinance shone in her gaze and body language. She wanted nothing more than for him to argue with her, just so she could prove him wrong.

"But—"

"Give her your sword," Valerio cut in. Shula didn't turn to look at the prince. "Let's see what she's got."

Clay reluctantly handed over his sword. It seemed realer then, and Shula hesitated a mere second before reaching for it and wrapping her hand around the hilt. Clay let go and her arm nearly fell to the ground. It was heavy, and she gritted her teeth as she lifted the weapon up, pointing it in Julius' direction.

The ginger Fae was smirking with malice that should have thrown her into a stupor, but she narrowed her eyes and focused. Her body mimicked his stance, feet set apart, both hands on the hilt, back slightly bent, arms strong. It was harder than it looked.

"I was waiting for the moment you stopped watching us and decided to join," Julius said, his tone implying a taunt. He dropped his arm to the side and prowled back and forth, sizing her up. "For you to finally get brave enough to want to learn something useful."

Shula knew what he was doing. He did it to everyone before they trained. He tried to distract them by getting them riled up. It wouldn't work on her.

"I'm no damsel in distress," Shula replied. "No matter what any of you may think."

Julius' bushy eyebrows shot up to his forehead. "Oh, really? I've heard the contrary."

Shula snorted. "Whatever you may have been told, *I'm* the one who escaped from the Brotherhood. Me. On my own. You Fae assholes didn't do shit."

"'Fae assholes.' You say that as if you aren't one of us."

Don't fall for his bullshit. Shula swallowed the lump in her throat. "I know exactly what I am, you think I could ever forget? I've been on my own for ten years. I did just fine surviving without you, and I'll continue to do so."

"Not anymore, Shula." Julius raised his sword, pointing it at her like an accusation. "Times have changed. Humans are growing bolder. Hiding your ears isn't going to be enough. You need to be prepared."

Shula just met his gaze with an equally cold one of her own. If he thought he could scare her, he had another thing coming. Shula had lived in fear so long, it took up a permanent place inside her; never resting, always there, waiting for just the right moment to strike into her heart.

"I am prepared," she challenged.

"You will be."

And Julius barreled towards her. The ground beneath his feet rumbled, or maybe it was the fear in her body making her shake. Shula had only a split second to throw the sword up before his was careening towards her.

The percussive clang of metal against metal vibrated through to her skull. She gritted her teeth and tried to push back, but he was stronger than she was. A single, forceful shove made her feet skid across the ground, causing her to nearly lose her footing.

Already, her breaths were coming out in labored pants.

"Arms up!" Julius snapped before charging again.

This time she didn't meet him in the middle but dodged as he swung, exposing her back to the hilt of his sword. Pain sliced up her spine and she went down, losing the sword in the process. She struggled for breath as she pushed herself up, but Julius was a relentless, cruel adversary.

"Use your nimble, quick feet to your advantage!"

Shula scrambled to get her sword back, dodging with only a few centimeters to spare as the sword came crashing down near her. Her muscles protested as she lifted the weapon once more and swung, switching to an offensive maneuver instead of defensive.

Julius weaved away from the frantic swiping of her blade. A flash of silver came crashing down and pain radiated up her wrists, causing her to drop the sword again. He didn't let her pick it up a second time. Her feet scrambled backwards as he advanced. She ducked, rolled, stood up, and felt pain in her face.

Blood spurted down her nose, stained her teeth as she gasped to regain her breath. Feet swiped at her own and the wind was knocked straight of her lungs as she collided against solid ground.

Julius loomed over her, the tip of his sword pressed to her neck.

"You have a lot to learn," he began, "if you want to survive the inevitable war."

Shula blinked as tears threatened her eyes. Not because she lost, but because of the pain. Her back scraped against the ground, reminding her of the still healing wounds carved on her flesh.

And because Julius was right.

She'd turned a blind eye to it for so long, accepting the defeat of her kind. Things changed. Shula's eyes were wide open now. She saw things she hadn't known before. Like the Resistance, like Castle Aileach and all who resided there, wishing for a better future. She'd known and lost Orna, and she had suffered at the hands of the Brotherhood.

She'd thought the war was over because there weren't any Fae left. It was a lie. There were still some, and she could tell by the burning fire in Julius' eyes and fierce determination in the rest of her Fae companions that until the last of the Fae fell, the war would still wage on.

A war Shula was now inadvertently a part of.

She pushed the blade away from her neck with the back of her hand and stood to her feet. Determination burned inside her in an all-consuming flame that was hotter than her own fire and more painful than the wounds down her back.

She walked over to where the discarded sword lay and she picked it up, turning to face Julius once again.

If there was surprise at all inside him, he didn't show.

Shula smirked at him and held up the sword and commanded with a single, fury-filled word.

"Again."

The Faceless Emperor

The long, grueling days had a way of being forgotten when she was getting her ass kicked.

All she knew was exhaustion and the thrill of power through her veins every time she learned a little more, *trained* a little more.

Every morning before breakfast, Shula trained with each of the Fae men, sans Ryker and Valerio, though that was no surprise. Ryker didn't want anything to do with her and that was fine. Besides, training with Ryker would be too... intimate.

That was something she didn't want. With either Fae.

Because training with the others was a close and personal affair. Sometimes with swords, sometimes with shields, sometimes with both. Other times it was with no weapons at all other than fists. And magic? She still wasn't comfortable enough to use magic, and they hadn't asked her yet. Either because of her own cowardice, or because they'd seen her destruction firsthand.

For now, she was content with dominating the other things first.

It was always rough and painful. There were no inhibitions when it came to her training. She sported dozens of bruises and bloody noses, scraped palms and elbows. Her muscles ached every morning and felt worse every night. But inside? Inside, Shula felt powerful. It was the only thing preventing her from asking Ryker to heal her wounds. That and she couldn't imagine him bearing anymore of scars that weren't his to bear.

Among her personal training with Clay, there was a moment where she had wrestled him to the ground, pinning him beneath her thighs and locking him in a chokehold. He never trained her with swords, and she wondered if it was some perverted delight on his end. He never got handsy; in fact, he was the perfect gentleman, never touching her in places he shouldn't, but their bodies were always pressed so close, and Shula felt deep in her bones that Clay thought in his deranged mind he was irritating Ryker by doing it.

It couldn't be the farthest thing from the truth.

It didn't stop Clay from trying, though.

Days converged into weeks, it felt like, and everything was the same routine. They were cautious, but there was no trouble, though if there was, Shula was confident she could take anyone on. She felt her strength growing every day, but there was still a restlessness inside her that stirred and slithered like a living entity.

Until the day Valerio tried to assuage it.

Shula heard the roar of the Arcana before she saw it. Her feet almost stumbled to a stop. "What are we doing here?" she demanded, looking from face to face.

Julius was the only one who replied, manic glee twisting his smile so he looked almost feral. "We're here for the *real* fun."

The woods descended on a downwards slope with trees that angled sideways and low hanging branches with bright orange leaves. They crunched under Shula's boots as she followed down. Dry dirt made way to mud, made way to the roaring river.

Roar wasn't the right word for it. Yes, it was loud, but it was in no way violent. It rushed fast over jutting rocks on the shallow end, mellowing out towards the middle in deeper depths.

Shula chanced a look around, suddenly nervous that there would be humans camping out near the place. She cocked her head to the side, listening intently for any sign of danger. There was none. Nothing but clear water and the steady breathing of her companions.

They spread out, Weylyn taking confident strides until his back leaned casually against a tree, Clay and Julius near the edge of the river on opposite sides, Ryker to sit against a boulder, Uric stopped at the edge, and Valerio... he shouldered off his belongings and handed them to his right hand man.

Shula watched as he began methodically taking off his jacket, his vest, and his tunic until he was bare-chested.

What the—

He waded into the water until it was waist deep and turned to Shula. "Today you'll be fighting me," he said.

She blinked at the Seelie Prince. "In the water?"

He gave her a single, firm nod. "No swords," he added when Shula started for the weapon. It made her blink at him again. "Today we'll be using magic."

She felt her throat go dry, smoke filled her lungs, and inside the magic stirred. Like it recognized Valerio's words and wanted out. She felt the fire stir her blood, banging against her inner walls like it could bust out and incinerate the whole damn forest. Which probably explained the reason for being near water.

Valerio's eyes were hard with authority. "If you do not practice, it will control you for the rest of your life. You will always live in fear; it will always get out of control."

He was right. Logically, she knew he was right, but fear still lodged in her throat. She'd thrown herself into training with them. Hands-on, sword, self-defense training. Because it was safe. Because human soldiers fought that way. And maybe it was just another way for her to push her magic further away.

But Shula wasn't human. The humans hated her; at the first hint of what she truly was, she'd been betrayed. They thought she was siding with them over the Fae; she said she wasn't siding with anyone. The truth was, she *had* been siding with the humans. Because it was safer that way. Safer to endure the humiliation upon her body; to walk, talk, and live like a human because it meant survival.

This wasn't just about survival anymore. Not to them. She didn't want a bloody war. She didn't want death.

But for the first time in her life, she wanted to test the magic inside her.

Everyone waited with bated breath until she dropped her bag to the ground and toed off her boots and socks. After pulling off her coat, her hands went to the hem of her tunic and she froze.

If she did this, they would see her scars. They would see the most unnatural part of her, a part she herself didn't understand and wouldn't begin to know how to explain. She wasn't ashamed of them, if only because she didn't know the full extent of their meaning yet. But they felt magical. Something about the scars held power in a way she hoped The Seer could explain. They didn't feel wrong, no matter how painful they still were. They weren't right, either. Not normal. But they meant *something.*

Steeling herself, Shula brought the tunic over her shoulders and left it on the pile as well. She twisted her long hair over her shoulder, standing there in pants and thin bustier that did nothing to hide the wounds on her back. Shula fought back a shiver.

She quickly walked to the water, flinching at the cold as she waded in. She knew they were staring, could feel their gazes hot on her back, their questions burning, but no one spoke. She didn't know if she should be grateful for it.

"Talk to me about your magic," Valerio urged when she was a few feet in front of him.

Her hands clenched. "What do you want to know?"

"Everything. What does it feel like inside you? How does it feel to release it? You are an Elemental, so you have no price to pay except your own energy. The stronger you are, the more magic you will be able to wield. Think of it like a muscle in your body. You must exercise it, nourish it, for it to grow."

"I've never really used it before. The last time—" She broke off. The last time she'd used her magic, it had been to kill humans and to rescue Orna's body from an iron prison.

"The last time was incredible," Valerio commented. She hated how her heart beat faster at the praise. "Your power was like nothing I have ever seen before. Shula..." He cocked his head to the side. "You *melted* iron. You melted the bars off a cage."

"I don't know how I did that." Her face flushed. "I was so angry... Iron affects me just like it does you, but my powers... they were out of control."

"They were. But if you could learn to control them, imagine all the possibilities."

Melting iron? Shula had hardly even remembered that she'd done such a thing. She'd been so focused on her friend, on that loss, that she hadn't thought beyond that. In fact, it had been the furthest thing from her mind until he brought it up just now.

"So, what does your magic feel like inside you?"

"It feels like... fire."

Somewhere, she heard Uric snort. Her face flushed, but she refused to turn and look at the mocking gaze she knew he wore. "What else?" Valerio urged.

"Have you ever stared at the flame on a candle?" she asked. "The gentle sway from side to side. Or the flickering of a bonfire? Have you ever really studied fire? Because that's what it feels like. It feels like fire that's dug into my body like the roots of trees dig into the ground. It's a part of me, and it's different, but it's *alive.*" *And it wants out.* Those were the words she didn't say.

Valerio nodded. "That's what everyone's magic is, to some capacity. But you are an Elemental. Your magic may be different, but we shall treat it like any other gift from Mana."

Shula nodded.

"I want you to feel your power, familiarize yourself with it, and I want you to summon the flames to your hands. Slowly at first and then we'll go from there."

That was easy, something she'd done before with little effort. It was putting out the fire that seemed to take more concentration.

Inhaling a steady breath, Shula held her palms out and focused, calling out to the fire that lived inside her. Calling to the part of herself that she so long kept buried, knowing that Valerio was right. She'd held it in too long, and now it was time to let it loose.

She'd never fight in a war with them, but she needed to learn about herself, her powers, and know how to control them. It would mean the difference between life and death.

Lungs filling with smoke, she inhaled deeply, and felt it cloud from her mouth on the exhale. Heat suffused her palms, warm enough to bring comfort, but not hot enough to burn.

Her eyes flew open, and she stared down at the fire encasing her fingers. Vestiges of panic started in her chest and spread, making her want to hyperventilate, but she shoved it aside with a louder voice of reason.

I am safe. I am safe. I am safe.

Suppressing her powers had given room for this sensation in her chest. Powers equaled death, betrayal, *bad.*

But she wasn't among humans. She was with her own kind. That alone kept the fire around her skin burning. It spread up her arms in long, ribboned tendrils, dancing around her like a friend welcoming another after so long apart.

And the release inside her? To finally let loose that small bit of raw energy that had begged for so long? Already, she could feel her insides relaxing, the mental strain of keeping it locked up tight lessened.

"Good. Now, I want you to hit the emperor."

Shula's eyes snapped up and she staggered back, nearly sinking into the water. A figure stood before her just a few feet away but within striking distance.

The figure was human male in appearance, with a shadowed, distorted face and features Shula couldn't quite make out. A gleaming crown sat on his head, and in his hand he held an obsidian sword.

His form flickered in and out of focus, like shadows dancing around the edges.

"The human emperor wants you. He'll mount your ears on his walls and chain you to his throne room floor."

The figure moved like a phantom, charging towards Shula. She knew it was nothing more than an illusion created by Valerio for this precise moment, yet fear snaked up her spine. For a moment, it wasn't just a spectral image charging.

It was the real Emperor of Illyk.

"Shula! Focus! Use your magic!" Valerio's voice broke through her paralyzing fear. Her body jerked into movement, hands shooting out, she willed the fire to obey. Eagerly, it did so, a jet of fire speeding towards the phantom figure.

It hit him square in the chest. The figure vanished, only to be replaced by five more.

Fuck.

They charged at her in tandem, nothing more than dark blurs of whispered fury in her vision. She couldn't see from where they attacked until it was too late. Until the blows were already striking her body from all directions. Pain ratcheted over her body. She turned, heart pounding, trying to tune into her Fae senses as best as she could, but they were merely shadows. They had no scent, gave no sound.

So Shula's magic responded against the threat before she could stop it.

The fire blazed into a protective inferno.

No, no, no!

Shula tried to call it back into herself, but it was too late; she could already feel it expanding. She was vaguely aware of someone slewing a string of curses, of the searing heat that didn't burn.

And then she plunged herself into the water, extinguishing the magic and the flames.

She emerged coughing and sputtering, dripping and shivering. Blinking away the icy bite of water from her lashes, she swept a glance around. Valerio was no longer in front of her but standing next to a soaked Uric on the riverbank. The silver haired Fae had likely transported his prince away from Shula's destruction.

She walked towards them with reluctant steps, feeling their gazes like a heavy weight on her shoulders.

She'd failed. Epically. And had likely put Prince Valerio's life in danger with her uncontrollable magic.

Shula stepped onto the riverbank in front of Valerio, her feet squishing into the mud. She took a breath. "The last time I used my magic," she explained, "was when Orna died. And before that, the day you found me, the day I got these scars on my back. Before *that,* I'd been twelve." She owed them no explanation, no deeper part of herself than they already had, but the words came out anyway. Not because she trusted them, but because she wanted them to *understand.*

She was desperate to prove herself to them so they would look at her as something other than the pathetic Fae who altered her ears. So they understood why she'd done what she did, why she suppressed her magic and why she lived in fear.

Deep inside, she *wanted* someone to understand. Validation was what she sought. Someone to accept that she'd done what she had to do because there'd been no other choice. So they'd stop looking at her with the same expression Fanny wore when she discovered Shula was Fae.

"I've never *really* used my magic before." She turned from Valerio and, like she couldn't help herself, her eyes found Ryker's.

He was propped on the very edge of the boulder, his hands warped into tight knuckled fists on his knees. His jaw was clenched, like he was angry, though if it was at her, Shula couldn't be sure.

"Then we will train you." Valerio drew her attention back to him with those words. "You do not have to hide who you are, and you do not have to suppress your powers anymore."

Instead of answering, Shula walked past him up the slope to where her clothes lay. She fought back her shivers and methodically got dressed. Her tunic clung to her curves and pressed to the wounds on her back. Their gazes felt heavy on that specific part of her body.

Don't ask, she pleaded silently. *Don't ask, because I don't have the answers.*

"You panic and you run away." The growling voice had Shula snapping up, turning to face Ryker. He'd pushed himself off of the boulder and was close to her. She hadn't even heard his footsteps. "At the first sign of trouble, you *run.* You'll never control your magic that way."

It was the first time he'd spoken to her in days, since the night before they'd left Castle Aileach and he'd basically told her she was a Fae betrayer. The fact that he was talking to her now, after ignoring her and pretending she didn't exist for days, really pissed her off.

"Oh, so you're talking to me now?"

"Don't be petulant," he dismissed. "You need to control your fear. Your magic reacts to it. Next time you just might kill one of us because you're too afraid of an illusion, and you'd let yourself explode rather than face the battle."

Fed up with him, Shula threw her pack to the ground and stomped barefoot over to face him. Her hands collided against his shoulders on impulse, shoving him backwards. Something happened to her body when she touched him, starting at her palms. Something that spread and electrified her system, or maybe that was just her fire sparking to life. But Ryker staggered back too, and it was like he'd felt it as well.

"I am so sick of you!" she shouted, her chest rising and falling with her rapid breaths. "You've no idea how difficult it is!"

He stomped a step forward, their chests kissing intimately. The brief contact made her breath hitch and awareness spread through her veins. He bent so their faces all but touched and growled, warm breath fanning across her lips. "All I hear are fucking excuses. It's difficult? Then *try harder.* You train until you're bruised and bleeding, but when it comes to magic, your fucking fear makes you shy away every single time. You're a Fae. Start acting like one."

Seconds passed, then dragged on into minutes and neither one of them moved save for the rapid rise and fall of their chests, pressing together with each harsh breath. She could feel his heart beating like a steady, pounding drum, completely contrasting her own nervous patter. Yet they fit. Somehow, their heartbeats fit. Like jagged puzzle pieces among a pile of smooth edges, it was like finding a match. Another broken piece.

The thought was startling enough to almost have her jerking away from his proximity. *Almost.* She couldn't quite bring herself to move away from him, as if they were tethered together by a stronger force.

Her tongue darted out and swiped across her bottom lip, and Ryker's eyes flared, following the movement before letting out a low growl. Then he was storming away, shoulder ramming into hers as he passed.

That jolt through her body snapped her out of those strange feelings, and she gritted her teeth together. She whirled and opened her mouth to snap at him again, not wanting to accept his word as final, even if a small part of her knew he was *right,* she didn't want to accept it. That meant he won a battle in whatever little war they had going on.

But she never got the words out, because a speeding arrow tore from the trees beyond and landed straight into Shula's shoulder.

As her body flew back and hit the ground, she cursed.

It looked like Ryker would get the last word after all.

Fire and Blood

The pain didn't come till later. Thirty seconds later, to be exact.

Shula groaned and stared down at the arrow sticking out of her shoulder. For a moment everything else disappeared as she took in the sight of it. At the fire pooling out of it. Fire and blood. Tendrils flickered from the opened wound, from between the spaces of her grasping fingers. Her magic responded, protecting.

She closed her fingers into her palms and was slammed back into the moment. She heard her name being shouted. It was a growl, torn from the deepest depths of a soul, vulnerable and foreign.

It took only a moment for her to realize it was Ryker calling to her.

He loomed over her, his face etched in grave lines. He didn't speak or give her any kind of warning before he yanked the arrow from her shoulder. She barely had time to scream or register the pain before his palm covered the wound and warm magic glowed from his hand. In a single moment, the pain vanished, and Shula pushed to her bare feet.

Dozens of men erupted from the trees clad in the dark leather of soldiers. Weapons gleamed beneath the sunlight and when they charged, the scene was nothing but chaos.

Swords clashed together, sliced flesh, maimed, killed. Ten outnumbered their seven, and with iron surrounding the humans, the Fae found their magic weakened.

Adrenaline spiked through her system. Her body moved, instincts of weeks of training taking over. Her feet ran, her body bent, and her hand grasped for the sword on the ground. With a cry, she yanked it from its sheath and ran, clashing to meet a charging human.

Fire swirled around her, its power flickering and waning against the proximity of iron. But she'd been suppressing her magic her entire life. She didn't need it, because now Shula had a new set of skills. And she meant to use every single one of them.

Julius' instructive voice rang in her mind as she parried. She used her strength to her advantage, pushing against her opponent with a fierce brutality until he slid back, leaving his side exposed. Shula didn't think before she sliced the sword out, cutting him down. He fell into a heap on the ground, but she was already turning, going for the next soldier.

She hadn't heard them come close. Her argument with Ryker had distracted her from watching her surroundings. It had distracted the others, who fought as fiercely—if not more—than she did.

Even outnumbered and the iron giving them a disadvantage, it didn't take long to dispose of the threat, and when they did, Shula hurried to slip into her boots and jacket, shouldering her bag.

"We need to leave," Valerio commanded, swiping splattered blood from his forehead. "I can hear more of them... the iron prevents me from knowing how many."

So they grabbed their things and ran, and they didn't stop. Even as morning converged into night. Even as Shula's lungs heaved until she was practically gagging between painful breaths. Shula's ears rang so loudly and pulsed that she didn't think she could catch sound or scent of the humans anymore.

When they finally stopped running, the sun was already rising. A whole day had passed of nonstop moving, and Shula could feel the effects on her body. Her knees vibrated from the impact as they hit the ground, her palms digging into the earth as she promptly vomited the contents in her stomach.

"No more," she groaned. "I can't go anymore." She craned her neck up to look at the others. They looked just as winded as she did, pink-faced and heaving.

"We are far enough away now," Valerio whispered. He was staring off into the trees, gauging the distance of the humans. Shula couldn't hear anything beyond her own pounding heart. "But we should keep moving."

Shula groaned aloud. "We've been running for hours."

"We're in Dana now. If we cross the river, we'll make it to Orknie and we can rest then."

"Not a good idea. We don't have a boat. It would take us two days of swimming to cross the river."

That's how wide the Arcana was. Shula imagined swimming across the rapid waters and failed. Her limbs were weak and aching, and there was no possible way she could make it across the river alive.

"If we wait, the humans will catch up to us."

"Then what do you suggest we do?"

Shula pushed herself up, groaning as her limbs creaked. Voices rose and fell in a rapid rush around her, planning in arguments and counterarguments. Her knees wobbled as she settled into a standing position in time to hear as they finalized the plan.

"I will transport us as close to the shores of Orknie as possible," Uric said. His words were uneven, a betrayal of the strain he felt.

Before Shula could question whether or not he was strong enough to even transport them, a portal opened behind him. His face scrunched up in pain-filled lines.

"Hurry," Valerio urged.

Shula's eyes felt heavy, threatening to close with exhaustion, but she managed to make her way to the portal and step through to the other side.

Orknie

Shock exploded through her system as she landed in freezing water. The icy freeze chased away any lethargy she'd been feeling as she gasped, taking cold air into her lungs. Her feet kicked on instinct as she was dragged beneath vicious waves, the arms of the river threatening her death.

Her arms flailed, helping her to break the surface. Blinking away fresh water from her lashes, she turned and found the other Fae breaching the surface and kicking towards shore. She followed, though it felt like it took them forever to reach the muddy bank.

She crawled up through the mud, inhaling grateful breaths. Her whole body shivered, demanding warmth, but she was so exhausted, too tired to summon even the barest flames.

Her fingers slipped as she found purchase to push herself standing again. "Please," she groaned, not afraid that she was reduced to begging. "I can't move another step..."

Her heartbeat was frantic in her chest. Her knees almost gave out when Valerio panted, "We make camp. And risk a fire."

She turned to see the Seelie Prince holding Uric up, like he was the only thing standing between the silver-haired Fae face planting into the mud.

Julius walked over to help the prince, hauling Uric's arm around his shoulder. Together, they dragged his limp body further up the riverbank. Shula followed, willing herself to go just a little further. When they finally found a place a way's away from the Arcana, Shula finally let herself drop to the ground. Her whole body shuddered at the impact, but she didn't care. The pain could come *after* the exhaustion in her body waned. She'd deal with it then.

Just as she started to fall asleep in the soft grass, gentle hands pulled her up from her position and she grumbled, hands colliding against a solid, naked chest.

Her eyes flew open.

"What the fuck are you doing?" she slurred, glaring into Clay's perfect green eyes.

"You need to get out of these wet clothes, Fire Dancer. We may be Fae with better immune systems, but you are weak and could still catch a cold..."

Right. Her depleted energy made her susceptible to human ailments. It was a reason a lot of the humans at the circus suspected her; she never got sick. But she'd been through a hell of a day and didn't feel like arguing.

She dropped her hands at her sides. "Help me," she demanded quietly. "Can't move." Or speak. She didn't want to speak more than was necessary.

Clay groaned. "Fire Dancer, I don't know if that's the smartest idea..."

"Just do it. Please."

She didn't see his expression because her eyes fluttered closed, but a moment later, she felt his fingers tugging at her wet clothes. They slid off her body along with her boots, her pants, until she was in nothing but her undergarments.

Cool air kissed her skin and she felt herself lowered to the grass once again. "Everything's wet, even the blankets," Clay explained in her ear. "But I'll get a fire going to warm you up."

Despite her shivers, despite feeling like she had one foot in dreamland already, Shula felt herself smiling. Warmth spread through her chest. "Thank you, Clay," she whispered.

It was the first time she'd ever said those words to him. Surprisingly, she meant them. She'd been a bitch to him when he'd been the only one really in her corner since the moment she woke up in their safe house.

"You're a good friend, Clay," she murmured, burrowing into the grass. As if she could pull warmth from the earth somehow. "One of the best..."

She wasn't sure, but she felt a hand on her arm and lips press to her forehead. She didn't open her eyes to see, because she was already falling to sleep.

Her mind came to slowly, groggily. Her eyes blinked opened and she turned to her back, finding herself staring up at the night sky. She'd been asleep for hours, though by the aches in her body it felt like it'd only been minutes.

Pushing herself up by the elbows, she cast a glance around. She was all but naked before a steady fire, surrounded by equally naked Fae men who rested uneasily against the grass.

Sitting awake and across from the fire was Clay, tossing twigs into the flames. He didn't look at Shula as she sat up straighter and stretched her arms over her head. "Your clothes are probably dry by now." He pointed to where they hung on a low branch of a tree.

But Shula didn't look at her clothes. Her gaze immediately snapped to where Ryker stood next to them. He faced the forest beyond, the darkness that resided there. Standing watch.

"He hasn't slept at all," Clay supplied.

She looked back to him and noted the shadows dancing beneath his eyes that had nothing to do with the flickering of the bonfire. "It looks like you haven't either."

His lips twitched. "Can't leave the big guy alone, can I?" While his words were humorous, his tone was strained. It was how Shula knew he was forcing himself, pushing too hard.

She stood. "Sleep. I'll keep watch." She started to turn away.

"He won't let you."

Shula threw a smile over her shoulder. "He doesn't *let* me do anything." She walked away, leaving behind Clay's soft, snorting laughter.

She should have felt self-conscious as she approached Ryker barefoot and in her undergarments. She didn't. Instead, she felt a surge of determination.

His whole body was stiff as she approached, and she had no doubt he'd heard her quiet footfalls on the earth's floor. She went for her clothes first, slipping the pants over her legs. They'd dried stiffly against the branch and scraped her skin as she slid them on. She turned away from him to reach for her tunic. She could feel his gaze burning on her backside, staring at the scars even when she covered herself with her tunic. Her jacket was still damp, so she left it where it was and finally turned to face him.

His gaze flickered away almost instantly.

Her lips pressed together as she dared to step beside him. He radiated unease and intensity.

"You should sleep," she suggested quietly. She didn't have to look at him to know he had circles under his eyes, and his lips were pursed in a firm, unyielding line.

"Keeping watch," came his gruff reply.

"Not anymore." Shula's arms crossed against her chest.

He gave out a resigned sigh and raked a hand through his hair. "Woman," he growled.

"Look, I know you don't trust me, but I promise I'm not going to run away. Also—" she snapped when he opened his mouth to interrupt. "I'm not going to slit your throats in your sleep. I'm coming with you on this journey, and I need you guys. You're no use to me dead."

The silence pressed on in which Shula could count her heartbeats to measure the time. A minute passed. Exactly one minute for Ryker to contemplate his answer.

"Wake me if anything happens." It was an order that promised retribution if she didn't comply.

"Okay."

"You still have the dagger I gave you?"

"It's in my bag. If you want it back—"

"Keep it."

His bicolored eyes stared intently into the darkness. He didn't reprimand her, didn't snap. Shula put it down to him being tired. He seemed to be a completely different Fae.

They'd gone toe to toe before, they'd yelled. This was new. It was almost... peaceful. Shula didn't know what to take away from this encounter.

"Here." It took her a moment to realize he was holding out a dagger to her. How many did he have on him? she wondered with amusement as her hand closed around the hilt.

"Another one?" she asked, her eyebrow raising.

He shrugged a big shoulder. "You can never have too much protection."

She brought the weapon close to her chest. "It almost sounds like you care."

But that was ridiculous. There was no way Ryker cared about what happened to her.

"I don't. I care about the safety of the group."

And there it is...

She didn't know why his words stung, but they did, and they had her muttering under her breath, "Fucking asshole."

He grunted as he walked away from her, and for a moment, Shula watched him go. The strong muscles on his back tensed with every step. She turned away, focusing on the darkness and the sounds beyond.

And while she stood there, helping to protect their camp, she could feel his gaze burning holes into her back, watching her, judging her, and despite the urge she had to turn around, she didn't. Not until she heard his breathing settle into an even rhythm as he fell into a deep sleep.

Ryker knew he was an asshole. He knew he was being unfair. But he didn't care. It didn't matter how much the Fire Dancer trained, how much better she got at fighting if she still couldn't face the truth of who and what she was.

Magic was what made the Fae unique, and she was the rarest of the rare. It infuriated him to see her hiding behind the mask of humanity that she didn't even need. She had so much potential, could be so much more than what she was, but fear held her back.

Fear was the enemy of success.

So, yes, he was an asshole. She probably thought he hated her, and while he hated everything she stood for, she'd also become something he could grow used to having around. Because whether he liked it or not, he knew she would accompany them for a long while. At least, until they learned the truth about what she was.

But he knew there was potential inside her.

He glimpsed at it while she fought. There was a ferocity she hid that came out in her honey colored eyes, glowing like fire that didn't want to be tempered, but she snuffed out her own light and she didn't need to.

Ryker prowled away from her, feeling her gaze on his back for a moment. When he reached the fire, he sat across from Clay, who was finally settling in to sleep.

"Tact, Ryker," Clay muttered.

"What?"

"You're about as gentle as a lion tearing through prey."

Ryker scowled at Clay. "What the fuck are you going on about?"

Clay sighed and slumped on his back on the ground. "Females like gentle words and to be treated delicately. And you're... well... none of those things."

"Why the fuck would I be that?" His hackles rose defensively. He wasn't sure why. Probably because he didn't need a pretty, noble Fae to list all his shortcomings. As if Ryker didn't know what the fuck he looked like or that the shitty circumstances in life had made him bitter. Still, he was offended.

"If you ever want her to like you, ease up."

"I don't care if she likes me or not."

"Riiiight."

"I'm serious." Was he? It didn't matter anyway. She had made it abundantly clear she was leaving. She'd rather live a mundane life at the fucking circus than fight for her people.

"Okay, Ryker. But if you keep acting like that, then she'll never want to stay and help us." Clay didn't say anything else. He turned, giving Ryker his back and went silent.

Ryker laid against the ground, staring up at the sky through the canopy of tree leaves. He hated to contemplate Clay's words because he was...well, *Clay*. But they resonated in his mind over and over again. *Was* he being too hard on the Fire Dancer?

Did it even matter?

He was hard on her because he could see the potential she didn't. Because she locked up so much of herself. And maybe because, in part, she reminded him of Mairin.

The two were vastly different; Mairin was sweet and the Fire Dancer—*Shula*—was made of tougher stuff. But he saw similarities. The vulnerability, the fear. It was the type of thing that could get Shula killed. Just like it had killed Mairin.

He let his eyes drift closed. After so long of running and staying awake, exhaustion pulled at him from every angle. He didn't want to give in. Not when Shula was awake and alone guarding their little camp. He wasn't sure he could trust her to keep them safe. Sure, she knew how to fight, but her magic would be a greater asset against humans any day.

He thought of her as he drifted off to sleep and began to dream.

Long auburn hair drifted with the breeze. Strands wet with blood clung to pale skin. Mairin always had the smooth, porcelain complexion that was so easy to blush and quicker to burn with anger. But this paleness was different from normal.

It lacked that brightness that gave it life and instead was clammy, cold, dead.

Hair stuck to her wounded cheeks, held in place with blood. So much blood. Ryker's big hand framed her lacerated face as he shoved the strands aside, smearing crimson against her cold skin.

A sound erupted from his throat that he didn't recognize before he even realized that he was the one making it.

Iron manacles were shackled around her wrists, holding her arms up so she was suspended from the ground and hanging on a thick branch of an old oak tree.

It was like a salt-coated knife digging into an already opened wound.

He'd told *her. Why hadn't she just listened like she was supposed to?*

"Mairin." Her name shook on his tongue. "Mairin."

Her head hung forward, her arms bent at an unnatural angle; he was unsure if they were injuries she'd sustained because of the way she was hanging or before...

He tried not to let his eyes venture down too far. To the wounds that sliced open her skin and were no longer bleeding, or the blood drying on her thighs.

"Mairin," he repeated her name like a mantra. There was magic in words sometimes; it was the oldest form of power, yet it didn't work here. A choked sound came out of his throat as he willed his own magic forth and ran his hands over the wounds on her exposed abdomen. All his life, he'd healed things like cuts and burns. Every time he needed it, his magic was there to save everyone else.

Only this time, it wouldn't save the one person he wanted to live the most.

Tears tracked down his unscarred cheeks and dripped down his chin. Of all the wounds he'd ever healed, these were the worst. Maybe he just wasn't strong enough, but even as those treacherous thoughts crossed his mind, he knew they weren't true.

It wasn't that he wasn't strong enough.

It was that Mairin was already dead.

Even then, his magic burst forth along with a scream from his lips. He ran them over her naked stomach and where his fingers touched, her body healed. He traveled higher, palming her face and the scar that bisected in jigsaw puzzle pieces across her skin. He pulled the pain she'd felt into himself, healing her wounds so Mairin was once again the beautiful woman she should be. He gladly took her scars.

But he still couldn't give her life.

Her soul had already departed into Mana, leaving behind a broken shell of a body that he healed with no essence to occupy it. Every broken bone, fuck, *even the pain between her thighs, he sucked into himself. As if that could make it any better. As if it could somehow reverse it. Even if she were alive, even if she wouldn't feel the pain anymore, it had still happened.*

And Ryker blamed himself.

When there was nothing left to heal. When he had absorbed every scar over his body and felt the difference settle over his face, his abs, his legs... He dropped to his knees before her and hugged her close.

The tears came, and they didn't stop. He knew, unfathomably, that this moment? It would live with him for the rest of his life. And he vowed over her lifeless body that he would never let what happened to her happen to anyone else ever again.

Even if he had to give his own life to save others, he would do it.

Because no one, no one, *deserved to suffer such a fate at the hands of the humans.*

"Mairin! Mairin! No! Mairin!"

Shula jolted out of guarding the woods to Ryker's distressed cries. She whirled, dagger in hand, heart beating against her chest, but there was no threat. Just Ryker thrashing against the ground. A sound came from his throat that was guttural and animalistic. A sound that weighed heavily on her heart, for it was a sound of immense heartbreak that no one deserved to bear.

She debated marching over and waking him up from his nightmare. Even if he was an asshole, he didn't deserve to suffer. She knew what nightmares could do. How the phantom limbs of the past could flicker into waking moments meant for torture.

Truth was, the sound broke her heart.

No one else woke. Or if they did, they pretended they were still sleeping. Were they so used to this behavior that they didn't bother waking him anymore? She'd been with them for weeks and hadn't seen him fall into nightmares. Then again, she hardly ever saw him sleep...

She took a step towards Ryker's body, but in a moment, he shot up from the ground, a primal growl roaring from his mouth. He breathed heavily and looked around, his eyes wild as he took a moment to gather his surroundings, to remember where he was. Who he was.

Then his eyes met Shula's, and she wanted to stagger back from the intensity of it but kept her feet planted firmly in the earth.

His breath hitched, and he pushed himself to his feet, staggering away from the fire. Shula's feet moved of their own volition, meeting him halfway. He tried to side-step her, obviously desperate to get away, but her palm pressed against his chest. He froze. His whole body felt too hot, too tense, primed and ready for a fight. She felt his muscles shaking beneath her touch, vibrating with the remnants of his nightmare.

"Ryker..." His nostrils flared at the sound of her voice.

She should have let him go. She knew that. But something about his distress, about the vestiges of the nightmare clinging to him physically hurt. Because Shula had been there before. She knew what it was like to wake up screaming, to wake up not knowing what was real and what was fake.

So often she dreamt of her parents and the day they were taken, what would have happened if their roles had been reversed. She dreamt that they'd shoved her in their iron ovens and fire consumed her from the inside out until she was reduced to ash.

"Ryker," she repeated, softly, but no less firm. "It's okay."

His black eye flashed, and she could see the fury in the single, dark color. Like the darkness of storms, it threatened destruction.

His hand clamped down on hers, tightening around her fingers. Not hard enough to bruise or even to hurt, but his grip was adamant. "Shula..." His voice was a gravelly sound. It was the first time he'd ever said her name. "Don't." There was a begging quality to the word that made her determination falter. "Let me go."

Shula knew he could easily break her hand and walk away. He could push her hand aside, shove past her shoulder, and rage away like he obviously wanted to do. But he didn't. Why didn't he?

Shula couldn't help but feel like he kept his hand plastered to hers to keep the two of them tethered. Because maybe, even though he demanded it, he didn't really want to be alone.

His heartbeat slammed against her palm, as rough as the edges of his scars. It was a sound that resonated in Shula's own soul.

"It wasn't real," she whispered. Those words were empty and she knew it, but she didn't know what else to say to him. She could feel his fear; it wafted over her like a powerful blow.

For a moment, his eyes flashed with clarity, and he snorted a breath. He gripped her hand tighter and using the other, he trailed his fingers down the side of her face in a surprising moment of intimacy. "It was real, Shula."

It was the strangest moment of vulnerability between the two. Shula's heart beat faster, and she wondered if he could hear it. Her throat tightened with so many emotions and this connection between them. Like a force of invisible magic that somehow pulled them together.

The humans, her power, the Emperor of Illyk... none of it frightened her more than their connection right then.

"Who's Mairin?"

It was the wrong thing to ask. His whole body tensed, and he looked down at everywhere their skin touched, as if just now realizing just how close they were, at how intimately their skin kissed. He dropped his hold on her, and then he did what she'd expected him to do in the first place.

He pushed her hand away gently and stormed away into the dark of the forest. Shula watched him go, feeling a burning sensation behind the backs of her lids. She willed herself not to cry for the scarred Fae man who dared showed his vulnerable side and open up even with something as simple as a touch.

She willed herself not to cry for the haunted look that mirrored her own.

She willed herself not to cry over the fact he woke up screaming another woman's name.

She willed herself not to cry because she didn't know why she was hurting in the first place.

Wounds of the Mind

The next morning, after everyone was well and truly rested, they decided not to waste any more time and marched onward. No one mentioned the fact that Ryker had woke up crying out someone's name in the middle of the night or that he hadn't gone back to sleep. No one talked about what they had no doubt heard between Shula and Ryker, or about the fact that he didn't show up to their camp until it was time to leave.

Not even Shula felt the need for that conversation. Not yet, at least, when the feelings were still so raw inside her, inside *him*, even though he seemed to have hardened his resolve under grim expressions and glares.

So Shula bit her tongue as everyone packed their bags and continued on through Orknie. The mood was quiet and somber, the silence only broken up by the sounds of birds and other wildlife. When they finally came to a stop as night descended, they prepared a fire, and laid down to sleep.

Ryker and Weylyn were set to take first watch, and Shula found her gaze on Ryker. Even while she laid down, using her hands to pillow her cheek, her eyes followed him as he stepped into the woods, wondering about *who* Mairin was. She figured the others knew, and she wanted to ask them, but she wanted to learn that information from Ryker himself.

An impossible dream, she thought, because of the way he'd closed up when she'd asked the first time. He would never tell her who Mairin was and why he thrashed and cried out like that.

Whoever she was, she must have been terribly important if Ryker lost sleep over her.

And that hurt.

Clutching the pain close to her chest, Shula finally let her eyes close and she drifted off to sleep.

⋙ ⋯ ⋘

"Wake up." A heeled boot nudged against Shula's side. Though the touch was soft, she jolted up on the ground, her heart pounding, her breathing all but erratic.

She glared up at Ryker through her grogginess, meeting his stern expression. "What the fuck?" she hissed, rubbing the backs of her hands against her eyelids. The sun hadn't even risen yet and darkness still blanketed the woods.

"Get up," he ordered.

The tone had her reaching for the dagger he'd given her, sheathed at her waist, and looking around camp. "What is it?" She listened intently but didn't hear anything other than the soft breathing of her Fae companions in sleep.

"We're training, Fire Dancer. Now."

She stared at him, a part of her wanting to flip him a vulgar gesture and go back to sleep, but the pressing bruises beneath his eyes made her stop and reconsider.

Ryker loathed her. Of all the Fae, he was the only one who hadn't yet trained with her. He'd been the only one who hadn't offered her any input at all, save to tell her what a frightened mess she was. And now he was staring down at her, an unreadable, hard expression over his features.

All the vulnerability from the previous day had vanished as if it hadn't even been there at all. In its place was the same Fae who had glared at her since the moment she'd slammed into his massive body. Only this time, there was one difference.

He wasn't looking at her with open disdain.

Perhaps that's what had Shula pushing to her feet, all traces of tiredness gone from her body.

"Okay," she agreed.

She couldn't be sure, but she thought there was relief flashing in his eyes for a second before he masked it again. Then he was leading her away through the trees.

They walked in silence while Shula tried to gather her thoughts. She wondered what had changed in the span of all these weeks to have Ryker taking her before anyone else woke to train. Perhaps it been the simple act of compassion from the night before, or maybe something else entirely.

The trickling sound of a stream pulled her out of her thoughts at about the same time that Ryker stopped and turned. Shula felt her body freeze at his sudden assessment. His eyes raked over her body, from her booted feet and up higher, landing on her face.

She didn't cow before his glare, no matter how intimidating. Just like she wouldn't admit that his intensity made goosebumps rise along her flesh, making her glad she was wearing a long-sleeved tunic and jacket over it. She tilted her chin in the slightest stance of daring defiance.

He was always judging her, always finding her lacking. Now wouldn't be any different, and just like all the times before, she refused to be embarrassed by what he thought he saw when he looked at her.

He turned away abruptly, staring at the steadily flowing stream. "The waters of Lake Degara flow all throughout Orknie."

Okay?

He turned back. "It's not the Arcana, but it will do."

In case she lost control. So she didn't burn the entire forest down.

He was taking precautions in case her powers got out of control, but for some reason those precautions made her hackles rise defensively. She had no right to even feel that when she knew her powers were erratic and unpredictable.

It wasn't that she was embarrassed about not controlling her powers, it was that he *knew*. Not that it was some grand secret, but it still made her uncomfortable because he'd done nothing but judge her for it since they met.

She was familiar with wanting the approval of those who hated her the most. It was an endless cycle in her life. First, the humans. She'd molded herself to become one, or as close to a human as she could possibly be. Now, the Fae were ripping that away from her and reshaping her into what they wanted. A weapon, a killer, their pet. And even if she didn't believe in this war, she'd still bend over backwards to do what they wanted. It was a void desperate to be filled. She wanted to be accepted, loved.

That, she realized, was why she felt such a strong pull to Ryker rather than the others. Because he was the one it was hardest to please.

The truth was, she didn't *need* his approval. Logically, she knew she didn't. She was leaving anyway, going to find a new life for herself, and she drowned in her own toxic need to make him happy. To have him smile at her. To have his acceptance.

Ryker stepped closer to the stream, over to where there were boulders and fallen logs. He lowered himself onto a boulder, one leg extended into the ground, the other bent against it to prop himself up. The move was very casual and unlike him.

He nodded at the rotting log across from him. "Sit."

Shula gripped the knife in her hand tighter, drawing comfort from the action, because *what the hell?* Moving almost too cautiously, she took a seat across from Ryker, moss and wet, rotting bark seeping through her pants.

That eerie gaze assessed her. Being the recipient of that stare made her feel naked. Not the type of naked that meant no clothes, but the other kind. The kind that seemed like he could see into her mind, her soul. Like he saw vividly every vulnerable piece of her.

Shula didn't like it.

"What are we doing?" she demanded.

It was a while before he responded. "Training."

Okay?

"Um—"

"Why are you frightened of your powers?" he interrupted.

She jolted at the question. "I'm not." His glare was pointed. "I'm not!"

"Do not lie to me. I can smell your fear every time you summon the flames."

She gritted her teeth together and averted her gaze, not able to answer because... well, because he was right. She *was* afraid of her magic.

Her fingers glided along the edge of the dagger's blade. It sliced her skin, but she didn't wince. The pain grounded her.

"What does that have to do with training?" she snapped finally. She had no desire for him to sit there picking at her wounds like a child poking at a dying animal. "Shouldn't we be fighting?"

Ryker slid one leg down, planting them both against the ground and leaning forward, his forearms resting against his thighs. "I am a healer. That means I can sense wounds. Any wounds. Even the wounds here." He pressed two fingers to his temple. "Like the body, the mind can be wounded, and sometimes the pain we can't see is the most harmful. If a Fae is stabbed and loses blood, their powers weaken and they cannot fight." He pushed himself from the rock and crouched in front of Shula. His fingers pressed to her temples, and she felt the touch down to the fibers of her soul. "This is wounded, and it needs to heal in order for your magic to work." He pushed away again, putting space between them. "So, I'll ask again, why are you frightened of your magic?"

Something clogged in her throat. Words she wanted to say, emotions she didn't let herself feel that blocked her from saying anything at all.

Ryker sighed, clearly impatient.

Shula scowled. "Well, what about your wounds, then?"

The eyebrow above his white eye rose. "What about them?"

"They're not healed."

His expression hardened, and she knew she struck a nerve. It wasn't any of her business, and she had no idea what his situation was that made him wake up screaming a woman's name in the middle of the night, but she'd be damned if she let him lecture her about the wounds of her mind when he was just as damaged.

When he didn't reply, Shula leaned back. "Exactly," she shot.

Ryker growled. "There's a difference between my wounds and yours, Fire Dancer."

"Oh? And what's that?"

"My wounds *fuel* my magic. Your wounds impede yours."

He was right, yet she still couldn't bring herself to say the words she kept tightly locked up. She couldn't give up that part of herself when he'd given her nothing but disdain.

So she pressed her lips together and glared.

A growl rumbled in his chest. "Talk," he ordered.

"No."

His lips pursed. "Do you need Fae wine to confess your secrets?"

Her face heated as she recalled that moment, how the coarse beard along his cheeks felt like thorns between her palms. The heaviness of the emotions clogging her throat, the looseness of her tongue, and the words that slipped out of her mouth.

"Fuck off, Ryker." She pushed to her feet, pointing the dagger accusingly in his direction. "While you sit there preaching at me about my life, take a good long look at *yourself*."

He straightened, something dark wafted over him. Something that could have been considered evil but wasn't. No, Shula had seen her fair share of evil. But there *was* something dangerous, a threat.

"At myself," he echoed, his voice nearly a purr.

"Yes, yourself." Her rage rose. "You preach at me every time you open that fucking mouth of yours. You aren't perfect, either. You like pointing fingers, to claim that I'm *wounded* in the head, but what about you?"

"What about me?"

Even him repeating everything she said irritated her. "You can't go a fucking minute without insulting me. You know what I think? I think you're projecting your own failures and insecurities onto me. You look at me and you see whatever failures live in that fucked up mind of yours, and *that's* the only reason you hate me."

He moved before she could even blink. He was a blur as he charged towards her, and she didn't have time to react. He was there, his hand closing around her throat, putting enough pressure to make her gasp but not enough to hurt. His body pressed against hers, and everything about this seemed like something *more* than what it probably was.

It felt sensual, and the heat that bounced back and forth between them was just enough to make Shula rub her thighs together. The danger of the situation melded into pleasure that shivered down her spine.

Ryker's nostrils flared as he scented her arousal, and humiliation swept over her. Just because he had that effect on her didn't mean she liked him or that she wanted to feel it.

They stayed like that, their breaths mingling, chests pressing in a heady rise and fall, hearts beating fast as if they meant to jump straight from their chests and mesh together into one single entity.

His calloused fingers slid up a fraction and gripped her jaw. It took only a second to register just how close his mouth was to hers, and when he spoke, his breath fanned across her lips. "You're right, Fire Dancer." It sounded like he was pulling the words from some dark place inside him. "I *am* afraid. I am afraid *for you.* Because I see your potential; I see how great you can be, and I see you lock it up tightly behind your fear. Don't let your fear rule you, because I believe you can be *great.*"

Fuck, if those words didn't reach into her heart and squeeze. She believed him. The truth was in the cadence of his tone, and she wanted to believe in herself as much as he seemed to believe in her.

"The truth is, I have lost too many Fae. That's why I save them." He paused, and she swore she felt the brush of his lips against her own because they were so close. "Believe it or not, I don't want to lose you, too."

Her breath caught in her throat. It was the raw and primal truth. A small, vulnerable part of himself that he shared. It wasn't a confession; it wasn't his story, but it was something. A piece of himself. So she would give him a piece of her, too.

"I'm afraid of the humans," she confessed. "I'm afraid they'll *hurt* me. And if I use my magic, then no one will truly love me."

His grip eased, and slowly his fingers trailed down the skin at the open neck of her jacket. His gaze softened, and it was like he *saw her.* Like he understood.

Maybe he did.

Maybe... maybe he was the only one.

"No one can hurt you, Shula. I won't let them. And with enough training, *you* won't let them either."

And Shula believed him.

One by one, his fingers extricated from Shula's neck, and he took a step back. "Summon the flames," he whispered.

Shula did.

And the flames responded in kind, appearing between her fingers, flickering and dancing.

"Direct them. Make them do what you want."

Shula followed Ryker's soft-spoken instructions, confidence surging through her body as she let the flames dance against her palms. She started small, molding them into figures; butterflies, fluttering pixies, a kitten...

She pushed the fire kitten out, and it prowled towards Ryker before bursting into sparks and falling into ash at his feet.

"Now draw it back into yourself."

Like he was the one commanding it, the flames listened, shooting back inside her body where they settled with the discreet taste of smoke in her lungs.

She exhaled smoke, and a smile pulled at the corners of her mouth. "I did it." The words were whispered. She looked up at Ryker. "I did it!"

And then Ryker surprised her.

He smiled.

"Where have you two been?" Clay demanded the moment Shula and Ryker stepped foot back into camp. It had been an hour since the sun had risen, and they'd spent every minute of it coaxing Shula's magic out, molding it, controlling it in small quantities.

There hadn't been a single accident.

Ryker had expected to at *least* put out a raging fire or two with the water from Lake Degara's streams.

After she'd confessed her fears, he'd felt fragments of her troubled mind start to mend, like bits of broken steel meld together once more. It wasn't much; it was the smallest of pieces, and yet it was progress just the same.

"Training," Ryker answered, though the word came out more a growl than anything else. Whatever. It didn't matter. He stormed over to his bag and hauled it over his shoulder. He didn't need to turn to know Shula's smile followed his every move.

He fought not to tense up at the attention he didn't want. While they'd made progress, a part of him felt... strange... There was no other word for it, because of what he'd given her. A bit of his own fragmented pieces. As if she could take them in her delicate hands and fit them onto her own broken bits. He'd given them up like an offering and didn't even know why.

It didn't matter, anyway. It wasn't anything that the others didn't know. He could pretend all he wanted, but they all knew exactly why he protected others so much. And while they were words he hadn't said to Shula, not completely, he still meant them.

He was saving everyone else because he hadn't been able to save Mairin.

Shula reminded him of Mairin. The misplaced trust in the humans was the same. Some would call him hypocritical, say that he despised the humans almost as much as they despised the Fae. While that seemed true, it wasn't.

Ryker knew that not all the humans were the same. But a lot of them were vile, evil, and would do whatever it took to eliminate the Fae. Their prejudice knew no bounds. The proof of that had been on Mairin's scarred face, her bruised and brutalized body.

He should know.

He'd felt it. He'd felt her pain as if it had been his own. Every bruised rib, every slash against skin, even the fucking pulsing between her thighs, he'd taken into his own fucking body. Every wound inflicted by the humans, he'd *felt.*

He didn't want anyone to ever live through that kind of torture, and he hated that Mairin had.

So, yes, he'd offered pieces of his secrets to Shula because she needed them to be stronger. And if given the choice between spilling the darkest secrets he held in his soul and saving Shula's life?

He'd save Shula's life every damn time.

"How did it go?" Clay asked.

"It went well," Shula chimed in.

Ryker turned and found her smile wide and unyielding. He frowned at it. Not because he didn't think she should be happy. She'd made a huge step towards unlocking her potential, but he didn't want her blinded by a single, miniscule stepping-stone when there was so much left in the journey to walk.

"She did passable," Ryker told them. "She still has a lot to learn."

His words broke Shula's smile and he hated doing that to her, hated himself for the expression that replaced the happiness.

But if he had to choose between letting that happiness blind her to a reality that meant death, or judge her harshly so she worked harder for her life?

Ryker knew which one he would choose.

Every damn time.

Mairin

Lake Degara did split into streams and rivers all throughout Orknie. The water was clear, fresh, and filled with fish. But most importantly, it was *clean.*

Shula stood at the edge of the river, cocking her head to the side, listening. The Fae had fanned out, looking for any sign of humans that would be near. When they'd found none, Shula had declared she wanted a bath, and no one had argued as she stormed over to the rushing water of the river.

She listened then, to make sure she was truly alone before she slipped her jacket from her body. She toed off her boots and discarded her clothes until she was naked.

Cool autumn wind caressed her skin, making her shiver. Toeing into the water, she figured the brisk cold of it was worse. But she needed to feel clean. Sure, when she'd traveled with Piriguini's Circus, she and the others hadn't bathed every day, but she hadn't gone so long without as she had traveling with the Fae.

She was starting to feel gross and had been willing to burn off all of Prince Valerio's hair if he'd argued. He hadn't. Better for him, she supposed.

The icy bite of the water enveloped her, trembles already wracking through her body. She hurried through the routine, having to go without soap, but scrubbing everything that was necessary until she felt normal again.

When she finished, she stepped out and used her discarded clothes to dry off with. Perhaps if she hadn't been so focused on her task, she would have heard the footsteps approaching, but she didn't realize until a figure was right in front of her.

She yelped and jumped back, glaring into Weylyn's golden eyes.

"What the fuck, Weylyn?!"

The tall, lithe man simply stared. His golden eyes were penetrating, like he was staring into the recesses of her soul. No, not staring; pulling out her thoughts, pillaging, murdering. There was a darkness around him, one she noticed as he prowled towards her like a looming predator.

She stepped back, her feet sloshing into the mud of the riverbank. But the ten feet of space between them still didn't feel like enough distance to escape that stare.

She held her clothes against her body like a shield, but it felt useless. Like he could see through that as well.

"Weylyn..." She hated how her voice trembled with the slightest edge of fear.

"I am not going to hurt you, Shula Azzarh," he said, and his voice was deep and smooth. Like if melted chocolate had a sound, it would be what just fell from his lips. The scent of him enveloped her from a distance. Something nauseating, too spicy like sandalwood or hot peppers and something thicker as well.

"What do you want? I don't know if you noticed, but I'm kind of busy at the moment."

"Have you ever heard of the mating bond?"

Shula blinked at him. "Weylyn, I don't think this is—"

"Have you?"

She shifted from one foot to the other uncomfortably. "Of course I've heard of it."

He cocked his head to the side and stared at her, the color of his eyes swallowed by the whites. He went immobile, like he was seizing standing up. Shula took a step forward, unsure if she should help him, but then the episode ended.

"Interesting..."

"What's interesting?"

"The fact that you know nothing. That you can't even see it yet."

"What are you—"

But he didn't reply, because he was already turning and walking away.

Shula held her breath and waited, counting his retreating footsteps until he was gone. Only then did she hurry and dig through her bag, pulling out a fresh change of clothes. Once she was dressed, she hurried back to camp, but there was no sign of Weylyn at all. He'd likely gone patrolling the area, but she couldn't get their encounter out of her mind.

She sat next to Clay by the roaring campfire.

"Hey, Clay?"

"Hmm?"

"What's Weylyn's power?"

He froze. "I don't think you really want to know."

She thought back to the way his eyes seemed to roll to the back of his head, his immobility. It wasn't the first time she'd seen him do that, and since all magic came with a price, she wondered if that was the price of his particular magic.

Whatever that may be.

Clay sighed. "Weylyn can read minds and communicate telepathically with others."

Shula felt all the blood drain from her face. "What?" she hissed.

Clay nodded. "Why do you think everyone is so wary of him? He knows all our secrets, all our desires, everything. It's why King Ashera keeps him so close. It's also why he sent him with us, so Weylyn can report back to the king, mind to mind."

Shula tried not to let the sliver of fear overtake her, but it was too late. Too many thoughts swirled in her mind. That meant that everything she'd ever thought, Weylyn knew about? He knew her past, her shame?

No wonder the others mistreated him. She would have said he didn't deserve to be treated like cattle, but if he was openly eavesdropping into everyone's minds...

"Yeah, exactly," Clay muttered. "Told you."

They spent the rest of the night in silence, Clay poking at the fire while Shula contemplated how hard it'd be to block her thoughts out from now on.

"Shula."

She startled, looking up into Valerio's eyes. The Seelie Prince worked tightly at his jaw. While Valerio was always so serious, she hadn't ever seen him look so... grave. His hand held out to her, expectant and patient.

"Come with me."

It was an order, and Shula didn't consider him her prince, but the effort it would take to argue was something she didn't feel like doing. She slipped her hand into his, and he helped her to stand. Once on her feet, he didn't pull his fingers from her grasp. He seemed to hold her tighter as he tugged her away from the fire and prying eyes of the others.

Once they were well out of earshot, protected by the dense copse of trees, he released her. They were facing each other, and in the darkness she could make out the sharp, slashing lines of his features.

"Is there something you needed?" Scrutiny from the Seelie Prince was almost as unnerving as receiving it from Uric or Weylyn.

"You trained with Ryker." It wasn't a question.

"Um... yes."

He nodded, and she watched the workings of his throat as he swallowed. She couldn't be sure, but she was almost positive the Seelie Prince was nervous.

"Was he... kind to you?"

She blinked away her surprise at the question, only to be swallowed by it once again. "I don't see why it matters." No one had seemed to care about how he treated her before. Why should it matter how he treated her now?

"I worry about him. After what happened with Mairin..."

Shula felt her ears twitch. "Who's Mairin?"

Valerio's lips pressed closed. He shook his head. "Not my story to tell."

"Yet you brought it up."

"You once asked me why I went after you if I thought Davina was rambling mad."

She remembered and chose to ignore the fact that he'd changed the subject so abruptly.

"After all, you were one Fae locked in a human temple with guards posted around the building. Why would we risk so much for you when we had already saved so many? Even if we were desperate for soldiers and to preserve our race, why risk it for *you*?"

Shula's heart pounded. Yes. She had wondered what method of persuasion Davina had used to convince the Prince of Seelie to go after her. It must have been something life-altering, something *huge* for them to risk their lives going to get her out of that place.

"What did she say?"

He looked away. As if it hurt to face her. When he turned back, she felt a storm of dark power around him, like he was drawing all the strength he could towards him. Hiding behind a mask of formidable power so no one would know just how truly scared he was inside. But Shula knew fear, so she recognized it.

"She said if we rescued you, I would find my mate."

Shula staggered back a step, her heart shooting up to her throat. Mates, like familiars, were held in the highest veneration. And this wasn't the first time in the day someone mentioned the word 'mate' to her. Were they trying to tell her something?

She took in the prince again, from head to toe. All slashing, dark lines and a face that could enamor and kill with a single glance. Yet when she looked at him, she felt *nothing.*

She may not know a lot about the Fae because of her upbringing, but everyone knew about mates. The bond that clicked into place like a missing piece of a puzzle pressing into two differently shaped souls to bind them forever. It was a love that was catastrophic and extraordinary.

The Seelie Prince *had* altered her life, but...

"I thought I would arrive there and find my mate in you. That our bond would snap into place."

"But it didn't..." Something tight in her chest eased. Something like relief, even if she felt a bit sorry for the hopes Prince Valerio had.

"I did not tell the others why I decided to go after you. Nor will I. Perhaps they'd understand, but if they do not..." He shook his head, his hair moving like strands of silk around his shoulders. "Regardless, I feel the fool. I allowed the seer to play me. She said what she knew I wanted to hear. The promise of my mate." He sighed. "The Fae live such long lives; it's only the promise of our mate that makes it bearable. I've lived centuries, and I thought you would be it."

"I'm sorry, Valerio." She didn't have anything to be sorry for, and yet she felt his sorrow and mirrored it. She couldn't imagine the hope he'd harbored for the Fae meant to be his only to find Shula instead.

"I suppose I thought if I kept you, a bond would fall into place, but now I see it is impossible." He took a step towards her, pressing his palms against her shoulders.

She allowed the touch because she knew it was for him, to ground *him.* "There still might be hope."

"Perhaps. But I will not hang on to that hope anymore." A moment passed, and then he was pulling her close. It was so surprising, she stumbled against his chest. His arms wrapped around her, and she knew this was him, saying goodbye to what he thought they could be. So she let him. He pulled away, and she felt the whisper of his lips across her forehead. "You are not mine."

Valerio took in a breath and stared at the darkness.

"Stare long enough and you will find the darkness staring back."

He closed his eyes as if blocking his sight could block out the voice as well. Of all the Fae that could come upon him then, it had to be the one he wanted nothing from.

"Leave," he ordered, his tone broking no room for argument.

But Weylyn could never do what he was told.

"You told her."

"I do not see what business it is of yours." He felt the ground shift as Weylyn stalked towards him. He despised feeling vulnerable, and there was no more vulnerable feeling than being around a Fae who could look inside his mind.

Everyone gave Weylyn a wide berth, but Valerio did not have that luxury. Not when Weylyn was Valerio's father's preferred Fae. It meant countless interactions, it meant learning to school his mind and compartmentalizing his thoughts whenever the other male was near.

Unfortunately, things still slipped through.

"You have not told my father."

"Yet."

Valerio's eyes opened on a glare in his direction. It was smarter to hide what he was feeling, but he was *tired,* his patience thinning.

He was a prince, and Weylyn stared at him as if he were scum.

"Let me reiterate that." He stepped forward until their chests were touching. "You have not and *will not* tell my father. In case you have not noticed, he is not here. That means I am in command."

If he meant to intimidate the Fae, it didn't work. Weylyn's lips curved into a sly smile, looking like a cunning feline ready to pounce. "You are truly a fool if you think you are in command. So long as the king lives and breathes, you will never be. Your desires come second to his own." He lifted a hand and tapped a finger to his temple. "He is in here always. So let me ask you, my prince, what do you think your father will say when he discovers the real reason behind saving the Fire Dancer?"

Valerio gave nothing away in his expression, in the beating of his heart, or the rushing of his blood. He'd given away too much already; he wouldn't give Weylyn any more.

"No?" Weylyn's smile widened. "Let me help you. He will be furious. You are his son, and so immune to his wrath, but Shula will not be. The seer played you for a fool, and the king will not take kindly to you besmirching the Ashera name for her."

"He wouldn't. She's too important for this war."

"A theory. One that until disproven protects her. But what if she is not? Your father will give me the order. If and when he does..." He stepped back, putting space between them once more. "My blade will taste the blood of fire."

The next morning, Shula got up and trained with Ryker before the sun even came out. They worked tirelessly, him coaching her as she molded fire, gradually making the figures she created bigger and bigger until exhaustion overtook her.

The figures died in a pile of ash at her feet. She slumped, dropping to the ground and heaving in breath after breath.

Ryker grunted as he sat across from her. "You need to build resistance," he said. "Once you control it better, we can move on to learning to fight with your magic."

She inhaled sharply and release the breath slowly. "Are you qualified to teach me that?" At his pointed look, she continued, "What I mean is, you're a healer. How do you use *your* magic in battle?"

"I direct my magic to heal the Fae."

Her brows pulled together. "Wouldn't that weaken you, though? It doesn't make sense to weaken yourself, especially if it could kill you. You're the ones who say that every Fae life is valuable."

"I know I am essential, but when it comes down to it, if it means my life to save countless others? I'll use everything I have left in me."

He said it with such conviction, she believed it was true. It gave her a glimpse at the man inside, at what he hid behind scars and a gruff demeanor. He was willing to die for what he believed in.

She remembered what Valerio had said, the name that Ryker had shouted for in his nightmares. She wondered if this willingness to die for the cause had anything to do with her.

"Why?" she found herself asking.

"Why what?"

"Why would you give your life?"

She knew what would happen if she were on the other end of the spectrum. It was what she'd done time and time again. She would run and hide, and that fact suddenly made her feel less brave than she thought she was.

She'd thought there was bravery in running and hiding; *surviving*, she'd called it. But was there truer bravery in standing and fighting, even if you knew you were going to die?

As if he could read her questions, Ryker answered, "A life of slavery and fear is not a life. When you know freedom, true freedom, nothing else can ever compare. And I would rather die fighting to give freedom to others than hide amongst those who would kill me without a second thought."

Those words were like a slap to her face. She felt the heat crawl up her neck because he was talking about her. About the decisions she'd made. They weren't said with their usual ire, and yet they still stung.

"I've never known freedom. How can I fight for something I've never seen?"

"You just do it."

But, how? All she knew was a life in shackles. It had grown comfortable. Familiar. Safe. Fighting wasn't safe. It was unknown and therefore dangerous.

"You hate me because I'm afraid to fight," she whispered. "But I haven't known anything other than hiding."

Ryker grunted but didn't contradict what she said. That hurt. Even after training together, he still thought so little of her, and all she'd tried to do was prove herself again and again. He couldn't see, and all she wanted was to hurt him for it. Like he hurt her.

"Don't you think your behavior is as bad as mine?" His eyebrows merely rose. "Is that why you heal everyone else so much, no matter the injuries? Not because you feel like it's the right thing, but because you don't care if you live or die? You're using the 'saving the Fae' thing as an excuse when it's not true."

"Shula…" His voice held a tone of warning that she didn't heed.

"Do you really want to save everyone because they're Fae and you want them safe, or are you compensating for someone you couldn't save?"

Ryker's glare slashed through her. Had it been a knife, she would have bled out on the forest floor. He pushed himself to his feet like he wanted nothing more than to get away from her and the truth she presented. Likely, a truth he never dared consider himself.

"Ryker…" Shula stood. She wouldn't let him walk away. Every time he threw something in her face, she took it and she listened. But when someone mentioned his own faults, he ran.

"Leave it alone, Shula."

"It's true, isn't it?"

He started to walk away. Shula followed. She was being incessant, she knew, but it didn't matter. He was making her face her demons, why shouldn't he do it as well?

Whenever they took a few steps forward, progressing in whatever strange relationship they had, he always trampled over it, pushed them backwards. Like he didn't want to accept where things were going.

Shula didn't even know where they were going, but she liked it. She liked the amicability between them. When he shoved her away, each shove harder than the last, maybe he hoped that with the right pressure, he'd push her away for good.

And it was working.

So Shula fought back.

"You don't know what you're talking about," Ryker growled.

"Don't I, though?"

"You don't know a damn thing."

"Who's Mairin?"

The words pulled Ryker back. He stopped, his whole body going taut. Then he was whirling, stepping towards her with eyes that were blazing with the force of his fury.

"Mind your own fucking business, Fire Dancer."

Those words were chilling, telling. They felt of violence and a promise of death.

Still, her stubbornness didn't allow her to keep quiet. She wanted to know. Needed to know to assuage the ache in her chest, like little claws tearing through her body and mind and soul.

"Tell me, Ryker. Who is Mairin?"

She was a fool if she thought he'd answer. He turned and stomped away, and Shula watched, the claws of truths unanswered digging deep in her chest.

Clay felt the weariness creep over him like smoke. It wasn't borne of being tired, even if he felt that too. Bone-deep and with all the eternity that came with a long lifespan, he felt that. Yet this was different. Not because they'd been walking for weeks.

His weariness came from something else entirely.

It came from the iron that seeped deep into the ground.

They'd left the lush woods behind, each tree becoming scarcer than the last until there was nothing left to cover their presence. Nothing but dried, skeletal limbs of old, dead trees and a vast expanse of wasteland. They had made their way into the lands where things didn't grow.

The middle point where Orknie met Tir na Faie. The blight on the earth.

The poisoned lands.

It was close. He could feel it in the aching joints of his bones and the struggle it took to breathe.

Valerio stopped walking and they followed suit, staring at the horizon where dead land lay. All they had to do was walk the slope and make it to what had once been called 'home.'

"Do you feel that?" Shula stood next to him. Her whole body shivered, and he placed a hand against her shoulder for comfort.

"The iron has spread," Valerio whispered darkly. "I feel it pulsing."

"How is that possible?" Uric turned to the prince. "It was not so far spread before."

"It's been years," Clay supplied.

Years since they last were anywhere near their homeland. Before they'd been driven out of it with iron. The humans had really assured that the Fae could never go back without consequences.

And here they were, ready to venture into it.

Clay remembered a time when these lands had been ripe with beauty. Even with the Ley Line separating the human from the Fae, he'd seen what southern Orknie had been once upon a time. It had been lush with bright fields and grazing animals.

The humans had never possessed magic in the traditional sense, but Mana had gifted them with their earth. That in and of itself was magical, and they couldn't see their own magic around them. They'd destroyed it all.

Clay's heart clenched as he remembered home. The Seelie Courts, his own home, with glittering castles and roads paved with blue gems.

But those castles had long since fallen, the roads dug up for their riches and set with iron and death.

Clay adjusted his bag and rolled his neck. "Well," he tried for a tone to lighten the mood. "What are we waiting for? Let's go."

Home.

And he didn't need to say the words that he knew everyone else thought.

Whatever was left of their home.

Ley Line

The Ley Line that separated Orknie and Tir na Faie wasn't a real line at all. Rather, it was an invisible border of magic. Even though the land was covered in iron and weakened Shula with every step she took, she felt the magic of the Ley Line the moment she passed over it.

It was the same pressure that enveloped her when she passed through Uric's portal. An invisible force that threatened to smother with varying degrees of temperature. Unlike Uric's portal, though, it *hurt* to go through this.

Iron was embedded into the ground, and though they couldn't see it, they could feel it, just like they could feel it in the air. As if it were somehow permeated into the wind, into the portal.

Shula gasped for breath as she crossed the invisible barrier and nearly tumbled to a fall on the other side. She righted herself and looked to the other side.

To Tir na Faie.

She never imagined she'd see the Feylands in her lifetime. Not as they once had been, and certainly not like this, either.

It was dead land where no trees or plants grew, though whatever plant life there had been just... decayed. Even after years, the trees hadn't crumbled. They'd just seemed to have lost the will to live, leaving dried, black husks in their place.

Shula could feel death around her, almost as sharp and as strong as the iron. She dreamt of the beauty of the Feylands before. The dead earth before her just made her want to weep.

"The iron is stifling," Clay complained, rubbing his palm over his chest. "I didn't expect it to be so strong."

"We need to hurry." Valerio began walking. "The faster we find The Seer, the faster we can get out of here. Eyes alert. We don't know if humans prowl these lands."

Shula unsheathed her dagger and held it close. More out of comfort for her rolling emotions—mainly, the sadness—rather than fear. Holding the knife controlled the storm.

"Do you feel it too, little Fire Dancer?" Julius came up beside her while Clay took the other side.

She gripped the knife tighter. "Yes."

"Curious, isn't it?" Clay added. "You melted iron bars, yet it can still effect you."

"The Elementals are not bound by the same rules as the rest of us," Valerio said from his place at the front. "They pay no price for their magic, are directly bound to Mana, and as we've discovered, can melt iron. It should not be possible, yet Mana works in mysterious ways. Do not question it in the land where Mana was born."

It felt like a bad omen to talk about, Shula had to admit. She didn't know why though. It was the ominous energy of the place. Not just the iron, but the memories of the near eradication of the Fae, of the wars, everything bad that ever happened seemed tied here. Like the land remembered, absorbed that negativity and slowly died from it.

She felt as stifled as the rest of them. They'd walked for days, rested, ate, and she hadn't felt a fraction of what she felt here. Her feet started to hurt, her chest started to heave as if she'd run for days instead of walking for hours.

"The Seer is rumored to be in The Iron Mountains," Valerio said. He came to a stop, and Shula soon saw why.

The earth they walked on crested and split into a mountain pass. The rocky ridges towered on both sides so high that it cast nothing but shadows through the middle. For a moment, it all looked like an endless tunnel with no exit.

The Iron Mountains were spread all the way down for miles to the Jade Court. It would be a treacherous trek; at least, that's what Valerio had said before they'd stepped over the Ley Line. From the entrance, Shula could see how it would be true. The ground rose and fell unevenly, and the shadows of the dangerous trench wouldn't help. They needed sunlight, and she doubted the rays even reached the bottom of the mountain pass.

"Stay together," Valerio ordered, voice firm. "We do not know what we'll find within."

The slide of swords against their sheathes sounded as they brandished their weapons. With the iron weakening them, they'd need to fight using other means. While Shula felt more confident now with a sword than with her powers, that wasn't a problem. The same couldn't be said for her companions.

They entered the pass and were swallowed up by the darkness.

Hours morphed into days. Or so Shula thought. One lost all sense of time within The Iron Mountains. They could have very well been walking for hours or days and she wouldn't have known. All she knew was that the pain was catching up to them.

The further they walked, the more iron made itself known. It eroded from the ground like the roots of tree trunks, creating a maze against the ground. Every time Shula stepped down, jolts of pain zapped up her legs like never-ending strikes of lightning.

She took a step over an iron ridge only to slip. She fell, throwing her hands out and barely breaking her fall. The dagger slipped from her grip, lost within the iron roots. Her face slammed onto iron, and she tasted copper on her tongue.

Groaning, she pushed herself up and her elbows shook with the effort. Heaving a breath, she sat on a piece of iron. "Let me catch my breath," she pleaded. "Just a moment."

"You okay, Fire Dancer?" Clay sat next to her. His face was pale, and there were shadows beneath his eyes. "You're bleeding."

It wasn't until the blood dropped from her nose to her top lip that she realized she'd hurt her nose, too. She moved to wipe it off, but before she could, Ryker dropped to his knees in front of her and swiped the blood away with the pad of his thumb.

"Shula...You're hurt." Ryker's palm started to emit a soft glow

"No!" She grabbed his wrist, snuffing the light of his magic. "Save your strength."

He looked ready to argue, but Shula was spared a lecture when Uric started letting out watery coughs. Her eyes widened as he doubled over and promptly vomited blood.

"Uric!" Valerio dashed to grab his friend before he fell. Uric's already pale complexion seemed even paler, sickly, with bruises around his eyes. The prince lowered his friend to the ground, holding his head up until his heaving stopped. "Are you well?"

Uric straightened, but Shula could see how it cost him. His whole body shook with the effort. "I am fine, my prince. We must keep going."

"No," Valerio said. "We will rest. Gather your strength, eat, drink. Then we will continue."

Shula couldn't deny the relief she felt at those words. They'd been walking tirelessly. After a few hours of walking, they'd realized there were no wild animals, no sound or sight of any, yet they'd still stayed alert.

"Here." Shula shook herself out of her thoughts to see Ryker handing her a skin of water. "Drink."

She took it with shaking hands and after a generous swallow, handed it back to him. "Fucking Iron Mountains." She scrubbed her hands over her face to take away the exhaustion.

"They didn't used to be named that, you know." Clay took a drink and wiped his mouth with the back of his hand. "These mountains got that name after the wars."

"Yeah? What did they used to be called?"

Clay got quiet then. "I can't remember. It's been so long."

Before Shula could reply, Uric started heaving again. Blood and spittle flew, staining the rusted iron on the ground bright red.

Ryker stood from his position and walked over to Uric. Ryker's palms pressed against Uric's chest. They glowed, the light infusing into Uric's body. He gasped, arching, wheezing in breath after breath.

"There's iron flecks in his lungs from breathing this air," Ryker growled. "We need to hurry and leave here."

Valerio looked away like he wanted to curse the world but held it back. The prince always looked so composed, even when facing the threat of death.

He loosed a breath.

"We need to keep moving," Valerio decided. "Uric, can you walk?"

Uric's face was grave as he nodded, though Shula suspected it was a lie.

"Then let's go. We need to make it to The Seer before we get worse."

Ryker grunted as he helped Uric to his feet. Julius positioned himself on the other side, throwing Uric's arms around the two Fae. Together, they helped him walk.

It had only been a few minutes rest, but Shula wouldn't complain. Valerio was right. They needed to leave and quickly. After picking up her discarded blade, she followed close behind.

Shula stared at the iron at her feet. She'd been able to melt the iron bars of Orna's prison, perhaps she could burn this too. At least, to create a pathway that would allow them to walk without feeling the pain in every step.

She held her palms out to the ground and concentrated, focusing on summoning the flames. She could feel a sliver of her magic respond, and even that brought her pain. She tried to push past the sensation and focused.

Flames shot out of her hands and enveloped the iron on the ground only to diminish into ash. The simple act depleted her energy and had her coughing into her hand until her palm came stained red with blood.

"Stop it." Clay grabbed her wrist. "It won't work. You'll just hurt yourself."

"It'll work." She spoke the words like a promise. She refused to stand back while they all got hurt, especially if there was something she could do about it.

"Save your energy," Clay echoed her earlier words. "You never know when you'll need it most."

Because he was right, she listened, tucking her palm into her pants pocket, her other enclosed tightly around the hilt of her dagger, where it stayed for hours, days.

They got little rest, all of them eager to make the journey quickly. The further they traveled, the denser the iron became. And while they hadn't come across humans or animals, Shula swore she heard the scuttling of feet against the ground. It made her scan the ridges of mountains at their sides, but her senses were dulling, and she was exhausted.

So when Valerio announced the words she'd been longing to hear, she almost fell to her knees with relief.

"We're here."

The Seer

"Mana save you." The harrying words came from Clay.

The line of Fae males came to a cautious stop, blocking the view. Shula's heart thrummed slowly up to her throat. And then Clay shifted, and Shula reeled back, a gasp tearing through the polluted air at what she saw before them.

A latticework of iron twisted up from the ground like rusted vines that formed a gnarled cage. From between the bars, a pale face peeked, skin clinging to a sharp facial structure, stringy strands of hair clinging to dirty cheeks.

Valerio braved a step forward, and white eyes flew open and thin lips curled into a smile. Shula flinched at that gaze, bereft of pupils and irises but seeing just the same.

"Are you The Seer?" Valerio's harsh voice cut through the space that separated them from... the creature.

Shula couldn't discern whether the figure trapped in iron before them was male or female. So twisted were the confines, they twined around a skeletal body, pinning The Seer in place.

"I have not been called that in a long time." The Seer's voice was hoarse with disuse, as rusted as the bars that kept the Fae in place.

A flicker of movement caught Shula's attention. The Seer's boney fingers twitched and curled around the bars. The Seer's nails were flecked brown with dried blood, and the movement caused fresh blood to drip down skinny wrists.

It was then that Shula realized how the iron was holding the Fae up. The twisted tubes cut through The Seer's body, impaling the Fae through many directions. Arms held up at the sides, toes barely grazing the ground.

The pain of that position was mesmerizing, making it hard to look away. Everyone seemed so entranced by it that their own pain was momentarily forgotten.

"I foresaw your arrival decades ago, much like I saw the fall of the Fae," The Seer continued.

The impact of those words had Valerio's hands tightening into fists and stepping back a single step.

"I see many paths of the future. It flows, like the currents of a river. There are many pathways, many currents, yet always only one outcome, destined, decreed by Mana."

Those words reminded Shula so much of Davina that for a moment her chest ached with the familiar pain of loss.

The Seer's head shifted, lifted. The bars and the Fae's bones groaned in unison. Blood slipped down The Seer's neck, staining the already brown ground even darker. Like blood had long since accumulated and soaked through.

"I know why you have come." The Seer's eyes found Shula's, and she felt the impact of that blind gaze keenly. "I know what you seek, Fire Dancer." That face shifted towards Valerio. "And you, Prince Ashera of the Seelie Court."

More blood dripped with each movement. Shula could only imagine the agony The Seer was feeling. That was nothing to say of Ryker, who seemed to stagger towards the Fae, his palms inadvertently glowing.

"Do not try to help me, Ryker Valda." The Seer stopped him before he could get close. "It is futile. I am one with the iron now. I have lived decades like this, and I will die like this."

"What happened?" Ryker growled. His hands furled and unfurled, like he was barely restraining himself from going forward and ripping the iron away.

"The humans happened. The iron chased the Fae from Tir na Faie. It killed the old magic of nature and evolved with this industrialized world, tainting what Mana should be and becoming something new. Something dark that spread and became a blight on the land. I have been trapped, hovering on the edge between life and death. To remove the iron would kill me, and I cannot die yet."

"But how is that possible?" Valerio demanded.

Shula echoed the sentiment.

Iron blocked magic, yet this iron had evolved and spread. It explained so much, and yet nothing at all.

"Mana works in mysterious ways," The Seer said. "Mana absorbed the iron. It evolved. It changed."

"Impossible," Julius dismissed almost angrily.

The Seer's thin lips pursed in what seemed to be amusement. "Yet the Fire Dancer burned the iron bars from a cage. Nothing is impossible. Magic evolves, and Elemental magic is the greatest mystery Mana has ever given."

"Why?" Shula boldly asked, stepping towards The Seer. She moved so close; close enough to feel the pain emitting from the iron and smell blood, old and new. "Why are Elementals so important, other than our direct connection to

Mana?" Her heart beat faster in her chest. The answers she so desperately wanted were grazing her fingertips.

"Mana lives within us, a phantom shadow within all the Fae. It connects us to life, to the elements, to our very magic like invisible threads. It is a single, soul-binding force. Yes, we have our own souls, our own magic, and yet the Mana in us all is the same."

There weren't many aspects of Mana. It wasn't divided or compartmentalized into separate bits and pieces. Mana was considered the supreme being to the Fae. God and Goddess. Fire and water, earth and air, ice and lava, mercury and spirit. Mana was all and lived within all.

Everyone held their breath as they took in The Seer's words.

"Mana *is* nature, and the Elementals are personifications of that force." The Seer's blank eyes held Shula's, and the Fae smiled. It wasn't evil or cruel but knowing, and that's what made Shula feel like there was just the slightest touch of malice beneath it.

Because The Seer knew all.

"The Elementals do not hold just a fraction. You are the pillars of Mana itself. The strongest, as you are the last of your kind."

Shula sucked in a breath.

"You did not know," The Seer mused. "What did you think the markings on your back meant? When the penultimate Elemental dies, the last one remaining receives the markings carved in their flesh."

Though Shula had never given much thought to other fire Fae, the implications of what The Seer said hit her hard. She was the last of her kind. The last fire Fae in existence. It was a difficult thing to know, that the humans had killed them all off. Like she'd lost family she had never known.

"There are others. Other pillars. Other Elementals that are the last of their kind."

"Why are you calling them 'pillars'?" Valerio cut in.

The Seer didn't even look at the Seelie Prince as they answered, "Because it is what you are. The pillars in the structure of the lives of other Fae. Another gift given by Mana. Direct fragments of Mana's essence that, when united, can either save the Fae... or eradicate us completely."

Those words gripped Shula like a vice, snuffing the air out from her lungs. The heaviness of them, of what she and others could do. Eradication of the Fae? She would *never...*

Ryker stepped forward until he was next to her. She drew strength from his heat like it was the most normal thing in the world to do. For a moment she pretended like they didn't have such a strained relationship and grounded her thoughts with his presence.

"Speak clearly, Seer," he ordered, his rage almost palpable.

A hoarse sound scraped out of the Fae's throat that sounded suspiciously like a laugh. "Join the Fae Elementals together, as direct fragments of Mana, and do you know what you can create? Life and death in equal measure. Together, you *are* immeasurable power and will open a doorway to release the full force of Mana on the lands. The Emperor of Illyk knows this. He knows that if he finds all six of you, he can use you all to sever Mana completely. And because all Fae have fragments of Mana within them..."

"He can kill us all in one sweep..." Valerio breathed softly.

"Smart prince." The Seer smirked.

"That's why the emperor wants Shula so badly," Clay supplied. "He's looking for the Elementals. Shula, you said you saw images carved onto the floor."

"Waves, flames, swirls, curling vines, stars, and a straight line." The images were etched as deeply into her memory as they had been onto the floor.

"Water, fire, air, earth, ice, and spirit." The Seer's blank eyes blinked quickly. "Scattered throughout Illyk, uncertain of what their future holds."

"How do we find them?" Valerio asked.

"Elementals can feel each other as prominently as you can feel the scars on your back."

"There are only six?" Ryker drew that blank gaze to himself. "Only six Elementals?"

"Yes. Lava and mercury breathed their last breaths." The Seer's head cocked to the side, studying Ryker for a moment. "Have you danced with fire yet, Ryker?"

Ryker's whole body froze. The words felt like a premonition that went ignored. Because The Seer spoke again, and this time, there was fear in every rasping word.

"Run," the Fae ordered. "The iron monsters have arrived."

Those were the last words spoken before the valley around them erupted into chaos.

Iron Monsters

The earth cracked down the middle. Iron splintered in half and geysers of dirt flew through the air, only to fall and pelt against their bodies. A groaning sound echoed through the air, like a great machine turning its cogs after disuse.

Behind them, The Seer cackled, but that didn't drown out the scuttling sound. Like thousands of spider legs running across iron, or the shrieking groans of machines.

Ryker held his breath as they emerged from the mountains.

Iron monsters.

That was the only way he could think to describe them. Massive things made of rusted machinery and iron legs that charged towards them like hulking predators.

"Blood will be shed," The Seer cackled in a voice that seemed like it would break and crumble to dust. "Run for your lives, Fae, or our race will fall."

Ryker drowned out the sound of The Seer's voice and unsheathed his sword. A second later, the monsters attacked.

Ryker's body hit the ground on a roll, dodging enormous, pointed legs that threatened to impale his body like The Seer's. He barely missed the striking iron limb as it cut through his leathers. He didn't feel the pain. The adrenaline didn't let him.

Gritting his teeth, he shot to his feet, swinging his sword. His aching muscles screamed from days of surrounding himself with iron. He'd grown weak, yet his will to survive was strong. Sparks flew as his blade met the metal, but it was too thick to shear through, and the impact of their collision blasted him backwards.

He fell to his back, the breath whooshing from his lungs. A creature came for him, aiming for his chest. He moved and the iron stabbed into his shoulder instead.

Ryker's scream came unbidden as the pain ripped through his body and out again. His hand clutched his shoulder, staunching the blood flow. The iron monster emitted a shriek that he felt down to his bones, and he knew the end was coming...

And the approaching iron combusted, clashing against waves of flames and sparks. Then she appeared over him, blocking the oncoming onslaught of violence with her own magic. The force of it was nearly impossible. Hours before she'd been coughing blood, and yet here she stood. Shula Azzarh, wielding fire to save his life.

Her screaming penetrated the haze of his thoughts, palms held out, fire shot from her hands. She made a pushing motion, her feet digging into the ground for purchase. She shoved forward, and the machine went backwards against the force of her magic, back and back until the iron began to melt.

When it became little more than molten metal on the ground, Shula turned back and ran, dropping to her knees between Ryker's spread legs.

"Can you walk?"

He sat up, never taking his eyes off her face, off the mesmerizing image she made, even paling and with blood dripping down her nose. The ferocity of those thoughts surprised him, and he winced as he sat up, still clutching his injured shoulder.

"I can." He got to his feet, and Shula followed. When he staggered, she grabbed his arm and wrapped it around her shoulders.

Clay ran towards them, limping and bleeding. "We need to get the fuck out of here!"

A machine charged towards them. Clay whirled and struck, pushed back with a curse. Ryker scanned the chaos. They were outnumbered and weak. There was no way they were getting out of here through those mountains because more kept pouring through.

"Uric!" he grunted. "Where's Uric?"

He was their only hope if they wanted to survive.

Through the striking iron monsters, he caught glimpses of his Fae companions, slashing their way out of the fray. Weylyn and Valerio cut through first, carrying an unconscious Uric between them. The silver haired Fae had blood over half of his face. They ran, dragging his body towards them, Julius breaking out of the chaos to follow.

As soon as they were within reach, Ryker shook away from Shula and cupped Uric's face in his palms. He turned his gaze over his shoulder, meeting Shula's eyes. "Buy me time," he ordered. After her firm nod, he turned back and let whatever was left of his magic loose.

It ruptured from him to Uric, and in return he received the pain. Uric's agony mingled with his own, but Ryker gritted his teeth through it. He couldn't stop, couldn't halt his magic once it begun. Because of all of them here, Uric was the only one who could get them out.

And that sense of panic was prominent in Ryker's chest. That need to save, to sacrifice. Because they couldn't die here.

And Ryker would give anything, even his own life, to make sure the others got out safely.

He screamed as the pain rippled through him, his power a dominating force unleashed against Uric. And Uric... his eyes flew open, his wounds healed, and he took in a sharp breath.

And then all Ryker knew was the darkness.

Darkness and fire.

Ryker wanted time? Shula would give him all the time he needed.

They came from all sides, whirring, unforgiving machines. The ground shook from the force of their stomping steps, and as they approached, Shula could feel a rush through her whole body, igniting her blood. For a single moment, all earlier weakness was replaced with adrenaline. It was a feeling that built low in her gut and spread, a strange energy that burned every inch of her body.

It built and built, a protective force rising. And it gave her no other choice but to unleash it.

She screamed as the magic within her exploded, enveloping the charging machines in a terror of flames. Hitting iron, her fire burned green with the heat, sending sparks flying across the sky like fireworks.

The iron monsters pushed against the fire, but Shula pushed harder. These monsters were human creations, meant to destroy them. Whether they'd been created with that sole purpose or if Mana had somehow evolved within them, it didn't matter.

Because Mana lived within Shula, too, and she intended to use it. She had friends, if her kidnappers could even be called that. Whatever they were, she was going to defend them, knowing she was the only one who could.

The power inside responded in kind.

It exploded against iron, burning so hotly that the metal melted. Using so much force nearly brought Shula to her knees. She could hear shouting, though it sounded far away. Her ears popped, and she barely tasted the blood dropping from her nose to her cracked lips.

Darkness started to settle into the corners of her vision.

Then she was yanked backwards, her feet giving out from under her. Her head whipped to the side in time to see Clay pulling her back and Uric, standing and bloody, a portal glowing behind him. Julius had Ryker thrown over his shoulder, and Valerio was pushing his way through the portal with Weylyn. Julius followed, and then Clay was pushing her forward, and she was swallowed up by the maelstrom.

Shula's face ricocheted off the dirt, and she tasted it and blood on her teeth. Her heart pounded against the earth, and she felt the scrape of her nails against the ground as she pushed herself up. Inhaling a deep breath into her lungs, she was met with fresh air and only the smallest tinge of iron.

She got to her knees, inhaling the taste of unpolluted air and looked around. Clay, Julius, and Weylyn were pushing to their feet, Valerio was helping Uric, whose face was now a latticework of wrinkles, into a sitting position, and Ryker lay immobile on the ground.

His name tore from Shula's lips, and without realizing what she was doing, she flung herself over his body, fingers pressing against his scarred skin to feel for a pulse.

"Ryker..." Her voice shook and so did her hands when she reached up to push his long hair away from his face.

Seeing him laying immobile on the ground made something in her chest fracture. It was an inexplicable sensation with no name, no beginning, and no end. Yet it was there, as prominent as the rapid beating of her heart and the magic in her veins.

"Wake up."

The silence seemed to pulse around them, around this very moment. Shula could feel everyone's gazes on them, taking in Ryker, their ears taking in every faint beat of his heart.

"You don't get to just save that asshole's life and die on us!" Shula demanded, feeling tears sting at the back of her eyes.

He was demanding, cruel, and spit words always laced with poison. He had secrets that he refused to expose even while ripping her own from her chest. He was as imperfect as the scars that marred his skin. And yet he was a healing force. He pushed Shula to do better and be better, not because he wanted her on their side for the war—he'd made it clear that he didn't—but because he genuinely believed in her.

He was perhaps the first.

She wasn't ready to let that go.

His pulse was a soft beat beneath his skin; he was alive, breathing, yet he didn't wake. Shula felt a tugging at her arms as someone tried to pull her off of him but she refused to let go. He would wake up. *He would.*

She waited with bated breath until Ryker's eyes slowly fluttered opened, and his chest expanded in a single, painful inhalation before falling into a steady rhythm.

"Thank Mana." Shula dropped her forehead to his chest and looked back up at him.

His eyes were on her, soft, while his thick brows pulled together. The next moment, his palm enveloped her cheek, and he swiped away the blood on her face with the pad of his thumb.

"You're hurt," he said in his guttural voice.

Shula choked on a laugh. "You can't heal everyone." When the tips of his fingers started to emit the softest light, Shula pushed his hand down to his chest. "No. You have done enough."

"I can't leave you injured," he argued.

"Will you stop with your stupid, reckless, impulsive need to heal everyone?" she spat, annoyed because he'd nearly died healing Uric for the good of the whole group. Did he have a death wish and didn't care what happened, or how much energy he pulled from deep within himself? He'd live his life morphed in scars by the thousand and absorb the pain until he died if they let him. It wasn't sacrifice. It was stupidity. "Not everyone needs to be healed."

The tender look was replaced with an annoyance Shula felt herself.

"Yes, some would rather let their wounds fester and infect until they're so wounded, they're left blaming the rest of the world for their ailments."

Beneath their joined palms, his heart pounded, and Shula couldn't move away from the evidence of his life. Like she needed this one moment to ground her own soul back into place.

For a moment, where hatred once reigned, caring was in its stead. She could feel it; *he* could too. Even if it felt so right, the perfect way it seemed to fit within their emotions was wrong.

"There's a difference between sacrifice and stupidity." She pulled her hand away and curled it into a fist so he couldn't see how badly she was shaking. "What you have is stupidity in abundance."

He bared his canines, snapping them in threat. "Get the fuck off me, Fire Dancer," he spat her name like an insult. On his tongue, it was.

Shula scrambled to her feet, her knees shaking only a fraction. A moment later, Ryker grunted as he got up and they faced one another, him baring his canines, her glaring.

"What the fuck just happened here?" Julius demanded with a hint of teasing in his tone.

Shula turned to them and saw Clay throw his arm around Julius' broad shoulder. The blond-haired Fae was smirking. "Romance, my dear Julius. *Attraction.* Pure, primal attraction."

Rolling her eyes and ignoring the slice of *something* down her back, but she decided she would analyze that later.

"If you're done spouting your fucking delusions," Ryker growled, "what are we going to do now?"

They all turned to Valerio. Even Shula, because she certainly had no idea what she was going to do. Information had not only dropped into her lap but had erupted. Everything she thought she knew about herself had changed within a few moments. Not like she'd known much about herself in the first place, but there was something special about finding out she was one of the keys to opening a portal directly to Mana to summon destruction.

Her life had taken a turn for the unexpected, and she suddenly found herself in a position she never imagined before. Killed by humans? Sure. Thrown into a camp and burned alive? Also, sure. But learning how much power she truly wielded wasn't what she wanted. It was a burden, one she knew others would want to exploit. One they *had* tried to exploit.

The danger of the situation suddenly hit her, especially when the Seelie Prince looked into her eyes, expression on his face grave. She wouldn't be safe. She'd *never* be safe again. Because if she was what The Seer said she was—and Shula believed it—then the Emperor of Illyk would never give up until he found her and the other Elementals.

Fear had her tucking her hands into her pockets and chewing on the inside of her cheek.

Finally, Valerio looked away from her. "We can do nothing now except rest. The iron still courses through us and we will need our strength to decide what to do next." He looked at their surroundings, a barren wasteland. Uric had transported them just outside the Ley Line, in Orknie. "Let us rest our feet for an hour, deal with our wounds in any way we can. The closest town is a few miles north of here. We have a safe house in Terryln. It's one of the nicer ones." He gave them a rueful smile. "I think we deserve to sleep in a bed tonight."

They'd been through hell and they looked it. A few hours to rest and a real bed sounded like a fantastic and terrible idea all at once. Her limbs screamed, aching and demanding, her stomach rumbled with hunger pains, and she was suddenly so, so tired.

So when Valerio suggested a safe house in a small village in Orknie, well, Shula just didn't have the heart or will to argue.

Hatred Tastes a lot like Chocolate Cake

Shula didn't argue with the idea of a safe house until after she rested her feet and cleaned the blood off her face with a torn part of an extra shirt, and with what little water she had left. When Valerio rounded them all up and told them it was time to go, she felt the nerves of the situation kick in.

"Are you sure that's such a good idea?" She usually tried to avoid Valerio because of who he was, and because the Seelie Prince unnerved her almost as much as Uric, his faithful hound, though not as much as Weylyn.

It wasn't the only reason she avoided him.

The confession he'd whispered a few nights ago had stuck with her. She tried not to think about it, but it still slithered through her mind on occasion. If not for what Davina said, he wouldn't have gone to try and save her at all. While she knew he didn't think she was his mate, it was still awkward that he'd thought so at one point.

That, and the fact that he'd kept her prisoner for days in his camp.

It was in the details.

"You dare question the heir to the Seelie throne, Fire Dancer?" Uric spat. His voice was grave, hoarse. Not from being tired, but from old age, the remnants of using his magic still clinging to him.

There was bite to his tone, but Shula just felt like she was being lectured by a senile senior and paid him no mind.

"Need I remind you that Illyk is full of humans who despise Fae and you plan on walking into a populated village in Orknie just like that?"

Terryln was a pretty populated place; Shula had been there oftentimes enough to *know* how many humans took up residence in the town.

Just the thought of doing something so reckless was fraying at her nerves. Her fight-or-flight instincts were kicking in, and every cell in her body was screaming at her to turn and run in the other direction. Away from the Fae and the humans that wanted them dead.

Valerio's lips pressed together, and she realized he was suppressing a smile. "I commend you for your worry, Shula, but it is misplaced. We have safe houses in plenty of populated places. We will be very careful."

Her fingers twitched. "I have a bad feeling about it."

"We have been through hell, Shula; we have been hiding in forests, we have fought, we have suffered, and I would like to eat something other than dried meat."

He must have seen the uncertainty on her face because he sighed.

"It will be safe. It's a tactic we have used many times before."

"Tactic?"

He smirked. "Hiding in plain sight. I am sure you are quite familiar with that one, so why are you so worried?"

She was familiar with it. It's probably why they were looking at her as if her slow-building hysteria was unnecessary. But she'd hidden in plain sight *alone.* Never with a big group of Fae. They were smaller than the refugees the Resistance had saved, but the fear was still there. With a bigger group, the outcome had been death and heartbreak. Even if this smaller group was filled with those who kept her held against her will, she had grown close to them and feared for what might happen.

It would have been a lie to say she feared for herself more, but Valerio was looking at her expectantly, as if he could read every thought that crossed over her mind, and the truth would not spill from her lips.

"I'm worried about *myself,* Seelie Prince. I've been avoiding danger my whole life only to have you come and try to throw me straight into it."

Valerio turned away, but not before Shula caught the smile on his face. She fell back a step, accidentally ramming into Weylyn's chest. The contact made her jolt away from him. His shoulder brushed against her and his feline features smirked down at her, as if he knew exactly what she was thinking and what a lie her words were.

She supposed he *did* know. That was unnerving.

She fell back again, if only to avoid his stare, only this time, it was Ryker who rammed into her shoulder. It was unkind but not painful, and with just enough force that let her know he'd heard every word she said.

And believed it.

Clay and Julius sandwiched her between their large bodies, Clay throwing his arm around her shoulders. "Don't worry about a damn thing, Fire Dancer. You'll like this safe house. It's disguised as a bed-and-breakfast. We'd get our own suite and a decent meal and dessert."

Julius bumped his shoulder against hers and smiled. "You like chocolate cake, little dancer?"

Her stomach growled at the very prospect. "Of course. Who doesn't?"

"All women love chocolate. It's magic, or science." Clay's hand squeezed. "Whatever you want to call it, it's just true."

"Is there really chocolate cake?" She'd always loved dessert for dinner, and at Piriguini's Circus there had been confections in abundance. The only thing preventing her from becoming as big as Illyk's fattest man was the fact that she danced. Sugared candies and glazed buns had become an everyday thing for her.

Ever since she'd been with the Fae, she hadn't had a single pastry. Just thinking about them now had her whole body shivering with anticipation and her tongue getting heavy in her mouth. She could almost taste the creamy goodness...

"What other kind of desserts does this safe house have?" she asked. And surprisingly, Shula felt all her fear melting away.

And all it took was the promise of a chocolate cake to do it.

They reached Terryln by nightfall but didn't walk through the paved roads of the populated, busy town. They crept in through the woods that bordered the line of houses and shops, hiding in the shadows.

Sweat stained Shula's palms, her heart pounded up to her throat, and her stomach twisted into knots. She fought hard not to give in to the rising panic that clawed through her body, taking deep breaths that did nothing to steady her and everything to make her sound like she was losing her mind.

"Breathe," Ryker snapped, the sound of his deep voice impatient.

"I am breathing," she hissed. She was breathing so much, making too much noise. If there was a soldier patrolling the woods or the back doors of shops, they'd hear her. Her body didn't seem to care, though, because it racked with nervous shivers.

"You're hyperventilating," Ryker said again.

She ignored him that time and focused on steadying her breaths. Valerio was confident there was nothing to be nervous about, but Shula didn't have the Seelie Prince's unwavering confidence. The last time they'd been near a safe house, humans had found them and murdered Orna.

Why did they have a safe house near humans, anyway?

They'd said it was disguised as a bed-and-breakfast, an inn, and was run by humans. It was easier to hide in plain sight rather than risk every safe house being within the woods, since soldiers combed solitary places more often than they did human locales. While it made sense, Shula still couldn't breathe past the nerves.

Death. Fire. Ashes. Water burning down her throat.

She grasped at her neck as if she meant to ease the pressure there, taking in gasping breaths.

They were hidden behind the tree line, staring at the back door of the safe house. It looked like any regular human building. A cabin-like structure made of stone and oak logs and glass windows. Candle and oil light glow from within, illuminating the sight of the humans inside.

They all had their hoods up, covering their ears and obvious Fae features from anyone who could be looking out at them.

Valerio stepped out of the shadows first, a blur as he dashed towards the back door, his fist rapping across the wood in a three-note tune.

Shula held her breath as the door opened to reveal a short, rotund human woman wearing drab, brown clothing and a dirty apron. Her frizzy hair was held behind a wool cap, and even in the darkness, Shula could make out the flush on the older woman's round cheeks.

She stepped outside and looked side to side before gesturing wildly at Valerio to walk inside.

"Come on." Clay's hand grabbed her elbow, but the touch wasn't calming. If anything, him dragging her forward quickly made her all the more nervous.

But she went, one forced step after another until they were all inside the house, the door closing behind them.

Shula took in her surroundings almost immediately. Born of years of instincts and hiding, of being near humans. She looked for possible exits, for soldiers, for iron, anything that would threaten harm.

A cozy interior snagged her attention. Candles dripped down their tapers, oil lamps cast dull glows against the walls from where they hung. They were in a kitchen, a hearth burning hotly with a cauldron over it. Scents of a delicious, home cooked meal wafted through her nostrils, making her stomach growl loudly.

There was one other human in the kitchen with the older woman. She was a young girl, no older than seventeen with smooth features and pretty eyes, hair pulled back into a white cap. Her eyes widened as she took in their small group of Fae, nearly bugging out of her head as Valerio lowered his hood to reveal his pointed ears.

The older woman bowed low. "Prince," she greeted. "I have the suite available with two adjoining rooms and a shared bath. The rest of the rooms are taken... I—"

Valerio placed his palm on the woman's shoulder. Her body went rigid, but Shula didn't scent any fear. "How full is it?"

"The suite is the last room. We're full of travelers and—" She trailed off, her eyes darting to the floor.

"And?" Valerio prompted.

"Prince, there is a soldier staying."

Valerio didn't even flinch, even when Shula's heart seemed to beat itself bloody against her chest.

"We will stay in our rooms. It is just for the night. Possibly two."

The woman worried at her apron. "I'll sneak you in through the secret entrance, prince." She pulled out of his hold and turned to the young maid. "Filomena, prepare a hot meal for our guests."

The maid nodded vigorously and set about preparing everything while the older woman led them deeper into the kitchen where she shoved aside a rickety wooden shelf that held pots and pans. Behind it, she pressed a pattern against the brick, and it opened to reveal a dark stairwell. The woman grabbed an oil lamp, hiked up the hem of her skirt, and climbed.

They followed after her. The stairwell stank of wetness and mold, though it wasn't overly unpleasant.

"Can she be trusted?" Valerio asked, his voice whispering through the darkness.

"Filomena? Of course. She may look young and impressionable, but I have never known one as loyal as she. Your presence will be a well-kept secret, I promise you that."

Shula wasn't inclined to be sure, but Valerio hummed. She supposed if they trusted this human enough to keep them hidden, then they could trust the young maid.

At the top of the stairs, a scraping sounded, and the woman pushed open a doorway. The oil lamp disappeared inside, and they followed into the suite she'd spoken about.

Shula's eyes adjusted well in the darkness, but even so, lamps were quickly lit all around. There seemed to be no other entrance or exit save for the one they'd just come from, and no windows, either.

It was a secret room, built to seem as if it wasn't there at all.

"There have been a few upgrades around the place," the woman stated as she wandered around, slapping her hands along pillows strewn against the small couches. "It's been so long, dust has accumulated, but there have been renovations. We have plumbing now."

"We can manage from here, Imogen." Valerio's fingers worked at his cloak, pulling it off his shoulders. "We are in your debt."

Imogen smiled warmly at him. "Long live the Resistance," was her reply. "Filomena will be up shortly with your dinner. We have dessert as well." With that, she left, closing the door behind her.

It wasn't until she was gone that Shula felt she could breathe again. She sucked in a breath and all but clawed at the drawstrings holding her cloak together.

Ripping it off, she tossed it on top of Valerio's and sucked in a breath that scraped against her lungs unpleasantly.

"I worried you were about to drop dead of nerves." Clay brushed aside her hair from her face. "Relax, Fire Dancer. They're bringing up dessert."

The thought of dessert had a calming effect on her frayed nerves. She nodded.

"Now, as much as everyone is anxious to talk about what The Seer said, I think it best if we rest first, don't you, Valerio?" Clay said.

"As much as I hate to agree with you, I think that's best. Rest now, gather your thoughts and your strength. Tomorrow we can speak about everything we have learned." His sharp eyes softened on Shula. "Take a bath, Shula. You look like hell."

She bristled at the judgment, sure she looked better than Uric, at least. The Fae was still covered in wrinkles and had been wheezing when they'd walked up the stairs.

Before she could say anything, Clay's palm pressed between her shoulder blades, giving her a gentle shove. "First door on the right. Go."

A warm bath sounded divine. Water that wasn't cold, no peeking over her shoulder to make sure she wasn't ambushed in the woods by humans or Weylyn's prying eyes...

"I can see your eyes glowing. Go." Clay gave her another nudge, and she stumbled forward a step before deciding to go ahead and bathe. She took her pack with her to the bathing room, closing the door behind her.

There was a small unlit oil lamp hanging from a hook on the ceiling. Concentrating, she sent the smallest flame, lighting it. A white claw footed tub sat in the center of the small room, a toilet and sink beside it.

Once the water was filling the tub, Shula undressed looked at her reflection in the single oval mirror there. She did look like hell. Bruises covered her eyes that weren't just there because of exhaustion. Cuts split against her golden-brown skin, dried blood, dirt and grime staining her cheeks and neck. She got into the tub, reached for the bar of soap there, and scrubbed the dirt from her body, washing her hair and detangling it twice. When she scrubbed herself raw, her stomach demanded she get out and search for food.

Because her clothes were dirty, Shula swallowed her pride enough to tuck a fluffy towel around her body. She'd ask Imogen to wash her clothes or see if she had a tunic and pants she could borrow for the time being.

Hair dripping, she walked back into the room where a table had been placed with heaps of food, goblets of a sweet-smelling wine, and a pitcher of water. A nice, thick stew with cow meat and veggies steamed from bowls sat on the plate in the center of the table, along with buttery bread.

Her companions were already eating by the time she walked in, but they froze as they caught sight of her in nothing but a towel.

Warmth flooded the apples of her cheeks that she ignored. They'd seen her in very little already, but still, their stares made her shift from foot to foot with discomfort. "My clothes were dirty..."

Ryker's jaw tensed at the declaration.

Clay merely kicked out the chair beside him, gaze dipping back down to his plate. "Come and eat, Fire Dancer. Filomena will bring dessert in a bit."

Not having to be told twice, she sat next to the Fae, wedged as usual between him and Julius, leaving Ryker, Valerio, and Uric across from them. Weylyn had taken his bowl to the couch, where he hunched over and ate in silence. Always apart from the others, but constantly watching with keen eyes.

But it wasn't his gaze she felt.

It was Ryker's.

She tore into a piece of bread and took a generous bite of stew. She'd never tasted anything so delicious, and it was unfortunate that she couldn't enjoy it because Ryker's bicolored gaze burned through her skin.

Spoons clattering against bowls filled the silence. A drop of water from her hair dripped down her neck and slid over her collarbones. Her fingers drifted to brush the moisture away, and she noticed Ryker's eyes following the beads of water trail down the valley between her breasts.

A low growl rumbled in his throat, and that sound was both inappropriate, given everyone around them, and possessive. It was a sound that was strange coming from Ryker's chest, and yet it was a sound that enveloped her whole body. It made goosebumps rise along her arms, a slow spreading thing that felt like the gentle caress of his rough fingertips trailing along her skin. Like he was touching her with his gaze, staking his claim and undressing her with his eyes.

But that was impossible, wasn't it?

Ryker hated her, after all.

Nothing in his eyes suggested hatred that moment. And if they did, it was underneath the scorching burn of desire that made her press her thighs together to stave the arousal that shocked its way through her system.

Ryker's nostrils flared as he scented it, and he bared his canines. It was a primal, animalistic gesture that Shula shouldn't have found appealing, but the evidence quivered between her thighs.

She liked that attention from him.

And she had no idea why.

"Put some fucking clothes on," he growled suddenly. He was holding his spoon so hard, he bent the utensil and promptly dropped it into his bowl.

"I kind of like her like this." Clay threw his arm around her shoulder, fingers brushing along her bare skin. There was a teasing note to his voice that Shula recognized right away. On her other side, Julius chortled a laugh.

Valerio's lips pressed into a thin line. Uric's eyes darted between the two Fae males, Clay and Ryker then back again. Like he was waiting for something, preparing for it.

Violence vibrated in the spaces between them. Ryker's canines snapped in Clay's direction, threatening and filled with rage.

Clay merely chuckled. "Why are you getting so pissed, Ryker? Something you have to say?" His fingers caressed Shula's shoulder, and she didn't push him away. In part because she was curious about why Ryker was so angry, and she wanted to see what he had to say.

"Yeah, Ryker?" Julius taunted between bites. "Why so pissed?"

Canines slapped together on a snarl that was aimed at the males on either side of her. His chair scraped back as he shot to his feet, shoving his bowl forward. A feral grumbling ripped from his throat before he turned and exited the room in hurried, hulking strides.

A door slammed. As soon as it did, their laughter followed, Clay's arm dropped from her shoulder, and he chortled into his bowl.

Even Shula found herself slightly amused by his reaction, but also confused. "What's his problem?"

They responded to her question with more laughter.

"That prick. Five gold coins says he fesses up." Julius slapped his hand down on the surface of the table.

Clay snorted. "He's too fucking stubborn. Ten coins says he doesn't."

"What the hell are you all talking about?" Shula demanded.

But they didn't give her any answers. If anything, her words sparked even more laughter.

Julius pointed at her with his spoon. "You're beautiful," he said, "but not very bright."

Filomena took down Shula's clothes, promising to launder them, then brought up a loose shirt and long skirt that fit Shula tight around the hips. The hem reached just below her calves, not quite touching her ankles. It didn't matter that it didn't fit. They were still clothes.

Dried and with her hair loose down her back, Shula sat on the tabletop, her long legs kicking out in front of her. A plate of chocolate cake, as promised, sat in her lap, half of the contents already gone. Shula sat alone and in contemplative silence. The others had long since gone to bathe and sleep to prepare for tomorrow and the talk they would all likely have.

Shula took the time to think. She hadn't really processed everything The Seer had said, but with the bursting taste of chocolate on her tongue, she thought. Plotted.

As she understood it, because she was an Elemental, she had a direct connection to Mana, like a master vein or artery in the body that flowed blood, life, and soul through the universe. Everyone else was also interconnected in a small way. If the Emperor of Illyk managed to gather all six of the remaining Elementals, he could use them to cut off the life source of the entire Fae race.

Why now? Shula wondered. The war had been going on for years, decades. The Fae were all but extinct anyway, so what was the emperor's purpose? Maybe they weren't as extinct as she thought. She'd seen their numbers for herself traveling with the Resistance, meeting the King of the Seelie Court. She had seen the safe houses, stayed at Castle Aileach. What if there were even more and the Emperor of Illyk knew this?

Whatever his reasons, the Emperor of Illyk wanted to use Shula as a weapon. Which meant the Fae would never want to let her go. Not after what they'd learned.

It didn't matter which way she turned; it seemed like Shula was meant to be a pawn in someone else's game, even though she didn't even want to be on the board.

Her future was clouded in uncertainty and fear.

She shoveled a bite of cake into her mouth before that fear could take root.

She'd lived with those things her whole life, had been molded from those negative emotions. She wouldn't let it root her into a sense of helplessness now. She *would* find a way to get through this.

The Fae could call her what they wanted. Coward. Damaged. Traitor.

Only one thing was certain.

She was a survivor, and she would continue to be one regardless of the circumstances or what fate threw at her. She'd rise from the ashes covered in blood if she had to. But she *would* survive.

Her thoughts were interrupted by heavy footfalls against the floor. Shula looked up from her dessert to find Ryker walking into the small room.

He was towel drying his dripping hair, wearing a loose fitted tunic and pants, feet bare of socks and shoes. While the shirt was loose, it still clung to the wet patches of his body. Shula could make out the scars behind the material but tore her attention away when she heard him growl.

His massive body seemed to take up most of the space around them, but really it was his presence that left her drowning.

It was the stare, the way those eyes roved over her figure, seeing something she didn't, *knowing* something she didn't. It was a stare that pressed between the thin lines of hatred and desire, and it didn't matter how many times she tried to expel it from her mind and body; that desire *flooded.* It consumed.

It also made her angry.

She wasn't sure when those lines had blurred between them. When things had changed from hatred, to tentative relationship, to *this.* There'd always been that strange push and pull. Ever since she smacked into his body, she'd felt something akin to touching pure, raw magic.

It was an all-consuming feeling that made her wonder if hatred and desire stemmed from the same place. She wasn't sure she could even differentiate between one and the other anymore.

All she knew was his gaze until he was closer. She hadn't even realized he'd moved until he tossed the towel to the side and stepped in front of her.

Shula's thighs widened like it was an instinctual thing to let him get this close. But her body demanded what it never had before.

Closeness.

She craved touch just as easily as she pushed it away. Fanny had left a hole in her soul that way, had dared to make Shula feel *unlovable.* Unworthy of touch and feeling.

But Shula *felt*; it echoed in the cavern of her chest, one beat after another. Her fingers trembled against the plate, her throat tightened, and her body seemed to curve towards Ryker as he stepped between her legs, with only the chocolate cake keeping them apart.

"What do you want?" Her tongue felt leaden in her mouth, but the bite she wanted to lace in her words wasn't there. It came out airy, almost breathless.

Wordlessly, Ryker reached between them and took the plate and spoon. Shula watched with a sort of fascination as he took a bite of chocolate into his mouth and chewed before he set the plate to the side.

Without anything to hide the trembling of her fingers, Shula grabbed the edge of the table as he pressed closer.

His silence somehow made the moment that much more intense. She traced the scars on his face, like puzzle pieces pulling skin together by jagged edges. He was a jagged edge, like a broken shard of glass, and when his chest brushed against hers, for a moment it was like clicking two broken pieces together to form something new and strong and perfectly imperfect.

"Tell me to fuck off," he whispered, and the way his voice rumbled from his chest to hers had her feeling the sensation down to her core. She ached to rub her thighs together and ease the foreign pressure there, but they were opened, his hips wedged between them.

She *should* tell him to fuck off. It only made sense after his angry display at dinner. But somehow Shula knew deep in her mind that those events had been the catalyst to set this off like an explosion.

And all they had to do was burn.

Her hands slid up his chest, where she felt the rising ridges of his scars through the material of his tunic. She traced them with her fingertips, over his hard pecs, his shoulders, ever careful with his wounds, and down to his stomach. The scars were just a testament to how *good* he was. And how much guilt he carried.

His hooded eyes were on her face, taking in every quiet gasp the more she explored, from the way her own eyes lowered as the pleasure threatened to consume.

"I don't want to tell you to fuck off, though." She wasn't sure where she found the strength to admit that. Somewhere in the energy pulsing around them, maybe. Or maybe just in this moment, as she finally decided to chase away the embarrassment with her own wants.

Ryker's nostrils flared. His hand reached up, cupping the back of her neck. He bent, merely a whisper away. He didn't offer her a smile, but an expression that was angry, stern. Like he wanted her as much as she wanted him and hated her for it.

"Hate me," Shula ordered.

That black eye flared, and then he was devouring her like he meant to do just that. The firm pressure of his lips against hers lasted a single second before he pillaged, his tongue pushing past the seams of her mouth to dive in, demanding, fighting.

He kissed like he argued. Like Shula imagined he fucked.

She responded with an almost desperation, her fingers grasping his shoulders for purchase as she pressed herself closer to him. One hand at the back of her neck, the other went to her hip, his nails digging in as he bent her over with his body, grinding his hips into her molten center.

Fire stirred to life beneath her skin with every press of his skin against hers. His tongue played, dominated like a jailor doling out punishment. Their hearts pounded together.

This moment felt more like a fight, primal and wild. It felt a lot like magic. Like hatred.

She pulled the hatred from his tongue with her own, tasting the chocolate in his mouth. She would have been content with devouring him for days, years.

But it lasted seconds.

Minutes.

And then Ryker pulled away, the harshness of their breaths mingling between the spaces of their lips. Slowly, it seemed like things settled back to reality. This was the aftermath of the explosion. Of burning.

Nothing but ashes and pain.

And a hatred that tasted a lot like chocolate.

With an almost visceral awareness, Ryker pulled away. Shula fought the urge to cry out and wrap her legs around him. Instead, she propped herself up on her palms and stared. Wishing for a moment that hatred and desire weren't so similar, because she didn't know which one exactly burned in the depths of Ryker's eyes.

"Goodnight, Fire Dancer." He turned and walked away on quieter footsteps.

Leaving her to heal the pain on her own.

WANTED: Alive and Intact

There was always so much work to do at an inn. Between the washing of clothes, windows, dishes, scrubbing the floors, cleaning the wax off tapers and tables, changing sheets, making beds, helping Cook in the kitchen, and busting tables... It barely gave Filomena time to breathe, let alone think.

And all she wanted to do was think about the secret guests hiding upstairs.

Filomena had never seen Fae up close until the night before. The moment they'd walked through the back door of the kitchen, she'd only caught flashes of feral, glowing eyes beneath their hoods. Then she'd taken the food up to their rooms and gotten her first glimpse of them.

Ethereal beauty came to mind. They were all too beautiful to be human. Even with hollowed cheeks and shadows beneath their eyes, they were something out of this world, so obviously not mortal. Their beauty was all sharp, elegant edges that cut like daggers.

The only female of the group was softer than the others, with rounded ears instead of pointed. Half-Fae perhaps? But she had the regal beauty of a full-blooded Fae.

They were a frightening bunch, but Filomena didn't *fear* them. Rather, for them. Especially that afternoon when the inn's dining room filled with humans, two of them soldiers of Illyk.

Her fingers fumbled with the pitcher of ale as she walked cautiously over to the table they occupied. The soldiers always made her nervous; every soldier she'd ever met held the same thing in their eyes: cruelty.

These ones were no different.

She poured ale into their tankards, trying to keep her fingers firm. Her eyes kept straying to their faces. Hardened like leather, their skin pulled tightly against their strong bone structure. Beards peppered along their jawlines, and their bodies were clad in tight leather that overlapped like the scales of fish. Iron shoulder pads jutted in sharp points out from their uniforms. Simple sacks hung from their shoulders.

Before she could turn away, one of the soldier's stopped her with a curt call. "Maid!"

She froze mid-step, fingers tightening along the handle. But she remembered she had to be obedient. If she showed even the slightest bit of rebellion, they'd likely use force against her. So she smiled prettily, even if it didn't quite reach her eyes.

He rummaged within his bag and pulled out a roll of parchments. "By order of the Emperor of Illyk, every locale is to place these posters on their walls. To refuse is treason." His voice was forceful and cruel, and he was staring at her with an imperious smirk tilting his mouth.

Like he was begging her to refuse. Like he wanted a reason to strike out.

Filomena wouldn't give him one.

"Of course. I will tell Imogen, the innkeeper, and she will follow the great Emperor of Illyk's orders."

Using one hand to hold the pitcher, she used the other to reach for the rolled parchments. The moment her fingers enclosed around them, the soldier's hand clamped around her wrist and he yanked.

Filomena all but fell forward, her stomach jamming into the edge of the table. She wanted to fight. Everything within her body screamed for her to fight back, but she pushed back that urge. It would only bring on so much worse.

Her heart slammed up to her throat and his touch felt like poison. It was a sensation that made her want to shed her own skin, to wear one his vile hands hadn't touched. Unfortunately, she was familiar with *that* too.

His smile was vile. "You'll tell us if you see any of these Fae and Fae sympathizer scum, won't you, pretty little thing?"

The name made her skin crawl, but she forced a smile to her face. "Of course, I will."

He gave her a jerking nod then turned to his companion, gesturing with his chin. "Take a look at these faces, pretty thing."

She forced her eyes away from him, nearly afraid to do so. It wasn't wise to take her eyes off a predator, but she knew the decision was forced. So she turned to his companion to see him holding up one of the posters.

"Recognize that face, pretty thing?"

It was all slashing black lines, a face painted to look vicious, more wild animal than Fae.

"No, sir."

He dropped the poster to reveal another one beneath it. This one of a human she didn't recognize. "This one?"

"No, sir."

"What about this one?"

Filomena froze, feeling everything inside her go tense as if ready to snap. She tried to school her expression, her breathing.

Because Filomena recognized the Fae on the poster.

Black lines curved and connected, forming the beautiful face of the Fae woman hidden above stairs.

But Filomena's voice didn't waver. "No, sir."

"Pity, that. If you see them, you'll let us know?"

"Of course, sir."

He released her wrist, and she fought the urge to rub it; it wasn't wise to show weakness before men like them.

Giving them one last smile, she turned and went back to the kitchen, dropping the posters on the table next to the vegetables, where Cook was chopping and Imogen was supervising.

"Soldiers," Filomena supplied. "The emperor has ordered the posters be placed on the walls."

Imogen's eyes strayed to the rolled parchments, but she didn't reply. It wasn't wise to do that, either. There were eyes and ears everywhere. Any whisper of rebellion could cost them their heads. So Imogen picked up the parchment and placed them into the pocket of her apron. As soon as she finished supervising Cook, the posters would go up. Every wall would be plastered with the face of the Fae they harbored in secret.

Tonight, Filomena would have to tell them. They were wanted.

And Filomena and Imogen would do whatever it took to keep them safe.

Midnight came and went, and the inn finally quieted down. Cook had left, and Imogen was in her office, counting the day's earnings. Meanwhile, Filomena was in the kitchen, preparing plates of food for their Fae guests.

There seemed to be an unspoken rule between Imogen and Filomena; they wouldn't mention the Fae or acknowledge their presence. Not even at night. So Filomena hurried through the motions to take their food up and come back down as quickly as possible. She'd tell them about the soldiers, and in a few hours, she was sure they would be gone.

The thought almost made her sad, if only because she could imagine how hard it was to be Fae, to fear being killed on sight simply because of what they were. Filomena understood fear. Being an unmarried young woman, she lived with it every day, but she would never know the fear they experienced. There was no way to compare the two, and it made Filomena realize how privileged she really was. She could walk openly down the street, ears exposed, without being skewered with an iron sword.

They didn't have that luxury.

She hoped that one day they would.

She was so lost in her thoughts that she didn't hear the back door to the kitchen open. Not until it was too late.

A blinding pain came as she was gripped by the back of the neck, her face slammed onto an empty plate she'd been in the process of serving. Her hands dropped everything. Food flew as her fingers reached back, grasping at her attacker. Nails scraped across leather, and that simple touch made everything within her still.

A deep chuckle sounded behind her that made her skin crawl. The hand on her neck squeezed, making Filomena gasp against the table. She knew she should kick out, fight with all she had to get out of such a vulnerable position, but fear kept her rooted. Fear of a blade to her side or worse.

"Remember me, pretty thing?" The soldier's voice slithered around her skin, full of vile promise.

"S-s-sir?" She hated how her chin wobbled, how the word came out more a fearful sound than firm like she'd trained herself to be.

"Ah, so you do remember." He pressed closer to her with each word, grinding his hips into her backside. She swallowed the bile coating the back of her tongue at the action and breathed through her nostrils. "You seem to be an intelligent girl. So tell me, pretty thing..." He kicked at her ankles, and a whimper escaped her as the action caused her legs to widen. "Why did you lie about the Fae?"

Her heart hammered up to her throat.

"S-sir, I d-d-don't—"

He slammed her face down again, and pain exploded behind her eyes. "Don't fucking lie to me, sympathizer scum. You recognized the female Fae. I could see it in your eyes."

Filomena was prepared to deny it until her very last breath, but the words caught in her throat, choking her in the rising panic. Her vision blurred around the edges. Not with tears. She wouldn't give this soldier scum that satisfaction.

"Don't even think about lying to me." His hand went to the curve of her backside and squeezed. A promise if she lied. A promise if she told the truth, too.

She was familiar with position, with the cruelty of men, of fists and worse. She'd lived through it once before; she could do it again. She could go far away into her mind. To greener pastures, to beaches and waves and sunlight. Whatever he wanted to do, she would let him.

But she would not betray the Fae.

Foolish, maybe, but she knew men like him. A confession wouldn't be enough to stave off his violent desires. He'd get the truth and rape her and kill her in the name of his murderous emperor.

Filomena would *not* give in. No matter what, she would protect the Fae.

Because they were perhaps the only chance everyone had at a better world.

And if she had a hand in creating a better place, even if it came at the cost of her own pain, then she would suffer in silence.

"Talk!" he barked, slamming her face down again.

This time, her skin grazed against the knife there, splitting open. She felt the warm rush of blood down her forehead, staining her vision red. She blinked it away from her lashes, sucking in sharp breaths. She refused to show pain. She didn't dare.

"So help me, if you don't start confessing..." He hiked her dress up, baring her legs.

Filomena couldn't find the energy to fight back against him. He was stronger, bigger. He'd kill her slowly. But she found the courage to speak. "Do what you have to do," she spat, "and go straight to hell."

He chuckled. "I like my women with spirit." The words were accompanied by the sound of clothes rustling. She bit the inside of her cheeks to avoid screaming and tasted blood. Her hands slapped against the table, grazing the handle of the knife.

A moment of clarity settled over her. Panic was a blinding thing. She'd felt the pain of the blade against her face, but it hadn't registered until her fingers brushed against the handle, until she opened her eyes through the haze of red and saw it gleaming in the light of the hearth.

Her skirts lifted higher, and she felt the press of his skin against hers.

Her hand closed around the hilt.

The soldier's hold loosened on her neck, the other hand holding her hip steady.

She breathed in deep, gripping the weapon tightly.

Before he could tear through her, Filomena angled her body and swung.

The blade sliced through the leather of his uniform, startling him enough that he cursed and jumped away from her. She whirled, brandishing the knife like it was her last protector in the world.

"You little bitch!" The soldier fixed his trousers and reached for his sword. It made a scraping sound as it was unsheathed.

She tried not to be intimidated by the sheer size of his weapon compared to her much smaller butcher's knife.

"I was going to spare your life, but now I think I'll kill you and fuck your corpse." His eyes gleamed with malice. "How about that?"

"Do what you have to," she heaved. "By the time you get to my body, my soul will have moved on and it won't matter anyway, you sick fuck."

He snarled. "Fae loving bitch!" And then he swung his sword. Filomena jumped back. She had no experience with weapons; she wasn't a soldier, didn't know how to defend herself. But she still swung with all her might, blade meeting iron with such a strong force, that the weapon fell from her fingertips.

Her head whipped back as the side of the blade slapped against her cheek, the edge splitting her skin. The force gave her whiplash and sent her flying to the side, hitting the shelf with pots and pans. They fell, pelting painfully against her body. Agony spread across the whole side of her face, traveling up her temple and skull.

She prayed Imogen had heard the crash from all the way on the other side of the inn while at the same time wishing she hadn't. If Imogen came in right now, she would protect Filomena and get killed.

Better Filomena than Imogen.

Yet her prayers weren't answered.

As the soldier charged towards her, grabbing her by the neck and slamming her against the shelf, Imogen burst through into the kitchen, brandishing a sword with all the rage of an avenging mother.

Filomena blinked as she was whipped up and around, her back pressed to the soldier's front. A moment later, she felt the blade against her throat and was staring through her pain at Imogen's murderous expression.

"You alright, Filomena?" Imogen asked, her voice steady.

The blade pressed tighter to her throat, drawing a line of blood that made her afraid to answer.

"In the name of the Emperor of Illyk, I reserve the right to sentence this maid to die under the crime of treason for harboring information regarding a Fae fugitive."

The blade bit into her neck and Filomena knew, almost on instinct, that she was drawing her last breaths. She could read the truth of it in Imogen's eyes. Her soul would move on. She'd suffered, cried, and fought her whole life. Perhaps she'd done nothing worthwhile. Nothing except for this night, protecting the Fae.

That alone would earn her a warrior's heaven. She knew, and she closed her eyes and prayed.

And before the last words to beseech whatever gods were listening were finished being uttered in her mind, she felt a shift in the air.

And then came the blood.

It exploded, bursting against her body, her skin warm with the rush of it. Her eyes blinked open to see Imogen. The magical portal shimmering beside her, and the most beautiful male—Fae or otherwise—she'd ever seen in her life, his palm facing her. Blood dripped down his nose, down his eyes like he was crying crimson.

The soldier froze behind her. His hold loosened, the sword fell, and a second later, so did his body.

Filomena stepped away, gasping, turning to look down at the body of the soldier.

Immobile.

Dead.

And covered in blood.

Clay wiped the blood from his nose but did nothing to clean the blood tracking tear marks down his cheeks.

Valerio's cousin always looked uncanny when he unleashed his magic. Because of the violent nature of what Mana had gifted him; to control and augment blood in such a capacity that it erupted from his enemies. In exchange, he lost blood as well, but only a fragment. Only in broken vessels of his eyes and nose.

Valerio felt his fellow Fae emerge from the portal behind him. The commotion from the kitchen had reached their ears, the crashing of pots and pans, and instinctively they knew that they were no longer safe here.

He took in the young maid's face. Busted and bleeding, bruises already forming against her skin. Her whole body shook, and she stared at Clay, at the hand he'd used to unleash his fury, at the blood still dripping from his eyes. But it wasn't fear in her eyes.

It was gratitude. Admiration.

"I didn't tell him anything." She trembled. "I swear it on my life. He came back because he knew I'd lied earlier, but I swear I didn't say a thing." Tears burst from her eyes then, and Valerio wished he had the bravery to run to her and hold her crumpling form to his arms, but Imogen beat him to it.

The young maid's body wracked up and down with sobs as she curled into the older woman.

"You are brave. Truly," Valerio said.

"How did they find out?" Julius demanded tightly. He didn't wait for Valerio's permission before he was looming over the soldier's dead body and dragging him across the kitchen floor. Blood trailed behind him in pools. Julius dropped the man's feet then reached down, rummaging through the bag hanging over his shoulder, coming up with crumpled parchment. "Ah," Julius declared. "This makes sense." He extended his arm to Shula, handing her the painted sign.

Valerio barely caught sight of it. He'd seen so many of them throughout the years, most with his face painted on them in sharp, angry strokes like he was some feral animal, that he knew what it said.

WANTED.

Shula's face, an incredible likeness of her, was on that parchment. The moment she took it in and saw the words *Alive and Intact*, Valerio could smell her fear.

Her hands trembled as she held the sign. He could only guess what was going through her mind. All her life, she'd lived hidden in the limelight of the circus, in plain sight yet away from the humans. She'd kept her Fae-self hidden out of fear and the bone-deep need to survive.

And just like that, the perfect little safety blanket she'd been holding tightly to had been ripped from her.

They had her face; there would be no more running. Valerio had told her. The Brotherhood knew what she looked like. So any dreams she ever had of returning to the life she had before had been only that.

Dreams.

Ryker looked over her shoulder at the portrait of her and growled, the sound low and protective.

"H-he had a friend," Filomena whispered.

Valerio turned back to her. "What?"

Her chin jerked. "The soldier. This afternoon he was here with a friend, but tonight he came alone."

"Fuck." Julius hauled the body up again. "Prince, we gotta go."

Emotions swirled within Valerio, building up to a storm that threatened a path of destruction. He wanted to keep a level head, but sudden guilt overwhelmed him.

"The safe house is compromised," he gritted out.

"Do you hear that?"

Hounds.

"His piece of shit friend went to get help."

"You have to go," Filomena said, straightening. Her voice was suddenly firm, her expression bereft of fear and replaced with grim determination. "Leave the body."

"We brought this mess to you," Valerio argued. "We can't just leave him here to be found."

Imogen smoothed her palms down her apron. "Filomena is right. There is no time. Leave or they will capture you."

Valerio knew what would happen if they left. They would be charged with treason for being Fae sympathizers. They would be charged with the murder of a soldier. The inn would burn to the ground and Imogen and Filomena? They wouldn't live through the night.

He couldn't do that. Everything within him screamed it was wrong. He knew what his father would say, what the king would do, but these women had risked their lives for him.

What kind of ruler would he be if he wasn't willing to do the same?

"Go! Now!" Filomena snapped.

"You know their lives do not equate to your own," Weylyn's voice whispered in his ear, through his mind. He didn't need to turn to know that the bastard was using his magic against the prince.

And damn it, he was right. Valerio was a prince. They were two maids. Yet the thought of their deaths didn't sit well with him. His life didn't feel any more valuable than theirs.

"They will kill you." He had to try one last time.

Filomena straightened. "I was prepared to die today, anyway."

The barking of the hounds came closer.

"Uric, open the portal."

The air shifted immediately after Valerio's command, and he could feel them passing through it one by one.

For a moment, Valerio stared, memorizing their faces, and they did the same to him. He wondered if they'd hate him in their last moments, for what he brought to their lives. He'd known Imogen for years, and he could have never predicted the end would come like this.

"Go," Imogen urged.

So Valerio did.

And he didn't look back.

Even when the sound of hounds grew louder and the women screamed and the portal closed behind him.

Declaration of War

Shula's nails tore through parchment on the other side of the portal. Shadows and forest greeted her. The world smelt like fresh, crisp air; earth and pine and grass. Just beneath that, the sharp tang of fear and the salt of her own tears.

"We left them." She didn't think anyone could hear the words she whispered into the night. The parchment crinkled as her hands smoothed out the crumpled edges. She stared down at her own face. At those damning words that changed everything.

WANTED: Alive and Intact.

She'd wondered what lengths the Emperor of Illyk would go through to get her, and now she had her answer.

He would send his soldiers after an innocent young woman, have her beaten, killed.

Her screams filled Shula's mind and seemed to slide down her back. Like Orna's broken body, those screams would haunt her forever.

So why hadn't she turned and grabbed them? Why hadn't she turned and pulled them into the portal behind her?

"Don't," a rumbling growl cut through her thoughts.

She blinked up at Ryker. Expression cut into stern lines, he reached out and brushed aside her tears with the backs of his scarred knuckles.

"Don't fucking think it."

How he knew what she was thinking, she didn't know. Were her feelings so easily read from her face?

"They made their choice. They could have jumped through with us, but they bought us time. They stayed."

She heard his words, maybe even a part of Shula could understand them, but they didn't *register*. "We left them. They'll be tortured or worse—" Her breath caught, a pained sound coming out of her throat. She looked down at the paper, knowing this was her fault.

If she hadn't been caught by the Brotherhood, if she hadn't told Fanny the truth, her face wouldn't be plastered on these wanted signs, Filomena wouldn't have had to lie to the soldiers, and she wouldn't have been attacked.

"I think it's finally time we talked," said Valerio. Shula turned and saw him nod once at Weylyn. "The human emperor wishes to use Shula to eradicate our race. My father needs to know about it. Tell him everything, Weylyn."

Shula observed as Weylyn's eyes rolled to the back of his head and his whole body stilled. Just like the first time she'd seen him, there was nothing but the occasional twitch of his body. She remembered what his power was, reading minds and communicating telepathically. She tried to clear her thoughts, her fears.

For a few minutes, Weylyn was still, his long black braid tugging with the breeze. Then he blinked, inhaled, and turned to Valerio, wearing a feral smile.

"Find the Elementals before he does." He spoke the words with command, like they didn't come from him but from the King of Seelie, and Weylyn was using the tone to match the formidable Fae's. "We have lived in the shadows for too long now. We have taken his abuse for the last time. The Emperor of Illyk wants a war with the Fae, then we will give him one."

"We don't have the numbers." Clay stepped forward. For the first time since she'd known him, she saw worry there.

"It matters not," Weylyn answered. "The King of the Seelie has made his declaration of war, and to battle we will ride."

The words were like a knife down her body. They were everything she'd ever tried to avoid. Danger. War. Death. Destruction.

"We barely survived the last war we were in," Shula argued, voice shaking. "Your numbers were bigger then. What makes him think he can win against the Emperor of Illyk?"

Perhaps those were treasonous words, contradicting him, but she'd said it before. The King of Seelie wasn't her king, and she was being logical.

There was no way they could survive the war.

"You did not listen to The Seer, did you?" Weylyn's eyes rolled with annoyance, while his smirk held in place. "The Elementals can *give* life as well as take it away."

"If the Elementals are a direct portal to summoning Mana, the human emperor wants to use that and eradicate us all. If we find the Elementals first, we can use that portal to heal, to give *life*." Realization seemed to dawn over Valerio. He stared at Shula like he'd just found the answer to all his problems.

"Precisely," Weylyn said. "King Ashera has ordered Shula to lead us to the Elementals."

Her whole body froze. "Wait a minute, I never agreed—"

"It's for the good of the Fae. Only you can find the other Elementals, and we need to keep you out of Emperor Laurel's hands, besides," Valerio interjected.

"I'm not some *weapon*—"

"You are. Open your eyes, Shula. We all have a duty to our race. This is yours."

Her heart pounded. Everything was spiraling out of control, becoming so overwhelming she didn't know what to do or say. She had never agreed to any of this. The only reason she'd even gone to Tir na Faie was to discover the truth of herself.

Now she knew it. She was done. She could go her own way, hide from the emperor instead of risk safe house after safe house, collateral damage, and close calls. Lives were at stake, and she'd already put enough of them at risk, just like they'd put *her* at risk.

"Shula..." She looked up at Ryker. His whole expression was softer than she'd ever seen. "This is your war, too."

War.

Since childhood, she'd traveled with her parents to avoid war. All she ever knew was a life of hiding and surviving. They saw it as cowardice, but there was bravery in hiding, too. They just couldn't see it.

They were asking her to give up everything she knew for a war she didn't want any part in. Hiding and going on her own was a risk. But a war? The risks were greater. She'd led a perfectly fine life alone. She didn't need to dive headfirst into danger by helping them.

But she knew if she said that, they would never let her leave.

Determined, knowing what she had to do, Shula dipped her head, feigning acquiescence. "You're right," she whispered. "It's my war, too."

"Good." Valerio nodded. "Tonight, we'll camp here. We have another safe house not far from here. We will go there tomorrow, make a plan, and decide how we will find the Elementals."

Shula nodded. "I'm not sure how to do that."

"One step at a time, Fire Dancer," Clay said. "We'll figure it out tomorrow."

"Yeah. We will."

Her heart beat fast as the lie left her lips. She found her gaze straying towards Weylyn often as they prepared to set up camp. Fear, an icy, biting sensation wound its way up her throat as those golden eyes stared hard at her. They didn't roll to the back of his head, so Shula knew her thoughts were safe for the time being. Yet, his eyes followed her, glittering in the night, his lips twitching with the smallest of smiles like he *knew*.

Surely, if he did, he would have said something to Valerio but when the time came for him and Ryker to take watch, he prowled into the copse of trees without a backwards glance, easing the anxiety in her chest as he went.

They all settled in for the night, believing she would be with them in the morning. She'd made sure of it so after they all fell asleep, they wouldn't suspect that she lay awake, staring up at the night sky, counting down the seconds until the pattern of their breathing steadied. As soon as they fell to sleep, as soon as those keeping watch were too far away to hear her, she got to her feet, shouldering her bag.

This wasn't her war, and she'd done what she'd set out to do. At least, that's what she told herself. She told herself she was being smart. That the Emperor of Illyk couldn't find her if she hid. That the Fae that were supposedly her friends wouldn't be able to use her.

She told herself she was protecting her life, her heart, from being used. Protecting herself from being killed. That it wasn't fear of the unknown driving her away, or the fear of what she could possibly mean in this war.

She was protecting herself and them.

Because the Emperor of Illyk would not stop looking, and the day would come when they couldn't protect her anymore. When a human soldier got lucky. Next time it wouldn't be an innocent like Filomena. Next time, it would be Clay or Julius.

Ryker.

Their deaths would weigh heavily on her, and Shula couldn't live with that on top of everything else.

No.

Sometimes, when the lives of friends were on the line, it was better to just be alone.

An Unwanted Mate

Her Papa's voice echoed with every step she took against the cold earth. As quiet as she tried to be, winter was approaching, which meant dry earth and crinkling leaves.

"It blankets us when we don't want to be seen, but it tricks us into thinking we are safe."

She should have heeded those words more than she had. It would have made her more cautious. It would have pulled her out of her own mind, her own tumultuous thoughts, and the severity of what she was doing, what she planned on doing.

Maybe then she would have heard the footsteps before the body stepped out from behind a tree.

But she'd been too wrapped up in her own fear, in the clawing way it choked through her lungs like the smoke had all those years ago. When she'd burned and burned and her parents had paid for what she was and what she did.

Everyone seemed to die around her. Mama, Papa, the sweet little old human woman whose name Shula never learned. And because of what she was, they would keep dying while she lived to watch them die or to be the weapon that would kill them.

It was a pattern in her life. Trouble followed where she went. Safety in numbers and in plain sight was an illusion.

Too bad it had taken so long for her to realize it.

Her feet skidded against the ground as the figure stepped before her. Far away, and yet the way his scarred hands scraped over her skin was imprinted on her body. She had his heat memorized and so she felt it like he was in front of her.

One white eye seemed to glow beneath the smallest sliver of moonlight as Ryker took her in.

She could read the disappointment, resentment, and anger from where she stood.

"Ryker..." Her voice sounded harsh in the quiet of the night.

"I knew you were lying the moment you opened your mouth," he cut in. "You're a fucking *liar* and a traitor to boot."

They shouldn't have, but his words cut. She should have been used to them; he'd said them often enough before. But that had been *before.* Things were different now. She was different. They were. Maybe it was the imprint of his mouth on hers, the scrape of his beard against her skin.

That alone made his words tear through her heart.

"Please understand—"

He snarled, cutting her off. Quiet followed where they simply stared at one another, waiting with bated breath. For what, Shula didn't know, but they waited.

Ryker broke the silence first. "You asked me who Mairin was."

Shula's heart beat faster.

She'd wondered, conjured up ideas of a lover and it twisted at her insides.

"Mairin Valda," he whispered the words like a prayer, filled with an eternity of sadness that should have been impossible. He took in a breath. "She was my sister."

Her mouth dropped. Sister. The reverent way he said it split her heart. *Was.* Because she was gone. Dead, because what else could she be in this fucking world of chaos and unrest? And the agony in his eyes said it all.

Ryker's sister was dead.

"Tensions were high between the humans and the Fae. The war had just reached its peak, laws of segregation were being passed, humans were invading Tir na Faie, and Mairin..." He broke off, swallowed his emotions. "Mairin fell in love with a human. A fucking soldier. She'd mated with a fucking human soldier."

"But how—"

"She didn't tell him what she was. She hid it with glamor, and he never suspected, never went around her with iron or ashwood. I don't know who the bigger fool was. Her for lying, him for not realizing it, or me for not stopping her from seeing him."

"If he was her mate, I don't think there's much you could have done..."

"I warned her. I told her not to hide it from him, but I didn't stop her. I should have fucking stopped her. She was so *ashamed* of our kind that she flounced around pretending to be human so he would love her. Then the day came when he found out. You'd think he would have been lenient because she was his mate, but he was a soldier, betrayed, and he despised the Fae."

"Ryker—"

"They tortured her. Raped her. Took turns." Hatred burned in his words, his posture, within every single inch of him. "They left her hanging from an oak tree for me to find, her face carved up, and I tried. I tried to save her, but all I got were these scars." He gestured at his face, the raised flesh pulling taut at the rest of his skin. "I got her pain, the pain of what those beasts did to her, and not just the cuts, but everything else, too."

She took a wavering step towards him. "Ryker..."

"All because she thought she should hide who she was. If she'd had the slightest bit of Fae pride, instead of betraying who she was to fit into what the humans want us to be. She betrayed herself for a human who didn't deserve her. She didn't have to say it, but I knew she was ashamed of what she was. Hatred does that. It makes us change. When it looks us in the eye long enough, we start looking back at it like we're looking into a mirror until we hate ourselves. Mairin hated herself." His eyes burned on Shula. "And I see that in you too. Cowardice. Fear. *Hatred.*"

Shula rocked back on her heels. "That's not fair," she choked out. Tears stung the backs of her eyes. "I told you why I had to hide—"

"But you *keep* hiding, Shula!" he screamed, and she flinched at the sound as if he'd struck her. He growled and lowered his voice. "You keep hiding from what you are and what you're meant to be."

"I'm not meant to be anything! I didn't choose this!"

"Mana gave it to you, regardless of what you want or wish you had. You're an Elemental Fae, and you have the power to change the world, but you're too fucking cowardly to accept it."

"It's not my fight," she argued.

Ryker scoffed. "Pathetic." Then he stepped off to the side and gestured to the direction she'd been walking towards. "Leave, then. It's better if you walk away now."

Shula swallowed the emotion rising in her throat. At this goodbye, the anger and evident hatred. Everything they'd built together, the hatred, the training, the understanding, the *kiss*, it all came back to this again.

She'd told him time and time again what she felt, what she thought, and he couldn't look past what had happened to his sister to see that maybe Shula was different. That maybe it wasn't shame driving her away at all, but the bad luck. The hurt. The fear of seeing everyone around her die. The helplessness. Being used and discarded.

She felt it all.

A sense that she'd never really belong anywhere because in the end she always brought more harm than good.

So Shula did what she had to do.

She walked away from him, but his voice trailed after her.

"I don't need a coward for a mate."

And it was those words that had her halting. That had the heaviness in her chest dropping. A sense of magic purred inside and clicked into place. Like those were the words she'd been waiting to hear her whole life. They settled. Right. Perfect. Pieces falling together.

She whirled. "What did you just say?"

His lips were pressed into a thin line, his eyes hard. "You're my mate, Shula."

She felt like he'd struck at her with a blade. The words tore through her body, slowly, painfully, and they settled. Familiar enough with the agony to embrace it as inevitable, as the truth.

Everything came to her, a flash of lightning through her mind. The laughter two nights before, Ryker's behavior at dinner, and everything in between. Talk of mates, Weylyn's questioning by the river.

Everyone had known.

Everyone except for her.

She gritted her teeth, hands tightening into fists. "How long have you known?"

He blinked. "I suspected when you ran into me outside the temple of the Brotherhood. I knew for certain when we arrived at Castle Aileach."

Months.

He'd known for *months,* and he hadn't told her.

And it explained so much. Her attraction to him that bordered between the lines of hate and desire. Because the bond had been pulling them together, jagged pieces that fit into a broken and fucked up relationship somehow.

"How?" The word broke out of her.

"It seems Mana has a sense of humor, as I don't understand it any more than you do. But it doesn't matter. Because I don't want a mate. I don't want *you.*"

Those words shouldn't have hurt as much as they did, but they were further proof that not even her mate, the one sent by Mana who was meant to love her regardless of anything else, wanted her.

No one wanted her.

Reality was a harsh thing, and she didn't think anything could ever be harsher than this.

"Good," she whispered, even if she wasn't sure she meant the words. "I don't want you, either."

"Good," he replied.

There was finality in the moment. Nothing left to say. "Goodbye, Ryker."

Leaving felt like cutting her soul up into thousands of pieces, but it didn't matter that she was walking away, dragging her broken heart behind her, leaving the only Fae she ever considered friends, even if they perhaps didn't feel the same.

She was a coward.

And cowards never got happy endings, or friends, or love.

Merely a life of hiding, of fear.

Of loneliness.

He'd known, the moment she'd seen her face drawn on that poster, he'd known she was going to leave them. That the fear would be almost too much.

What he could have never predicted was how it would make *him* feel. Betrayed, hurt. He shouldn't have been surprised. She'd been trying to run since they'd found her. But she'd *changed.* He hadn't imagined that, the shift between them. Not just because of the kiss, not just because she was his mate.

He almost scoffed.

Mate.

He'd suspected what she was since the moment he saw her. When she'd slammed into his chest and looked into his eyes, the mating bond snapped into place inside him. He hadn't contemplated it at the time, had thought it was a fluke of his own magic somehow. Afterwards, he'd felt the pull. Something about her had felt *right,* and yet Ryker wanted no part of her.

Not this fearful, shaking Fae with curved ears and an unhealthy love for humans that reminded him of Mairin. Seeing Shula brought memories of his sister back, the pain, the anger, the sorrow. It had made him all too aware of his scars and the way Shula's eyes traveled over them like she was studying the pathways on a map.

He wasn't ashamed of them; he no longer felt shame. He just knew that it had to be some kind of joke. He didn't want Shula, and Shula didn't want him. She didn't want the Fae at all.

It was better to push her away than to form bonds, to see her become so jaded in her beliefs that she followed in the same footsteps as Mairin, lying, hiding. The truth of the matter was, she wasn't safe with the humans and never would be, but she couldn't see that.

So, yeah, it was better to watch her walk away. It was better to not want her at all. To not acknowledge what Mana had thrust unwillingly upon them both so that the bond became nothing but ash before it could even ignite.

He didn't need to care just to watch her die.

He stepped back into camp, his footsteps beating against the ground loudly until they jostled awake. He reached for his bag, shoving his things inside and pulling the straps on his shoulders.

Clay got up, looking at the empty spot where Shula once lay. "Where's—"

"We need to leave," Ryker snapped.

Uric and Valerio untangled themselves from their sheets, standing slowly. The prince's features were set in hard lines. "Where is Shula?" he demanded.

Ryker had known they would ask, just like he knew that when he told the truth they'd want to go after her. Which was why he'd taken his time coming back to camp, giving Shula just enough time to flee so they couldn't catch up to her.

"She's gone," Ryker growled. "Good fucking riddance."

A collective silence washed over the small group. Then, "What the fuck do you mean she's gone?" Valerio stepped towards him, snapping his canines.

"She ran away just like she always does." Ryker had never struck his prince, but in that moment he contemplated doing just that.

"We can't just let her leave." Julius pushed to his feet, staring at the darkness of the woods as if he meant to run and catch up to the Fire Dancer.

"She won't help us. She's too scared."

"Well, what the fuck are we supposed to do? Just let her walk the fuck away? The soldiers would find her in a minute and take her to the emperor!"

Ryker knew better than anyone what he had let walk away. A weapon for Illyk. Their only chance at saving the Fae.

His fucking *mate.*

"She would have kept fleeing from us." It would have been a special kind of punishment to watch her leave, walk away from them, and have to bring her back every time. "It's better this way."

"Better for who?" Clay growled, shouldering aside his cousin so he was in front of Ryker himself. "For us or for you? Because it sounds like you let her go out of pure selfishness." Then Clay's palms collided with Ryker's shoulders, shoving him backwards. "We *need* her, you asshole!"

"She's *my* mate!" Ryker shouted, shoving Clay back just as hard. The Fae stumbled, his eyes widening with surprise. Ryker didn't blame him. He'd avoided speaking about what she was to him ever since they all realized what she really was. He hadn't even wanted to admit it to himself. "Not yours! None of you get a say in what she does."

"I am your prince," Valerio interjected, his voice containing the cold of his fury. "We had orders."

Fuck your orders, Ryker wanted to snarl but somehow held the words back.

"We have to go after her." Valerio's hands began waving around, a silent issue of orders that set everyone in motion.

"It's too late." Everyone froze and turned as Weylyn emerged from the shadows of the trees, his golden eyes glittering in the dark, a devilish sneer pulling at his mouth. "The Fire Dancer is gone; we cannot possibly catch up to her."

It took a moment for everyone to absorb this, and a moment later for Ryker to feel the blow of a fist against his cheek.

"You asshole!" Clay pounded into him and Ryker staggered back. Blood burst inside his mouth and he spat it out, a growl ripping from his throat. Soon, they were nothing but a scuffle of fists and tangled limbs on the ground. When Clay's fist dug into Ryker's still-healing shoulder, he screamed.

"Enough!"

Clay was yanked off of Ryker and hauled backwards. Ryker took a breath before he slowly pushed to his feet and turned to meet his prince's stern gaze.

"This is a fucking disaster! You may have just fucked over the entire Fae race by letting her go. Do you know how much danger she could be in? The emperor could find her and she has no one to protect her now."

"Sounds like her fucking problem," Ryker bit out. But he didn't feel the words. In fact, they felt vile. Untrue. He hated them as soon as they left his lips and they made an ache build in his chest, more painful than the wound on his shoulder.

Valerio looked at him with pity in his eyes like he could see right through him. "What you did was an act of treason. My father could have your head for this." He said it softly, sadly, and Ryker almost believed that the prince really cared.

Too bad Ryker couldn't bring himself to in that moment.

He didn't have it in him to respond.

"We will go to the safe house and think about what to do next. Perhaps we can somehow track her."

Ryker did not want to track her. He didn't think he want to see Shula Azzarh ever again.

"Ryker..."

The sadness in that tone undid him. "Let's go," he cut off the Seelie Prince. There was no point in staying here when he knew she wasn't coming back. That final glimpse of her walking away was probably the last he'd ever see of her.

"Ryker, we can't just—"

"Let's *go*," he barked, snapping his canines together.

He was not their leader by any means, but it was suffocating to be here, to stay with that hope that she would come running back. But they hadn't seen the look in her eyes.

The finality.

It didn't matter how long they waited.

The Fire Dancer wasn't coming back.

Will-o'-the-wisps

The further Shula walked, the quicker the tears threatened to form behind her eyelids. She blinked them away, scrubbing the back of her hand against her eyes furiously. She didn't want to cry, refused to do it for them.

For Ryker.

And those damning words.

Mate. Mate. Mate. Mate.

It didn't matter. What was the point of crying over someone who didn't want her? It wouldn't make her feel any better, and there was no point contemplating what *could* have been. There was no room in life for what ifs. That was something she was starting to learn.

Things just happened, good or bad, and you dealt with them in any way you could.

That's what Shula was doing. Fleeing before things could get bad. Because, eventually, the Emperor of Illyk would find them. He was actively looking for her and she would bring death down upon those around her.

She wouldn't be the death of her friends. Her mate.

She stopped, leaning against a tree. Since when had she started thinking of them as her friends?

Sure, they'd kidnapped her, wouldn't let her leave. But through it all, relationships had slowly built. She'd gotten to know them at a level that surpassed the surface.

Ryker, who healed those that were hurt and asked for nothing in exchange. Who bore the scars of cruelty with Fae pride. Who was rough and brutal and cranky, a personality born deep from heartbreak and sorrow.

Clay, who was the first to make her feel welcome. Who was kind and flirtatious, patient and quick to help. He'd lifted her up when she'd been kicked down, had stood up for her simply because it was right. Not because he wanted to use her, but because he loved women and treated them all with kindness.

Julius, who was rough, loud, *funny*. His antics made her laugh, and there was a protective side to him shown in those moments when their swords clashed, when he knocked her to the ground and screamed at her to do better. Because he believed that she could do better. He'd given her the means to fight with both precision and brutality.

Valerio, the Seelie Prince, he was... He was complicated. Their relationship hadn't bloomed. She'd harbored a resentment towards him because of him taking her but it didn't burn at hotly as it had then. Because she saw it. The pain in his eyes when they'd had to leave Imogen and Filomena. The softness in his expression as he'd confessed he thought Shula would possibly be his mate. Prince Valerio cared deeply, but he hid it behind masks of sharp glares and serious expressions.

She hadn't gotten to know Uric beyond his standoffish demeanor, but he was made of loyalty through and through. The way he hovered over Valerio protectively, was alert at all times to any danger, the way he would put his own life at risk to protect his prince... He was good, and Shula knew she just couldn't see it yet.

And Weylyn? Shula didn't know what Weylyn was. She didn't know what motivated him. Beyond the feral grin and prowling saunter, he was unreadable. Even while he could read everyone else.

And yet, they had all fit together. A perfect little unit. A family. And Shula had slowly felt herself being drawn into that, being included in their jokes, their banter, their *training.*

Maybe she even felt a part of them already.

It took a moment for her to realize that the tears were falling. They slid down her cheeks, to her chin. Annoyed with herself at showing emotion, she swiped away the tears. Clear from her face, she looked up and promptly froze.

Her Papa had always told her stories of the faerie lights that guided travelers to their futures and made clear their destinies. His words were spoken whispers in the reservations, in the dark of the night where nothing illuminated their faces but the flickering campfires. He'd whisper tales of simple Fae travelers going through the wood and coming across the floating lights, following, and being led to greater things.

"There is one integral rule when it comes to will-o'-the-wisps, Shula," he would say. "Always *follow the lights."* He would precede to bump his finger against her nose. *"You never know where they'll take you."*

She would stay awake for hours after that, staring at the stars in the sky, wondering what the faerie lights actually looked like. If they were as bright as stars or if they burned hot like fire. If they danced or were gentle, if they were many lights clustered together to form a giant ball of illumination. Or were they something else entirely?

She didn't know then.

She certainly did now.

The pull of the light was ethereal. She could *feel* the magic surrounding it. As otherworldly and preternatural as Tir na Faie must have been, once upon a time. Shula had never seen a faerie light before, but she was looking at one now.

Like a spectral of a ghost, it floated in hues of blue and white. Wisps of light the glowed in the darkness, like a swirling phantom of smoke that coalesced into a single ball. It bobbed up and down like a leaf in the water, slow and patient.

Shula could swear it had eyes, and they were trained on her, waiting for that first step.

Always follow the lights.

She pushed herself away from the tree. The will-o'-the-wisp stirred. She took a step and it moved, further away, but still within her line of sight. Beckoning, begging, and she was weak to resist the call.

You never know where they'll take you.

The thrall of the will-o'-the-wisp wasn't something Shula could forcibly break herself out of. It was an enticing, ancient magic that pulled her towards it, faster and faster until she was running through the darkness, with it as her only beacon of light.

Branches slapped against her skin and drew a thin line of blood against her cheek. Her heart pounded up to her throat, her breaths heaved, but nothing mattered more than catching the faerie light. Within the span of a few seconds, it had become an obsession. It hypnotized her, pulled her into its thrall.

It burst past the forest and into a clearing, becoming a dull red glow that she ran after. Shula abruptly skidded to a halt outside of the tree line, gasping.

She hadn't known what to expect the light would lead her towards.

It hadn't been this.

Not a camp full of human soldiers brandishing swords of iron.

You never know where they'll take you.

Shula's light had led her straight to her death.

Shock and fear kept her rooted firmly to the ground for a mere minute before Shula whirled. She wasn't quick enough. The human soldiers surrounded her, and not even the knife Ryker gave her was enough to keep them at bay.

Steel barely met her little blade before the knife was knocked from her grasp, her arms wrenched behind her back and clasped in iron manacles. The touch of it diminished her magic almost immediately. She tried to will the flames to emerge, but there was nothing inside her but a dull flicker of light.

And so much fear.

"The emperor will reward us tonight," one of the human's said as he shoved her to the ground in the middle of their makeshift camp. Her knees buckled and her ankle twisted as she hit the ground, sending sparks of pain up her leg. "This is that fire bitch he's been looking for."

They had her face memorized.

Shula tried not to drown in the despair that suddenly gripped her. Everything had happened so fast. Leaving. Ryker. The faerie lights. She'd been so deeply rooted by her fear that she had barely even fought back. Months of training for nothing, only to be caught in iron manacles once again.

She thought she was stronger than this. That the next time she came face to face with anyone who wanted to harm her, she'd strike them down with sword and magic, and flee.

She should have known she could never be strong enough; she wasn't a fighter. For Mana's sake, whenever things got hard, she would *flee*. She wasn't a warrior. She wasn't strong and brutal like Julius, as elegant as Clay, or as selfless as Ryker, as imposing as Valerio.

She was the coward who fled from what she was and who was too scared to accept what Mana had thrust upon her.

Neither human nor Fae, but something in between. Something ugly and afraid, with all the faults of both and none of the advantages of either.

And she was as good as dead. Even if she was trapped in her own mind, she still tried to summon the flames, yet nothing stirred to life within her. Because of her foolishness, they would take her to the Emperor of Illyk. He would use her.

And the Fae would be no more.

"We'll be ascended in rank, boys. We'll turn in this bitch and present him with the heads of wanted Fae by morning!"

A raucous cheer rose up after that declaration.

Shula stared at the burning embers of the dying fire, feeling tears sting behind her eyelids. She felt the swords pointed in her direction, and even if they weren't so close as to cut her, she still felt the threat radiating through her body.

"Their safe house isn't far from here. If we surround ourselves with enough iron, we'll catch them unawares."

The words from one of the human's had Shula's body stiffening with awareness. She blew out a deep breath, lifting the strands of dark hair fallen against her face.

Awareness slowly came back to her, as if she'd been experiencing this outside of her own body the entire time. Living in the fear, the uncertainty, even her own memories. But it was those words that pulled her back to the moment and made her realize her position.

She was laying on the ground on her side, arms twisted at her back, one shoulder screaming in pain. Her ears were exposed, her hair curtaining her vision. Pushing it away, she cast her gaze around and got a good look at the soldiers when she hadn't before.

There were about a dozen or more of them, the dying embers of their fire and the packs secured on the sides of their horses was an indication that they'd been about to head out.

To the safe house.

She swallowed the rising lump in her throat and steadied her breathing.

"The key in any fight is to breathe," Julius had said. *"Control your emotions, your breath, and you can control your body's reaction."*

So Shula breathed, letting the words Julius had spoken so long ago take hold of her mind and eventually, her body. She breathed in and out until her whole body was no longer taut with tension, but relaxed. Then she could see clearer.

Only then would she be able to fight her way out of this. Perhaps not with magic, but somehow.

"Watch her while we go chop off some Esses heads." One of the human's slapped a hand down against his horse. No. Not a horse. Shula's vision homed in on it, realizing that it was much bigger, taller, wider. A structure that Shula hadn't noticed at first and wondered how she'd even missed it. But something about it screamed with familiarity in a way that sent shivers down her spine.

Probably because it was made entirely of iron.

But...

She swept her gaze around. There were more of those things in all varying degrees of sizes, each bigger than the last.

The human used a ladder built in on the side of the metal device and climbed, straddling the back of the machine like a horse. He started pulling at various levers, and then Shula watched as the thing sprang to life and became something she was intimately familiar with.

An iron monster.

She jerked against her bonds and fought to sit up.

"No!" The word croaked from her throat, and she regretted speaking immediately.

A steel toed boot came crashing against her side, knocking the air right out of her. Even as she tried gasping for breath, it didn't come. Her lungs constricted painfully, and she turned to her back, staring up at the black sky and streaks of stars until her vision started to blur.

"See what you fucking did? Don't kill her before we get her to the emperor!"

It was a slow process, inhaling grateful breaths of air.

"Just fucking watch her while we go get the Esses scum. These iron monsters are hungry for a taste of Fae blood."

The ground vibrated as the monster moved. One, then another, and another. Shula couldn't pull her gaze away from the sky to turn and look, but she'd counted at least four.

Four iron monsters against six Fae, maybe more, if the safe house was occupied.

"No..." The word was weak coming out of her mouth.

Ryker, Julius, Clay, Valerio, Weylyn, Uric...

They were at the safe house.

Somehow, the humans had discovered where it was and were going after them.

After her friends.

Tears slipped down to her temples, staining the ground beneath her. Helplessness threatened to invade her.

Her friends were in danger and there was nothing she could do. It was everything she ever feared would happen. Everything that *had* ever happened, and she was too helpless, too pathetic to stop it.

Her friends were as good as dead.

Her *mate* was as good as dead.

Just thinking those words made everything within her rebel. Her stomach heaved at the thought and she swallowed down the bile. Even her soul hurt thinking those words, because she didn't want them to be true.

Not Ryker. Not kind, selfless Ryker. Who saw something in her and believed in her, coaxing it out. Perhaps it hadn't been in the way she wanted, but it had been in the way she *needed.* He wouldn't coddle; he was brutish, rough, growling, and he'd helped with healing her mind.

He saw her, and it was like he *knew* everything she harbored inside. Whether it was because of the bond, because he was observant, or because of something else entirely.

He'd helped her heal.

The magic she used to be so afraid of, he taught her to hone it into something great, into something she never thought it could be.

She'd melted the iron bars off of a cage. She'd melted the iron monsters in the mountains in Tir na Faie.

She was *strong.*

Against all odds, against everything she ever thought she could be, the Fae had made her strong. They'd taught her to wield weapons, to fight against an opponent much bigger than herself, to use skill and magic.

They'd turned her into something she never thought she'd ever be.

They'd made her Fae.

Because she *was* Fae, she realized with a jolt. She always had been. The power inside her had always been there. Her potential had been there, waiting to be unlocked.

Something indescribable surged through her soul, but she knew what it was just the same. Mana awakening, demanding, and filled with realization.

It burned brightly inside her like the hottest of fires. Spread throughout her body. Mana whispered through her, a sensation of a powerful magic, stronger and fiercer than anything she ever knew.

Acceptance.

Of herself, of what she was, of what she could be.

Tears burned her eyes as everything surged through her at once.

She was enough. She was strong.

And her friends needed her.

Because she knew they wouldn't stand against the iron monsters on their own. And maybe she was an Elemental for other reasons, but none seemed as important right then as this. As rescuing them, rescuing the males who had unlocked the potential she'd dared to bury deep inside her.

And that fear? It still lived inside her. She knew it always would; it would be there, a sliver of doubt tainting her thoughts. Yet right then, a bright light shoved it away with the knowledge that there were things she couldn't control.

The deaths of her parents.

The death of the old woman.

Davina.

Orna.

Filomena.

Imogen.

So many more Fae would die unless she used her strength, and she *fought*. Not just for their lives, but for hers.

She would fight for the little girl she had been, barefoot and afraid, feet bleeding as she ran through the streets of Tuath away from soldiers who threatened her life. She would fight for the Fae who wanted a better world.

For Mairin.

For the humans who had a skewed view of what she was and who couldn't accept the truth of her like Fanny.

She would fight for the Fae who wished for a better world.

And for herself.

The time for hiding was over, and she was tired of being a coward.

Her friends needed her.

Her *mate* needed her.

Shula felt the flicker of heat ignite and spread, fueled by anger and determination in equal measure. She guided it to her wrists and felt the iron melt away from her skin.

"What the fuck!"

The words drowned out with the roaring sound of fire in her ears. Smoke swirled through her lungs and when she exhaled, it clouded over her face. Her body moved, and she pushed to her feet. It was then that she realized she was glowing, her skin bright like molten lava.

"How—" The human pointing the sword at her didn't get the rest of his sentence out.

Fire shot out of her palm and engulfed him. His screaming didn't last, because her magic burned too hot, too angry, and she wasn't playing games.

She was a Fire Elemental, a gift straight from Mana.

She erupted, and every human in the vicinity suffered her wrath and *burned,* and when there was nothing left but smoke, ash, and the stench of burnt flesh, she turned back to the woods and bent to pick up her fallen dagger. She straightened, looking into the darkness.

And saw a floating will-o'-the-wisp.

Shula smiled. "Will you lead me to them?"

In response, it flickered away.

And all Shula could do was follow.

The safe house was a rickety cabin of rotting wood, no candles, and minimal space. It didn't exactly give Ryker a moment to brood in peace. Everyone was near, and everyone was staring between him and the prince, waiting to see what he would do. If he would tell his father what had happened.

Prince Valerio hadn't. Not even Weylyn had.

As if they felt sorry for him because of what he'd lost. A mate he hadn't even wanted in the first place.

It didn't matter if his chest was pounding, the strings of the threads in his soul pulling uncomfortably. He rubbed absently at his chest to rid himself of the sensation. He shouldn't have bothered. It felt like it would be just another prominent ache in his soul. First Mairin, then Shula.

Perfect.

Just perfect.

Ryker pushed himself to his feet, feeling a rush of sudden fatigue. He should sleep before they left. He knew that, but it was either deal with nightmares or keep watch. Sometimes if he stayed awake enough, his body just crashed when he finally did fall onto his makeshift bed for the night, no traces of memories or dreams slithering through his mind.

He didn't announce what he was doing or where he was going. They were all familiar enough with one another to know their routines. Like how Ryker and Weylyn always took the night watch. Ryker, to avoid sleeping, Weylyn, because Valerio didn't want him near.

Weylyn was already outside, combing through the perimeter. Ryker avoided looking at the rest of the males as he went outside himself. His pointed ears perked as he listened.

The earth was telling. One could always know its secrets based on its silence just as much as its noise. Like Weylyn's booted feet scraping against the bark of trees as he climbed for a better vantage point from a distance away.

Other than that, the night was quiet.

Too quiet.

Assuming a defensive stance was almost instinct. He'd lived out in the woods enough to recognize the sounds of animals rushing through the wood. Of deer, birds, squirrels... But there was nothing.

His nostrils flared, and he tilted his head up to the air and inhaled sharply. Earth. Dry leaves. And something else. Something that didn't belong.

It was then that the groaning pierced his ears, the groaning and whirring of cogs like a well-oiled machine and rumbling, heavy steps that shook the ground. He'd only ever felt something like it once before in the lands that used to be home.

Iron monsters.

As soon as the thought broke through his mind, the monsters burst through the trees, splintering them like twigs. They fell towards his direction, and he could feel the earth shriek in protest.

Six monsters molded and bent into the jagged image of a bulky elephant. Atop sat human soldiers, working at cogs and knobs to propel it forward.

A beast so big shouldn't have been so fast, but it was.

It charged, and Ryker barely had time to shout a warning to the others as it neared. Ryker jumped to the side, narrowly missing the iron tusks, as sharp as swords.

The others burst out of the rotting cabin, brandishing their weapons, eyes taking what they'd been sure had only existed beyond the Ley Line.

Ryker's sword slid through his sheath and in a mighty swing, it collided against a metal monster. Sparks shimmered and the monster jerked against him, shoving him away.

The close proximity was already making Ryker breathless, his knees shaking and barely able to keep him upright. But still he fought. Strike. Dodge. Duck. Strike.

His sword sawed through iron, barely making a dent. Above the machines, the humans laughed, the sound maniacal, a singing promise of death. Metal trampled through the wood of the cabin, tearing it apart like it could somehow tear apart what it stood for as well.

Ryker's breaths came out of him painfully. Iron collided against him and the agony that raced up his body made his vision blink in and out. He was shoved back, his back making an impact with the ground, the sword flying from his grasp.

His vision cleared in time to look up at the machine hovering above him and the human soldier laughing. Just in time to see his companions faring no better than him, iron weakening them, blood dripping from their faces. Just in time to see Weylyn drop from a nearby still-standing tree and run into the fray, sword colliding against a tusk that threatened to impale Valerio. Just in time to see wisps of faerie lights dancing through the pathway of destroyed trees and disappear just as quickly.

Just in time to see Shula Azzarh follow right behind, her brown skin glowing like molten lava.

Fire bursting from her fingertips.

Revenge in her eyes, and anger bursting past her lips as her magic shot out and consumed a machine. Licks of fire kissed the sky as her gift consumed, melted.

Destroyed.

And it was at that moment that Ryker thought with certain clarity that Shula Azzarh had never looked more beautiful.

A Wanted Mate

Destiny came in many forms.

It came in the form of death, heroism, sorrow, agony.

And it came in the form of melting iron.

The will-o'-the-wisp had led her down the path of destruction. Trees tumbled towards the clearing where the little cabin was destroyed and the Fae were fighting for their lives. And when Shula saw them bloody, exhausted yet determined, she exploded.

Fire shot from her palms, and her feet began moving, running. Her toes barely touched the ground as she ran, no, *flew* across the earth, finding momentum to jump. Her body vibrated with pain as she landed on the edge of the thick tusks of the machine. She ignored the pain, fueled by her rage and all the sudden overwhelming realization of what she was and what she could do.

The human screamed as fire trailed against the iron behind her. She tip-toed along the metal like a dancer along a tightrope. And when Shula came face-to-face with the human, she didn't give him another chance to scream before she incinerated him from the inside out.

The fire spread beneath her feet, but it didn't burn. The machine groaned and fell. She balanced herself, finding purchase as it went crashing down. Only then did she jump again and land against the ground, squelching the fire to not harm the earth.

She saw Ryker on the ground in front of her, a machine looming above him. He cried out as he turned, rolling on the ground, making a dive for his sword. The human manning the thing laughed, a cruel sound that scraped against her bones. He attacked Ryker and everything else fell away.

Everything else but this.

Her mate.

In danger.

Shula screamed, her feet and fire propelling her forward. She jumped onto the machine, slamming behind the human. Iron armor embedded into her skin, but she barely felt it. All she knew was rage, protection, that this bastard was trying to harm Ryker.

Something primal and possessive came to life inside her. Maybe it had always been there. Time and time again. She just hadn't noticed why she was so willing to jump in front of him when danger was near, why he had been so willing to protect her. When the human had a knife to her throat, when an iron monster had nearly killed him.

Because even then, some part of her recognized that he was *hers.*

The soldier cried out, bringing his elbow back to collide against her side. The breath rushed out of her in a gasp, and she nearly fell back. Her fingers grasped for purchase even while he bucked and hit, and pain seared against her. Shula's nails dug into the skin at his face and the flames came out to kiss.

Skin melted from muscle and bone until his screams diminished into echoes throughout the night. The fire caught on the machine, but Shula didn't move.

She needed to end this. Now.

So she dug deep inside herself for the last reserves of her magic until it exploded against the remaining machines and humans and the iron melted to the ground.

And all was silent save for the flickering remnants of flames.

Shula stepped down from the still-burning machine and as quickly as she let it loose, pulled her magic back until the flames doused to ash. Her body lost its glow and her knees felt so weak, she wanted to fall to the ground but she somehow managed to keep herself upright and take one step and another until she faced Ryker.

The pain of their goodbye and the words exchanged was still raw in her heart, yet there was no denying the relief at seeing him relatively unharmed.

She counted five separate footsteps close in around them, but she didn't turn. She stared at Ryker, and it was like she was seeing him for the first time all over again. Like when his hood had dropped to reveal the creature underneath.

Scarred and imperfect, brows furrowed, jaw tight. Raised flesh pulling his face together like jagged broken pieces of a puzzle, one eye different from the other, but were so focused on her like she was the only one in the world.

"Why did you come back?" he growled.

Because a 'thank you' could never suffice. He had to growl, yell, sharpen his claws and dig them deep into her. Because that's who he was, and she would respond with equal disdain. Because that's who she was.

It's who *they* were.

"I'm not a coward."

"That's not an answer."

She stepped forward until their chests brushed. "Isn't it? Since we met you've been accusing me of being a coward. Maybe I was, but I'm not anymore. All my life, I may have run from camp to camp, but when the soldiers finally came for me, my Papa and Mama bought me time to run. So I kept running, so much that I forgot what it was to be selfless and face my fears like my Papa did."

She knew everyone was listening, but she didn't care. She'd already given them the brunt of her story, with bits and pieces missing. These were the pieces that were missing.

Her parents had protected her, and they'd died because of it. Their ashes had coated the streets of Tuath for *her.*

"I couldn't let you die," Shula confessed. Just like her parents protected her, it was high time Shula protected others.

The time for running was over.

"And I'm tired of being afraid. This won't truly end until the Emperor of Illyk is stopped, and if I'm one of the six who can do it, then I'll do everything I can to end this war."

Ryker's nostrils flared. And it was a long moment before he spoke, so long that Shula thought he wasn't going to say anything at all. "I was wrong." The hand not holding his sword came up to brush aside the tears she hadn't even known she'd been crying.

"You weren't. You were a dick, but you weren't wrong."

"So, you'll help us?" Valerio asked from behind them. And Shula heard it in his voice.

Hope.

"I'm not running away. Not anymore."

Ryker's fingers slipped through the hair at the back of her neck, angling her head back so he could look deep into her eyes. Her palms slid against his chest where she felt the rapid beating of his heart.

"Good." The word rumbled through his chest and against her palms.

Then Ryker bent and he kissed her.

The collision of their lips set off an explosion of fireworks behind her eyelids. Magic built from somewhere deep inside her, Mana rising and settling in place. A bond tangled at the seams and shoved into a dark corner suddenly unraveled, threaded together, and *snapped* into place.

A shudder rippled through her body, leaving her gasping. Magic flowed between them, a joined feeling that had them pressing closer until no inch of space was left. Light flared brightly around them, the strings of their bonds pulling, enveloping.

It was everything Shula never knew she wanted, a desire hotter than her Mana-given gift.

Tongues tangled together, not in a fight but a *dance*, an understanding. It healed raw, opened wounds and became something fresh and new.

It made them whole.

Shula's hands lifted on instinct and wrapped around the back of his neck. Using all the strength she could muster, she pulled herself up against him, creating a friction at her core against the tight ridge pressed against his pants.

A throat cleared, shattering the moment between them. They came down together slowly, pulling apart, gazes holding, breaths mingling.

"I hate to interrupt, but we have to go." Shula could hear the amusement in Clay's voice, but she ignored it.

She could feel the air shimmering behind her as a portal was created. Then slowly, without taking his eyes off her, Ryker walked her backwards and into the pressurized surface of the portal.

For a moment, there was nothing but darkness and silence.

And Ryker's arms wrapped tightly around her in reassurance.

That she was safe in his arms, joined by their bond and something more that had no name or face yet, but it made her feel, perhaps for the first time in a long time, what she'd only dreamt of at night.

Wanted.

A Dance with Fire

Ryker knew where the portal took them as soon as his feet touched the stony ground, and the warmth of the hearth enveloped their tightly clinging bodies.

He couldn't let her go. He didn't want to.

"My father will want to see us. He'll want to know the safe houses were compromised." Valerio's footsteps echoed against the ground of Castle Aileach. The fluttering wings of Unseelie echoed across the vast ceiling above them, offering blankets, drinks, food.

But Ryker didn't want any of that.

He didn't want to waste another moment when desire was coiling low in his belly, ready to strike.

His eyes still hadn't left Shula's, and her golden-brown depths seemed to flare, like she knew what he was thinking, and a slow smile teased her lips.

It was Ryker's undoing.

"Later," he growled at the prince.

The sword he held to so tightly slipped from his grasp and clattered to the ground. He usually didn't treat his weapons disrespectfully, but Shula was back. Here, in his arms, and everything he'd tried to convince himself to believe melted away like her magic melted iron.

She'd come back for them, for him. And no words could ever express how wrong he was about her, and no apology could ever make up for the things he'd said in his own fear and heartbreak. But he would start with this.

His hands slid across her back, spanning against her ass. He squeezed before he lifted, sliding her body up against his until her legs wrapped around his waist. Then he was kissing her all over again, something prominent inside him urging he consummate the mating bond. Raw and primal urges that he'd shoved away for so long since he'd met her came out all at once. And this time, he listened.

His legs swallowed up the space towards the stairs, then he climbed and made his way down the hall, listening for any sign of movement behind the closed doors, all while Shula's lips devoured him.

He groaned, feeling every touch like bolts of lightning across his skin and made it to his room, kicking the door open and closed again once they were inside. Only then did he set her to her feet. She swayed a little, which brought a smile to his face.

The room wasn't the most romantic of settings. It smelt like damp stone, and the small hay-stuffed pallet meant as a bed was flat. A single white sheet that smelt clean was folded neatly down on it. There was no illumination save for the single beam of moonlight peeking through the only window. Candles burned to the wick were tapered against the walls, but they didn't burn.

There was so much Ryker wanted to say, so many words that were on the tip of his tongue, apologies that wouldn't be half as worthy as what she deserved, and yet he couldn't bring himself to say a thing. The time for talking wasn't now. Not now, when this buzzing heat had been building between them for weeks. When desire was so close and still so far away. It was vibrating through his body, making his limbs tremble with wanting.

His need for her was a slow spreading ache.

So he touched her, his hand reaching out to cup her cheek. Shula leaned into his touch, like it was as hard for her to keep to herself as it was for him.

"Be sure, Fire Dancer," he whispered. "Be sure it's me you want. Because I want you. All of you."

Ryker had never been self-conscious about his scars. But if Shula let him go further, she would see the rest of his body. She would see the maze of pain he wore against his flesh. He knew it was nothing to be ashamed of, that they were a testament to the lives he'd saved. Yet in a moment of weakness, he wondered if she would be repulsed by the amount there.

In response, Shula's fingers drifted to the lapels of his jacket, pushing it over his shoulders. Heat burned in her eyes, a seductress ready to take. And he let her, dropping his hand so she could pull the jacket past his arms, his hands, and drop it to the floor. Her fingers lifted the hem of his tunic, pulling it up slowly, heat grazing across the panes of his bared stomach. His whole body tensed, waiting as she pulled it over his shoulders. Once the garment was out of the way, Ryker held his breath. Waited.

Flames danced behind her golden-brown eyes as she took him in. All his imperfection laid bare for her to see.

Scars bisected along his body, a spiderweb of them that traced jagged edges. Some marks were older than others, some more prominent, white, red, in angry, slashing figures across his body. They traced along his arms, his back, even his navel.

A tentative touch was all it took to break him. As her fingers lifted to gently trace along the old wounds, a guttural growl pushed from Ryker's throat.

"Shula..."

Like his voice had been an invitation, she leaned forward, eyes fluttering closed, the starred points of her lashes kissing her cheekbones, and she pressed a kiss to the scar right over his heart.

His heart pounded, and he was sure she could feel it against her mouth.

Ryker tried to reach for her then, but Shula pulled away, a slow curling smile on her mouth as she stepped back. Her eyes said the words her mouth didn't. She didn't break contact as her fingers slowly worked along her own clothes.

It was a teasing, sensual dance she gave him. Toeing off her shoes and socks first, she turned, moving and undulating her body like a flame. One by one, lights flickered on above them.

Not light.

Little balls of flames that curled and molded into figures to illuminate her in a brighter light. She still had magic inside her, and she let it burn brightly until her skin glowed golden and every step around the room was a promise of seduction. She moved, *danced.* It was nothing like that night so many weeks ago. The night when she'd been hazy with Fae wine and moved across the bonfire for entertainment.

This was different, because it was for *him.*

Fire sparked to life around her body like a whip, trailing sparks around her with each firm movement. Shula Azzarh danced like fire. One with the heat, flickering seduction, a hypnotism that held him enraptured in her very essence.

And each step brought her articles of clothing off.

One by one.

Jacket.

Tunic.

Pants.

She whirled, hands reaching to her back to grasp the hem of her thin shift. When it hit the floor in a puddle at her feet, Ryker felt the breath leave his lungs. Then her fingers were against her undergarments, hooking into the waistband and tugging. Slow, low, revealing inch by inch the soft curves of her ass as she bent over to tug the material away from her ankles.

She stood.

She turned.

Her whole body glowed something ethereal and Ryker's own went taut, his cock tightened painfully in his pants.

His gaze flickered over her body, memorizing every inch. From the curve of her breasts to the shapes of her pointed nipples.

And then he saw the bruises and a snarl tore out of him, angry and murderous. In a couple of strides, he was in front of her, dropping to his knees. For a moment, her nudity was forgotten, his own desires quenched as he took in the mottled bruise around her ribs.

A fierce, foreign wave of protectiveness drowned him. His nostrils flared.

"Who did this?" Ryker's fingers grazed underneath the edge of the bruise, careful not to touch, to hurt. His magic reached out on instinct to get a feel of the pain.

Shula's fingers raked through his hair. "No one who is still alive."

Of course.

A smile touched his lips before he leaned forward and pressed a soft kiss to the bruise. That's where he kept them for a few seconds as his magic took over and healed her skin, took away the pain.

He barely winced as he absorbed it.

"You didn't have to do that," she whispered, fingers dancing along his scarred shoulders.

He tilted his head up. "I did. You are my mate."

He felt her body tremble at those words. Her nails dug into his skin, and pain had never felt so good.

"Say it again," she ordered.

Desire flared to life as if it had never been extinguished in the first place.

Ryker pressed a kiss to her stomach. "Mate," he growled against her flesh. "You are my mate."

A groan urged another kiss from Ryker. Lower, his beard scraped across the soft flesh of Shula's body and lower still to the dark hairs beneath. Her hips bucked against him and he held her steady with his hands, nails digging into soft skin to keep her still.

"Ryker..."

"My mate," he growled. *"Mine."*

His mouth closed over her clit, and it was like the very essence of Mana exploded onto his tongue. Euphoric, enticing, addictive. Those were a few words that came to mind as he sucked her clit between his teeth.

Shula cried out, gripping him tighter as she ground herself against his mouth, wanting friction. He craved it as much as she did. Ryker pulled back a fraction, enough to let his tongue slide down the folds of her pussy.

His tongue dove between her folds, tasting the evidence of how much she wanted him, lapping it up with deep, even strokes. He explored every inch of her with his tongue and teeth, using her gasps and whimpers to learn what she liked. Releasing one hip, he thumbed her clit as he found a steady rhythm, one he matched a moment later with his fingers, curling them inside her and stroking deep until she was writhing, pleading... begging.

"Ryker!" Her nails dug into his shoulders, and he knew she was close to falling over that delicious edge. He felt it in his own body, the sensation building, his cock aching, and above all that, wanting to *please* her, drive her into oblivion.

He curled his fingers, sucked her clit into his tongue, using his teeth to apply the lightest of pressure.

She fell.

Her screams echoed through the room, and he felt the heat of her fire explode above them. He dared a glance up, seeing figures dancing above them.

Have you danced with fire yet?

The Seer's words came back to him, a prediction of the bond he'd denied but that was now consuming them both.

Her magic was reacting to the orgasm, so he pushed her higher, drew it out longer until she was begging, chasing the release with quick undulations of her hips. Until the fire dulled to the colors of burning embers and her knees buckled beneath her.

Only then did Ryker pull away, missing her heat as soon as he did, but he still tasted her on his tongue. It was a primal urge to kiss her, to leave her breathless and let her taste herself on him. So Ryker did. He slid up her body, looked into her heavy-lidded eyes and kissed her with the same enthusiasm he'd applied to her pussy.

So she'd never doubt he wanted her.

Even when he'd said he didn't.

Let her know his words had been a lie.

He conveyed that in his kiss, his mouth against her mouth, his tongue against her tongue. He bent her over his arm, one hand digging into her hair, so he could delve in deeper. Consume her, merge their souls together, complete their bond.

He pulled away just enough to walk them backwards to the makeshift bed and lower her against the clean sheets.

"I tried to deny you," Ryker found himself confessing. Hurt flashed behind her eyes. It was a brief flash, but it was there, and he hated himself for putting it there. He grabbed her wrists and pinned them above her head. "Never again," he vowed. "I swear on Mana, I will never deny you again."

Just like that, her expression softened, and she smiled.

And Ryker knew he'd never seen anything so beautiful.

"I promise," he whispered, lips skimming across her collarbones.

She let out a content sigh, body squirming beneath his. "Ryker..." It came out as a groan that he felt jolt through his body. "I have to tell you..."

"What?"

"I've never done this before."

Her words registered and something like elation rippled through his body. He pressed a kiss to her chin, to her lips, and smiled against her mouth.

"Don't worry," he whispered, just another promise he intended to keep. "I'll be gentle."

⟡

Worship.

That's the word that came to mind as Ryker's hands and tongue roved over Shula's body. He worshipped her with his mouth, from her mouth, sending kisses down her neck, over the sharp ridges of her collarbones. His hands danced along the surface of her skin, fingers strumming her clit once again pulling her towards heights of desire.

Until she was squirming beneath him, until a haze swirled over her and she *begged.* "Ryker," she gasped. *"Please."*

He lifted and she heard the rustle of his pants as he undressed quickly and lowered over her once again. The delicious friction of his skin against hers had her moaning, lifting her hips in search of his cock.

Desire had never felt so foreign or so necessary before. She'd never wanted anyone this much. In fact, she'd never wanted *anyone.* Her whole body quivered with anticipation, and then she felt the head of his cock slide against her folds. Warm, wet, *hard.*

Ryker held himself up with one hand, with the other he poised his cock at her entrance, running his head up and down her folds, pressing it tightly against her clit.

The mere touch was enough to send sparks of lightning across her nerve endings; it was electric, and she wanted more.

Slowly, he pushed the head of his cock inside her. One slow inch at a time. She took him, her whole body tight as she felt a pinch of pain. He wasn't even halfway in when he stopped.

"Look at me, Fire Dancer," he groaned.

Her eyes snapped open and she hadn't even realized she'd closed them.

"Eyes on me. Relax."

Her body melted into the makeshift bed, her legs widening and wrapping around his hips to keep him right where he was. He smiled, and she committed the image to memory before he surged to the hilt inside her. A brief flash of pain was what she felt before it faded and made way for something else.

He rocked his hips in short thrusts, his length pressing, drawing out her cries. The walls of her sex hugged him close, pulling him in, and every time his hips slammed back down onto hers, he created the friction her body desired until he pushed her, the sensation rolling through her whole body, at the base of her spine and rose.

Flesh slapped against flesh, their cries and breaths mingled, and her magic soared above the ceiling like streaks of fire flying across the darkness.

Every scrape of his scarred hands traveling up her body sensitized every nerve, elicited gasps of delight that he swallowed with his mouth. They only pulled away to gasp for air. Her neck arched and his lips pressed to her pulse, feeling the rapid beats like the fluttering of a pixie's wings.

All the while his hips moved, pushing into her channel, and every thrust against her clit was done with a restless need, a fierce certainty. Every other moment in their lives was unpredictable, but not this, not their lust for one another.

The need expanded into a restless energy, and when that sensation exploded into an orgasm that made her see more than fire, more than light? Her magic exploded with it, raining sparks down against their skin until everything was bright. Perfect.

And as Shula's body climbed down from the euphoria, she felt Ryker's teeth graze her neck. It was a silent request, the final step to seal their bond.

She swallowed against his lips.

"Do it."

Make me yours.

Teeth elongated into canines that bit into the soft part of her flesh. Pain was immediate, but then so was the bond. She felt it slam inside her like a separate entity, like a foreign magic taking root somewhere deep inside her soul.

Above her, Ryker bared his neck, bared a rare space with no scars.

Shula leaned up and willed out her canines. The moment they made contact with his skin, she bit, piercing past his tan flesh. Blood burst against her tongue. Blood and magic.

And the bond finally settled.

And they were officially mates.

Ryker's fingers pushed aside her hair and slid along the edge of her curved ear. It took everything within Shula not to shy away from his touch, to get used to the caress.

She'd hid them for so long, saw them as human for years, that she'd all but forgotten what it was like to have them elongated like his.

Her own fingers reached up to touch his ears, the sharp points of them. He shivered at the contact.

Shula took her bottom lip between her teeth and chewed on it before Ryker's thumb pressed against the indent in the middle of her lip.

"What are you thinking?"

The breath loosed slowly out of her lungs. "About how much the surgery hurt. About how I'm missing what I used to look like right about now."

He touched her ears again. "There are some half-Fae without the pointed ears..."

"I'm not half-Fae," she interrupted, feeling a flush creep over her face.

She'd never been ashamed of what she'd had to do to survive, but she had always been self-conscious about her ears. She always hid them behind head scarves or long hair. Somehow it felt more vulnerable to bare her ears to him rather than her body.

She supposed he felt the same way about his scars.

Her fingers slid over the new scar against his neck. A bite mark, still fresh and pink, slowly healing, but just another mark to add to his collection of old wounds.

"Do you..." She trailed off, unsure if she should suggest it right then.

"What?"

"Do you think you could heal them?"

He paused. "I suppose it's possible..." He bent her ear, looking at the scars behind it, the proof of what she'd done and what humans had always seemed to overlook. "Scars are just the evidence of wounds. If I healed Mairin's body when her soul was gone, I could try to reverse this." He pulled away. "But think about it first. I—"

"I want you to try it."

He blinked and her flush deepened. "You're sure?"

Because this was big. It was finally leaving behind a life she thought she'd been happy in. It was leaving behind her humanity for good. No more hiding behind surgically altered anatomy, behind a façade that had never belonged to her. It was leaving behind Piriguini's Circus, Fanny, a life of hiding.

But it was embracing a life of fighting and war. It was their bond. It was taking back her power and strength, taking in pride in who and what she was.

It was the freedom of finally being herself.

Unwavering, she tilted up her chin. "I'm sure."

"Then brace yourself, Fire Dancer." His hands cupped the sides of her head, fingers pressing against the tips of her ears. "Because this is going to hurt."

And the first surge of his magic zapped through her.

And Shula screamed.

And screamed.

To Teg

An opulent, rich feast awaited them in King Ashera's royal meeting room. His circle of trusted Fae stood along the shadows of the walls, alert and staring curiously as Shula and Ryker made their way inside.

Valerio, Uric, Clay, and Julius were seated around the table while Weylyn was standing behind the king's shoulder, looking alert and like a feline ready to pounce.

"Good of you to finally join us," King Ashera purred, his eyes going over Shula and Ryker, paying extra attention to the marks along their necks, stopping on Shula's now pointed ears, which she displayed with pride, hair knotted on top of her head so everyone could see who she had chosen. "We could hear the screaming from here."

Ryker dropped into a deep bow that Shula mimicked a moment too late.

Even if she'd chosen the side of the Fae, she felt uneasy about the Seelie King.

"I believe congratulations are in order," the king went on. "It is not every day a male finds his mate." Shula swore she could hear his envy as he stared at Ryker. At his own ears that he displayed just like she did and the scars behind them, the proof of her twelve-year-old decision of survival. "Let alone one as powerful as her. If Weylyn is to be believed..."

"Thank you, your Majesty," Shula murmured. She didn't like to think that they'd all been talking about her, but she supposed she had to get used to it.

She was an Elemental, after all.

"Now, we can commence our meeting. As I understand it, two of our safe houses have fallen?"

"Both in Orknie," Valerio supplied with a nod of his head while Shula and Ryker took their seats at the table.

"It stands to reason the humans Imogen and Filomena were tortured for information on the second safe house," the king said, stroking his bearded chin. "As Imogen only knew the location to the ones in Orknie, I think it's safe to say the rest of them are safe. Still, I will dispatch troops to quickly move everyone here within the week."

Thoughts of Imogen and Filomena made Shula's throat tighten up, but she tamped emotion down. They'd known what they were getting into. Now, all that was left was to avenge them. Make the soldiers pay.

"Now, let's move on to the Elementals. We need to find them before the human emperor can." King Ashera's eyes snagged on hers. "How do you plan on finding them?"

Shula felt her heart pound. She hadn't thought about it, didn't know *how.* The Seer said she could, but her magic was the magic of fire. She wasn't a tracker.

She must have given something away on her face, because King Ashera pushed back in his chair, expression darkening.

"I may have an idea on how to track the Elementals, Your Majesty." It always felt so odd to hear Weylyn's voice since he spoke so little. But when he did, it held a note of superiority in it. Like he wasn't the king's lackey.

"I'm listening."

"I'll need a map and stones. Six stones, to be exact." Weylyn snapped his fingers and someone rushed to get what he ordered, coming back as quickly as they'd left to spread the map out on the center of the table. "Give the stones to Shula." She held her hands out as the stones were placed in her palms.

They were unimpressive, gray, and smooth.

"Now what?" She looked up at the eerie Fae.

"Stand over the map." She did what he asked and only then, did he speak again. "Now, close your eyes and take deep breaths. Channel Mana, call it to you while thinking about that special link, that *bond* you have with the other Elementals. Picture it, give it form, and then open your hands and let the stones fall on the map."

She found herself doing what he asked, picturing Mana. She didn't know what it looked like, but she birthed its form. A thread of light interconnecting her and the other Elementals. They were one with Mana, the gateway to the world of magic that connected every living Fae. She imagined it glowing brightly, spreading through her body like the blood in her veins. She sent it outwards, tugged on the thread as if she could find five other Fae on the other end.

Then her hands released the stones and they bounced against the map.

When her eyes opened, she saw each piece on a different space of the map, each further away than the last.

"There you have it," Weylyn said, coming up beside Shula. His long fingers traced against the map of Illyk, pointing to the mountains in Tuath where one of the stones landed. Where Castle Aileach was located. "This is where you are. The rest of the stones depict where the others are."

Shula stared hard at the map, at the stones. Her body began to buzz in little aftershocks of magic, and then something strange happened. She started to see what she'd pictured in her mind. A silver thread spreading across the map connecting each stone. The threads transformed, became colors and figures that looked similar to the marks etched onto her back.

Her gaze darted around the map, taking in each location, each different city.

Ielwyn.

Dana.

Teg.

Vellm.

And the fifth stone, the fifth symbol, it wasn't tied to one place. It moved along the map, jumping erratically from one end to the other.

"Is that the Valley of the Dead?" Clay demanded, leaning across the table to look at where one of the stones had landed in Vellm. "Are you fucking serious?"

The Valley of the Dead had a reputation as frightening as the Iron Mountains beyond the Ley Line. Shula didn't know details except what she'd heard in whispers at the circus, and they'd certainly never traveled there.

It was home to murderers, monsters, and a vast expanse of cold, dry miles where not even nature thrived. To set foot there meant death.

"Dana is closest," Valerio said. "We should go there first."

"The Valley of the Dead," Clay scoffed. "It's suicide."

"Maybe we should start in the west and work our way east?" Julius suggested.

But Shula drowned them out. The lights on the map brightened, flowing like a river of glittering starlight, pushing, expanding, molding, until a single line formed and pointed to the city of Teg. The light burned. Brighter and brighter. Voices raised around her, but Shula *knew* they were wrong.

She knew where they had to start.

Her hand slammed down against the map, right over the stone where Teg was. Where another Elemental was.

The sound shut everyone up.

"Here," she ordered. "This is where we have to start."

"Teg," Valerio read. "Why? Dana is closer."

"Call it a hunch." She smirked. "Mana is telling me to go here. It doesn't matter who's closer. Mana wants us in Teg."

And because every Fae believed in the magic of Mana, Shula knew no one would argue.

"Alright," Valerio agreed. "Then we'll go to Teg. We leave in the morning."

Tranquility settled over her bones, a message from Mana that Shula had made the right decision. She didn't know why, but it felt right. Whoever was in Teg needed them before the others, so it was there they would go.

"Who do you think it is?" Clay asked curiously. "Water? Earth?"

"I'll know it when I see it." But Shula had a feeling it was neither of those Elementals waiting for them.

Julius clapped his hands. "Excellent. Let's celebrate with some Fae wine before we leave, yeah?"

Ryker's hand rubbed along Shula's back, but she couldn't take her eyes off the map. Off the bright light that still glowed. It was a warning of what was to come, she was sure of it. And fear, old and familiar friend that it was, crept through her blood. But there was something stronger in her now.

Determination.

Shula's hands picked up the stones and pocketed them before reaching for the map and folding it neatly into her pocket.

"Shula." Ryker's knuckles brushed along her cheek, drawing her attention to him.

"Yeah?"

"Do you want wine?"

She felt a smile pulling at her lips. "Can I have dessert first?"

"Chocolate cake?"

She smiled at the memory of his body on hers, of the taste of hatred and chocolate shared in the dead of night.

"My favorite."

So they left the king's meeting room, and they ate, drank, and partied.

For tomorrow they'd leave and start a new journey.

To Teg.

To find another Elemental, another ally.

And hopefully?

Another friend.

To be continued...

Acknowledgments

It looks like we've reached the part in the book where I get to thank the people who've helped me make this book possible. I'm constantly amazed as I look through my books and all the people who have helped me in my journey becoming a self-published author. As the years go by, I see myself changing. I see my writing changing, my circle of friends expanding.

A Dance With Fire, in my opinion, is some of my best work as an author. It's been a crazy journey and I know I wouldn't be writing 'the end' were it not for the following amazing people.

To Lisa. Thank you for helping me brainstorm at midnight and for sending me messages telling me how much you hate me for killing off your favorite characters. This book wouldn't be possible without your guidance and critiques.

To KD over at Storywrappers. Thank you for bringing the image I had in my head of Shula Azzarh to life. You made her shine in a way I knew only you could. Thank you for that.

To my pack of sexy mamis. Kathryn and Crustal (that's never, ever going away). You two have been so encouraging in this whole process. I never imagined I'd be friends with two amazing authors that I love and who I now adore with every single bone in my tiny omega body. Thanks for putting up with my thousands of "teasers" and questions and moodboards. I never thought it'd be possible to have such encouraging friends and I'm truly grateful to call you my sexy mami pack. *insert flirty winky face here*

Lastly, firstly, and for all eternity, I want to thank my readers. For always being so encouraging and kind and for reminding me every single day with your words and amazing reviews why I started writing in the first place. I appreciate you all.

Also... *runs back into the acknowledgments section* I want to thank my husband, for your encouragement and support as I went from stay at home mom to full time author. *Te amo mi amor.*

About the Author

Aleera Anaya Ceres is the USA Today Bestselling author of several series including the Origins of the Six series and the Daughter of Triton series. Like most introverts, Aleera prefers to curl up with a good book, listen to music, paint, read tarot cards, and snack on the tears and heartbreak of her readers. A proud Mexican-American from the state of Kansas, Aleera currently resides in Tlaxcala, Mexico with her husband and children.

You can find/contact her here:
aleeraanayaceres.com
aleeraceres@aacbooks.com

Also by Aleera Anaya Ceres

Adult Fantasy Series
Fae Elementals

A Dance With Fire

A Sword of Ice

A Shield of Water
The Dark Waters series

Riptide

Reverse Harem Series
Royal Secrets

Secrets Among the Tides

Whispers Beneath the Deep

Caresses Between the Sand

Death Beyond the Waves
Royal Lies

Slave to Ice & Shadows

Princess in Frost Castles

Queen of Frozen War
Origins of the Six series

Academy of Six

Control of Five

Destruction of Two

Wrath of One

A Daughter of Triton series

Triton's Academy

Triton's Prophecy

Triton's Legacy

A Daughter of Triton Box set

Reverse Harem Standalones

Queenie & the Krakens

Lourdes & the Mafia

Paranormal Romance Series

Deep Sea Chronicles

Fall in Deep

Siren Queen

The Blood Novels

Love Bites

Blood Drug

My Master

Last Hope

Young Adult standalone

The Last Mermaid

www.ingramcontent.com/pod-product-compliance
Lightning Source LLC
Chambersburg PA
CBHW020245030826
48979CB00030B/2622/J